PRAISE FOR

Saving Grace

"Lee Smith opens the human heart. . . . We're privy to the charged atmosphere of fundamentalist belief—the goodness it attempts to conjure, the evils beneath, the inherent loneliness and rationalizations that God forgives all who repent. Humility and humanity are present everywhere in this novel."

—*The Boston Sunday Globe*

"[Smith's] style is lilting, resonant with the rhythm and accent of Appalachia. And she fashions compelling plots in which innocence is often overshadowed by circumstances that are at once humorous and harrowing."   —*Chicago Tribune*

"[An] extraordinarily interesting, lively, and well-made novel."

—*The (Raleigh) News & Observer*

"A funny, frightening odyssey of love, hate, repulsion, pity and redemption . . . Imagine a steamily erotic Eudora Welty, or Flannery O'Connor on Prozac, and you'll have a feel for the essence of Smith's modern Southern fable."

—*The Virginian-Pilot and Ledger-Star*

"Smith is peerless at evoking an entire world with a detail or two. . . . The comedy is rich, and the sense of place is intense."

—*Detroit Free Press*

"A heartrending book."   —*Kirkus Reviews*

Saving Grace

LEE SMITH

BERKLEY BOOKS, NEW YORK

THE BERKLEY PUBLISHING GROUP
Published by the Penguin Group
Penguin Group (USA) LLC
375 Hudson Street, New York, New York 10014

USA • Canada • UK • Ireland • Australia • New Zealand • India • South Africa • China

penguin.com

A Penguin Random House Company

Berkley trade paperback ISBN: 978-0-425-26728-8

The Library of Congress has cataloged the G. P. Putnam's Sons hardcover edition as follows:

Library of Congress Cataloging-in-Publication Data

Smith, Lee, date.
Saving Grace / by Lee Smith.
p.   cm.
ISBN 0-399-14050-6
I. Title.
PS3569.M5376S28   1995   94-43904 CIP
813'.54—dc20

PUBLISHING HISTORY
G. P. Putnam's Sons hardcover edition / May 1995
Ballantine trade edition / April 1996
Berkley trade paperback edition / December 2013

PRINTED IN THE UNITED STATES OF AMERICA

10 9 8 7 6 5 4 3 2 1

Cover images: John Oliver Cabin, Great Smoky Mountains © Pixtal/SuperStock;
Reagan Tub Mill, Great Smoky Mountains © age fotostock/SuperStock.
Cover design by Royce M. Becker.
Interior text design by Tiffany Estreicher.

I would like to thank Kaye Gibbons for calling to my attention *Powerhouse for God* by Jeff Todd Titon, and Katherine Kopp for suggesting the title of this novel. I am indebted to Sarah Dessen for her help; to Jane and Vereen Bell for inspiration; to Allan Gurganus for his encouragement during the dark times when I was writing; and to Susan Ketchin for her inspiring faith and friendship. And to Hal, again and always, my thanks and my love.

Source notes appear at the end of the book.

For Annie

We shall not cease from exploration
And the end of all our exploring
Will be to arrive where we started
And know the place for the first time.

T. S. ELIOT
"LITTLE GIDDING," FROM *FOUR QUARTETS*

Scrabble Creek

MY NAME IS Florida Grace Shepherd, Florida for the state I was born in, Grace for the grace of God. I am the eleventh child of the Reverend Virgil Shepherd, born to him and his third wife, Fannie Flowers. They say I take after her, and I am proud of this, for she was lovely as the day is long, in spirit as well as flesh. It isn't true, however. I am and always have been contentious and ornery, full of fear and doubt in a family of believers. Mama used to call me her "worrywart child."

"You've got to trust more in Jesus, Gracie," she'd tell me again and again in her pretty voice which always reminded me of running water, of Scrabble Creek falling down the mountain beside our house. "You've got to give over to Him," she'd say. "Hasn't He always took good care of us? The Lord will provide," she'd say, smoothing my long yellow hair and pressing me against her bosom where I could smell the familiar smell of cotton dried out on the line. She'd hold me until I quit crying, maybe sing me a little song. Mama was never in a hurry when we were kids. She had all the time in the world for us, putting down whatever she was doing in order to catch us up and comfort us. Mama took good care of us, as good as she could.

This was not true of Daddy, nor of Jesus either, as far as I could see. Daddy and Mama talked about Jesus all the time. I loved Daddy and Mama, but I did not love Jesus. And I actually hated Him when He made us take up traveling in His name, living with strangers and in tents and old school buses and what have you.

I couldn't understand why we had to do this, why this was required of us alone when other children I knew from school got to live in a nice brick house and have Barbie dolls and radios. I was full of resentment and raged against Him in my heart, but I knew better than to say it out loud, for then they might decide I was possessed by the Devil and try to cast him out as directed by Acts 10:38. I had seen this done, and did not want it done to me. But I worried and worried, about everything. I worried that the Devil might really be in me after all, growing like a baby inside of me until I got so big that everyone could see, and everyone would know my awful secret.

When I think on my childhood now, it appears to me as a wild mountainside where I was lost. Often over the years I have dreamed about it. In these dreams I always have a duty—to take something to somebody, to tell somebody something—but the trees are thick and the path disappears beneath my feet. I never know where I'm going, and I never get there.

I reckon I never did get there.

This is why I have had to come back now, traveling these dusty old back roads one more time. For I mean to tell my story, and I mean to tell the truth. I am a believer in the Word, and I am not going to flinch from telling it, not even the terrible things, not even the part about Lamar nor how Mama died nor the true nature of Travis Word nor what transpired between me and Randy Newhouse. I have entered these dark woods yet again, for I've got to find out who I am and what has happened to me, so that I can understand what is happening to me now, and what is going to happen to me next.

MY BEST MEMORIES come from Scrabble Creek. This is where we lived the longest, in the house God gave us when I was seven years old. We had come to North Carolina from Georgia in an old car that blew up in the mountains near Waynesville in the summer of 1949. The car was a blue humpbacked Studebaker. A used-car dealer in Stone Mountain, Georgia, had given it to Daddy free for healing his baby daughter of croup. It made a funny noise but it ran pretty good until that August afternoon when it just flat exploded on a high narrow mountain road with Daddy driving of course and Evelyn and Billie Jean and Joe Allen and me crammed in the backseat and Mama nursing Troy Lee in the front. All of a sudden there came a big "pow!" noise and the car lunged over to the left—*away* from the edge of the mountain, thank the Lord—and came to rest at an angle against a rocky cliff. Black smoke poured out from under the hood. We scrambled all over each other trying to get out, which was hard since the left side of the car was pushed against the mountain and the right side was up in the air. One by one we jumped,

"We're wrecked, we're wrecked!" Joe Allen shouted, running around and around.

"Joe Allen, stop that foolishness this minute," Mama directed from inside the car. "Evelyn, come over here and get Troy Lee," she said, and handed him out to my older sister. Troy Lee was crying like crazy, his face bright red. Mama jumped out lightly after him, like she was entirely accustomed to jumping out of burning cars, and took Troy Lee back from Evelyn and comforted him. "Now, now," she said. "There now." I clung to Mama's skirt and wished that Troy Lee had never been born, or that he would die, so that Mama would hug *me*.

My handsome daddy followed Mama out, yelling, "Praise be to Jesus!" as he hit the ground. For traveling, Daddy always took off his jacket and drove in a white shirt with the sleeves rolled up. Daddy was fifty-six then, but he seemed younger, because he was so full of energy. The Holy Spirit kept him hopping, as he said. His eyes were a sharp, bright blue. His long curly hair had been turned pure white by God in a vision on top of Roan Mountain, in Tennessee, when he was twenty-five years old. "All right children," he said calmly, "help me now," and we untied the bundles that were lashed to the top and the back of the Studebaker and got them over to the far side of the road just before the car exploded in earnest, its hood popping off, a great plume of smoke shooting straight up in the air.

"My goodness!" Mama said. Billie Jean was sucking her thumb and Evelyn was crying. "What will we do?" Evelyn sobbed wildly. "What will we ever do now?" Daddy fell to his knees in the road and started praying. I knew he would take the explosion as a sign—Daddy was ever on the lookout for signs and wonders, which were vouchsafed to him accordingly.

"I guess we'll just take to the tent again," Joe Allen said darkly, kicking at our biggest bundle, the green canvas gospel tent which we had slept in before, and plenty of times at that. I wished with all my heart that it was burning up in the Studebaker. I hated it when we stayed in the gospel tent. One time we had slept out in that tent in the blowing snow. Another time, in summer, I woke up one morning and found both my eyes swollen shut from bug bites. That was in Dahlonega, Georgia.

Now Mama sat down on the rolled-up tent and unbuttoned her blouse and set in to feeding Troy Lee some more. A piece of her long blond hair had come loose from its bun and it fell in a screen across her face as she leaned over Troy Lee. The rest of us pulled back from the heat of the blazing car but continued to watch it closely as it shimmered and snapped, except for Daddy, who stayed right where he was.

"I'm hungry," Billie Jean said, but nobody answered her. We were all hungry. We had slept in the car the night before, piled on top of each other, and breakfast had been half a loaf of white bread, hours and hours before. I'd never cry, though. I'd die first. I took pride in not being a whiner like Billie Jean. I ignored my empty stomach and looked up the dark column of smoke, past the tops of the dusty green trees, to a patch of deep blue sky. I wished I could just float away with the smoke, away from there, away from them all. "I'm hungry," Billie Jean said again, and again nobody answered her. We knew there was nothing to eat. Mama buttoned herself back up and placed Troy Lee facedown across her lap. Butterflies fluttered around her. She smiled at us. "I'll swear," she said, "if it's not the prettiest day!"

About five minutes later, a gray truck came rumbling along the road and stopped. God had answered Daddy's prayer. The back of the truck held three boxes with hunting dogs in them, and all the dogs started barking at once. A man got out as quick as he was able. He had a long red face and a nose with a knob on it. "You folks okay?" he hollered over the sound of the fire and the barking and Billie Jean's crying and Daddy's praying.

"Why yes, praise Jesus, we are," Mama said sweetly.

The man walked over to get a closer look at Daddy. "Son of a gun," he said. He stood there in the middle of the road and waited until Daddy finished praying and got up.

"Virgil Shepherd, minister of God," Daddy said, grinning his big grin and holding his hand out. "Mighty pleased to meet you."

"Likewise." The man said his name was Carlton Duty, and he was going on to say something else when the other door of the truck swung open and a woman stuck her curly red head out. "And this here is my wife Ruth," he said. We would learn that Ruth Duty loved children, and hadn't ever been able to have any. She had the kindest heart in the world.

"Why this is awful!" she cried. "You poor little things! You all look like something the cat drug up! I tell you what, I've got a coconut cake in here that we was taking over to my sister's." She pointed at me. "Honey, you come on over here and help me."

So I ran right up to the Dutys' truck, and Mrs. Duty handed me a platter holding a great big cake covered all over with little white strings of coconut, which we had never seen before. I took the cake and put it down in the road beside Mama, and then Daddy came over and sat on a rock and cut it up with his pocketknife. Though we were about to faint with hunger by then, we knew better than to start eating before Daddy had said the blessing. He stretched out his arms and set in, "Hallelujah! Oh, He's a good God, that has led us up here from Georgia and give us His sign of holy fire and provided us a feast in the middle of the day. He's a good God, hallelujah!" Daddy went on and on, the way he always did, but I peeped out from under my eyelids to watch Carlton Duty just standing there leaned up against his truck staring at Daddy with his mouth open. Daddy had had this effect on people before. I thought I would die of starvation before he finally hollered, "Amen!" and picked up a piece of cake.

In my whole life, I have never tasted anything to equal Mrs. Ruth Duty's coconut cake. Even today, it makes my mouth water just to think about it! I reckon we ate like we were about starved, which we were. The Dutys came near to watch us eat, Carlton Duty smoking a cigarette and Mrs. Ruth Duty hovering around our little circle like a big old moth. We didn't even have anything to wash the cake down with. We just ate. I thought we had died and gone to Heaven for sure. We ate until every crumb of that cake was gone, and then we stretched out our legs and lay back against the mossy bank and blessed God and watched our car finish burning up, and Daddy told Carlton Duty how we had got there.

"Mr. Duty," he said, "I preach the Gospel of Jesus Christ as it is written in His Holy Bible, amen, and not in no other place, and I am out here on the road follering His divine plan where He said, 'Go ye into all the world, and preach the Gospel to every creature.' My religion is not a mouth religion, Mr. Duty. No sir. I am follering the plan of God. I will do what He tells me to do, I will go where He tells me to go, and stop where He tells me to stop, praise His sweet name."

"But what about all these poor sweet little younguns?" cried Mrs. Duty, looking at us.

"I cannot think of no better plan for them than to foller the plan of God," Daddy said. "These children may not have new clothes on their back nor new shoes on their feet, but they are going to Heaven with me. These children are on the road to salvation. Isn't that right, Fannie?" Daddy asked Mama, not taking his eyes off Carlton Duty's face, not even nodding when Mama smiled and said, "That's right." I snuggled over closer to Mama and the sleeping Troy Lee, while Evelyn held Billie Jean in her lap and Joe Allen poked around in the woods with a stick.

Carlton Duty swallowed hard. "Do you mean to tell me, sir," he said, "that you-uns wasn't even for sure where you was a-going? That you did not have no more definite destination in mind than Heaven?"

"That's right, brother," Daddy said seriously. "As it says in the good Bible, this world is not our home, we're only passing through. We're follering the plan of God, brother, and we have given our lives over to Him. He is leading us where He wants us to go, and today He has brung us to—" Here Daddy paused and narrowed his eyes and asked, "What place is this?"

"Well, you're about nine miles outside of Waynesville," Carlton Duty said.

"Bless Jesus!" Daddy said, reaching his arms up in the air and bowing his white head to the will of God. His left hand was still blue-black and swollen from where he had gotten bit in Clayton. "Bless Jesus," Daddy continued, "who has showed us by the sign of fire in His holy woods nine miles outside of Waynesville, North Carolina, His plan for our life today, by freeing us from the things of this world and casting us wholly on His mercy, amen, and by bringing us His blessing as a gift of food from his good servants Carlton and Ruth Duty, amen."

"Shoot, it's just a *cake*," Ruth Duty said in the silence that followed Daddy's prayer.

But Daddy appeared beatified, gazing around at the smoking skeleton of the car and the thick green woods and the blooming black-eyed Susans beside the road as if he had never seen such sights in his whole life. Bumblebees droned and yellow butterflies fluttered around us.

Carlton Duty cleared his throat. He looked at his wife.

"Well," he said, "seeing as how things are, I believe I might be able to help you out. You-uns stay right here, and I'll be back directly."

"God be with you," Daddy told him.

They climbed back in the truck and rattled off down the road with the dogs all barking at once. Mrs. Ruth Duty waved out the window. We sat there and watched them go until there was nothing left of them at all except a puff of dust that hung in the hot, still air above the rutted road.

Then Joe Allen came crashing through the underbrush and reported that he had found a spring, and Evelyn and Billie Jean and I started off down the steep hill after him. Down, down, down we went until we came to a deep shady spot where the spring bubbled up between the mossy rocks like a fountain. We cupped our hands and drank like we were dying of thirst, like it was our last chance for water in the world. The spring water was cool and sweet, delicious. Finally I quit drinking and raised my dripping chin and looked back up the mountain.

And there stood Daddy, black against the sun. His white shirt and his white hair appeared to be shooting off rays of light behind his dark form. I did not wave or holler at him. I started playing with Joe Allen and Evelyn and Billie Jean. We built a dam, and made a little lake, and sailed leaf-boats in it. The whole time we played, I knew that Daddy was watching over us.

THROUGH THE MEDIUM of Carlton Duty, God provided us with a completely furnished four-room house on Scrabble

Creek, the nicest place we ever lived. This house was actually owned by a woman named Elvie Mayhew, who had
left it for good the minute her husband, Lester Mayhew,
died one night while they were having supper, a year
before our arrival. They had been eating green beans and
mashed potatoes, now dried forever to the plates still on
the table. Mama had to throw these plates out, and also the
pots on the stove. Daddy cut back the trumpet vine that
had grown in through the open kitchen window, and
swept out the chicken droppings on the floors. The chickens themselves were long gone, probably eaten up by animals, Daddy said. The well was choked by ivy. We boiled
the linens in a big iron pot on a wood fire outside the
house, and beat out the corn-shuck mattresses in the sun.

Carlton Duty brought a scythe to cut the waist-high weeds
in the yard and clear a path to the toilet. Mama was so worried that Elvie Mayhew might come back, but everybody said
she had lost her mind and been sent to live with her sister in
Ohio. Finally Mama just quit worrying and delighted in the
house, which had everything—an oilcloth-covered table and
four chairs in the kitchen, a tufted horsehair sofa and a rocking chair and a faded velvet easy chair in the sitting room,
plus a heatstove, one bedroom for Mama and Daddy and
Troy Lee, then a great big bedroom for us kids.

The sitting room, kitchen, and Mama and Daddy's bedroom were built in a row, and then our bedroom went out
at the side, so that the house was shaped like an upside-
down L. A porch ran around the inside of the L. Most
every night we'd sit out there till it got pure dark, reading
the Bible out loud to Daddy, one after the other.

Of course he wouldn't let us read anything *except* the Bible; he said that was all we needed to read. We were not even allowed to read the newspaper, as the only news we needed to know was the good news of the Gospel, and anything else would distract us from it. One time Daddy caught Evelyn with a love magazine and beat her with his belt until her back was covered with welts. Daddy believed in "Spare the rod and spoil the child," and practiced this for our own good.

Anyway, we had climbing red roses on the porch rail, and two pictures hanging up on the walls—one of a vase full of flowers, in the sitting room, and the other of an Indian brave in a canoe, paddling through a swamp, on the wall in our bedroom. I thought Daddy would make us take these down, but he didn't. He said something about it when we first moved in, but then he appeared to forget them. Daddy was so busy following the plan of God that he didn't pay us much mind in general as we settled into the only real house we would ever have, that house which always comes into my mind along with the happy sound of Scrabble Creek.

THE MOUNTAIN WAS steep beside our house, and the creek proceeded down it in a line of little waterfalls all the way to the road. Each waterfall had its own pool, some of them big enough to fish in, or to swim in when it got real hot. We couldn't really swim, of course, at least us girls couldn't. We were not allowed to learn how, and we had to keep our skirts and blouses on even when we waded. Holiness girls have to stay covered up. Still, it was exciting. A great thrill would shoot through me whenever I held my nose and dunked myself all the way down under the cold rushing stream, even though Mama had said not to. But she didn't really seem to mind when Daddy was gone and it was sunny so our clothes could dry out.

Mama was that way about a lot of things when Daddy was gone off preaching. We got to play more, and even dress up sometimes in the clothes we had found in the Mayhews' attic. For me and Evelyn and Billie Jean, who had always lived in a single dress apiece and passed those down from one to another, this attic was a treasure trove. There was even an old yellow wedding dress, which Evelyn soon found and put on. This was when I first realized that Evelyn was beautiful. Though she was only eleven at the time, she held herself erect in that dress and walked in a way I'd never seen her walk before. I helped her pick a bouquet of blue flowers that grew by the creek, wild phlox I think it was, and then we called Mama to come and watch Evelyn hold her bouquet in front of her and walk down the length of the porch.

To our surprise, Mama covered her face with her hands and started crying as if her heart would break. We ran over to her, me and Evelyn and Billie Jean, but she would not be comforted. "Oh me," she sobbed. "I just want you girls to be happy." Then she sat down on the porch step, and cried and cried and cried.

"Take it off," Mama finally said to Evelyn, and Evelyn,

scared to death, did so that very minute, to stand thin and white in her shift on the sagging porch, our old Evelyn again.

"Don't you never let me see you in such as that," Mama said. "You know what your daddy would think. I've got a good mind to tear that dress up for underthings," she said, looking at it where it lay in a fancy yellow heap. But she did not. The dress went back into its box and back up in the attic, and none of us ever mentioned its existence to Daddy.

From that magic attic we all got real coats for the winter—a plain green one for Evelyn, a blue one with a white collar for Mama, a hunting jacket for Joe Allen, a ripped black greatcoat that Mama made into coats for Troy Lee and Billie Jean, and a navy pea jacket that went to me. I dearly loved my pea jacket, which had anchors on the buttons.

Also it looked like a boy's jacket, and I wanted to be a boy then, like Joe Allen, and go off to play ball or hunt with the other boys, and cut my hair short like the girls in town, and not have to stay home all the time and help Mama. If I could just be a boy, I wouldn't even mind going to work at the sawmill like Joe Allen did as soon as he was old enough, at thirteen. Daddy himself did not work a regular job. He was too busy. He had to travel a lot, like the apostle Paul.

Mama explained it all to us. "Your daddy is a saint," she said, "a precious saint of God."

And in spite of the frequent sadness in her pale gray eyes and the shadow that sometimes fell on her face, we never doubted for a minute that she loved him. Maybe she loved him even more since she knew she could lose him at any time, because of what he had to do.

Whenever Daddy walked in the door, everything suddenly got real exciting. All the familiar sights and objects of our lives—the bright flapping quilts on the line, the silvery falling-in barn halfway down the hill, the green forest around our house—took on a deeper, richer hue. Nobody could laugh louder or pray longer or swing you up higher in the air than our daddy. And when he looked at Mama, something passed between the two of them which I didn't understand, something which scared me and made me lie restless in my bed, straining to hear them in the other room. Often I heard Daddy's voice talking and talking deep into the night, mixed with Mama's softer tone. But I could never make out the words. Sometimes Mama would call out in a way I could not account for.

On those nights I'd lie awake for hours while Billie Jean slept in the bed beside me. Sometimes I'd hear the serpents rattling in their boxes under our beds, but I was used to the sound, and finally it would put me to sleep.

THE FACT IS, I felt safe in that house on Scrabble Creek, the safest I ever felt in childhood. I was raised to believe that the things of this world are not important, and I know it is true, but a house is different. A house will give you a place on the earth. If you know where you live, you know who you are. I loved being the girl who lived in the house by the musical creek, with blue willow dishes in the corner cupboard and a little army of gladiolas that sprang up every summer around the white quartz rock in the yard, red glads that stood straight and proud as soldiers. They were blooming when we first moved in, and Mama had a fit about them. She loved flowers, any flowers. After we got settled, she started weeding all around the yard, with Troy Lee beside her on a quilt.

"Looky here," she'd say, "there's a rosebush under this honeysuckle," or once in a tone of rapture, "Oh, Gracie! Peonies!" though we would not get to see the peonies bloom until the next spring.

Evelyn and Billie Jean and I got to stay at home to help Mama, but Joe Allen had to go with Daddy and Carlton Duty to build the brush arbor.

God could not have sent a better man to Daddy's side than Carlton Duty. He lived on land that had been in his family for a hundred years, and ran a store down at the crossroads named Duty's Grocery, where Ruth sold her famous pound cakes and fried pies. People went out of their way to get some of Ruth Duty's cooking. The Dutys were well-known and liked throughout that community, but it was not generally known that Carlton had been having a hard time of late, with black days and sleepless nights, for no good reason. It was like a heaviness had come over him from the heart, and everything was turning gray before his eyes. He had stopped going to church and didn't even want to go down to the store. Ruth had been worried sick about him. She told Mama that Carlton's brother Ruel had shot himself in the head when he was exactly Carlton's age, thirty-five. Now she was scared that

Carlton was fixing to do the same thing. She was afraid it ran in the family. Carlton's daddy had done it too. Ruth Duty told Mama all this as she stood in our yard holding a lemon chess pie, with her big bosom heaving and her blue eyes swimming in tears. "If we could of just had us some children . . ." Ruth said, looking at us ranged solemnly up and down the steps watching her sob and wondering when she planned to hand over the pie.

Mama, barefoot, held Troy Lee on her hip and smiled at Ruth Duty. "Things is fixing to change," she said. "Watch and see." For Mama had the gift of discernment.

As usual, Mama was right. Carlton Duty caught religion from Daddy in a big way and soon was Daddy's right-hand man and an elder in his new church.

First they built the brush arbor. The Dutys' land was too poor to farm good, but there was one piece of it right off the road down from the store that was tailor-made for the Lord, Daddy said. Not to mention the Little Dove River behind it, which was great for baptizing. They had plenty of help. Once people met Daddy, they couldn't stay away. He was more alive than anybody else, with energy to spare, and in that poor place of hardscrabble farms and hand-to-mouth lives, he was the main thing happening. People were drawn to Daddy like bugs to a flame. He had something they wanted, and they'd stick around to find out what it was. The men made the roof out of poles and brush, and the floor out of wood shavings and sawdust, and finished the brush arbor up with sawmill slab benches.

The whole time they were working, Daddy was preaching. I don't think he was ever not preaching—he often said that a preacher is a preacher twenty-four hours a day, that the Lord's work is never done.

When the brush arbor was finished, they put two loudspeakers on a plank and mounted this across the top of Carlton Duty's truck. Speakers like that were against the law, but Daddy always said he obeyed God's laws, not man's, quoting from Acts 5:29. Then Carlton Duty drove Daddy all over that part of the county, announcing the revival meeting that would start the following Saturday night. But they drove by our house first, and stopped in the road at the bottom of the hill.

Evelyn and Billie Jean and I were sitting in the grass under the big tulip poplar, making daisy-chain jewelry.

"Fannie Shepherd," Daddy said over the loudspeaker. "Fannie Shepherd and little children," he said, "come see what the Lord has wrought." His voice filled our whole holler. Billie Jean started crying and hung back, but Evelyn and me ran down the hill along with Mama.

"What in the world!" Mama said. Rosy-faced and breathless from running, she wore a daisy-chain necklace, which we had made for her. Holiness women cannot wear real jewelry, and she had said she didn't know if she ought to put it on or not, but she'd been too surprised by the loudspeaker to take it off. Daddy was leaning out the truck window laughing at her, and then his eyes narrowed as he looked at her good. "Hang on a minute," he said to Carlton Duty, and then he swung down from the truck, his white shirtsleeves rolled up and his collar open, still looking at Mama.

We were scared, we didn't know what he meant to do.

He pulled Mama over to him and kissed her long and hard, right there in the middle of the road in the middle of the day. "You're a beautiful woman, Fannie," he said when he let her go. Then he got back in the truck and Carlton Duty drove him away, and me and Evelyn waved goodbye until they were out of sight. Mama stood there giggling like a girl.

EVEN TODAY, I don't know how to describe Daddy's voice, for that was surely one of his greatest blessings from the Lord. To start off with, he did not sound like a preacher. He did not fall into the singsong chant you hear so often. No, Daddy had a deep, ringing voice and spoke real slow, so that every word he said registered, and seemed to settle directly on the soul. He talked to God like he was sitting right across from Him, like they were old friends. He talked to everybody that same way, in fact, not like most preachers, who will yell at you and shame you and try to make you feel bad. Daddy's voice made you feel good, like you were strong in the Lord, and proud to do His will.

"I declare," Ruth Duty said one time to Mama, "that man ought to have been a salesman! Why he could sell anything to anybody! He could have made a fortune."

Of course I wished Daddy would have turned his talents more in this direction, so we could have had decent school clothes at least, but he said that he could not afford to waste his time studying on the things of earth. Jesus wouldn't let him. Daddy did not even take up money at meetings unless it was a special offering for somebody whose house had burned down or their child was sick or something like that. He would not take up money for *us*, so we never had any, and I don't know what we would have done without people coming by the house all the time to bring us food, and vegetables from their gardens, and such as that. People were real good to us up on Scrabble Creek.

It was Daddy's voice that started it all, and even now, years and years later, I can close my eyes and hear him so plain, talking over that microphone hooked to the top of Carlton Duty's truck as they drove around the county. "Folks, we're having a big meeting on Saturday night over here by the river, about a quarter-mile down from Carlton Duty's store. You know where that is, folks. You all come on out. You'll see the other cars there. You'll see Jesus himself there, for it's Him that's calling this meeting over here on Saturday night. It's Jesus, my beloved! He hopes to see you there." Daddy's voice was soft and pleading. It made you want to do whatever he said. Then he'd add, "And if anybody finds a big rattlesnake, why bring him along, and we'll take him up in Jesus' name. In Jesus' name, beloved. In Jesus' name. Come on out in Jesus' name."

This is what Daddy would call his church when they built it—the Jesus Name Church of God—for he loved to say Jesus' name, as he told everyone. In fact Daddy always baptized in the name of Jesus and not in the name of the Father, Son, and Holy Ghost, for those were not *names*, he said. Daddy had thought long and hard about the Bible, and drew his own conclusions. He was dead set on what he believed, and neither the threat of jail nor the fear of death could sway him. "I'm not running a scared race," he often said. "A man ain't alive if he's scared to die."

Everybody admired this.

We were too little to go to that first meeting, but we were to hear about it for years afterward, as what happened there passed into legend. We heard it first from Mama. She used to tell it to Evelyn and Billie Jean and me on the days when she washed our hair.

Some sinner boys from up on Holt Branch, the Graybeals, learned about the meeting and determined to break it up out of sheer meanness. So they laid off work and went around gathering up snakes until they had a huge yellow rattler and a smaller rattler and a big old lard can full of copperheads. They got in their truck and drove down off the mountain where they lived, and arrived at the river after the meeting had been going on for some time. Cars were parked up and down the road. It was nearabout dark, so lanterns had been lit all around the brush arbor. Daddy had placed his own serpent box under the first bench the way he always did, in case God did not send him one, and had started off with prayer and singing. It was Daddy, and a young man named Doyle Stacy on guitar, and Ruth Duty with her tambourine. Ruth had a high trembly voice that would raise up the hair on your arms. The brush arbor was full, the benches packed and people standing in the back. Some of these were believers from churches all around there, but most of them were doubters and sinners who had come along just to see what would happen. After the singing stopped, Mama stood up to read the Scripture, as was usual. She would read while

Daddy paced back and forth with his eyes closed and his head bowed, listening. Listening as intently as if he had never heard these words before and his life depended on it. This time Daddy called for her to read from the fourth chapter of the Acts of the Apostles which she did, ending with verse 31, "And when they had prayed, the place was shaken where they were assembled together; and they were all filled with the Holy Ghost, and spoke the word of God with boldness."

"With boldness!" Daddy shouted, making everybody jump. "With boldness, my beloved! And as believers, can we do any less? God calls for us to be bold tonight, beloved, to turn our lives over to Him and open our hearts to His holy spirit, and He will fill us with rapture, oh my beloved. He will grant us powers which we have not dreamed of. I mean *power*, beloved. Oh, I know you're out there tonight saying, 'What do you mean, Brother Shepherd, why I have not got no power in this world, I have got laid off and my wife is up sick in the bed and my children are lost to Jesus and it's hard times everywhere I look. It's a sea of trouble, Brother Shepherd, and you come in here talking about power. Why, you're just a joke! You'd just as best go back to wherever it was you come from, fast as you can go.' But I say to you here tonight, oh my beloved, it don't have to be this way. No sirree. For God is the great-est source of power in this here universe, and all we have to do is open our hearts and minds up to Him this very evening and let Him work, and His power will run through us and we can do anything. *Anything*, beloved! We can cure the sick! We can cast out devils! We can speak with

new tongues, beloved, we can take up the deadly serpent in His name, and there is no harm in it, for Jesus has given us the power. Oh, He's coming down on us here tonight, beloved. I can feel it. I can feel Him right here, can't you feel Him, brother? Can't you feel Him, sister?"

As he preached, Daddy paced back and forth with his white shirt and his white hair gleaming in the lamplight. Doyle Stacy and Ruth Duty were playing music over to the side while Daddy went on preaching, and before long, folks all over the brush arbor were leaping up to shout or pray or clap or start dancing. It finally built up to where the anointing came down on Daddy as it always did, and he yelled, "I can feel the power! Oh, I can feel the power right here tonight, Lord Jesus, oh thank you, Lord, thank you, thank you, sweet Jesus!" Then Daddy reached under the bench and opened up the box and took a serpent out and draped it across his shoulders. All of a sudden the air went electric, and some people were scrambling back and others were surging forward and the singing got louder and louder.

This was the moment when the Graybeals chose to make their appearance.

They came running in from the road side of the brush arbor, all liquored up. One of them carried two sacks and the others were holding the lard can between them. "You want a serpent, preacher man?" they were hollering. "Here's a serpent for you!" They made their way to the front of the brush arbor and dumped those snakes out everywhere. People were yelling and crying and climbing all over each other and running ever which way. Mama said you could not believe a place could clear out so fast. She ran to the woods, but Daddy would not go with her. The Graybeals hooted with laughter.

Daddy stood right in front of the wooden cross and raised his arms and prayed for power while the snakes slithered and struck at his feet. Then he bent over and started scooping them up and hollering, "Oh, He's a great God!" and "Hallelujah!" Daddy unbuttoned his shirt and stuffed it full of copperheads and laid the big rattler across his shoulders and wrapped the little one around his neck and reached down to gather up the rest of them in his arms. He walked down the middle of the empty brush arbor until he got beyond the last slab bench. He stopped there in the wild light of the flaming lanterns and looked into the darkness past the circle of flickering light where many stood huddled in the trees, waiting to see what would happen. Daddy was fully anointed and covered in snakes, which writhed around his arms and his body and popped out of the open front of his shirt.

"It was something to see," Mama would say softly, her eyes shining when she came to this part. By now, she was plaiting our hair.

Daddy raised his arms and stretched them out to the darkness. "Come back here, beloved," Daddy said softly in that voice which would not take no for an answer. "Come back, come back to Jesus." And they did, many of them, crying and sobbing and calling out to Jesus, pouring back into the brush arbor almost as fast as they had rushed out of it. Doyle Stacy grabbed his guitar and Ruth Duty started in again on the tambourine, joined by one of the

Dotsons on Daddy's guitar and by the Cline sisters, who loved to sing, and as Daddy walked slowly back up the middle aisle to the front of the brush arbor, the Lord came down hard on the whole crowd, so that everybody started to dance and shout or fell down on their knees to pray.

There were those present who will swear to this day that Daddy gave off light like the sun. Many were blessed that night to come forward and pluck the serpents off of Daddy and handle them too, and nobody was harmed in any way, and tongues of fire came down on several, including Carlton Duty, who flung back his head and shouted out in the unknown language of the Lord for upwards of an hour. The Holy Spirit was so strong that night that three of the copperheads died from it, Mama said, right there in the service.

Rufus Graybeal, who had been converted on the spot, was holding one of them when it went limp as a dishrag in his hand. "I went in there as a sinner and a fool," Rufus Graybeal said later, "and come out as a true believer." Though Daddy cautioned him not to think the whole thing was a show put on by God for his own benefit, Rufus was later to fall into the pit of pride, as Daddy called it, anyway.

But this was a great meeting in which the spirit of the Lord rested upon the brush arbor for an hour or more, and it was not over until late in the night, when Daddy took a torch and led a large group of people down to the Little Dove River and baptized them one after another in Jesus' name.

"And when the last one was baptized," Mama always

said, "now that was Mrs. Goody Keene, don't you know that the moon broke out from behind the clouds and lit up that whole riverbank bright as day! We could see every rock and pebble on the shore, and laughed at how Mrs. Keene had got so caught up in the Spirit that she had took her pocketbook right down in the river with her. We all rejoiced," Mama said, "and thanked God for it, and the moon stayed out for the rest of the night. The road looked like a silver ribbon," Mama said, "as we were coming home."

Mama timed the story of the first brush arbor meeting so that it always ended just when she got to the last rubber band.

MANY UNBELIEVERS WERE convinced that night, and from then on, the brush arbor meetings were full to overflowing, with cars parked all up and down the road. Mama and Daddy took us children over there sometimes, but often we stayed home with Evelyn. When they were gone overnight, off preaching someplace, Ruth Duty or one of the other ladies would come to stay with us. Sometimes Ruth brought a chicken to fry up, and one time we had a pork roast. Another time she made us a batch of sugar cookies and we ate them while they were still warm, and washed them down with sweet milk she'd brought from the store. The cookies had little sprinkles of sugar on the top of them that stuck to your lips while you ate. Ruth would patch our clothes too, and clean the house, claiming it was the least she could do. She taught us how to sew on buttons and crochet. It was not that Mama couldn't do these things—it was just that she was so caught up in Daddy's ministry.

For Mama was truly religious, and believed that Daddy had saved her, in Atlanta, Georgia, where she was a dancing girl, actually a young widow with three little children to support—now this is Joe Allen, Evelyn, and Billie Jean, who was nothing but a baby when Daddy came to town with a tent crusade. Their own daddy had been shot in the back for good reason, Mama always said. This was a Mister Bevel Reed, Mama's first husband. And since Mama had run off from her home on the farm at a tender age to join up with his traveling show, she had no one to turn to at his death. She found a woman to keep the children so she could work, but Billie Jean was sick all the time and Mama got real low. She was down real low when she met Daddy. She didn't care about anything, not what she did, nor what happened to her. She was mad at the whole world.

It was in a spirit of making fun that she went to his tent crusade for the first time, on the arm of a fancy gentleman, for it had been in all the newspapers. Daddy had been arrested, then released, and everybody was waiting to see whether he would obey the judge. Mama and her gentleman friend had been drinking. They went to the crusade like it was a freak show.

But Daddy knocked her socks off, Mama said. Though he was arrested again that very night—or perhaps because of it—he made a big impression. As the police were hauling him off, they ran right into Mama, who was wearing high heels, a green suit, and a little green hat with a bird on it. Daddy stared down at her with his piercing blue eyes, then leaned over quick as a wink and kissed her on the mouth. "You're all right, honey," he said. The police jerked him back and pulled him away, and of course Mama's gentleman friend was furious. Mama laughed it off at the time, but the next day she went to visit Daddy in jail, where he stayed for thirty days, refusing to pay the fine. When they finally released him on the condition that he would leave town, Mama went too, taking her children along.

She never looked back.

I was born about a year later, in Kissimmee, Florida.

Up on Scrabble Creek, even our home life revolved around Daddy's ministry. He held meetings on Wednesday nights, Saturday nights, Sunday nights, and every other Sunday morning. Sometimes we'd scarcely get back on Sunday before we had to go over there again.

Even when Daddy was at home, he talked to God all the time. You could hear him on the porch, or even out in the toilet. Sometimes you could understand the words and sometimes not. We had to pray and pray at bedtime, on our knees. We had to pray over our meals even if we had scarcely a thing in the house to eat, even if we were praying over nothing but cornmeal mush. We'd pray till the food was cold. Daddy did all this, I understood, because Jesus required it of him, and Mama did it because she loved Daddy. Mama loved Jesus too, but I think she loved Daddy even more.

She went with him to meeting, and read the Bible out

for him to preach, but she did not take up serpents herself. Many believers did not. It was only a few—some people called them the saints—who were blessed to do so, with special power that came from God in the form of anointing. It was not given to everyone, and I was real glad it had not been given to Mama.

So I cried and cried the first time she handled fire, one winter night up on Scrabble Creek.

CARLTON AND RUTH Duty had come over, as they often did, and they were in the front room with Mama and Daddy reading the Bible and talking about it and praying all together while me and Billie Jean played jacks on the kitchen floor. We could not play cards or have a radio, but we could play jacks and paper dolls. Billie Jean was thin, with pale brown hair that came down in pointy wisps all around her thin little mouse's face. She did not look a thing like Mama, which I did. Maybe she looked like Mister Bevel Reed, but if so we did not know it, as we had never seen his likeness. Billie Jean counted all the way up to five without missing. Daddy came out for his guitar and rumpled our hair on his way back through the kitchen. Billie Jean missed.

They started singing in the front room, "I'm on my way to Heaven, I can see that other shore, and I won't be coming back anymore." It was a real catchy tune which I loved, I threw out the jacks and got up to six and then missed. We could hear them singing and dancing in the other room. The glasses in the kitchen cabinet started to rattle.

Without a word, Billie Jean and I looked at each other and she gathered up the jacks and the ball and put them in her pocket and we went in there.

It was clear that things had reached a certain point already. Ruth Duty was dancing, with her fat white arms held out to the side and her stomach and her bosom bouncing up and down. Mama had her eyes closed, and bright spots of color on her cheeks. She looked like she was wearing makeup. Daddy was dancing around with his guitar. Carlton Duty was shuffling away by the heatstove with his hand over his heart, singing off-key, which didn't matter because the women were so loud. From the door, Billie Jean and me joined in. "Lord, I won't be coming back anymore, Lord, I won't be coming back anymore. . . ." Then all of a sudden Mama flung her head back and started jerking and crying out in a scary way, no words, just sharp animal noises. I tried to go forward to her, but then Daddy was there, barring my way. I watched across his arm as Mama rushed over to the heatstove, still shrieking, and opened it up and plunged her hands in there and grabbed up the red-hot coals. Smoke poured into the room.

"Je-sus! Je-sus! Blessed Je-sus!" Carlton Duty was yelling as Mama danced all around the room with the burning coals in her hands. Ruth Duty fell down on the floor moaning and sobbing.

"Thank you, Lord! Thank you, Lord!" Daddy said over and over. "Pray, little children! Pray!" he said to us.

Billie Jean and I got down on our knees and fell forward, but I was not really praying, I was banging my head on the floor and saying, "I hate Jesus! I hate Jesus!" over and over in my mind, because He was burning my mother. I fainted dead away right there, and they all thought God had come over me, but He had not.

It turned out that Mama was just fine.

I had a bruise on my forehead for two weeks, while she had nary a blister. The next day, she told us how it had felt.

"It was a good feeling, Gracie," she insisted, smoothing my hair away from my face, "a *good* feeling. It was a pleasure in the Lord. Oh honey, I don't know how to explain it. It was just too good to explain, First it was like chill bumps come over me, and then my arms and my hands went numb, and I could hear that cold wind blow, and I got kind of a cold feeling in my heart. I could feel my hands drawing to do something, and before I knowed what was going on, the Lord had led me over there to the heatstove.

"Now you *listen* to me, Gracie," she said, for I had put my hands up to my ears, "it was a perfect pleasure in the Lord, you silly girl!" But I could not understand, and though Mama was anointed to do this many times later, I never could bear to see it.

IN THOSE YEARS up on Scrabble Creek, Mama was like a child herself, never too busy to stop her work and play with us. She was always happy and singing—church songs mostly, but also other songs, from her days in the traveling show, "K-K-Katy, Good-bye," "Bill Bailey, Won't You Please Come Home," "My Blue Heaven," and "A Bicycle Built for Two," my favorite.

Joe Allen actually had a bicycle, which his boss at the sawmill had given him, and he used to ride it over to give Mama some money every payday. He was living in the bunkhouse at the sawmill. If he had not done this, we never would have had any cash money, since Daddy didn't even carry a wallet, trusting always in the Lord to provide. Mama kept the money hidden, and used to slip us some if we went to town.

I never thought about this one way or the other until the day I heard Joe Allen arguing with Mama about it.

"Just keep *some* of it back, Mama," he was saying earnestly as he stood by the porch holding the handlebars of his red bicycle. "He won't know the difference anyway." Joe Allen had freckles all over his face and one piece of brown hair that kept falling down into his eyes no matter how often he slicked it back. He could not have told a lie, or been mean to anybody, if his life depended on it. "You can't tell what might happen, Mama. You never know what you might need it for."

"Why, we don't want for a thing, honey," Mama said, laughing, as she looked around at the bright day and her blooming roses and Troy Lee down in the dirt with a spoon. I was stringing beans on the porch.

"That's just what you think right now, Mama," Joe Allen said. "You keep some of this back, you hear me? You put it away someplace where he won't know, so you'll have it, like an insurance policy. I'm not going to give it to you if you're just going to give it all to the kids, or let it go to church folks." Joe Allen stood up straight and talked as serious as a man.

"Joe Allen, I'm ashamed of you!" Mama had a little fit of temper. "What would your daddy say?"

"Number one, he ain't my daddy, and number two, I don't care what he would say," Joe Allen announced. "You can tell him if you want to. There's other ways of looking at things, Mama. You ought to hear what they say in town, some of them." Joe Allen pushed the money into her hand and got back on his bike.

"What do you mean?" Mama clutched the porch post real tight.

"Never you mind what I mean, Mama," Joe Allen said. "You put that money away like I told you. I've got to get on back now. I'll see you, Mama. I'll see you next week." Joe Allen looked like he was fixing to cry. He kicked off and rode down the hill at a furious rate of speed, and disappeared down the road to town. I watched him go, and wished that I could go with him.

"I'll be praying for you, Joe Allen," Mama called after him in a wavery voice that seemed to hang in the hot still air like the butterflies over the flowers. She looked at the money in her hand and then at me. "What are *you* looking at?" she said in a voice that was as close as she ever came to being hateful. Then she went inside, and I never knew if she saved any of that money, or any of the money that Joe Allen gave her every week until he had the big fight with Daddy. I didn't think Mama was capable of keeping anything from Daddy, though. For he was the master in our house, and she was often like one of us kids.

Daddy was really *old*, for one thing. Whenever I pictured God, especially the God of the Old Testament who parted the Red Sea and sent boils to people and burned up Sodom and Gomorrah and smote His enemies dead, I pictured Daddy, with his white hair and his sharp bright eyes and his deeply lined face. His hands and arms were black and blue from serpent bites. He had lost a whole finger—the little one on his left hand—and most of the fourth finger too. I used to hold that hand when we went to town, and when I felt the rough bumps where the fingers had been, I loved my daddy so much I could hardly stand it. For I knew—I guess we all knew—that we could lose him at any moment, and this made our time with him so precious. It gave everything an edge.

And Daddy could be really sweet too, and a lot of fun. Sometimes when it got real hot in the summertime, he would help us make pallets out in the yard, and him and Mama would sleep out there with us. He'd tell us stories out of the Bible, like the one about the baby Moses in the bulrushes, and Mama would tell us other stories she knew from childhood, like Jack goes to seek his fortune. We'd lie on our backs looking up at the stars, all of us together. Sometimes we made up stories ourselves. Daddy would start off and then everybody would add on, even Troy Lee.

"One time there was a little girl that wanted a pony," Daddy began one night, and I said, "A *magic* pony that could fly," real fast, for that was me. Everybody knew I wanted a pony.

Daddy said, "One time there was a little girl that wanted a magic pony that could fly," in his beautiful deep voice which made everything true. "And so she prayed to the Lord for the pony to come, and because she was a real good little girl who helped her mother and did everything she was supposed to, God sent the pony to her."

"At Christmas," Billie Jean added, for we never got much at Christmas. I didn't like this story very well so far, because I hadn't wanted the pony to come from God, I had wanted it to come to me all by itself, appearing from the forest. But I reckoned I couldn't be choosy.

"And she got on the magic pony and rode and rode," I said, "she rode all over the whole world, way up in the sky, and she could look down and see all the houses and everybody sleeping. She could see in every house," I said, seeing it all in my mind. I lay looking up at the sky, which was full of big winking stars though heat lightning flashed in the distance.

"And in one house there was a sick little boy," said Evelyn, who was so morbid and dramatic, "and he needed a—a special kind of syrup, and it was real far away, in Africa, and he was going to die if he didn't get it, and the only way he could get it was if the little girl would ride the magic pony over there and get it for him."

"Giddyup," Troy Lee said, and everybody laughed.

"So she started off for Africa," Evelyn went on, "but she had to go mostly all around the world to get there, and when she finally did get there, it was dark, and the bottle of special syrup was up in a hollow old tree that was guarded by lions—"

"And niggers," Billie Jean stuck in, "with rings in their nose."

"Don't say 'nigger,' " I said, for my teacher had said this hurt their feelings.

"They *love* to eat little girls," Evelyn said. "Their best kind is little blonde girls." This meant me. "And ponies. They love to eat pony stew."

"They do not!" I said. Everybody was laughing. I knew they were teasing me. "Make them quit, Daddy," I said, though Daddy was laughing too.

"And her poor little pony was so tired—" Evelyn went on, but I started talking up louder.

"That she had to give him a vitamin pill, and then he was just fine, and then she rode her pony home, and kept it forever and ever. *The end!*" I was practically screaming.

"Gracie, honey," Mama said, "it's all right," and it *was* all right, for I had gotten the pony after all.

I knew it was the only pony I'd ever get.

"Now give me your hands, children," Daddy said, and we all scooted around to where we could hold hands, and Daddy started to pray. "Oh Lord," he said, "bless these little children who have not got much in the world, and give them the keys to your kingdom, Lord, and help them to understand that they have been singled out for a special mission on this earth, Lord, as your own special servants. . . ."

I quit praying. Daddy told us this all the time. I didn't want to be a special servant of the Lord. I didn't want the keys to His kingdom either. I wanted a pony, or at the least a bicycle, and as Daddy went on and on praying, I imagined that I really had a little black-and-white spotted pony of my very own, with a silver saddle, and that I rode it across the summer sky, jumping stars.

ONE WINTER NIGHT when we were all sound asleep, there came a great pounding on the front door. I sat straight up, my heart beating out of my chest. "Billie Jean!" I shook her. "Quit it, Sissy, I'm awake," she said. The pounding continued, and now we could hear shouts. "What do you reckon it is?" I asked, and Billie Jean said out loud what I was thinking, *It might be the sheriff*, for the law had been giving Daddy a good deal of trouble. We held each other tight and listened hard.

But before long we could hear voices, Mama's and Daddy's among them, and by their tone we could tell it was not the sheriff.

"I'm going to go see what it is," I said, and I got up and pulled on my clothes though Billie Jean begged me to stay with her. Even at eleven, she was a fraidy cat. I buttoned up my sweater and listened. It sounded like they had moved into the kitchen. Billie gave a big gulp and pulled the covers over her head, and I left. Evelyn was still asleep, dead to the world. I grabbed an old quilt as I tiptoed out, and closed the door behind me. Its white china knob was smooth and cool to my touch. Once I got outside, my breath hung around my face like a cloud. I could see it in the light that spilled from the kitchen window onto the porch, and stepping up close to that window, I could see everything that happened, and hear it too.

Everybody was gathered around the kitchen table, where they had laid out the body of a little dead girl under the hanging lightbulb. I saw this. I know she was dead. She was about my age, ten years old. They had stripped off her coat and her nightdress, so she lay there wearing only her white panties and socks. She was real thin. I could have counted her ribs. She was not breathing. Her chest was sunken in and did not move. Her face was blue, her lips were blue, and her eyes had rolled back in her head. I was glad Billie Jean had stayed in bed, though I couldn't have left that kitchen window if my life depended upon it. Of course it was cold on the porch, and I was barefoot, but I didn't even notice. I let the quilt fall down around my feet.

The girl's daddy was telling my daddy how it had happened, and how they had come to be here. His name was Dillard Jones, and his freckle-faced young wife Leanne, big with another child, stood by him crying and wringing her hands. The dead girl's name was Lily. She had died that evening, but she'd been sick for a long time, most of her life, in fact. She'd take croup at the drop of a hat, and pneumonia, and lately she'd been having these spells where she couldn't breathe. The doctor said it was asthma. He had come and looked at her and given her some pills, but they didn't do her much good. Nothing had done her much good. Dillard Jones was a big tough strapping fellow, a long-distance trucker, with black hair. He looked like he could take care of any problem that ever came along, and couldn't believe that this one was out of his hands. Ever since Christmas she'd gotten worse and worse, he said, and so they'd known it was coming. She had died about an hour before.

Dillard Jones stood tall as a tree, with his hands clasped behind his back and his belly hanging over his pants, and related all this in a strong voice, like he was giving a recitation.

Daddy, in his long johns, stood with his hands on his hips and listened hard, his eyes going back and forth from Dillard Jones's face to his daughter's, there on the table. I couldn't help but think for a minute how funny it was that she lay on the new oilcloth, which featured a cartoon pattern of dogs and cats. I'd picked it out, and Mama had ordered it from Sears and Roebuck. Daddy's hair stood out wildly all around his head. Mama's pale hair fell in its long rope down her back as she clutched her old blue robe around herself with one hand and hugged the dead girl's mother with the other. Leanne Jones hardly looked old enough to have a ten-year-old child.

Daddy asked a question, and Dillard Jones answered that right after Lily died, somebody came to their door, and it was one of their cousins that they had not seen in a long time, and when he saw what was going on, he advised them to bundle Lily up and get in the car with her and drive her over to see the Reverend Shepherd, who had healed a little boy at Scrabble Creek not a month previous.

Daddy nodded. This was true.

The cousin said that if it was him, he'd do it, and so Dillard Jones had figured it was worth a try. Besides, he said, crying, he was afraid that Lily's sickness was a judgment on him for his own sins, as he had been a bad one, and run liquor and shot two people before he found the Lord. He would do anything if the Lord would give her back, he said. Tears came streaming down Dillard Jones's red face.

"Now I can't speak for the Lord," Daddy said in his deep calm voice, "but we'll all pray here together, brother, and He will let her go if He wants to, or keep her, as He sees fit."

Dillard Jones wiped his face on his sleeve and nodded.

"Fannie, get the Bible," Daddy said, but Mama had already slipped off for it, and when Daddy called for the fifth chapter of James she had already turned to it. Daddy paced the kitchen floor while she read. Then he beckoned for Mama and the Joneses to draw near to the table and put their hands on Lily while he prayed, and then he started in praying, and this went on for a long time, I don't know how long. I do remember stomping my feet to get the cramps out, and thinking how big Lily's daddy's hand looked on her thin waist. I looked up at the stars, which were tiny pinpricks of light, far away. There was no moon. The only sound in the dark cold night was Daddy's voice as he prayed.

Then, little by little, Lily came back to life. I don't know when it started happening, or when I started realizing it. But after a while her lips were not so blue, and then her face was not so blue, and then after a long while her eyelids fluttered and her eyes closed.

At this, Dillard Jones bit his lip and looked over at

Daddy, but Daddy was praying hard with his own eyes closed and gave no sign, and so it continued on, and at some point I could see that Lily's chest had started to move up and down just barely beneath their hands. It got light as they prayed, and by the time the sun rose in a fiery burst over Coleman's Ridge, she was breathing in through her mouth and her face was as pink as mine.

"Thank you, Jesus!" Daddy said when he was done. He looked old and worn-out.

Lily lay wrapped in a blanket and seemed to know what was going on, though she could not speak. Her mother held a little tin cup of water up to her mouth.

My mama waved at me through the kitchen window like it was the most natural thing in the world for me to be standing out on the porch at the crack of dawn. "Gracie, come in here and start the coffee," she called. "This is Gracie," she said to the Joneses, who were in a daze as was Daddy, slumped over in a kitchen chair. Mama disappeared and came back shortly in her housedress with her hair pinned up, and started frying bacon and breaking eggs. As soon as I smelled the bacon cooking, I realized I was just starving, which must have been true for everybody there, for we all ate the biggest breakfast.

Because of the miracle that had happened, Dillard and Leanne Jones packed up and moved over to Scrabble Creek so they could go to our church, and Lily and I came to be fast friends. We used to spend the night at each other's houses, and sit together in meeting, and I never forgot how I first saw her when she was dead.

* * *

DADDY HEALED OTHERS, including a woman who cried all the time because her nerves had gone bad, a baby that wouldn't suck, a man with a sore on his leg that wouldn't stop running, another man that couldn't hold a job because of his headaches, a girl possessed by the Devil, and many more. So there was a lot of wonder and joy in the Jesus Name Church. Daddy did not handle the serpents at every service, not even after the other saints began to take them up too. It was done only at the meeting on Sundays, after the preaching, and when a crusade was going on, where it could convince an unbeliever like nothing else. Often serpents were not present in meeting at all, and sometimes when they were present, the Lord didn't move on them, and nobody was blessed to take them up. It was only *one* of the signs that followed believers, as Daddy used to remind everybody. He hardly ever preached on those verses anyway, often letting the Bible just fall open willy-nilly and getting Mama to read out loud from whatever page the Lord had picked. Daddy could preach a good sermon on any verse. People marveled at him.

But when the time was right, and the Lord blessed him to do it, why then Daddy did take up the serpents, as did the other saints, including of course Ruth and Carlton Duty and Rufus Graybeal and Dillard Jones and the Cline sisters, and many more. Sometimes the Spirit would be so strong that the whole congregation appeared to catch it, shouting "Hallelujah" and jumping up in joy to dance, and passing the serpents from hand to hand.

People in the Spirit will often act like children—laughing out loud, giggling, patting their feet or clapping, sometimes talking baby talk. I saw old Mrs. Duke Watson, who had to be almost carried into meeting whenever she came, get up and dance the hula. I saw Lily's mama get up and throw her new baby at the nearest woman she could find, then grasp a copperhead in each hand. I saw my own sister Evelyn dance right down the aisle with a yellow rattler, popping her gum and grinning. Later, she wouldn't talk about it much. "*You* do it, Sissy," she said. "Then you'll see."

But I had never been anointed, and prayed that I never would be.

I always sat way in the back with Lily, watching what all went on. We played tic-tac-toe on a little pad of paper when things got boring. A lot of the time I got to stay home and keep Troy Lee anyway. Meeting was not really the place for children. God would send for you when He was ready for you.

There were several teenagers active in the Jesus Name congregation though, besides Evelyn. There was Evelyn's best friend Patsy Manier, a plump funny girl that everybody liked—Patsy would talk your ear off—and Darlene Knott who wore harlequin eyeglasses, the first I ever saw, and her brother Robbie Knott, who played drums sometimes in meeting, and Doyle Stacy, the thin boy with a thin mustache who played electric guitar and lived with his sick mother and worked for the Appalachian Power Company. I had a little crush on Doyle Stacy. I had a little crush on beautiful Rhonda Rose too, who had quit cheerleading in ninth grade because God told her to. This amazed me.

If I *ever* made cheerleader, I wouldn't quit for anything. I used to plan how I would hide my cheerleading outfit in my locker at the high school and just get it out when I had to wear it, so Mama and Daddy would never have to know. But this was pure fantasy, and by the time I was old enough to be a cheerleader, I was long gone from Scrabble Creek anyway.

Of course people did get bit in meeting sometimes, but nobody ever died of it. As Daddy liked to point out, the Bible says, "They shall take up serpents," *not* "They shall not bite you." Daddy himself had been bit over two hundred times, so often he had quit counting. Whenever it happened, he cried out "Glory to God," for he believed always in the perfect will of God, and turned himself over to it. He said that God has His reasons, which we know naught of. Sometimes He's just testing you. And when the serpent bites, you have to keep your mind directly on the Lord, and He will recover you. If you let your mind get off the Lord, you'll swell up.

Carlton Duty swore this was true, for he was hurt bad by a copperhead that he attempted to handle when he was thinking about buying a new truck. "The Lord taught me a good lesson," he said later, "and I thank Him for it!" though he was laid up in the bed for months afterward.

Whenever anyone was bit, we'd all go to their house and pray over them night and day, as long as it took to get them out of danger. I liked going to the people's houses, since we didn't get out much. I also liked it when they came to our house, though I couldn't stand to see Daddy get bit. It made me get the worst feeling deep in my stomach, like *I* might die. I saw this happen many times as a child, and I never got used to it, though frequently Daddy was back at church for the very next meeting, his faith was so strong.

Once I saw a rattler strike the upper part of his arm so hard it actually hung there swinging until some other men pulled it off, but by the next day you could scarcely see its fang marks. Then there was old Lonnie Ratchett, who swore that getting bit had helped his arthritis, and recommended it.

Many were healed at the Jesus Name Church, and many were baptized, and signs and wonders, such as speaking in tongues, were commonplace. Tongues of fire were seen to come down on Ruth Duty, and several people saw golden wings in the air over Daddy's head.

THIS WAS BEFORE all the bad things started happening. I always thought that a lot of the trouble had to do with the size of Daddy's ministry. At first it was small, so that the church the men had built near the old brush arbor held everybody just fine. The whole congregation came from right around there and had known each other most all their lives, so the meetings were filled with love and unity, and God was always present, and sent His anointing down accordingly.

But after Rhonda Rose's mother flew into a panic and took her to the big hospital in Waynesville for serpent bite, we got written up in the newspapers, and the crowds started getting real big. They tore one wall out of the church and added on to make it bigger, and then added on again. People were coming from miles and miles away to worship at the Jesus Name Church, believers and unbelievers alike, and troublemakers too.

Then came the time when Daddy was hurt bad. There were a lot of unbelievers present, a lot of people we didn't know, and the very air in the church house felt wrong. I don't know how to describe it. It felt to me like it does before a thunderstorm, I could smell it the way you can smell lightning. I was watching Daddy real close to see if he could feel it too, but it seemed that he could not. He was preaching and playing his guitar to lead the singing just as usual, when some of the people in the back started to yell out and heckle him.

"Hey, preacher man!" they yelled. "Where's them snakes?" And such as that.

Daddy tried to ignore them, but people in the congregation kept turning around to look, and the Spirit was slow to move among them. My heart sank when one of the men in the back hollered, "Hey, preacher! Let's get to it! We've brung a big un for you!" For I knew that they would torment the serpent before they brought him in, and sometimes put red pepper on him so he'd be ready to bite. This had happened before, and Daddy had amazed all, but tonight it didn't feel good.

"Get to it, preacher!" they yelled.

Then finally the Lord moved on the congregation, and Rufus Graybeal, always the first, brought out two rattlesnakes, and Carlton Duty took off his shoes to tread on one of them, and Doyle Stacy put his face down in his serpent box, something he had taken to doing which bothered me a lot. People were crying out and singing and dancing as usual, having forgotten about the strangers.

Suddenly a heavyset man ran up from the back, past me and Lily, and flung a huge cottonmouth onto the floor in the midst of everybody. The Spirit fled. People began screaming and trying to get away.

Daddy had to come forward then and try to grab the serpent up, and I saw it bury its fangs deep in the fleshy part of his right hand, between his thumb and index finger, and then rear back and strike his leg before he could even try again to pick it up. Carlton Duty had to help Daddy get it off his leg.

Then Daddy held the cottonmouth—the biggest one I had ever seen—up above his head with both hands, and cried out, "Glory to God!" in a strong deep voice before putting him into a sack. Daddy went on preaching to those that remained, but he had been hurt, I could tell. His speech grew slower and more halting, and he stumbled as he walked. Finally he sat down on a chair and slumped sideways.

The service was over.

Rufus and Carlton rushed to catch Daddy before he fell on the floor, and they supported him out the door and into Carlton's truck and brought him home. It would be the next day before we would learn that in all the confusion, Doyle had also suffered a serpent bite on the cheek.

By the time we got home, Mama was crying at Daddy's side and his whole arm was swelled up like a ham. His hand was black. The skin on his leg was black too, with red streaks fanning out around the serpent bite. Mama had cut his pants leg off above the knee. "Pray, children, pray!" Mama told us, so we fell to our knees and prayed and prayed, but as the night wore on, Daddy seemed to get worse instead of better. He lost consciousness and vomited blood. We understood that Daddy had been hurt because he was not anointed when he worked the signs, and we knew that he would die if it was God's will to take him on home.

Along with others from the Jesus Name Church, we prayed all night long, and it was noon of the next day before it grew clear that Daddy would live. In fact Daddy astonished everybody by going back to church that very night and handling the same serpent, the giant cottonmouth, which was now gentle as a little kitten in his arms. Doyle Stacy was not so lucky. The whole left side of his face was paralyzed, so that one eyelid drooped shut and he drooled out of the left side of his mouth. It also affected his vocal cords. He sounded real funny when he talked, and now it would be hard for him to become a preacher as he'd hoped. But you had to admire Doyle's attitude. He said that God had been testing his faith, and he thanked God that he was equal to the test.

Around this time, Rufus Graybeal was going more and more out of control. This happens sometimes. He gathered up serpents from the mountains until he had a roomful of them at his house, it was said. His wife left him one day while he was gone to meeting. She took both his little girls. They went down to Florida on a Greyhound bus, to where her people lived. Then Rufus got fired from his job at the highway department. After this, he was over at the Jesus Name Church all the time, night and day. He practically lived there.

He took money out of the bank and ordered off for some exotic serpents from a place in Florida—coral snakes, bamboo vipers, a python. They came in a special wooden box on a cargo plane. Rufus had to drive to the Asheville airport to get them. Afterward, he was real proud of those serpents, and drove around showing them to people. He had them in coolers in the back of his truck. I know that Daddy was very worried about Rufus, and talked to him many times about the sin of self-exaltation, and told him he was setting himself up to get bit if he could not rid himself of it.

So nobody was surprised when it happened, nor when he died, though we were all real sorry. Carlton Duty, speaking at the funeral, said that maybe Rufus had gotten too puffed up in the Lord. Then Daddy said that while this seemed to be the case, we were not to second-guess God, and reminded us of Jesus' words, "He that loses his life for my sake and the Gospel shall find it." Daddy said that while the ways of God are mysterious and passeth understanding, he had no doubt that Rufus Graybeal was in the heavenly kingdom of the Lord right now, having found that perfect peace which he was so far from having on this earth.

Serpents were handled at Rufus's funeral, of course, where everybody outdid themselves preaching.

They ran a picture of Daddy on page one of the *Waynesville Times*, plus a picture of Rufus in his open coffin with quarters on his eyes and a rattlesnake coiled up on his stomach. After the funeral, his brothers snatched him up and carried him to West Virginia to be buried and then came back and started talking against Daddy and the Jesus Name Church. An editorial against the church appeared in the Asheville paper, mentioning Daddy in particular. I hated that. For I had a real hard time at school anyway, without us making the paper.

IN ELEMENTARY SCHOOL, I had gotten used to them all teasing me and leaving garter snakes in the top of my desk, and to not ever being elected to anything and not making good grades because I had to miss school so much, taking care of Troy Lee or praying over those who were sick or had gotten bit. I fought a lot too, just like a boy, though Mama said not to. Mama said to ignore them for they know not what they do, but I just couldn't. I'd get mad as fire, and when somebody did something like stick out their foot to trip me as I went by, I'd turn around and kick them as hard as I could. I didn't even care if the teachers spanked me for it, which they did.

But this one year was going to be different. This year I had the chance to start all over, and I meant to do it right. I had been assigned to a new school closer to town because of redistricting, and I had already made one true friend there named Marie Royal, a regular girl from a regular family.

I thought Marie was the most beautiful girl. She had long jet-black hair, like Rose Red in my fairy-tale book, and skin as white as snow, and delicate features. When she giggled, which was often, deep dimples appeared in her cheeks. She had long willowy legs, like a deer,

I felt awkward and country around Marie. In fact I stumbled over a stool when we met, the second day of seventh grade. Our teacher was showing us how to use the school library. I was real excited, since I had never gone to a school that had a library. I had noticed Marie because she was so pretty and because she looked different from all the rest of us, but of course I hadn't said anything to her, and didn't plan to. For I had determined not to talk to *anybody*, so nobody would find out about me and tease me.

I planned to be a girl of mystery in the seventh grade.

Billie Jean was a year behind me in the new school because she had flunked twice, and I had already sworn her to secrecy. This was not hard, as she was too shy to talk to anybody anyway. Lily went to a different school because of where she lived, and Evelyn had dropped out of school altogether in order to sing with Daddy when he went out street preaching and evangelizing, which was all the time now. So the coast was clear. I was off to a great new start.

I had even gotten Mama to cut me some bangs, which I wore long, right to my eyebrows. I kept my eyes down and didn't say anything to anybody, thinking, *Girl of mystery, girl of mystery. I am a girl of mystery.*

But I got so excited in the library that I forgot myself and made a beeline for the little display of horse books on a table. I didn't even see the stool until I had knocked it into Marie.

"Ooh!" she said, hopping on one foot and clutching the other.

"I'm sorry," I mumbled, eyes down. Actually I didn't care. I couldn't wait to check out as many of those Walter Farley Black Stallion books as I could get at one time. I reached past Marie to grab.

"That one's real good," she said with authority. "That's where he goes down in these secret caves at the ocean. I'm going to get this one." She took *My Friend Flicka* off the table.

I could feel her looking at me, though I tried to hide under my bangs.

"Aren't you in Miss Black's room too?" she asked, and I said I was, and then she said, "What's your name?"

"Gracie Shepherd." I held my breath, but it was clear from the way she nodded that she had never heard of us.

"I'm Marie Royal," she said. "I can draw horses. I can draw a horse that looks just like this." She pointed at the stallion on the cover of *The Island Stallion*, which I stood there holding.

"Can't," I said immediately.

"Can," Marie said. "Look, I'll show you." She pulled one of the little wooden chairs up to a table and motioned for me to sit down on it next to her, and I did. Then she opened up a pink plastic three-ring note-book I would have given anything to own, and took several colored pencils out of a clear plastic pouch that fitted right onto the rings. I watched while she bit her tongue, concentrating, and drew the best horse's head I had ever seen. I couldn't believe it. "My mother's an artist," Marie said without looking up. "She's giving me lessons." Then she went on to draw the horse's body, which was not as good as the head, and four legs that were too short. "Here," she said, ripping out a sheet of paper for me and giving me a purple pencil. "You try it." My purple horse's head looked like a dog's head, which made me admire Marie's even more.

"Girls!" Miss Black, our teacher, bore down on us from her great skinny height. "Marie! Florida Grace! What are you doing? I've been looking everywhere for you all!" She grabbed our horses and crumpled them up. "That'll be ten minutes out of lunch for you young ladies." Miss Black talked through her nose.

"She *sounds* like a horse," I whispered to Marie as Miss Black jerked us along the hall to our room, and Marie giggled, and then we were friends.

When Miss Black kept us in at lunch, we drew four horses apiece and named them. Marie's were Jumping Jack, Hot Potato, Queen of England, and Blackie. Mine were Shadrach, Meshach, Abednego, and Judas. "Wow! Neat names," Marie said. She had never heard them before because her family didn't go to church, not *ever*, as I would learn.

"Can you come home with me one afternoon?" she asked later that day, and though I wanted to go so bad, I had to say no.

"I don't know how I'd get back to my house," I said, "if I was to miss the bus. We live way out of town on Scrabble Creek."

"Oh, Mama will drive you home," Marie said instantly, to my amazement. I couldn't imagine a mother who even knew how to drive, but Marie's mother turned out to have a car of her very own, and she was perfectly willing to drive it anyplace Marie wanted her to. Marie got to call the shots around her house. For she had been adopted, like a princess in a story. She was an only child, which seemed to make her extra generous, instead of spoiled. For lunch her mother always packed two sandwiches for her, as well as potato chips in a waxed paper bag and an apple and a Peppermint Pattie or maybe a cupcake or some cookies. I was embarrassed about my own lunch, which was nothing but a piece of cornbread usually, and sometimes a mason jar of buttermilk to break the cornbread up in, or maybe a biscuit. Some days I didn't have any lunch at all, and then I always said I was on a diet, but Marie would put half of her lunch on my desk anyway, and not say a word when I ate it up. Sometimes she had pickle loaf sandwiches, which I had never heard of, and sometimes she had peanut butter and marshmallow whip sandwiches, which were wonderful. It took a long time of begging Mama, though, before she'd ever let me go home with Marie. I knew better than to ask Daddy about it, of course. I was sure he would say no, and that would be the end of it. At first Mama said no too, but I kept at her about it.

"Why not?" I asked one day in late September. "Her mama will bring me home by dinner. She's got a red station wagon, I've seen it. She's our room mother. She's real nice. I'll do all the wash," I said. "I'll do anything. I'll be real good."

"Oh, Gracie honey—" Mama sighed while I was going on and on about it. She stroked my hair and played with my new bangs. "You *are* good, honey. It's just that—oh, it's better if . . ." Mama stared out over my head, beyond me, at the blue fall sky and the yellow leaves tumbling across our yard in the wind. She set her jaw. "Don't ask me no more." Her voice sounded funny, and when I looked at her, she turned her face away.

I waited another week or so, until Daddy went on a crusade to Tennessee, taking Evelyn with him. Then I cleaned up our room and washed all the floors in the whole house and asked Mama again. She was just coming in the door with Ruth Duty. Mama always seemed stronger, somehow, when she was with Ruth Duty, as if Ruth's good spirits and pluck had rubbed off on her too. She had this effect on everybody.

"Why, look here!" Ruth exclaimed. "I wish you'd just look at what all this child has got done! Aren't you something, Florida Grace. I know you're real proud of your girls," Ruth said to Mama, who nodded and beamed, taking off her hat, and so I popped up and asked her again if I couldn't go home one day after school with Marie.

Mama looked at Ruth.

"Honey, I'd let her, if it was me," Ruth said. "I'll swear I can't see no harm in it."

So I got to be picked up after school by Marie's mother in the red Chevrolet station wagon and driven in toward Waynesville to Marie's house. She lived in a white brick ranch house with grass in the yard and a picture window that bowed out from the living room and had about a million little panes of glass in it. Inside, the entire house looked like a magazine, with everything matching.

Marie's mother gave us olive and cream cheese sandwiches on white bread with the crusts cut off, set out on plates at the kitchen table, and Coca-Colas. At home we were not allowed to have Coca-Colas. I thought I had never tasted anything in all the world as good as those sandwiches, and I loved how the Coca-Cola fizzed on my tongue. I tried to drink it real slow, so this would go on for a long time.

Marie's mother, whose first name was Irene, sat at the kitchen table with us and smoked Salem cigarettes, which she held at an angle that I admired. I admired the way she blew the smoke out too, in a thin stream toward the ceiling, pursing her mouth. Mrs. Royal had a pixie haircut, which was popular then. Her made-up eyes pointed out at the end, like a cat's eyes. She wore pale pink lipstick and tight black pants, and her hands were stained with paint because she was an artist. I did not think much of her paintings, which were mostly just blocks of color with black lines running every which way between them. I thought Marie's horses were a lot better, and said so when Mrs. Royal asked me what I thought of her work. She threw back her head and laughed. She told me, in her strange hard Northern voice, that she found me "very refreshing." I was surprised to learn that Marie's dad was at home too, reading a book. Mr. Royal was called Dr. Royal, but he wasn't a real doctor, he just worked over at the college in Cullowhee. It must not be much of a job,

I thought, for him to be home in the afternoon. He asked me a lot of questions and listened hard, nodding seriously, to my answers. I wasn't used to being asked questions, or listened to. I knew I had to be real careful about what I said, and though I told them all about my brothers and sisters, I just said that my daddy traveled, which was true, Dr. Royal nodded in a way that made me feel grown-up, and sucked on his pipe. I felt like I got drunk on smoke in that house every time I went over there, and I resolved to start smoking myself, the first chance I got, and hold my cigarette at an angle like Mrs. Royal.

Marie had a big dollhouse and a closet full of dolls, a shelf of books, a pink-and-white indoors bathroom with a lacy cover on the toilet seat and—best of all—a television set! This was the first television I had ever seen, and I will never forget the chill which came over me that day as we sat down before it and watched Kate Smith sing "When the Moon Comes over the Mountain" in grainy black-and-white. I started crying, I was so surprised! And then I got tickled, and Marie got tickled too.

That afternoon passed so fast I couldn't believe it when Mrs. Royal said it was time to go. Marie and I sat in the backseat and giggled while her mother smoked Salems and played the radio. Sometimes she sang along.

I had to pay attention and give directions for the last part of the drive. "Are you *sure* this is the road?" Mrs. Royal kept asking when we left the pavement and took the gravel road up to Scrabble Creek. "Yes ma'am, I'm sure, yes ma'am, this is right," I kept saying, and then I was home and she stopped the car and we all stared up the hill at my house, which looked so poor to me suddenly, like a picture in a book about olden times.

"Oh neat, look at the creek!" Marie said, and Mrs. Royal said, "Is that your mother on the porch?" and then Marie was saying, "Mama, can we go in for a minute? Can we, can we?"

I looked up the hill and saw my mother stand up and go in the house, closing the door behind her. She did not wave.

"I've got to go," I said. "Thanks a lot, I'll see you tomorrow, Marie." I slammed the car door and ran up the hill as fast as my legs would carry me, stumbling over rocks and roots on the way because my eyes were stinging with wind and tears.

MAMA LET ME go home with Marie once a week from then on throughout the fall, but she never let me spend the night or the weekend, though the Royals asked me to. I couldn't miss meeting, Mama said. I told Marie that I had to stay home and keep Troy Lee because Mama worked, which turned out to be sort of true, after Mama started helping out at the Dutys' grocery. Mama never came down to the car to meet Mrs. Royal, or told me to invite her in. Mama did not go to PTA, or come to the school on Parent Day. Billie Jean was real jealous of my friendship with Marie, and whined about it, accusing me of being stuck-up. She asked me lots and lots of questions at first about the Royals' house and what all Marie had—what toys, what dolls—but I wouldn't say. I wanted to keep it all to myself, just for me, though I knew it was a sin to be selfish. I didn't care. I wanted something just for myself, and I wouldn't tell Billie Jean a thing. Finally she quit asking.

I didn't tell Billie Jean that she was invited to go to the Halloween fair at the Waynesville Lions Club with me and Marie in late October. I just told Mrs. Royal that Billie couldn't go. "Billie Jean has asthma," I said. I knew about asthma because of Lily. "She has to rest a lot." "Oh dear," Mrs. Royal said, and at the Halloween fair she bought a gumball necklace for me to take home to Billie Jean, but I kept it. I didn't care if I went to Hell or not.

Marie and her family were *mine*.

One thing Marie and I always did together was write horse books—that is, I'd write the story, and Marie would draw the pictures. We had made up a talking roan named Spice and a girl named Melinda who owned him. Nobody except Melinda knew that he could talk. They solved mysteries together, and the names of the books were the names of the mysteries—*The Secret in the Hollow Tree*, *The Clue of the Broken Flower*, *Melinda Saves the Day*, and *What Went On in the Meadow*, which was Mrs. Royal's favorite. She was just crazy about our books, and used to bring lemonade for us into the dining room, where we got to work on our books at the big table under the fancy hanging light.

While I was visiting, Mrs. Royal was usually in the kitchen cooking, or reading magazines and smoking cigarettes, or sewing. She made a lot of Marie's clothes, but you could never tell that they were homemade. I didn't understand why she did this. "If I could buy my little girl any dress she wanted at Wilson's, I would," I said to Marie one day. "I'd *never* make it!" Wilson's Department Store was the biggest store in downtown Waynesville. I had stood on the street corner outside it with Daddy while he preached.

"Oh, Mama just likes to sew," Marie said.

I still thought it was stupid to make something if you could afford to buy it.

Then one day Mrs. Royal showed me some sky-blue corduroy and a matching piece of cotton with flowers all over it. "I thought I might make you and Marie both some jumpers out of this," she said, kind of offhand but watching me, "and blouses to match. What do you think of that idea?"

"I wouldn't mind," I said, though my heart was jumping right out of my chest. The only time I'd ever had anything brand-new to wear in my whole life was when Ruth and Carlton Duty gave each one of us an outfit the Christmas before. So Mrs. Royal spread the blue corduroy out on the carpet in the living room, covered it with crinkly pattern pieces, and started cutting. The next time I went there, Mrs. Royal asked me what Mama had said about us having the matching jumpers, and I said Mama was tickled to death. This was a lie. I kept the jumpers secret from Mama, just as I kept other things secret from Marie and Mrs. Royal.

I had a lot of secrets that fall, so many that sometimes I thought my head would burst and they would all fly out into the room like hornets from a nest, stinging everybody.

* * *

THE SCARIEST SECRET was Daddy.

Ever since Rufus Graybeal's death, Daddy had gotten more and more religious, so that there was never a time when he didn't have his mind fixed directly on the Lord. He was trying to get to a new plateau. He wouldn't play with us anymore, or make up stories. In fact he wasn't hardly ever at home, and I have to say I liked it better when he was gone than when he was with us, because he was acting so scary. He fasted a lot and got so thin that he had to keep his pants up with a rope tied around his waist. He looked like a scarecrow then, with his long white hair sticking out in every direction and his eyes all wild and glowing. I wanted a daddy like Marie's, who wore a gray vest and sat in a chair and read books and talked to me. We couldn't understand what our own daddy was saying half the time now, as he often spoke the unknown language of the Lord. Mama's eyes were always red from crying, and she had lost weight too, and one time, when they didn't hear me coming in the door after school, I heard her say sharply, "Virgil, do you *have* to do this?" and he answered in his deep God voice, "Yes, Fannie, I do."

Then I went in the door to find Mama sobbing, but as soon as she saw me, she wiped her tears on her apron and said, "Why, Florida Grace! You mean you're home from school already?" and gave me a big fake smile. Later, when I asked her what was the matter, she said, *"Nothing. Just nothing,"* and went all stony-faced, so I didn't have a clue until Evelyn told me.

"He's gearing up to drink poison," Evelyn said.

"*What?*" I asked.

"They do it over in Tennessee, and Daddy's getting ready to do it too. He's getting right with God so he'll be ready." Evelyn's voice was matter-of-fact, but her beautiful face looked holy. She was still into it lock, stock, and barrel at that time, and traveled everywhere with Daddy, and her high pure voice was a big help to him in his mission.

I was present at Sunday-morning meeting in the Jesus Name Church to see Daddy bring in the mason jar of water with strychnine in it for the first time, and I saw him drink it with no ill effects, though an unbeliever grabbed it up to try it and then went screaming from the church house clutching his throat. Soon all the other saints were drinking poison too, whenever God moved on them to do it, and this was a regular feature of Daddy's ministry, but he did not let up even then. He kept right on fasting and praying nonstop.

It was like he had gone into high gear. He'd hold meetings in people's houses or vacant lots or anyplace, sometimes all night long. He'd travel from town to town in our area, then go over to Tennessee, where a great crowd of believers was gathering, he said, and God was working hard.

But Evelyn said something else, and this secret was harder to keep than any other. She came back from one trip to Tennessee all mad at Daddy, and though she was too scared of him to let on, she told me about it. She said she just had to tell somebody, so we went out in the yard by the tulip tree where we could talk.

"I was in the Ben Franklin five-and-dime over in Elizabethton, where we've been going to preach," Evelyn told me, "buying me some shampoo, and all of a sudden I heard this voice—*his* voice—and I don't know why, but I kind of ducked around the counter to where I could see him but he couldn't see me, instead of coming right out and saying 'Hi, Daddy.' There was something in his voice that made me do that. *Then*," Evelyn said, real dramatic, popping her gum, "you wouldn't believe what I saw next!"

"What?" I couldn't imagine.

"Daddy had him a hoor, right there in the five-and-dime!"

"A what?" I said.

"A *hoor*," Evelyn was all wrought up. "It's a bad woman, Sissy, that goes with a lot of men."

"How did you know it was a hoor?" I was dying to find out.

"Well, you can just tell. If you was ever to see one, you'd know it right away. She had on a whole lot of makeup, and black net stockings. She had bleach-blond hair, real curly, and a chiffon scarf."

"But what were they doing?"

"He was buying her just whatever she wanted, that's what. He was buying her some nylon hose and some bubble bath."

"Bubble bath?" I couldn't believe it. Of course I thought about how Daddy wouldn't buy us anything at all, and never had any cash money for Mama.

"That's why he goes over there all the time," Evelyn said in her fierce whisper.

"But what about those big meetings he's been talking

about? Is it a lie?" For he had whipped us from the cradle if he caught us in a lie.

"No, it ain't a *lie*, exactly," Evelyn said. "I mean, that's true too. He's got them all worked up over there, Sissy. You know how it is when he takes the message to a new place. He's got them coming in by the hundreds." She paused and took a deep breath. "You know what's wrong with Daddy? You know what I think is wrong?"

My heart was beating real fast, for we had never said anything against him in our whole lives. I shook my head.

"He does everything too much," Evelyn said darkly. "Whatever it is. If it's God or if it's a girlfriend, it don't matter. He does it too much."

"But what about you?" I asked. "Don't you feel funny about being his little angel of God now?" This is what Daddy still called Evelyn, though she was almost sixteen by then.

"You're damn right," she said.

I sucked my breath in sharply. A thrill ran through me as I looked at her set face. Evelyn was a lot like Daddy, in a way. There was no telling what she might do if she put her mind to it, She was breathing hard and staring off down the hill, her eyes fixed on something I couldn't see. I felt like crying.

"Evelyn, what are you going to do?" I asked.

She grinned at me all of a sudden, her old flashy self. "You can't tell on me if you don't know," she said.

Just then Mama appeared in the doorway. "Supper's ready!" she called in her sweet voice. "Florida Grace and Evelyn, you all come on."

Evelyn clutched my arm so hard her fingers left white strips on my skin. "Don't you say a word!" Her face was right up in mine, "Swear!" she said.

"Swear," I said. "Cross my heart and hope to die."

Evelyn acted just as natural at supper, like nothing had happened, and in a few days she went back over to Tennessee with Daddy, and I never told a soul about the hoor.

This is the time that Daddy was arrested over there, after a man died in the meeting from a combination of Red Devil lye and serpent bite. Daddy had to serve thirty days, and we thought that Evelyn would come home while he was in jail, but she didn't. She wrote that she had taken a job and was staying with some church people and was fine. She didn't say what the job was or who the people were. Mama's face got thinner than ever, and worry lines appeared between her eyebrows. The circles under her eyes got darker. "God's will be done," she said, and I didn't say a thing. Mama went to meeting, where Carlton Duty and Doyle Stacy and Bobby Gayheart were preaching in Daddy's absence, and came back full of the Spirit. "God has been testing me," she said earnestly. "He has found me wanting in faith." And she set in to praying like crazy. I could hear her in the bedroom praying, long into the night.

If ever anybody was a real saint in this world, it was my mother.

MEANWHILE, MARIE'S PARENTS knew all about Daddy, though I was pretty sure they hadn't told Marie. They never said anything to me about it either, and the way I found out was the purest chance.

I confess I was always a snoop in that house, looking in closets to finger the clothes, opening drawers just to see what was there. It was like I wanted Marie's *whole life*, right down to her underwear, right down to her mother's monogrammed stationery, right down to the Cuban cigars in her father's desk.

This was where I found the clipping.

Marie and I had just started a new book about Spice, and her mother was busy painting in what she called her "studio," which was really an empty bedroom, when the telephone rang. It was Marie's grandmother, who called up long-distance all the time from Wilmington, Delaware, just to see how Marie was doing. I didn't know my own grandparents—I didn't even know if I had any. We didn't have a telephone at our house either. In cases of extreme importance, such as when Daddy called to say he was in jail, the message came through the Dutys, and if any of us ever had to make a call, we went to the Dutys' store to do it. I had called Marie from there a couple of times, but I had never made or received a long-distance call.

Marie talked and talked to her grandmother, just like she was right there in the room with us. She told her grandmother about the new book we were writing and that she had gotten all A's in school—I had too—and that her mother was going to Asheville to learn how to be a Girl Scout leader so we could have a troop. This was the first I had heard about it, and I got real excited for a minute or two before I realized that I would never be allowed to join. Those uniforms cost money, and Daddy always said we had a higher allegiance whenever anything like that came up, like when Joe Allen had wanted to join 4-H. I imagined Marie in that beautiful green uniform, covered with merit badges, going on a cookout with other girls.

While she talked to her grandmother on the kitchen phone, I got up to go to the bathroom. But as I was going through Dr. Royal's study, something made me head for his desk instead, where I started opening all the drawers to see what I could find. This included a whole lot of baby pictures of Marie, plus some pictures of Mrs. Royal wearing a bathing suit, at a beach with the *real ocean* in the background, and a wedding picture of Mr. and Mrs. Royal looking like movie stars, several dollars in change which I did not touch, a lot of paper clips and rubber bands and little pieces of paper, an old watch, and—surprise!—a whole cubbyhole full of seashells. I took one of these, a small pink one I was sure Dr. Royal would never miss. Then I opened a drawer which turned out to be full of more papers and newspaper clippings, some of them old and yellow, some of them not.

Right on top was a brand-new one with a picture of my own father preaching and holding a copperhead while other people prayed and danced in the background. They were people I had never seen before. The headline said SNAKE HANDLER SEIZED.

I was going to read on, when suddenly Mrs. Royal reached around me from behind and took the clipping away. I jumped a mile, she scared me so bad. She put the clipping back in the drawer and closed it. She had paint on her hands. She didn't say anything to me about going through Dr. Royal's desk. "Oh honey, it's okay," was all she said. Then she hugged me real tight for a long time, until Marie hung up the phone and called, "Gracie?" from the kitchen. Mrs. Royal gave me a final squeeze and let me go. I went into the bathroom and she went in the kitchen with Marie.

Later that afternoon, she gave us a special treat of red Jell-O cut up in little squares with Dream Whip on it. Nobody ever said another word about the clipping.

I felt like I was walking on eggs all the time, I had so many secrets to keep.

THEN TO TOP it all off, Troy Lee got sick. Actually, Troy Lee had not been feeling good for a long time, and here is another secret I never told anybody—I was convinced that Troy Lee got sick because I had lied about Billie Jean, telling Mrs. Royal that Billie was sick when she wasn't, so I wouldn't have to share Marie's family with her. I knew it, was selfish when I did it, but I did it anyway. Now I was sorry. I felt like God was making Troy Lee sick just to get back at me for lying. I felt like it was all my fault. Plus, Troy Lee had always been my favorite, I had taken care of him so much, it was like he was *my* little boy in a way, and I just couldn't stand it for him to feel bad.

He had always been easy to take care of, because he was quieter than most little boys and didn't run around much.

He never did. He didn't have all that energy that most children have, and lately you couldn't hardly get him to go out and play. He was always tired. He was real little for six. His skin looked kind of gray to me, and most of the time he just sat in the porch swing with the cat that Ruth Duty had given him, kind of quivering on the air. It was like he was too weak to push the swing. When it started getting cold, he sat inside on the horsehair sofa in front of the heatstove, holding his cat. The cat didn't have a name. Ruth Duty hadn't named it, and Troy Lee wouldn't. I don't know why that bothered me, but it did. I was so worried about Troy Lee that I was mad at him half the time.

I joined in when the church people came over to lay hands on him and pray him well, I squeezed his small bony shoulder and prayed the hardest I ever prayed in all my life. I told God that I would never tell another lie if He would heal Troy Lee, and that I would try to open my heart to Him more, and join the church whenever He sent me His sign, something I had never promised before. Everybody was gathered up around Troy Lee and his cat on the sofa in the front room, praying out loud. It sounded like the Tower of Babel.

Finally, when they quit and stepped back, Troy Lee did look better, kind of flushed in the face, and said he felt better too, and he went outside to play for a while. But he was worse than ever when he came back in, and had to go right to bed.

Of course Mama and the Dutys took him to meeting as well, and Doyle preached and Carlton led the laying on of hands, and this time they used Wesson oil, so I was hoping that would help, but it did not. Troy Lee got weaker and weaker. He wouldn't hardly eat a thing, but he kept wanting water all the time. Mama was praying and counting the days until Daddy would get out of jail and come home to heal Troy Lee. She expected him on November first.

After that day came and passed, Mama took to standing on the front porch for hours on end, watching for Daddy to come down the road, while Troy Lee laid on the sofa with his cat. Naturally I wasn't going to school very regular, with all this happening.

But Troy Lee just kept getting worse and worse, and Daddy never showed up.

My birthday came and went, and nobody remembered it. Nobody told me Happy Birthday.

I was fourteen years old.

And then one day in early November, everything happened at once. It was a Saturday morning, a beautiful cold sunny day with the sky so blue and the air so crackling that it made me feel like running all around the yard shouting.

"Let's you and me climb the ridge," I said to Billie Jean, who looked at me like I was crazy. Even then, Billie was a more beat-down and slow-moving person than I was, perfectly content to do whatever Mama was doing, as if she was a grown woman already.

"What do you want to go up there for?" she asked me in her flat little voice. "There's not anything up there." Which was true, but that was just exactly what I liked about it, the miles and miles of nothing but sky and mountains stretching out from Chimney Rock, and I wanted to feel the wind that always blew up there, I wanted it to chill my very bones.

"Well, I'm going by myself, then," I said. "See you later."

"I'm going to tell Mama," Billie said. "You know she don't want you to go up there."

So I hurried to put on some pants and an old jacket that Daddy had left, and ran out the back door and headed up the trail past the toilet and the cedar trees before Mama could stop me.

I was out of sight by the time I heard her calling me. "Florida Grace! Florida Grace! You come back here!" Her voice got fainter and fainter as I went on. I was cold at first, but the more I climbed, the warmer I got. To get up the mountain, you had to climb a winding rocky trail and then pass through a laurel slick where it was dark and steep, almost a tunnel, but it was all worth it when you came out on a grassy bald at the top of the ridge.

Sunshine was everywhere. The trees around the bald were taller than down below, with grass between them, almost like a park. Most of the leaves had fallen. I loved it up there. I kicked through the bright leaves as I went along, looking up through the tree limbs which were like lace against the deep blue sky. I took big deep breaths of the cold air and felt my blood race all through my body. I felt bigger. I knew I could do anything. I walked the ridge until I got up so high that the tall trees gave way to brush, and then I was above the tree line in a windy place of flat table rocks and scaly lichen and low-growing tough little plants. I had to climb up and down over the table rocks, which appeared to have been flung out there by a giant.

Now I was up so high that I could look off to my left and see the whole valley spread out like a picture down below, like a faraway land of make-believe, dreaming in the sun. I couldn't see our house, but I could see the Dutys' store and their house and the Jesus Name Church and the road winding in and out of the hills, and the Little Dove River, a sparkling silver chain. Cars looked like toys from where I was. I wondered what Ruth Duty was doing, and if anybody was in the church house. I wondered if Marie was up yet—she got to sleep late, which was a sin at our house, and not only that, but her *mother* slept late too. Marie had said so. I wondered what Marie was going to do that Saturday, and what her mother was going to do. Maybe they would drive over to Asheville, where I had never been.

But I didn't care too much what Marie was going to do, as I climbed that ridge so high above her, so high above them all. That morning I felt too good to care. I thought I would rather be me than anybody.

I climbed all the way to the end of the ridge, right out to Chimney Rock, and then I climbed up Chimney Rock itself, surefooted as any boy. I remember it was the first time I'd ever climbed Chimney Rock, which was actually two rocks, two huge boulders perched on top of the last cliff looking out over the whole county, so you could see distance on every side, wherever you looked, three hawks swooping great circles through miles of air, smoke rising here and there down below. I remembered that it was hog-killing time, and that we would probably get some fresh meat later on in the day from the Pearsons, who were butchering. We didn't get meat often, so it would be a special treat. I stood on the rock and thought about how good it would taste. Maybe Troy Lee would eat some and it would make him feel better.

In spite of the cold up there, I was hot from climbing. I took Daddy's jacket off, then took my shirt off too. I didn't know I was going to do it before it was done. The wind felt great on my chest and my back, I reached up and took off the rubber band that held my ponytail, and let the wind blow my hair all around. I stood at the very edge of Chimney Rock with my feet wide apart and my arms folded, like an Indian brave. I looked out and pretended that my tribe owned everything I could see, mountain after mountain until they grew blue and hazy in the distance over toward Tennessee. I drew in big deep gulps of cold air until I got dizzy. Then I sat down beside a pile of smaller rocks, where I found a pointed white rock which I used to scratch my name GRACIE in big capital letters right across the flattest place on the top of Chimney Rock, I went over and over the letters, so they would last. I stood back up and took one more look around before I put my shirt and my jacket back on and started down.

As I climbed back over the table rocks, I thought about the vision Daddy had had on Roan Mountain when he was twenty-five years old, which I had heard him preach about many times. Daddy had started out as a young preacher but had backslid real bad, to where he was gambling and running liquor and drinking it too, and one morning after a big drunk he woke up alone laying by the side of the Roan Mountain road. His hands were cut and swollen, so he knew he had been in a fight, but he couldn't remember who with, nor what they were fighting about, nor where he'd been. Daddy said that when he tried to raise up his head, he felt so bad he almost died on the spot, so he just laid real still, and wished he *would* die. He was in a low distress, he said, when all of a sudden the whole world went dim and the voice of the Lord spoke out of the darkness loud and clear.

"Virgil Shepherd, get up from there," God said, and so Daddy got right up, and his pain was gone. He stood on that dark road and waited to see what would happen next. "Virgil Shepherd," God said, "I am calling you to be my own special minister, and go out to all the people, and spread my word."

But Daddy held back and said, "How do I know you are the Lord talking and not the Devil?" and God said, "I will give you this sign."

Then lo the darkness gave way to sunlight, and there in the middle of the road appeared a dazzling white serpent, and Daddy was anointed to walk over there and pick it up, and it grew tame as a toy in his arms. "Now go forth and spread my word," God told Daddy, and this was the true start of Daddy's ministry. Next God sent a truck to give him a ride down off Roan Mountain, and when he got back to town everybody that knew him shrank back upon seeing him, for his hair had turned pure white.

I thought about all this as I was climbing over the table

rocks on my way back, and for the first time I dared to wonder if it was true or not. I wondered if it had really happened as he said, or if it had all happened *in his mind*, which might also make it true, but different, I thought. That would be different.

I looked all around me real careful as I climbed, but I didn't see any sign of God or Jesus either one. I didn't see a thing but the bright cold day, and I didn't feel a thing but the hard rough rocks beneath my hands and the wind and the sun on my face.

I was getting real hungry as I walked across the bald and clambered down through the laurel slick and came out by the cedar trees to where I could see our holler. There was a truck parked on the road below. It was a truck I didn't recognize right off, and so I thought it must be the Pearsons bringing us some pig meat, and I started running down to the house.

I kept running until I got close enough to hear, and then I slowed down, and then I got to the back door and stopped. I knew that voice, all right. I would have known it anywhere. I felt like I ought to go in there, but I just couldn't move. I felt awful. I felt I had turned to stone or to salt, like Lot's wife. Then Billie Jean came tearing through the house and out the back door, and ran smack into me. She was sobbing as though her heart would break. We held each other tight as she told me what was going on, the best she could through her tears.

Joe Allen had come by to visit and give Mama some money, Billie said, but when he saw how sick Troy Lee was, he pitched a fit and said that he was going to take Troy Lee to the hospital. He had a borrowed truck and he was going to take him in it. Mama was welcome to ride along with them.

"What did Mama say?" I asked Billie Jean.

"Well, at first Mama was crying," Billie told me, wiping her face, "but then she started getting Troy Lee's things together, like Joe Allen said. When all of a sudden, there was Daddy a-standing in the door. Didn't none of us see him come, nor hear him, nor nothing. He just about scared us to death!"

"Then what happened?" I asked Billie Jean, while inside the house I could hear Daddy invoking the Lord to rid Joe Allen of whatever demon possessed him. The sound of Daddy's voice gave me the chills.

"Mama dropped all of Troy Lee's things in the floor and ran to Daddy, but he didn't kiss her, nor nothing," Billie said. "He put out his hand to stop her, looking first to Troy Lee, and then to Mama, and then to Joe Allen. It was like he took it all in real fast. Then he fell to his knees and prayed out loud to thank God that he had come back in time to take care of his family." Billie Jean was sniveling. "But Joe Allen said, 'No sir, you might as well get up from there, because God don't have anything to do with this. This little boy is sick, and he is going to the doctor, God has done drawed a blank on this one.' So then Daddy said, 'Son, I forbid you to take that boy from my house,' and Joe Allen said, 'I wouldn't hardly call it your house, you're not ever here, everybody in the world has got to take care of your own family for you.' Then Daddy stood up and stepped forward and said, 'Son,' again, and Joe said, 'Don't you call me "Son." Don't you never call me "Son" again.' "

"And then what?"

"And then Daddy started praying for Joe Allen, and then he switched back over to Troy Lee," Billie Jean said, and sure enough, we could hear him in there going at it. Daddy could pray for hours on end, he was famous for it.

"Where's Mama and Joe Allen now?" I said, and Billie said she didn't know.

She clutched the sleeve of Daddy's old jacket. "Don't let's go in there, Sissy," she said. "Let's walk down the road."

But I was bound and determined to see what was happening. I held Billie Jean's hand and we went around the side of the house to the front porch, where we found Joe Allen sitting on the porch steps, smoking a cigarette.

"Well, there you are, Billie Jean," he said. "I was wondering where you had got to. Hello there, Sissy." He grinned at me.

"Hi," I said. I looked at Joe Allen good. There was something different about Joe Allen. He had a new job now, working at Mister John Ritter's lumberyard, where he was in charge of filling the orders and sending out the trucks. But Joe Allen had been living on his own and working for years, first at the sawmill, then at the lumberyard. He was a man now. That was it. Joe Allen had become a man, Though he was still skinny as a rail and that same old piece of hair fell forward into his eyes, he held himself in a certain way, like a man who meant business. He took one last drag on his cigarette and ground it out under his boot heel and then threw it out in the yard and stood up.

"What are you going to do now?" I asked him.

"I am going to take Troy Lee to the doctor," he said, "come Hell or high water. Troy Lee is fixing to die, Sissy." That was something I had been knowing and not knowing at the same time, I realized. "It don't matter if Daddy's back or not. Daddy'll kill him."

Billie Jean made a sound and Joe Allen looked at her.

"I mean he'll let him die, which is the same as killing him. Sick people need medicine, they don't need no mumbo jumbo," Joe Allen said. Then he looked at me. "Come on and help me, Sissy."

"What do you want me to do?" I asked.

"I don't know exactly," Joe Allen said. "But you come on in here. Billie, you go sit in the swing," and Billie did it, crying hard again. Joe Allen shook his head. I followed him into the front room and stood still for a minute while my eyes got adjusted to the dimness. There was Daddy all right, big as life, praying on his knees before the sofa where Troy Lee lay in a kind of sleep, his little face dead white. Mama sat in the chair, wringing her hands. She looked up at us with her eyes wide, as if she didn't know who we were. Daddy didn't even turn around.

"Step aside, sir," Joe Allen said in an even voice.

Daddy didn't move.

"Step aside, sir," Joe Allen said again. Mama stood up and I went over to her. Daddy had both hands on Troy Lee, and was leaning across his little form all wrapped up in the quilt. Joe Allen moved forward and put his hand on

Daddy's shoulder, pulling him back. Quick as a flash, Daddy flung out one arm and hit Joe Allen in the stomach. He doubled over for a minute and then straightened up and pulled Daddy back with both hands, flinging him to the floor and then jumping on top of him, his hands at Daddy's throat. Daddy rolled back and forth, clawing at Joe Allen's hands, his face terrible. It was red and splotchy, the way it sometimes got in meeting. Daddy threw Joe Allen off and leaped to his feet and started kicking him, and then Joe Allen was up too. He hit Daddy real hard in the face, and blood started spurting from Daddy's nose, It poured all over his white shirt. Daddy sat down with a jolt.

Out of the corner of my eye I saw Mama go in the kitchen and come back with her big pickling crock, which she raised above her head. I reached up and grabbed it and sent it rolling out the door and off the porch. I put my arms around Mama from behind and held her tight, which was easy, for she was so slight and I was strong. Daddy's nose was bleeding, but he sat still, half propped up against the chair, which had been overturned in the struggle. He sat still because Joe Allen had pulled a knife on him. Joe Allen held the knife out toward Daddy in his right hand, his eyes never leaving Daddy's face as he moved past him to pick up Troy Lee in the quilt and throw him over his shoulder like a sack of flour.

"Stay right there, sir, that's right," Joe Allen was saying in an easy voice like a chant. "Don't you move none. That's right," he said, backing out the door. When Joe Allen got on the porch and turned to go down the steps,

I could see Troy Lee's head bobbing against his back. Troy Lee didn't open his eyes.

I let go of Mama, who turned around and looked at me in a tragic way. "Oh Sissy, the devil has done claimed you for his own," she said, and rushed over to Daddy, who still sat there against the chair like he didn't know what was going on. Mama knelt down on the floor and covered his bloody face with kisses.

Right at that minute, two more things happened.

Troy Lee's cat, which I had completely forgotten about, went dashing out the open door, and as I leaped after it, thinking to grab it and keep it for him, I almost ran into Marie, who appeared in the doorway at that very moment and then stood there frozen, her mouth in a perfect round O. She and her mother had just showed up to surprise me. Behind her I could see Billie Jean's scared white face, and down at the road I saw Joe Allen's truck peeling off past that familiar red station wagon. Then I felt Daddy's hands like iron on my arms just above the elbow.

Marie started crying and pushed the brown paper bag she'd been carrying into my arms. Her mother got out of the car and started screaming for her to come. Without a word to me, Marie turned and ran down the hill and got in the car, and then they were gone. Daddy pulled me back in the house and whipped me with his belt until I bled, but I didn't even care, and when I finally started crying, it was not because of the whipping, it was because I knew that was the end of my friendship with Marie.

I saw her at school of course, but it was not the same. It

was never the same again. Marie didn't ask me to come home with her anymore, nor talk to me much at lunch. When Mrs. Royal came to school to be our room mother, such as at Thanksgiving when she brought all the stuff and helped us make Indian and Pilgrim costumes, she treated me just like she treated everybody else. Nice but distant.

For a long time I kept the brown paper bag containing my blue corduroy jumper and my flowered blouse hidden in the corncrib, so I could go out there and try them on whenever I felt like it. Then one cold day in January, I took Mama's scissors and cut them to ribbons, and threw the pieces down the toilet hole.

When the Girl Scout troop started, I wasn't in it, which didn't matter because we had a lot of snow that winter and so Billie Jean and me couldn't get to school much anyway. It turned out that Troy Lee had had scarlet fever. He stayed in the hospital for a long time and then he was well, but Joe Allen kept him in town, which seemed to be all right with Mama. She was real busy helping Daddy with his ministry because Evelyn had up and gotten married, over in Tennessee. Daddy wouldn't talk about her or let us answer her letters. He said Evelyn was lost. I kept thinking about what I had promised God I would do if Troy Lee got well, that I would open my heart more to Him, but though I did go to meeting the same as ever, and though He came down on people to the right and the left of me and even on Lily Jones—they had to break the ice in the Little Dove River to baptize her—He never came down on me, nor sent me any sign. Sometimes I'd think about Marie and her family, and Melinda and Spice, and all the things I had seen and done at her house, but it was like it had all happened a long time before, in a book or a dream.

And as for Troy Lee's cat, we never saw it again.

IT WAS A hard winter, as I said. Billie Jean and me were alone in the house a lot, and to tell the truth, she was not much company, or much help. Billie Jean had always been real shy, but this winter she got more shy than ever, and something else. I don't know how to say it exactly. It was like she moved back in her mind someplace, away from everything. I believe it started when Joe Allen took Troy Lee away. The first time I really noticed it was not long after that, when we got snowed in for a whole week while Mama and Daddy were down in South Carolina. I was about to work myself to death keeping wood chopped and the stove fed, and hauling water in from the well. We didn't have any gloves in the house, and my hands got chapped, with big red cracks in them, and bled. One morning I slipped in the snow on my way back from the well and spilled a bucket of water. I just laid there and let the snow fall in my face and closed my eyes. It was so early that you couldn't even tell yet whether the sun was going to come up or not, and I was already exhausted. I wanted to lay there forever. But I knew I couldn't, for I had to take care of Billie Jean, and so finally I pushed myself up, and after a while I went and got some more water and struggled back to the house with it. I didn't know what we would do if the well froze solid—so far, I'd been able to break the ice by dropping the bucket down on it a lot.

"I made it!" I yelled to Billie from the porch. I figured she'd be worried about me, since I'd been gone so long. We both woke up before the light, because we were so cold. I'd gotten the fire started, and she was supposed to tend it while I went for water.

"Billie!" I hollered.

Nothing.

I stamped my feet, which felt like solid blocks of ice, and pushed the door open. Billie sat in the velvet chair in front of the heatstove holding a piece of firewood, exactly like I'd left her, her head cocked to the side a little, as if she was listening to something.

She was smiling. The fire had gone out.

A chill went through me which had nothing to do with the cold.

"Billie!" I said sharply. She turned to me and her face lit up as if she'd just noticed me. "Why, Sissy," she said. "How are you?"

"Fine," I said. I took the firewood out of her hand and threw it in the stove and stuck in some kindling and old catalogue pages. We had about used up that catalogue.

"Billie, what were you thinking of, to let the fire go out thataway?" I asked her.

Billie Jean just smiled at me, the nicest smile. She was humming a tune I didn't know. She got closer to the stove and held her hands up before it, spreading her fingers. She had pretty hands, like Mama. "That feels so good," she said. Then she went back to humming. Later that day we went out in the snow to make angels, and we had made them all over that hillside by the time Carlton Duty and Dillard Jones came walking around the bend to get us. I was never so glad to see anybody in my whole life! Billie Jean went home with the Dutys and I went home with Dillard Jones, where it was nice and warm, and Lily's mama took my shoes and stockings off and hung them by the fire to dry. I wore two pairs of somebody else's thick wool socks while my own were drying, and since it kept on snowing outside, Lily's mama let us pop corn in the middle of the day, just like it was Christmas, and drink coffee, and her daddy played his guitar and we all sang "I'll Fly Away." We had a real good time. I quit worrying about Billie. But I felt different about her from then on, like she was my younger sister instead of older.

I missed Evelyn. I missed Troy Lee. I missed Mama more than anybody. Even after the big thaw, when Mama and Daddy came home and I went back to school, I kept on missing them. I felt like I had a big hole in my heart. Ruth Duty asked me one Sunday right after meeting what was wrong. "I'll swear, Gracie, you don't hardly look like yourself," she said. "You're nothing but skin and bones, youngun." She pinched my arm, then hugged me tight. "Come on over here and let me give you some of this chicken and pastry before everybody else gets a shot at it." Ruth Duty thought food could cure anything. She took me by the hand and led me into the new fellowship hall, where women were putting the food out on a big long table, and piled me up a paper plate full of her own chicken and pastry, Lorene Bishop's baked beans, green Jell-O salad, corn-bread, and a piece of German chocolate cake. Then she sat me down and watched while I ate like a pig, for suddenly I was starving.

"Honey," Ruth said, leaning forward on her folding chair, her heavy knees spread wide beneath her skirt, "I have been thinking about you all a lot lately, you and Billie Jean too. I know it ain't easy. I know you've got a hard row to hoe."

At this, I started crying.

But Ruth wiped my eyes with a paper napkin. "No, now, honey," she said. "I want you to listen to me for a minute. Listen to old Ruth, sweetheart. The ones that Jesus loves the best, he sends the heaviest crosses for them to bear. But He don't never send more than you *can* bear. And you are a blessed child, honey, a blessed child, to live in the company of one of His own true saints, though it might not seem like it sometimes, I'll grant you. You will understand it all better by and by," Ruth promised. Her broad red face was full of kindness, which made me cry even more.

The funny thing was, I knew she was right. I knew it as well as I knew anything. I looked over at the door just then, as my daddy came in surrounded by men and women pressing up to him as close as they could get, like they hoped some of him was going to rub off on them, and his handsome face was beaming as he laughed and clapped some man on the back.

There were so many people in the Jesus Name Church now that I didn't know all of their names anymore. But I knew they loved my daddy, for he had saved their souls. I knew my mama loved him too, more than she loved anybody—more than me, more than Jesus even. But Mama loved Jesus too. I felt like if I could love Jesus then I wouldn't mind anything and I would *feel* like a blessed child, as Ruth Duty said. But He never had sent me a sign, and right now I did *not* love Him. I watched Mama over on the other side of the fellowship hall, helping the other women set out the food. Mama was smiling at everybody. She was still real pretty. She looked over at me and Ruth Duty and waved, and both of us waved back. I was fairly sure I was going to Hell, but I couldn't think what to do about it.

"I tell you what," Ruth said. "Anytime you start to feel lonely, you or Billie Jean either one, you all just come over and stay with me for a while. I need me some girls around. Will you all do that?"

"Yes ma'am," I said. I knew I wouldn't, though. I couldn't, any more than I could tell her about Billie's teacher sending those notes home to Mama, and how Mama burned them up in the heatstove so Daddy wouldn't see them, and said it was more than she could bear, and Billie would just have to do the best she could, and they had better *not* send anybody up to the house, that it wasn't anybody's business.

I couldn't tell Ruth how Daddy just *never* stopped ministering these days, preaching and praying and carrying on, way up into the night and sometimes all night long, it was like he didn't need to sleep. I couldn't tell her about that morning I woke up real early just as the day was breaking, and went out on the front porch—it was like something was drawing me, pulling me out there—to find Daddy bare-chested in the pearly light, serpents running like water over his arms and hands. I couldn't tell her that Daddy had taken it into his head now that he was going to walk the French Broad River come spring, and was preparing. She'd hear it soon enough anyway.

"Well, you're a mighty sweet girl," Ruth Duty said, "and a big help to your mama. Now, are you going to eat that cake or not?"

"No ma'am," I said, and so Ruth reached over for it and popped it into her own mouth and ate it all in one gulp.

"Too heavy," she said.

ONE FRIDAY AFTERNOON in March, when Mama's daffodils had come up like little spears and the mountains all around our house were full of redbud, Billie Jean and I got off the school bus at the mouth of the holler, and headed for home as usual. The wind blew first one way, then the other, the way it does in March.

"Slow down," Billie Jean begged, but I could not.

I ran ahead of her up the hill, so I was the first to see a boy sitting at the top of our steps like he belonged there.

Then Billie Jean saw him too. "Who's *that?*" she whined, hanging back.

"Somebody for Daddy, I reckon," I told her. As Daddy's fame grew, strangers showed up at our house fairly often. I slowed down to a more ladylike walk as I went on up the hill, for the boy on the porch was staring at me. "Hello,"

I called, and he called back, "Hello." But he didn't get up. He sat on the top step real easy, and watched us.

Something about him made me nervous. For one thing, he was good-looking—too good-looking to be sitting on our porch in the middle of the afternoon, for no purpose in the world that I could think of. He had dark brown curly hair and black eyes and looked like a foreigner, maybe an Italian, I thought. I had never seen a real Italian, as far as I knew. I had never thought of a boy as good-looking either. All of a sudden I felt that I myself looked awful. I was getting more and more nervous. I wished the boy would say something else, but he didn't. He just kept watching us come up the hill.

Finally I said, "Hi! If you're looking for Daddy, he's not here right now."

"Who is your daddy?" the boy asked. He had a funny way of speaking and I could tell he was not from around here, though he didn't sound like he was from a foreign country either. He was about Joe Allen's age.

I stopped at the bottom of the steps. "My daddy is Virgil Shepherd, minister of God," I said.

"That's him," the boy said. "He's my daddy too." He grinned at me then, a slow one-sided grin that ran all over me.

"He is not," I said immediately, though even as I spoke, I knew it might be true. For one thing, I never knew what to expect of Daddy, and anything might be true. *Anything.* Also, this boy *looked* like Daddy, I realized. I could see it in his face, and in the cocky way he held his head.

He stood up. "My name is Lamar Shepherd," he said.

"Pleased to meet you." He looked down at me and at Billie Jean, who had come to stand beside me, clutching my elbow.

She surprised me to death by speaking right up. "I'm Billie Jean," she said. When I turned to look at her, she was smiling, and I had the biggest urge to stand in front of her, or send her in the house, or something. "This here is my sissie," Billie said like a little girl.

"Florida Grace," I added.

"I was born in Florida," the boy said. "If you'll give me a drink of water, I'll tell you all about it."

And because I love a story, and because he was the kind of boy that you have to do whatever he wants, I said yes, and we took him into the house and gave him a drink of water out of the jug and a piece of cornpone, which was all we had. He wolfed it down and then we went back out on the porch.

Billie and me sat in the swing and Lamar stood leaning against a post, smoking a cigarette. He was easy in his body, like a cat. He grinned at us. Billie smiled back. She sat in the swing with her head tilted, like she was at some kind of a show. Lamar Shepherd kept grinning at us. "So I've got me some new little sisters," he said. "Well, well, well, I'll be darned." I hadn't thought of this. It made me feel funny. But then Lamar Shepherd made me feel real funny in general, I couldn't figure out why. I didn't trust him.

"Just tell it," I said.

"You're a pistol, ain't you, Sis?" He threw his cigarette butt down the hill and paused. "Okay. I don't know how much you know about your daddy," he said, very serious now.

"I reckon we know all we need to," I said, for no matter how ticked off I ever got at Daddy, I was always the first to stand up for him if anybody *else* said anything.

"Do you know where he was born at, and where all he lived before he married your mother? Do you know how many other children he's got?"

"We don't need to know that." I was getting mad, but I was real curious. I have always been too curious, it is one of my biggest failings.

"Maybe not," Lamar said. "Hell, I don't know all of it myself. All I know about is my own mother." He paused again and looked off down the mountain. The sharp wind blew his hair around. "My mother was not even his first wife. She was his second wife, as far as I can figure out. Mama said that the one before her was a woman named Orpha Crumpler, up in Virginia, and that they had several children, but I don't know their names, or where they are now. She died, I reckon. At least I think she died." He gave a short laugh. "My own mother was named Lantha Rogers, and she worshipped the ground he walked on, always did."

I nodded. This was true of a lot of people. It was true of my own mother.

"Until he took off and left us high and dry," Lamar went on. "Took off with a dancing girl."

I looked at him. "That was Mama?" I wasn't really asking, for I knew the answer already.

"I reckon so," Lamar Shepherd said. "I don't remember

none of it real good myself, for I wasn't nothing but a boy. Mama said he went off to Georgia on a crusade, and never come back, and that's all she ever said about it. We lived down in Florida, in the swamp. See, Mama used to have consumption, and then he cured her of it, but then after he left, the consumption came back and she got real poorly and just dragged around until she died. It didn't take too long. The county took us when she died."

"You and who?" Now I had to ask, had to know everything.

"I had a little sister named Susie and a little brother named Sam. They was twins," Lamar said. "They was little and cute, and they got adopted right off by some rich people."

"What about you?"

"I was twelve years old by then, and not little nor cute either one," he said, lighting another cigarette. He struck the match on his boot sole. "Nobody wanted me. I got sent around from here to yonder, but didn't nobody want a big old boy like me, and I can't say as I blame them neither. I wasn't too easy to get along with in those days."

"So what did you do? Where did you end up living?"

"Oh, I lived with first one, then the other," he said, grinning now like it had all been nothing but a lark, "and then when the circus come through town, I went with it. Since that day I ain't never looked back. Ain't never going to look back."

"The circus!" I said, for I had never seen one. "What did you do with them?"

"I was just a regular roustabout. I'd put up the tent, run

the games, take care of the animals, drive the truck, whatever. I can do just about anything." Lamar was not bragging but stating a plain fact, and looking at him, I could sure believe it. He looked like he could take care of himself just fine and move through the world on his own. It made me jealous, for a girl can't do that.

"So how come you to be over here?" I asked.

Billie Jean didn't say anything, but followed our conversation as bright as a bird, looking back and forth. Every now and then she'd push the swing with her foot.

"We were over in Tennessee," Lamar said, and I began to see how it was going.

"Outside of Knoxville," he added. "And some people was talking about a big tent meeting that was going on, and I heard his name, but by the time I got up with them, he was gone, so I found out where he had gone to, and come along. I been working odd jobs along the way."

"But why?" I asked. *If I could travel with a circus*, I thought, *I'd never leave.*

"I reckon I just wanted to meet him," Lamar said, "and say howdy."

He *did* look like Daddy. The more he talked, the more I could see it.

"Then are you going back to the circus?" Already I was wondering if I could go too.

"Maybe so, maybe not. I reckon I could find them if I've got a mind to. But it don't matter one way or the other to me. I don't care."

"You don't?"

All of a sudden his face looked different. "One place is

the same as another, Sis," he said. "You'll see. It don't matter what you do neither." I stared at him and he stared back at me, not smiling. Beyond him, in the yard, Mama's forsythia bush was in full yellow bloom. But Lamar looked dark and old, the opposite of forsythia.

Right then I heard a car on the road below. I knew it was Daddy, driving the old green Dodge which somebody had recently donated to his ministry. It was loud because it needed a muffler. I watched Lamar watch the car as it came up the road to the mouth of the holler, then pulled off and stopped.

"Is that him?" Lamar asked, not taking his eyes off the car.

"Yes," I said.

"I always did intend to see him again," Lamar said softly.

"Well, this is your big chance, then," I said as we all watched. Daddy and Mama get out of the car. Mama shaded her eyes and waved at us. Daddy carried a traveling bag.

"You better look out," I told Lamar as they came up the hill. "He's liable to save you."

"It ain't likely," Lamar said.

But I believe I planted a seed in his mind.

MY HEART WAS beating so fast. I thought, *I wouldn't miss this for anything.* I tried to imagine how I would feel if I was meeting my own daddy after such a long time, what I would say, what I would think of him. I tried to look at Daddy as if I had never seen him before.

He looked like a preacher, that's for sure. But he looked

like a workingman too. He moved forcefully. Even though he was thin, he had a large frame. His white shirt and blue pants flapped on his bones like clothes on a clothesline. It was his face that struck you, though. A big old face like a lantern. Nobody else I had ever seen looked anything like Daddy, except for the boy on our porch. Lamar Shepherd. Except for Lamar Shepherd.

But Daddy looked at Lamar as if he had never seen him before.

"Well, son," he said. "What can I do for you?"

Lamar grinned that grin. "You are Mister Virgil Shepherd," he said. "I heard about you in Tennessee, and come over here to see if you can help me."

"What kind of help is it you're after?" Daddy asked, climbing the stairs one at a time. Sometimes, not often, you could tell how old he was.

"I need the kind you've got, from what I hear tell," Lamar said. "I'd trade you for it. I can do anything, sir, iffen you'll hire me on. Chop wood, electric work, carpenter work, you name it. You won't be sorry."

Mama stood waiting to see what would happen. Daddy did not consult her.

"I reckon you can stay for a while, then," he said, "and we'll see what it is you're after. We'll see if we've got any of what you want." He winked at Billie Jean and me sitting side by side in the swing. "I reckon you can start by building you a room off to the back there. We have been needing us another room, now that my girls is growing up so big."

"Yessir," Lamar said.

"I'll be going to a meeting in Zionville in the morning," Daddy said. "You can come along if you've got a mind to. Nine sharp. Take off that shirt and let Fannie wash it."

"Yessir."

Daddy paused as he went in the door. "Now what did you say your name was?"

"Lamar Dickens," that boy said just as smooth as anything. If I hadn't known he was lying, I couldn't have told it in a million years. He pulled that name out of a hat in his mind, he told me later. He didn't know what he was going to say until he was saying it. He didn't even know he was going to lie to Daddy until he was doing it. I couldn't believe it! I sat in the swing and stared at him.

The main thing I couldn't figure out, then or later, was how he knew that I wouldn't speak up and give him away. Or Billie Jean—for he couldn't have known at that time how fast she forgets what you tell her.

So I had another big secret to keep, and I vowed that Hell would freeze over before I'd tell a soul.

Daddy paused to look back at Lamar. "On second thought," he said, "maybe you ought to take a look at that car down there before we go off in the morning. You know anything about cars?"

"Yessir," Lamar said.

So THIS IS how Lamar came to live with us when I was fourteen years old, and this is why I was bound to him from the very beginning, bound by secrets and something else, for I soon found I could not quit looking at him as he worked around the house fixing things. Sometimes I'd walk through a room just to see him, and at night when I fell asleep, his face was the last thing I saw in my mind. When I slept, I dreamed of him.

From the first, Lamar and Daddy got along great. Daddy saved him, and baptized him, and before long Lamar was blessed to work the signs too. I overheard Daddy telling Mama that Lamar might even get the call to preach. Meanwhile Lamar had got Daddy's car running great and had built a room onto the house and had everybody at the Jesus Name Church eating out of his hand. Daddy thought God had sent Lamar to him as a special gift, since Joe Allen and Troy Lee and Evelyn had been lost.

Daddy took Lamar's coming as a sign.

And he received many more signs that spring as well, as did others in the Jesus Name Church, which was planning its big Homecoming service for June, an event that would bring other sign followers from all around, and last for days. It would be like a great camp meeting, Daddy said. He planned to walk the river at that time. Dimly I remembered other camp meetings we had gone to when I was little. I remembered sleeping on a pallet on the ground and playing around with all the other kids. That had been fun. This would be different, though. I was not a kid anymore, I'd have to act like a grown-up girl. This knowledge made me feel sad but also excited, at the same time.

I FELT THAT way all spring, as if I was about to jump out of my skin. It was like my senses had been tuned up—

colors were brighter, sounds were louder, and everything seemed so important. I had a feeling that I was living in a mystery which I was about to solve. I felt like Melinda, but a more grown-up Melinda, without the help of Spice. And there had never been a prettier spring—or maybe I just hadn't ever noticed it so much before.

I remember one day when the school bus let me off where it always did, next to a grove of dogwood trees, how suddenly I *saw* them, all in bloom, white and pink, like I was seeing them for the first time, or like they were the first dogwood trees in the whole world. I dropped my books in the road and ran over there to stand in the middle of them, so that wherever I looked, I couldn't see anything except blossoms, and then I *was* the blossoms, all blossom—me, Gracie. I drew in great sweet breaths and then I was crying.

I stood there for a long time. I remembered the poem that Miss Black had read to us about the legend of the dogwood tree, how it used to be a big tall straight tree before they made Jesus' cross out of it, and now ever after, it grows little and twisted in shame. Each petal has a drop of His blood on it. I looked at the flowers all around me, and it was true. Every petal of my beautiful blossoms had a drop of His rusty blood. Fear shot through me then, and I started to shake like a leaf, for I was not on good terms with Jesus. I still went to meeting the same as before, and tried to pray, but I was paying too much attention to Lamar playing the guitar up at the front of the church house, and I knew Jesus knew it. If He knew anything about me, He knew that. I was afraid Lamar knew it too.

* * *

EVER SINCE THE public health lady came up our holler, Billie had stayed at home. I didn't know what the public health lady had said to Mama, or Mama to her, but the lady had soon left in her black car, with her back as straight as a poker. She had short white hair and a blue suit and didn't turn around once as she stomped down the hill to her car. Mama stood on the front porch and watched her go, hugging Billie, who was just about as big as Mama herself.

So now Billie stayed at home, which she was real happy to do, as school had been making her nervous. Every afternoon when I got home, she was glad to see me, but she never once acted like she wanted to go with me. And now Billie was a big help to Mama, for she had always liked doing house things—sweeping, sewing, cooking. She never got bored the way I did, nor longed to run down the hill or up the mountain or *anywhere* out in the world at all, like me. Billie was content doing nothing for the longest time, hours on end. She could just sit in a chair and be happy, it seemed.

One of my own jobs was to gather the eggs, and I dearly loved to go out back to the tobacco barn, which smelled like noplace else I have ever been—a smell I would know instantly anywhere, anytime, even now—and feel around for the eggs, straining to see them down in the shadowy straw. Even at noon, it was always half dark in the barn. I thought of it as my secret place, my private place. This is where I kept my jumper and blouse in the corncrib, before

I cut them up. This is where I went to be by myself whenever too much was happening in the house. I'd rush out there with my heart beating fast and my legs pumping furiously, to stand in the sweet dusky stillness until I calmed down. Most days I went out there at least twice, even though we never got all that many eggs, but nobody ever questioned me on it. They were used to me "running around like a chicken with its head cut off," as Mama sometimes said—the same way they were used to Billie staying put. You know how patterns will get set up in a family.

But after Lamar came, I started feeling funny whenever I went out there. I thought I could feel his gaze like little arrows in my back as I left the kitchen. It made me real embarrassed and real nervous. This was how I always felt with Lamar in the house, like he was watching me constantly, even when he couldn't have been. I felt his dark eyes on me through my clothes.

"You're getting so big, Gracie," Mama said. "Why, you're outgrowing everything!" She made me some skirts, and Ruth Duty bought me three brand-new blouses at Wilson's Department Store, one pink with a round jewel neckline, one plain white with a button-down collar, one short-sleeved white camp shirt for the summer ahead. I loved the name of this one, "camp shirt." I knew I would never get to go to a camp, not even a church camp like the other kids at school talked about. These blouses fit fine, but I could still feel my own skin inside them, rubbing up against the fabric. It was like I had grown new nerves.

Lamar had a way of lounging back in a chair wherever

he sat, even in a kitchen chair. He reminded me of a big black cat. He used to sit in the kitchen talking to Mama and Billie Jean and me for hours on end, telling us tales of life in the circus, or asking questions about people in the Jesus Name Church. Mama loved to tell him about all the people. She got bright spots of color in her thin cheeks as she told how Daddy had started the church, and how he had brought Lily back to life, and about the death of Rufus Graybeal. Mama seemed more like her old self these days with Lamar in the house, just because she had somebody new to talk to. Watching her, I remembered how she used to tell stories herself, and I thought about how lonesome she must have gotten when Daddy went off on a crusade or whenever he shut himself away to pray and fast. No wonder she went with him every time he'd take her, now that Evelyn was lost. Lamar kind of distracted us all from Daddy, who was getting thinner and thinner, with eyes that seemed to glow in his head. He was already working up to Homecoming.

As long as I live I will not forget that morning in early April when Lamar touched me for the first time. It was the nicest day, puffy white scudding clouds high up in the blue-blue sky, a breeze like perfume. We were all in the kitchen drinking coffee, everyone except Daddy, and then he came stumbling in, looking like a skeleton who had not slept, and Lamar leaped up to give him a chair. "Here, sir," he said.

Daddy grabbed onto Lamar's broad shoulders instead of sitting down, and started praying on him. "Oh Lord," Daddy was saying as I slipped out the door to get the eggs, "here is one of our own that has come a hard, rocky way, Lord, and stands before you now—"

I looked back from the door and saw Lamar's black eyes staring over the top of Daddy's wild white head. Lamar's eyes looked like shiny lumps of coal, intent, watching me.

I knew for sure he wasn't praying.

Nor was I surprised when he followed me out to the barn five or ten minutes later. I was bent over, feeling for eggs in the straw with one hand, holding Daddy's old black hat in the other. I used the hat to put the eggs in. Sunlight from the doorway fell in a solid yellow bar across the ground, and then it didn't. My breath caught in my throat. I didn't hear a thing, for Lamar always moved so quiet. Suddenly he was there behind me, his hands all over me, his hot breath on my neck. He had my new white blouse half off in a flash and was rubbing on me and sticking his tongue in my ear. "Don't," I said, but it came out more like a moan. "Don't." I didn't know if I meant it or not, and he kept on doing what he was doing until he got ready to quit. By the time he quit, my pants were as wet as if I had peed them.

Oh, Lamar knew what he was up to, all right. He knew exactly what to do and when to stop. He was working me like those circus barkers he'd told us about would work a crowd, showing folks just enough to where they surely couldn't stand it, to where they *had* to put their quarter on the table and go to the show. That first day, he even helped me tuck my new blouse back in my new skirt.

"I'll tell you, Little Buddy," he said, which was what he had started calling me, "you're something. You know that?"

"No," I said, for by then I felt so full of shame I wished I could die on the spot.

"Well, you are," he said. "You believe me?"

"No," I said.

Then he kissed me on the lips, which he had not done before, and stuck his tongue in my mouth, which surprised me. I felt like I was going to faint, or die, and I nearly fell down in the straw.

Lamar held me up.

"Are you my pardner, Little Buddy?" he asked me then, and I said I was. I didn't have to ask him what he meant. I knew what he meant, and he knew I would never tell.

Lamar was the first person I ever met that knew me instantly, as I knew him. This does not often happen. He knew me by the bad that was in me, I know now. I was not really a bad girl, but I had some bad in me, which Lamar could sniff out like a bird dog. It was what he was going for.

"Lamar? Lamar?" Daddy started hollering out in the yard.

Lamar drew my hair off my forehead and patted it back. "There now," he said. "I'll go on. You wait and come after while. Now where's them eggs?"

"What?" I said.

"Eggs," he said. "I want one of them eggs."

Dumbly I leaned down and picked up Daddy's hat from the barn floor, and quick as a wink Lamar grabbed one of the three eggs that I'd found. "Thanks, Buddy," he said. He gave me a squeeze and turned to go.

"You Lamar!" Daddy yelled outside, closer now.

Then sunlight streamed into my eyes so that I could

scarcely see, but I could see enough to watch Lamar pause for an instant in the doorway, tilt back his head, and break that egg right into his mouth. He dropped the shell in the straw and was gone. I pressed my back up against the corncrib and stood like that until I could breathe, and by the time I finally left the barn, Lamar was long gone, driving Daddy someplace in the car.

SOMETIMES DADDY WENT off by himself, leaving Lamar to "look after all the girls." It was especially then, with Daddy gone, that I would find myself lingering in the barn when I went to get the eggs, hardly able to breathe, hoping Lamar would come out to me. Sometimes he came, and sometimes he didn't. Sometimes when he didn't come, I'd start crying, and other times I'd get mad as fire. This seemed to tickle him. "Cat got your tongue?" he said one day when I came back in the house and passed by him without a word, "No!" I spat out, real mean, and he just laughed. I never could stay mad at him when he laughed. Lamar had me wrapped around his little finger. I'd do anything he told me to. "Come on out to my room tonight, Buddy," he'd say sometimes when Daddy and Mama were both gone, and I'd tiptoe out to his lean-to room in the dark, though I trembled with fear the whole time, afraid Billie would wake up and come looking to find me.

It got to where I was even wilder, more of a daredevil than Lamar. One time when Mama *was* home, I waited until it got way, way late, and I slipped out there, only to find that he had latched his door. When I knocked softly, he came to the other side of the door, and whispered, "Sssh. Go on now. It ain't safe. Go back to bed," in such a scared voice that I never went out there again with Mama in the house.

I felt like Lamar was trying to take care of me, in his way.

Another thing was, he *made* me go to school every day, even when Mama and Daddy were both gone. He made me, for after a while I wasn't interested in it anymore. It was like I was sick. The other kids at school seemed like nothing but little children to me now, and I had a hard time reading, for Lamar's face would come up in my mind. I said as much, one morning when he was pushing me out the door and down the holler.

"What if I don't want to go?" I said. "What if I'd rather stay up here with you all?"

"You wouldn't. That's just what you think right now. That's just what you think today." Lamar looked real serious all of a sudden, and older. He had been washing up at the kitchen sink and his curly black hair was slicked straight back on his head. He was not smiling.

"What do you mean?" I said.

"They's another day coming," he said. "You go on to school." Lamar's eyes were so serious that they didn't have any white in them at all, they were black, and deep, and old. His face looked like it was cut out of rock. I didn't say another word. I went. And after that morning I didn't try to skip anymore.

Lamar himself could not read. This came as a big surprise to me when I found out, because he was so smart in so many ways. I learned this when he had me read some instructions out loud to him as he was putting in the electric stove for Mama, after we got power up in our holler. Mr. Arnold of Arnold's Electric had donated the stove to us. Lamar listened intently while I read, and then started fitting things together. I sat cross-legged on the floor and watched him. "Read that last part one more time," he said, and I did, and he hooked the oven door in place. Then he started twisting wires together, looking at the diagram that had come with the stove. This diagram was real complicated, but Lamar seemed to understand it fine. Watching him work, I got a bright idea.

"Lamar, why don't you let me teach you how to read?" I said, all excited. "Me and Mama could teach you in no time flat, I bet."

But Lamar shook his head, keeping his eyes down on his work. "It ain't for me to know," he said in a flat voice, and his face went hard in that way I had seen before.

Sometimes I felt like Lamar was following a diagram himself, that everything he did was already set by some grand design that he knew about and I didn't, the way Daddy always said he was following the plan of God. I felt this so strongly that I knew better than to say anything about us getting married when I grew up, or anything like that, even though when I played paper dolls with Billie Jean—for this was always her favorite thing to do—I called the bride doll Gracie in my mind, and the bridegroom Lamar. But somehow I knew that was only for the paper dolls.

When the weather started getting real warm, I'd meet Lamar down at the mouth of the holler where Scrabble Creek formed the biggest pool, and jump right out of my clothes, and let him unbraid my hair, and we'd lay on the ferny bank in the shade. Later he talked me into getting in the water with him, and he taught me to float. I loved how it felt when Lamar's hand dropped out from under the small of my back and my hair drifted out around my head like the rays of the sun. I felt so good then, as if I didn't even have a body. I felt free. Other times it was like Lamar and me were both boys together, when I'd take him to the caves I knew about up on the mountain, and the limestone spring. I never did take him all the way up to Chimney Rock, though.

I have to say this. Except for that first time, when he followed me out to the barn, at no time during that spring did I ever feel like I was a sinner girl, which I was, not even when we went to meeting, which we did all the time of course, and Daddy or Doyle Stacy would tell the sinners to come forward and throw themselves on the mercy of God. I never had the slightest desire to go forward then. I knew His mercy was everlasting anyway, so I figured I could always do it later. I figured this, that is, when I thought about it at all. Personally I didn't think of God one bit that spring, even though our whole church was being seized with a great fever as Homecoming drew near.

Many new people joined, and sometimes when the handling started, there'd be so many at the front that some would have to wait their turn. Lily was right up there with the rest now, since she'd been saved. I felt like I didn't know her anymore. I sat on that same hard pew I'd been sitting on for years, with those I knew and loved, but I felt like I was a stranger. I saw Lily put a copperhead around her shoulders like a stole. I saw Lamar hold a four-foot rattler up above his head with the same hands that had touched my most private parts, but I couldn't make any connection between this Lamar that was a saint in the church and that other Lamar that came to me in the barn. No connection at all. So I didn't even try to. I sat with the others, and sang the same old songs.

ONE DAY LATER in the spring, I got home from school and when I stepped onto the porch I heard a voice that I didn't recognize coming from the front room. Then I heard Mama's voice, and something in it made me hold my tongue and not cry out hello as usual. I tiptoed across the porch, avoiding the plank that squeaked, and pressed up against the wall by the door. But it appeared that the conversation was already over. Mama was saying, "I wish you a safe journey, then," in a very formal way, and I heard the sound of chairs scraping, and I leaped away from the wall not a moment too soon, for here they came out the door.

I knew immediately that this was not the hoor Evelyn had described.

No, this was plainly a Holiness girl, for there was something old-timey about her. Maybe I thought that because I had just come from school, where most of the kids were more up-to-date, or modern. I wondered if this was how the other kids at school saw me. For I wore my own long hair in a ponytail too, and no jewelry, and no makeup. But it was more than that.

This girl looked like she came from another world. Her skin was dead white, with golden freckles all over it, and her long red hair was so curly that it made a fuzzy little fringe all around her face, though she had pulled it back with a rubber band. Her eyes were like deep blue pools, and her pale little mouth was as perfect as a rose. *Snow White*, I thought. *She looks like Snow White.* She smiled at me right off, and there was such a curious old-fashioned sweetness about her that I smiled right back.

"This is our daughter, Florida Grace," Mama said with some effort. She had a glint in her eye and looked like she was about to bust, one way or another. She was holding a blue wool sock with something in it, and it came over me in a flash that this was where she'd been keeping the money that Joe Allen used to give her, before the fight. I never knew if she had kept any back, the way he had said, or not. Mama hid the sock in the folds of her skirt. "How was school?" she asked me brightly.

"All right," I said.

I stood aside to let the girl pass by. She moved in a slow graceful way, clutching her white plastic purse. She wore a green-and-white print dress, homemade, and brown shoes run down at the heels. She was not too much older than me, about Evelyn's age, and suddenly I was shot through with longing to see Evelyn. The girl went down the steps and stooped to pick up a small cardboard suitcase, which I had not noticed before. Then she turned to look at me and Mama.

"I won't be bothering you no more, ma'am," she said in a musical voice.

Mama didn't say anything, She was breathing hard, with her lips tight together.

The girl set off down the hill, walking slow but with a purpose. I felt that she would get wherever she was going. I thought she would make it okay.

"Who was that?" I asked Mama.

"That was nobody." Mama bit off her words and stomped in the house. I stood on the porch and watched the girl go, until she was out of sight around the bend.

I never heard her name.

Later that night I was woke up by the sound of something breaking. I sat bolt upright in the bed, feeling for Billie beside of me, for I knew she would be scared. Mama was yelling in the kitchen. But Billie wasn't there. I was so amazed at Billie being gone that I couldn't hardly pay attention to Mama's voice. Part of me was listening, but another part of me was wondering where in the world Billie could be. Out at the toilet, I reckoned. It was all I could think of. Mama was hollering, "And you *dare* to call yourself a man of God, a preacher, you *dare* to tell everybody else how to behave! Well, this is the last un. The *last* un! And let me tell you one thing, sir, if you think I am going to keep my mouth shut this time, you've got another think coming!"

Even in my nervousness, or maybe because of it, I had to grin. Mama was always saying this to us, that we had another think coming. Meanwhile the drinking glasses were shattering one by one. I guessed that she was breaking them in the sink, or maybe throwing them against the new electric stove. Daddy wasn't talking back. He was letting her holler herself out, which she done before long, and then set in to crying like her heart would break. And then after a while I could hear Daddy's voice, slow and steady and powerful, talking on and on under the sound of Mama crying. I couldn't hear what he said, though. Billie came back in the middle of it all with her feet cold and the bottom of her nightgown wet with dew, so I relaxed some. She got in the bed and held me tight and I patted her hair. I didn't have to tell her to shush—she had *that* much sense, anyway. I fell back asleep in the bed, holding Billie and listening to the sound of Daddy's voice going on and on in the night.

But in the morning it was almost like I had dreamed it all, for Daddy was not anywhere to be seen, though Mama still had fire in her eye and a spot of red on her cheek. I went in the kitchen to find her standing at the stove stirring grits in a cookpot, with her tangled hair falling down her back.

"Where's Daddy?" I asked. "I thought I heard him last night."

"He had to drive over to Waynesville today," Mama said evenly. "He's picking up some kind of newfangled PA system he ordered off for. It's coming in on the train."

"Oh," I said, watching her.

"What's a PA system?" Billie said, stepping along behind me.

Nobody answered her. Out the corner of my eye I could

see a little pile of broken glass in the corner, but I knew better than to say anything about it.

Mama spooned grits into two bowls and plunked them down on the table. "Eat your breakfast," she told us.

Billie sat down and started to eat.

"I ain't hungry," I said. My stomach was turning over and over.

"Eat it," Mama said. She set her mouth.

I started crying, so Billie started crying too, just to keep me company. Mama walked over and slapped me smartly on the cheek. I vowed I would never eat those grits then—I would die first.

But Lamar saved the day. He appeared in the doorway right then, buttoning his shirt. "What's for breakfast?" he asked. "Grits? Gimme some." He grabbed a spoon from the sink and sat down, pulling my bowl of grits over to him. He ate a mouthful, then looked up at me and grinned.

"Ain't you fixing to be late, Buddy?" he asked. "You better get on down that hill." And I went. I ran down the hill as fast as my legs would carry me, looking all around at the sunny day, trying to fill up my eyes with the bright blooming flowers and new green trees, trying to push that horrible picture of Mama, the witchlike stranger by the stove, out of my head forever. For my sweet loving mama was gone by then, and gone for good.

THINGS WENT ON like this until the Homecoming, with everybody building up to a fever pitch. Mama was like a piece of bowed wire. Daddy was a man possessed, full of the Spirit, mumbling and praying full-time, the skin stretched tight on his bones. Even Lamar seemed to be caught up in the general excitement, his black eyes glittering. When he hunkered down on the porch to smoke a cigarette, the way he always did after dinner, I felt like he was all coiled up, ready to spring. I couldn't take my eyes off him then, but it didn't matter. Nobody was paying any attention to me.

In fact, we had a seventh-grade graduation ceremony at school, and I didn't even bother to tell anybody in my family about it. I knew they wouldn't care, and I didn't want them to come. It would have embarrassed me. This was the last time I was ever to be in a schoolhouse, at my seventh-grade graduation, though I didn't know that then. Now I can't even remember what the graduation was like. I can't remember who all was there, or what was said. I know we marched in. Marie made a speech because she was the valedictorian. I hadn't even been in the running, for my grades had slipped so. I didn't care. I didn't care about *anything*, I told myself as I sat on that stage in a folding chair and looked out at the other kids and parents in the auditorium. Marie's grandmother was there, all the way from Wilmington, Delaware. She had blue hair and wore pearls. They introduced me to her after it was over, and Marie's mother tried to hug me, but I got away from them as quick as I could. I didn't need their sympathy. I wouldn't have it. I balled up my diploma in my hand as we marched out the door. I didn't want it. I didn't need it. I didn't need anything or anybody.

Except Lamar.

Someplace back in my mind I had started thinking that Lamar was going to take me away with him sometime, if I could just hang on long enough. The only reason I'd stayed in school till the end of the year was because he sent me off down the holler every day. School had changed in my mind, into something I did for him. Not for me. It was that simple. What I did for me was what I did with Lamar. Riding home on the bus that last day, I felt so much older than all the others, even the girls from the high school that rode with us. They talked about boys and who had a crush on who and what they were going to do over the summer. Two girls were going to 4-H camp, and one said she had a job at the dime store in Waynesville. Their chatter blew past me like the warm wind from the open bus window. I felt that I knew more things than they had ever thought of, and had more secrets than they could even imagine. I felt like a woman grown.

I CAME UP the hill that day to find Daddy and Lamar washing off serpents in the creek, and Carlton Duty standing on the bank with his hat in his hands trying to talk seriously to Daddy, who did not appear to be paying him much mind. Daddy had his shirt and shoes off and was splashing around like a kid. My heart started beating faster, as was usual when I saw the serpents. I did not see them much now except in meeting, since Daddy had took to keeping more of them, and had moved the boxes out to the old smokehouse.

"Hi, Buddy," Lamar called, and I called back, "Hi." I flung my bookbag down on the mossy bank and sat beside it, at a safe distance, to watch what they were up to. They had some big old serpents that I had not ever seen before, and so I knew they had been up in the mountains snake hunting. Daddy was telling about it.

"I woke up before the light," he said, "with a picture of the place in my mind. I seen a whole bunch of big flat white rocks all jumbled up on top of each other, and under one of them rocks I seen two rattlesnakes all coiled up together a-forming the number eight. God put it in my mind as clear as day. So I got my sticks and a sack and gone up there, and sure enough, hit was just like God had showed me, and I thank Him for it,"

I knew where it was that he was talking about.

And I knew how Daddy used the sticks when he went out serpent hunting, how he slipped the noose on the end of one of them over the serpent's head to catch it up, then pinned its head to the ground with the fork on the end of the other stick, till he got the serpent around to where he could slip it into the sack, Daddy had not been serpent hunting in a long time, though, to my knowledge. Nowadays he relied on sinner folks to bring them in to him, and they brought him plenty. I couldn't see any need for him to go hunting others.

So I said to Daddy, "I thought you had plenty of serpents," and he grinned up at me in my spot on the bank.

"You can't never have too many, Sissy," he said, "nor too few." Sometimes Daddy didn't make any sense, especially when he spoke in parables like Jesus. "It's all up to the Lord, honey. I just go where He tells me to go, and do what He tells me to do. That's all. I am naught but a instrument. A instrument of God." Daddy seemed struck by his own words, standing tall with the creek flowing around his ankles, holding up a four-foot rattler in his hand. The rattler writhed and glistened in the sun. It kept twisting its head back like it was trying to look at Daddy. But I couldn't look at him without remembering that pretty girl who had come to see Mama. I remembered Evelyn saying that Daddy did everything too much.

Carlton Duty stood down by the creek in an awkward way, all bony knobs and angles. His chin jutted out and his whole face was red, the way it got whenever he spoke up in church. He looked real earnest and real upset. I knew he'd never so much as look at a pretty girl.

"It is my understanding," he started off nervous-like, "it is my understanding that the anointing is required, sir, for those that takes them up. For God said in Exodus Forty, Fifteen, 'And thou shalt anoint them, as thou didst anoint their father, that they may minister unto me in the priest's office: for their *anointing* shall surely be an everlasting priesthood throughout their generations,' " Carlton Duty emphasized "anointing." He twisted his hat around and around in his hands. Carlton was always worrying over the fine points of Scripture, and agonized about following it exactly. He was questioning Daddy for handling serpents without being anointed, which some of the saints held to be wrong, while others practiced it at home or in their yards or wherever, anytime they felt like it.

"Carlton," Daddy said, swinging that serpent side to

side with its tail swooping in and out of the creek, "Carlton, my beloved, all I can tell you is, I am follering the plan of God just as He reveals it to me day by day, I ain't a-going to quibble with Him, nor split hairs. I ain't a-going to say, 'But away back there in Exodus, Lord, you said such and such.' Oh no. *Oh no*, my beloved! For if Jesus says, 'Jump, Virgil,' I am going to say, 'How far, Lord? How far?' I ain't about to question Him. I am going to do whatever He tells me to do, from now on until the end of my time, until He takes me home. That is the long and the short of it," Daddy said. Sun sparkled off the shiny serpent and in the splashing drops and in the drops of water caught in the hair on his chest and head. He stepped out of the creek and slid the top of a snake box back and stuffed the serpent down in it, as if it was nothing but a rag. Lamar was watching Daddy close, watching his every move. Lamar's eyes had gone real narrow, and I couldn't tell what he was thinking, though they were so intent that I knew he was thinking something. Something big, something mighty. Again I had the sense that Lamar was following his own plan just as much as Daddy was following his. Lamar had kept his white shirt on, though he'd rolled up the sleeves so he could dip the serpent box in the running creek. This was how most people washed their serpents off, though Lily's daddy sometimes took his out and put them in the bathtub, Lily said. Like Daddy, he didn't think you had to be anointed if you wanted to take them up. He just did it, and they didn't bite him either.

"Why are you washing them off, anyway?" I said when Daddy had snapped the catch on the serpent box.

"Why, shoot, Sissy, they's nasty enough as they is. We're cleaning them up for the big day coming." First I thought Daddy meant Judgment Day, but then I realized he meant the Homecoming. His whole face was lit up by his smile, and I smiled back at him, down in the creek. I couldn't help it. He was so sweet at such times, and so sincere, he was just like a little child.

But Carlton Duty had more on his mind. "Virgil," he said, "there is also this matter of that money that I have been trying to talk to you about." His nasal voice came floating up the hill.

"Well, talk on, then, good buddy, talk on," Daddy directed, as we fetched up at the smokehouse and he and Lamar stooped to put the boxes inside the door.

I reckon he did talk on, but I didn't hear him, for just then I looked up to see Ruth Duty standing out on the porch with Billie Jean, both of them waving at us. "Yoo-hoo!" Ruth called. I ran on up there. Sure enough, Ruth had been over at our house cooking all afternoon. I was so glad, for Mama had not had the time nor the inclination to do any cooking in those days right before the Homecoming. In fact, she had gotten just about as bad as Daddy for praying all the time and not eating hardly a thing. We would of all starved if Lamar had not brought us food from the store, Chef Boyardee spaghetti and such as that. But now Ruth Duty had cooked us enough food to last for a while, a big pot of green beans with onions and potatoes and fatback in it, a tuna noodle casserole with potato chips crumbled all over the top, which she knew that Billie and me loved, and pineapple upside-down cake. Lamar ate two big helpings of everything when we sat down at the table, but Mama just picked at her food.

Later, when Mama and Ruth and me were in the kitchen washing up the dishes, Ruth said to her, "Honey, I can read the Bible as good as the next one, and I'll be darned if I can see anyplace where it says not to eat. You've got to keep your strength up if you want to serve Him, it seems to me. He wants us to *enjoy* the fruits of the spirit, Fannie. That's what I think."

Ruth Duty herself was a walking advertisement for these ideas. She jiggled all over, and had four chins, and energy flowed out from her in every direction. Everybody in the Jesus Name Church loved her, and respected her too.

I dried the last plate, looking from Ruth to Mama. Mama sat in a kitchen chair, fluttering her hands in her lap. She was as fragile as a moth, with her dry white papery skin. All of a sudden I knew that Daddy would leave her if she didn't get better, and that this would kill her, as it had killed Lamar's mother.

For Daddy was all her life.

"You don't know everything," Mama was saying darkly to Ruth. "There's a lot you don't know. God has been testing me lately. He has been severely testing me, and I can't pass the test. I ain't got a big enough heart. That's the truth." Mama started crying then, and Ruth hugged her.

I went out on the porch to play paper dolls with Billie Jean. She didn't even have any idea she was too old for paper dolls, and I wasn't about to tell her. It was the only fun she ever had, those paper dolls. She had a whole bunch of them propped up against the rocker of a rocking chair. "Now this is a great meeting," she said, "and here comes a sinner girl." She made another paper doll come walking across the porch. This was one that I had cut out of a *Teen* magazine and pasted onto cardboard for her. The doll was wearing slacks and a pink angora sweater. "Her name is Susan Brown," Billie announced, smiling sweetly. "Here she comes now!" Billie walked Susan Brown across the porch and into the paper doll meeting.

Billie thought it was all a game.

I got up and stood at the porch rail looking out into the night. Lightning bugs were rising one by one. I felt almost sick, I had eaten so much supper. I could hear, but not hear, Mama and Ruth in the kitchen. Lamar was gone. He had driven Daddy and Carlton someplace in the car. Beyond the porch, beyond the tiny fireflies, darkness stretched out as far as I could see. Homecoming would begin in two days, and it was not a game. It was a matter of life and death.

PEOPLE STARTED COMING in from out of town that Saturday morning, and by afternoon there was so many that Lamar had to stand out by the road like a traffic cop, telling them where to go. He parked them up and down the road and then lined them up in rows in the field, leaving the center open for the meeting. After they got parked, they unpacked their vehicles, setting up tents and folding tables and chairs around the field and back in the trees and all along the river. I had never seen so many cars or people in one place, or so much going on. It looked like gypsies had come to town. The church house and field and river were all changed, all new, a bright busy anthill with people going every which way on errands of their own, or just to see each other. There was a lot of hugging and laughing and crying and grabbing hands. Kids played tag in and out of the parked cars. Here and there, people were tuning up instruments. Somebody was already playing the banjo off in the trees where we couldn't see him, though the notes floated out sassy and solid on the summer air. Some boys from out of town asked Billie and me what our names were, but she giggled and ran away, so I ran off after her. Even Billie seemed to be caught up in the general excitement as we walked around watching it all start up. Some men from our church were building a kind of stage in the middle of the field and putting the new PA system up, stringing wires out over the grass. Lily's daddy hauled in some portable toilets they had rented in Waynesville, and set them up at the edge of the woods. Daddy wanted everything "modern" and "top of the line." He'd been saying this for months. He was nowhere to be found while the preparations went on, however.

The last we had seen of Daddy before the meeting was his white shirt disappearing into the laurel on the mountain path behind our house. I knew he was going up there to be alone, to pray and prepare.

Mama was preparing too. She wouldn't pay any attention to me and Billie. She got all dressed but then sat on the horsehair sofa in the front room with her knees pushed tight together and her white-knuckled hands clasped on top of them. She squinted, staring at nothing we could see. Her mouth moved. Billie and me passed in and out of there, getting ready ourselves, watching Mama. Once she jumped up and ran out onto the porch and vomited over the rail, but not much came up, as she had not really eaten for days. I got scared, seeing this. I went out on the porch and put my arm around her thin shoulders, but she shook me off and ran back in the house to sit again on the sofa in that frozen way. She gave me the creeps.

"Let's go," I told Lamar. We were going to ride over to the meeting with him.

But Lamar stood in the middle of the floor, jingling the keys and looking at Mama. He was studying her real close. "Fannie!" he said sharply.

Mama didn't even blink.

"Fannie," he said again. "Come on, we're fixing to go. It's the big meeting. It's the Homecoming." Lamar spoke as if to a child. "Come on now, Fannie."

Mama turned to look at him then, her eyes like searchlights, her face like a knife. She was not even pretty anymore. I was scared of her. "Come back for me, Lamar," she said. "I ain't ready to go yet. Come back for me later, honey."

"Okay," he said.

But then Mama started shaking her head back and forth. She was all wrought up. "You won't." She sounded real pitiful now. "You won't never come for me. I know it. I can feel it in my bones. You won't never come."

The way Mama was talking didn't make any sense. It made me feel funny in the stomach, like *I* might have to go throw up too. Things flew in and out of my mind. For the first time I thought Mama might be going crazy, and craziness is catching, to a certain extent.

"Oh, for God's sake!" Lamar was real disgusted. "I'll be back after while, Fannie. Come on, girls." He stomped out of the house with us following, and I must say I was glad to get out of there, and glad to get into the car. Both of us sat up in the front seat with Lamar, me in the middle, next to him. The car had been sitting in the sun, and I loved the way the hot seat burned the back of my legs. It made me feel real again, and not crazy. And I loved the feel of Lamar's leg against my own.

"Where's Daddy? How's he going to get over there?" Billie asked.

Lamar gave a short ugly laugh. "I reckon God is going to pick him up. I reckon he'll drive over here and get him whenever the time is right." He reached past my knee to turn on the car radio. Hank Williams was singing. I knew Lamar would never have done that if Daddy had been in the car with us.

But Billie was puzzled. "What kind of a car does God have?" she asked. I swear, you never knew what was going to come out of that mouth of hers.

Lamar turned and grinned at us. "A Cadillac, of course," he said. "Coupe de Ville. Ain't that right, Buddy?"

"That's right," I said.

Lamar smiled at me.

Then we were there, and then we were swept up in all the people and the excitement, and I kind of forgot about Mama because there was so much going on. That is, I didn't *forget* about her exactly, I just put her in another place in my mind for the rest of the afternoon. It is amazing how many different things you can keep in your mind at one time.

We met other people, from places all around, even as far as West Virginia, and then the women put the food out at suppertime, and everybody fell on it like they were starved to death. Billie and me ate with the Dutys, the Maniers, the Roses, and a group of others from the Jesus Name Church. After supper the women cleared off pretty quick while the men smoked and the shadows of the trees stretched out long on the grass. A little breeze started blowing when the sun went down. A new tone was coming into everybody's voices now. People clustered together, talking about God and about their lives in a serious way. Some more cars came up the road, driving slow, and then some men that nobody appeared to know walked to the edge of the field and stood there. We knew they were not Holiness men because of how they looked and carried themselves. Two of them had black cameras on straps around their necks. One of them was fat, and panted to keep up with the others. He had a pencil stuck behind his ear and carried a notebook. Rhonda Rose poked me in the ribs when she saw him.

"That's a reporter," she said. "I can tell."

This was because she had been interviewed so much

after she got bit and her mother took her to the hospital in Waynesville for treatment. Her picture had been in the paper four times. Rhonda had cut out all these clippings from the newspaper and taped them up on her bedroom wall. Since that time, Rhonda's mother had gotten mad and left the family, so now Rhonda had to take care of her daddy and her two little brothers all by herself, but she had still managed to get herself engaged anyway. She was going to marry Robbie Knott. Everybody in our church was tickled over it. Robbie was one of the people up on the platform that evening, testing the PA system, getting everything ready to go.

"Robbie has got him a new drum set," Rhonda told me. "Wait till you see." She squeezed my hand. Up close, she was beautiful, like a movie star. I could see why Robbie Knott or anybody else would want to marry her. I thought, *I am going to marry Lamar*, but I didn't believe it for a minute, even then. It was the only way I knew to think about what we'd done. Anyway, where was Lamar? I told Rhonda I'd see her later, and darted off in the crowd, leaving Billie with the Dutys. I was too nervous to stay in one place.

Everybody was moving now, though no general announcement had been made, moving out into the field, gathering around the platform, which stood about three feet off the ground. Big black speaker boxes were fixed onto poles at the side of it, and lights were strung all around. People I didn't know were jostling me. "Hidy," said a boy I'd never seen before, right up in my face. I couldn't find Lamar. Finally I gave up looking for him and allowed myself to be swept along, like a person caught up in a big slow flood. There was no turning back now.

THEN BOBBY GAYHEART and Dillard Jones came along with some rope and some poles to string it on, and got everybody to move back from the platform about thirty or forty feet, and roped that area off. The roped-off place would be for them that was handling. This made it more legal, or something. More acceptable, I reckon, as it was not legal in any case. Most of the time the law just acted like they didn't know what was going on, and left us alone, but in the rare instances when there'd be a death or when somebody would go to the sheriff's office and complain, why then they would feel obliged to show up and carry on for a while, arresting people and what have you. It would be in the paper. Then it would all die down again, and things would go back to normal. This was the cycle we lived by in the Jesus Name Church, but there were those who felt that Daddy should never hold a big meeting such as Homecoming—that the Jesus Name Church should never do anything to attract attention in any way. "So the work of the Lord can proceed in peace," is how Carlton Duty put it. He came up to our house and had a big argument with Daddy about it. Carlton did not hold with new PA systems and stringing lights and publicity. "These things gets in the way of the Spirit," he said.

I had seen myself that whenever lots of strangers were present in a meeting, anything might happen to break the mood and scare the Spirit off. It was real dangerous when the Lord just up and left somebody holding a serpent, without anointment. So I agreed with Carlton Duty and the others—but in secret, for the Holiness girl or woman does not have a voice in such as that. A woman can handle and she can preach, but she can't decide things.

Daddy, on the other hand, always claimed that there was nothing like a rattlesnake to advance the cause of the Lord. "I ain't preaching to the converted," he said. "I am in the business of saving souls, right here on this sweet earth, and I'm going to use everything the Lord gives me to further His purpose and fulfill His plan. If He gives me a truck, I'll take it. If He gives me a load of gravel, I'll take it. I ain't proud. I ain't too proud to carry on His work as He sees fit, and use whatever He sends me. If He gives me a new pair of shoes, I'll wear them. If He gives me a sack of potatoes, I'll eat them. And if He gives me a rattlesnake, why, I'll take it up in His glory and honor, in His glory and honor, a-men." So that had been the end of it, though Carlton was not alone in his views, and there were even some who whispered that Daddy was exalting himself instead of God in the signs.

A day or so before the great Homecoming, when I asked Lamar what he thought about all this, he looked at me like I was crazy, like there was something he knew and I didn't, or I wouldn't even be asking the question. He curled his lip and seemed about to speak, but did not. I remember I grabbed his hand. "Tell me, tell me," I said. "Tell me what you really think," for he was supposed to be one of the saints himself, after all. But he just stared at me with eyes so black and deep that I feared I might fall into them and be forever lost.

"I don't think nothing," Lamar had said. "I ain't here to think."

And now the Homecoming was upon us all, regardless of what anybody thought about it. I took my seat in a folding chair next to Patsy Manier, well back from the rope. Patsy never went forward either. She was a pretty girl who had actually graduated from high school and then gone to the beauty academy in Asheville, but she got pregnant and had to come home. Now she had the cutest little boy, Thomas, who was the apple of everyone's eye. Patsy and Thomas lived with her parents, Bill and Ruby Manier, who had been staunch members of the Jesus Name Church all along. Patsy's daddy had bought her a beauty shop chair that went up and down and swiveled, and put it in their family room, so Patsy ran a business right there at home, cutting men's hair as well as women's. At first Bill and Ruby were criticized for letting Patsy do this, as she gave permanents and even frostings to non-Holiness women and girls, not to mention touching men's heads, but the Maniers ignored the talk, and it soon died down. People will get used to anything and decide it's all right.

I was pretty sure that Patsy put something on her own hair, as it was a bright shade of red not found in nature. But Patsy was always real nice to me. That night, she hugged me. "You doing all right?" she asked, and I said I was, and we settled back in our seats as they started playing music up on the stage.

It was Slim Dotson on the electric guitar, wearing his familiar black cowboy hat and a belt with a great big JESUS buckle. He was so thin that when he turned sideways he was almost invisible, I'm not kidding. Slim's older brother, Darrell, was on bass, a heavyset man who ran a small engine repair shop and could fix anything, a man to depend upon. The Dotsons had been in the Jesus Name Church forever too, going back to the beginning days in the brush arbor when we first came. Their mother, who had died in the spring, was a handler herself. But she had not died of serpent bite, she had died peaceful in her bed, of natural causes.

Robbie Knott was playing on his fancy new drum set, grinning at the crowd, and Doyle Stacy was up there too on guitar. His left eyelid still drooped, and he spit out that side of his mouth when he got excited preaching, but really he did not look too bad, and once you got used to it, you didn't hardly notice it. A man and a woman I had never seen before were up there singing into the microphone, harmonizing together as good as professionals. Most of the folks from the Jesus Name Church sat together, I noticed, with the handlers up toward the front and the rest of us back some. It was getting dark. The electric lights shone on every face, making them somehow different, naked and new. I felt like I was seeing everybody for the first time, and, yet I felt I'd known them all forever and ever too, as if they were part of me.

There were the Cline sisters, old maids both, with their soft wrinkled faces like apple dolls. Lily sat up front with her daddy and her mama. Since she'd gained so much weight, she looked more like her mama every day, with big new breasts and a fat stomach. I didn't have much in the way of breasts yet, though I was hopeful, and wore a bra because everyone else did. The Dutys sat up front too—I could see the back of their heads—but I couldn't find Mama. Where was she? She usually sat with Ruth, but she wasn't there. I craned my neck to look around. There was lovely Rhonda sitting with her soon-to-be sister-in-law Darlene Knott, narrow-faced and nervous in her harlequin glasses. She worked at the courthouse in Waynesville now. There was Mrs. Duke Watson, rumored to be up in her nineties now, sitting with her son Earl, who never said much but was faithful as the day is long about coming to meeting, and ran a barbecue business. The Pearsons sat close to us—Della and one-armed Gobel and Gobel's daddy, old man Ed Pearson, who used to be an engineer on the railroad before he retired. Lorene Bishop sat off to herself a little, with a wild look in her eye. She'd been searching for a man ever since her own husband, Lovis, had died in the mine. In meeting, she was often the first to be claimed by the Spirit, and the last to quit dancing and speaking in tongues, which was how the Spirit generally took her. I smiled at Mr. Arnold, a new member of our church who was so taken with Daddy that he had loaned the church a truck which said "Arnold's Electric" in curli- cue writing on the door. But where was Mama? And where was Lamar? I turned around to see Truman Hart and his whole family sitting right behind me, and said hidy to them. Tommy Love and Wade Tilly were back there too, and Maudine Meadows, and Bucky Dollar, who was on probation. Before I got so taken with Lamar, it had crossed my mind that Bucky Dollar was kind of cute. I smiled at them all and turned around in time to see Billie walking up to join the Dutys at the front. She walked with her head down, real shy, but a big pretty girl nonetheless, with a round fair face like the moon, which nothing had ever made a mark on. I wished she was in the back with me, where she would be safer, but I wasn't about to go up there and get her.

I stayed put, butterflies in my stomach, as the music got faster and louder. "What would you give in exchange for your soul?" they sang, and before I knew it, I was singing too, and moving to the beat of Robbie's nice new drums. I couldn't seem to sit still. Next to me, Patsy Manier had one of those high, clear, heartbreak voices. Everybody was singing and clapping, and I gave up on finding Mama and Lamar. I was sure they were here someplace.

The wind came off the river and moved through the trees. The green leaves of June shimmered softly in the big circle cast by the light, and I thought all of a sudden that it was God's breath—God's breath touching the leaves, and touching each one of us. I guess I was not used to being outside in the nighttime like that, for there was something about it that really got to me. I felt like I was being caught up in something, like we were all of us caught up and held in something beautiful and solemn and grand. Each face seemed to me beautiful in that light, even old Mrs. Watson's, even Doyle Stacy's.

Bobby Gayheart led us in prayer, his huge arms outstretched. I knew about him not only because he was Lily's uncle but because he had preached it all to us before—how he had been a famous football star in high school, and then took to liquor and bad women and fighting, until he killed a man with a broken wine bottle and got sent off to the Brushy Mountain State Penitentiary in Tennessee, where he had not repented but continued on in his evil ways, fighting and whatnot, I forget, and then on a visit to his sister Leanne he had learned how his own little niece Lily had been brought back to life by God and he had pondered that, and on his next visit he had witnessed Daddy subdue a cottonmouth in the signs, and had given over to God on the spot.

"I was a sinner," Bobby Gayheart used to say, "but I was not a fool."

Bobby prayed for us all, and asked God to come down on the meeting and touch us every one. He talked about how far the different people had traveled to be there, and blessed their vehicles, and blessed God for bringing them safely. Then he told how God had worked in his own life, saving him from sin and giving him a good woman and a little son to boot. Bobby's wife Abby, holding one baby in her lap and big with yet another child, sat in front of me but over to the side some, so I could watch her while he was preaching, and I was struck by how she followed him with her eyes, hanging on every word. It was easy to see how much she loved him. Bobby stomped back and forth across the platform, preaching into a hand mike and getting everybody worked up so that when the music started again, people were jumping up everywhere to clap and sway and dance. "I am a pilgrim and a stranger," we sang, "traveling through this wearisome land." Patsy's voice rang out above the rest. Lorene Bishop was already up and dancing in the aisle. Before I knew it, I found myself standing and clapping with the rest. The breeze touched my face and lifted my bangs, and it was somehow different, all different, being outside like that. Patsy and I rocked from side to side in rhythm, like backup singers.

It was during the singing that Daddy made his appearance at the side of the stage, along with Lamar, both of them wearing white shirts though Daddy had on a tie too, which I knew he would fling off at a certain point in his preaching. He always did that. My heart started going double time at the sight of Lamar, who gave Daddy a hand up on the stage at the end of the singing. Daddy took the microphone from Bobby, and a current swept through the crowd. This was the man they had all heard about, the man that many of them had driven so far to see. Daddy prayed a long prayer during which my attention wandered, and I spent the time peeping out from under my bangs and trying to see where Lamar had got to. But I couldn't find him, nor Mama either. A woman I had never seen before read out the Scripture for Daddy that night, a dark-haired woman from some other church. She read from John 20, "And many other signs truly did Jesus in the presence of His disciples, which are not written in this book: But these are written, that ye might believe that Jesus is the Christ, the Son of God; and that believing ye might have life through His name." Daddy nodded as she read, as if she was confirming something he'd suspected all along.

"Oh my beloved," Daddy began, "what more do you need to know? For it says here in the Bible plain as day that Jesus himself has worked the signs—*Jesus himself!* my beloved—risked life and limb before His time, to take up the serpent and convince all them that was there to follow after Him and accept the gift of Life Everlasting, amen. And now He offers it to you tonight, beloved, His most precious gift of life eternal in the Spirit is right here available to each and every one of you tonight, just as it was back in them old Scripture days. For I say unto you tonight, beloved, the Spirit is as real right here and now on the banks of the Little Dove River as it ever was on the shores of Galilee." Daddy went on preaching while people yelled out "Amen!" and "Tell it!" By the time Daddy took up a timber rattler, the whole crowd was jumping and hollering "Move on him, Lord!" and such as that. Daddy laid the serpent across the pulpit and went on preaching, stopping to drink occasionally from the mason jar of water and strychnine on the pulpit.

By the time he had done preaching and the music had started up again, the Spirit had filled the whole crowd as it does when all are in joy and accord. All were on fire with the Holy Ghost in such a way that we were truly one in the Spirit, and you could see a smile and tears on every face. Even sour old Rupert Ball was nodding his head in time to the beat and grinning from ear to ear. Many were smiling and chuckling. Young mothers were trotting their babies on their knees, and old folks were tapping their feet. And I have to say, I felt the Spirit running through me like a grass fire. I guess Patsy Manier felt it too, for suddenly she was gone, up there at the front taking a copperhead from Ruth Duty, crying and laughing at the same time. Ruth jiggled all over as she danced.

Now the space at the front was full of so many that I couldn't even see who all was up there, it was such a crowd. The holy wind sprang up again and blew around and touched us every one, them up at the front with the serpents, us at the back, and everybody was full of the spirit for about twenty minutes until it moved off right fast and then everybody started jamming the serpents back in their boxes and straightening their clothes and touching their hair. I felt all self-conscious, like I had been caught with my clothes off.

But there were many, many to baptize that night, and Daddy led them down to the river straightaway, and the sound of their singing floated up the hill to Lamar and me where we lay in Daddy's car.

For Lamar had appeared at my elbow the minute the service was over, and put his hand on my arm, and I went with him. Yes, I did. I'll admit it. I was swept along, carried away in the general fever of that night. I did not feel I was doing wrong either, even then. I did not think about that. I did not think at all. Yet I remember that moment so clear. I will always remember it. I remember laying there on the backseat of Daddy's car, listening to them sing. I remember how those little knobs on the scratchy seat covers bit into my back, and how I looked up past Lamar's dark head to the tops of the trees, green and feathery against the enormous black night which waited there beyond our circle of light.

I FINALLY ENDED up sleeping on a pallet next to Billie, over in the woods by Carlton Duty's truck. The Dutys themselves were nowhere to be seen, nor was Lamar, who had left after he took me to find Billie. Robbie Knott and Rhonda Rose were not far off, though, laying on a blanket together whispering. I was jealous of them. I knew they would get married and live together always, and own a brick house, and have children. I was afraid that I would not have any of these things. Abby Gayheart sat holding her baby on a lawn chair nearby. The baby looked blue in the moonlight flickering through the trees. There was so much noise that I thought I would never get to sleep—you could hear folks praying and singing and testifying and hollering out all over the field and in the woods. Many of them would stay up all night long, too filled with God to sleep. But I was worn-out, and I believe I was asleep before my head ever touched the balled-up sweater I was using for a pillow.

I woke to find myself sitting bolt upright on my pallet surrounded by white faces, some of them people I didn't even know. Carlton Duty knelt beside me on the ground with one arm around me, holding a flashlight in his other hand. Billie's scared face was the first thing I focused in on. "Sissy!" she screamed, and then burst into tears. She flung herself facedown on her pallet, sobbing. I looked over at Carlton Duty.

"What is going on?" I asked. My heart was beating real fast and my mouth was dry and my head felt hot, like I might have a fever.

"You have been possessed of the Spirit, Sissy," Carlton Duty told me gravely, his good homely face as honest as all get-out in the light from the flashlight he held. "You have been sitting up in your sleep, and praising God and prophesying."

"Oh I have not," I said, for this was the last thing I wanted or expected to hear. I did not, I did *not* want to be like Daddy and Mama, I did not.

But, "Sissy, we do not always have a choice in these things." Carlton Duty spoke quietly and with absolute authority. "The Lord goes where He chooses, and visits those He loves."

"I don't—I don't want—" I was trying to tell Carlton that I did not want to be chosen or loved either one, but I was too sleepy to speak, and fell into a profound slumber that would last until ten a.m. the next day, later than I had ever slept in my whole life. When I woke up I felt sore all over, but especially my legs, as if I had been running a great long way. Actually I felt awful. It was what I imagined a hangover would feel like. *If this is how it feels to be visited by God*, I thought, *count me out*. Plus a lot of people looked at me funny as I made my way to the toilet and then into the church washroom, where I splashed water on my face and combed my hair, making a new ponytail. I did not want those people to look at me funny. I did not want to be visited by Jesus in the night. I did not want to be visited by Jesus at all, and was terrified that He might return.

"Don't come back," I whispered to Him that morning in the washroom of the Jesus Name Church. "Just leave me alone," I prayed, for I was scared to death.

The worst part of it was, nobody wanted to tell me what I had said when I sat up and spoke in the night. At first, Carlton Duty just shook his head and would not answer, even when I pestered him. I pestered him for a while.

"Come on!" I was getting upset. "I'm the one that said it, ain't I? I reckon I've got a right to know."

Carlton sighed a deep sigh and looked at me. "You was talking about the wind," he said, "and then about the Devil."

I was amazed. "I was?" I couldn't remember any of this. "What did I say about the Devil?"

"You was talking in tongues, Sissy," Carlton said gently. "Couldn't nobody really tell."

The last thing I wanted to do was talk in tongues.

"Could you tell *anything* I said?" I asked him.

Carlton hesitated, then took off his glasses and cleaned them and put them back on before he looked at me. "You said, 'The bite is coming.' "

"I said that? 'The bite is coming'?" I felt like we were talking about somebody else, as I had no memory of this at all.

Carlton nodded slowly. " 'The bite is coming,' you said." He looked over toward the platform area, where folks were gathering for the morning meeting. "Well," he said heavily, "I guess it's time to get on over there." He trudged off like a man going to do a hard job, and I followed, puzzling.

What bite? I wondered. Who would get it? Was it Daddy? Something shot through me, from the top of my head to my feet. *I don't have anything to do with this, just forget it*, I was screaming inside. *Just forget the whole thing*. But a part of me kept wondering, Is it Daddy?

THINGS WENT WRONG that Sunday morning from the first.

For one thing, a lot more people showed up, all of them strangers and some of them drunk, and they made such a racket at the back of the open meeting that it was hard to preach or pray or conduct services. At one point some of them fell to fighting amongst themselves, and had to be separated. Plus it was real hot for June. The sun beat down on our heads. People kept coming and going, starting cars, driving up and down the road. Somebody even had a car radio on real loud for a while. Mama was not present, and so I was worried about her, and couldn't keep my mind on what was happening. I couldn't imagine why she hadn't come, unless she was sick. It was the only thing I could think of. I was sure Lamar would have gone back to get her as he promised, but if she was sick, then why hadn't he told me? I'd go home and take care of her. I'd fix her some tea and brush her hair. I was thinking this while I watched Lamar, who was up there now with the others on the platform playing the guitar, which he was really good at. He could have played music for a living if he'd wanted to. He could have gone to Nashville. He could have done any number of things. But what *would* he do? What did he want to do? I didn't even know that. I didn't know anything about him. I was feeling faint and fidgety there in the sun. Out of the corner of my eye, I could see one of the sheriff's men, chewing tobacco and spitting to the side. Sun flashed off the gun at his belt.

It was not a good day to work the signs. But Daddy was not likely to be put off, not with so many folks gathered and the reporters present. And as expected, it was not long before some men made their way up to the front with a dynamite box that turned out to hold a mess of copperheads, which Daddy lifted high, praising God. One of them twisted out of his upraised hands and flew into the air, causing a wild scramble of people who turned over their chairs and pushed toward the back. But Daddy leaned down and plucked the serpent up off the floor, and the man that had brought in the dynamite box fell to his knees, and the meeting was on in earnest, though it still felt wrong. I was watching Daddy close when he straightened back up, and I saw his expression change in a way that showed he had received a bite. Usually when this happened he would go right on, and you could hardly tell it. For a while, this was the case. But about fifteen minutes later, he paused in what he was saying and his face turned white and he sank against the pulpit and closed his eyes. Doyle ran forward with the dynamite box for the copperheads. The reporters rushed forward too, clicking their cameras. Daddy lurched to the side.

When all the shouting and carrying on was over, Daddy

was hauled off to the hospital by the police, despite him rallying enough to swear he would refuse medical treatment of any kind, so they might as well just go ahead and take him to jail and be done with it. By then he seemed mighty strong for someone who had just been hurt in the signs, and all remarked on this, and called it a victory for the Lord. The last I saw of Daddy that day, he was sitting in the backseat of a deputy's car behind that little grill they've got, waving his fist as they drove him away.

It was only then that I noticed a knot of people around the Dutys' truck over there in the trees where Billie and me had spent the night. I went to see what was happening. The first thing I saw was Carlton in the back of the pickup, crying like a baby. The next thing I saw was a whole bunch of men lifting Ruth and placing her in the truck bed on her back. Her right arm and hand were swollen to twice their normal size, and her eyes were closed, and she was gasping for breath. She looked like she was dying. Her flowered skirt was hiked up so that you could see her rolled-down hose and the big blue veiny globs of fat just above her knees. *Ruth would be so embarrassed*, I thought, *to have herself displayed thisaway.*

"Gracie! Billie! Get in here!" It was Doyle Stacy hollering at us, and he was at the wheel of the Dutys' truck, and so we jumped in it and he drove us over to their house, where folks were already gathered when we got there. They carried Ruth in and put her on the couch, and folks crowded up close to lay their hands on her, falling to their knees on the carpet all around. Everybody was praying out loud at once, but I could hear Doyle's voice from time to time above the rest. "Almighty God, send down your healing power on this sweet lady, touch her right now Lord, and make her whole again, oh Lord we ain't telling you what to do or not to do, bless Heaven, but we beseech you to use your awful power to give her back to us for yet a while, dear God, for yet a while—" Doyle clasped his hands behind his back while he prayed. His whole shirt was wet with sweat. It was real hot in there. I leaned up against a big footstool that Ruby Manier was sitting on, and prayed as best I could, but all I could think of to say right then was, "Jesus Christ, don't do this, Lord Jesus, please don't do this." I said it over and over. For a while it looked like Ruth would not make it, but sometime in the late afternoon she started moving restlessly and then opened her eyes and smiled weakly at Carlton, who had never left her side. He cried like a baby, out of joy.

We all got up then, and praised God, and ate some cheeseburgers which the Gayhearts had brought over from the new drive-in on the bypass. Nothing ever tasted as good to me as those cheeseburgers when I knew Ruth would live! I ate two of them. Then Don Roy Privette gave Billie and me a ride home, since he was going our way, and it was sunset when he dropped us at the bottom of the hill.

The car was not there, so I figured that Lamar must have gone off in it to see about Daddy. It was the longest walk up that hill. The sun was setting behind our backs, throwing long shadows out in front of us, and the soft June air smelled mysterious and sweet. We stopped to rest by the creek and splashed water on our faces to cool off. It seemed to me like months since we had left here for the

Homecoming, yet it had been only the day before. The water of Scrabble Creek made a bitter taste in my mouth. "Let's go," I said to Billie, but she pulled on my sleeve, holding back.

"What's the matter with you?" I started to get mad, for I was dog tired, but she just shook her head with the funniest look on her face. I looked at Billie, and then I looked up the hill at our house, and then I knew something was wrong, knew it as clear as if somebody had whispered it in my ear.

It was the gift of discernment which came to me then though I did not want it, any more than I had wanted the gift of prophecy. I climbed the hill with a heavy heart, dragging Billie along. Everything looked strange to me that evening—the white quartz rock, the old black kettle, the chairs on the porch—all with wild purple shadows splayed out behind them.

"You stay here," I told Billie, and put her in a rocker on the porch.

The front door was standing wide open.

"Mama," I hollered as I went in the house. "Mama!"

I CHECKED ALL the rooms and then the toilet, saving the barn for last. By the time I walked out the back door, I knew she would be in the barn. I knew it as well as I ever knew anything, but at first I didn't see her. I pushed open the door as far as it would go, and stepped inside and stood straining my eyes to see into that familiar sweet-smelling darkness, but I couldn't connect what I saw with my mother.

It swung from a rafter, turning slightly in the breeze I'd made opening the door. It was as limp as the rag dolls Ruth Duty made for me and Billie years back, its head flopped over crazily to the side. The dark face was swollen past any real recognition, mouth open, tongue out, eyelids drooping, eyes not really closed but not open either. I grew terrified that it would raise its head and look at me, that I would have to know what was in those awful sightless eyes. It didn't, of course.

Of course, it was my mother.

She had looped some clothesline around a rafter, then made a noose, then climbed up on the corncrib and put her head in it, then jumped off the corncrib. She had planned everything perfect. Her feet hung about a yard off the straw, one of them bare, the other still wearing one of the old brown shoes I knew so well. Her work shoes.

The small bare foot looked white and ghostly dangling there in the gloom, not scary but pale and sad. I sank down onto the straw and pulled her foot to me and kissed it. It was cold. A bit of red remained on a couple of her toenails—she had been vain about her pretty feet and still painted her toenails sometimes, when Daddy was out of town. This was the only trace left of that dancing girl from long before, the girl I could scarcely imagine, but as I sat crying in the dark barn and covered her cold bare foot with kisses, the harsh stranger she'd become just disappeared, went out of my mind entirely, to be replaced by my sweet young mama of old, who had told us stories and sung to us by the hour, and kissed all our hurts away. I'm not sure how long I stayed out there in the barn with Mama, but I have always been glad of that precious time, for I was able to say good-bye to her then in my own way.

It was full dark when I saw a light on the path outside and heard Lamar's voice calling me. "Buddy?" he said cautiously. "Buddy?"

I tried but could not speak.

Lamar stepped through the open door and held the lantern up. What he said then was not words really, just an awful sound in his throat. He put the lantern down and reached for me, but I crawled back, back into the darkest corner of that little old tobacco barn, away from the light, away from his touch. I felt that if he touched me, I would be lost—utterly, utterly lost. I cringed down in the swinging shadow cast by Mama's body, and when I could finally speak, I spoke the truth as it was given to me in that moment, through my new and dreadful gift of discernment.

"This is your doing and your fault," I said, and my voice was not my own. I did not call him Lamar, for I was no longer sure it was his name. I didn't know what his name was, or who he was, or what he was. All I knew was that Mama's death was his doing, and I knew that absolutely, that she had been lonely and desperate and that he had come to her then, had lain with her as he had lain with me, and that she could not stand it, and now she was dead. Her body hung between us, turning in the lantern's yellow light.

"You've got it wrong, Buddy," he said. "It wasn't me. It wasn't never me. It was him, all along."

"Who?" I said.

"Him. That son of a bitch," Lamar swore softly in the reeling light.

I stared at him until he turned black before my eyes, the edges of his form crinkling as flames ate in toward the middle, like a photograph on fire, burning inward until he was gone, leaving nothing but a dark place in the air.

I never saw him again. None of us did. He stole our car and Mama's little bit of money that she had left—he threw the empty blue sock down on her bedroom floor—and lit out for parts unknown. Straight for Hell, I reckoned, though later it was said that the highway patrol found the car broke down and abandoned someplace in Louisiana.

I did not take in much of what went on for a while after that, and I don't have any memory of who came and got me out of the barn, or who cut Mama down, or where they took me next. I do remember that they buried Mama in the Duty family graveyard up on the mountain in the pouring rain, after a funeral where everybody cried and cried. Daddy didn't come because he was still in jail. I remember them shoveling dirt onto Mama's pine box, and how it turned into runny red mud in the rain, and Ruth Duty kneeling and getting all muddy and they had to help her up.

Then I don't remember anything at all for a long time, until one day when I kind of came back to myself and found that I was sitting in Ruth and Carlton's kitchen, at their round oak table, eating homemade vegetable soup out of a blue bowl with a big spoon that said "U.S. Navy" on it. I was surprised to see that it was still summer, and that I was still alive. The soup was delicious.

BILLIE WAS WORKING at the Dutys' grocery store now, and made two-fifty an hour. She was pleased as punch with herself. She smiled at everybody that came in the store, though she wouldn't talk to them much, since she was so shy. She was getting real fat too. I started going over to the grocery store myself, as I didn't have anything else to do. But I hated the way everybody stared at me and Billie, pitying us. Everybody that came in there knew who we were, and knew what had happened to us. I couldn't stand this. I couldn't quit thinking about it either. For more and more it seemed to me that it was all my fault. What if I had just refused to give Lamar that drink of water, and sent him on his way? None of it would have happened.

I felt dirty. Nasty. I felt like anybody could just look at me, even there in the store, and see what I was, and know what I had done with Lamar. For I did it first, I started it all. Mama would still be alive today if it wasn't for me. The worst thing was, I couldn't figure out what to do about it now. I knew that I had sinned, and that I had been a slave of sin. I knew that the wages of sin is death, but the gift of God is eternal life in Christ Jesus our Lord, as in Romans 6:23.

The big problem was that God wouldn't have anything to do with me now, though I tried and tried to pray. He was as far from me as He had been close at the Homecoming. He had turned away His face. So I couldn't think what to do next. I felt that I was waiting for a sign. I was not surprised to look out the open door of the grocery store one day and see Daddy get off the Asheville bus, which always stopped at noon. He was carrying a black suitcase. He looked all around for a minute, blinking in the bright September sunlight. Then he walked right in the store. Billie Jean started crying the minute she saw him, and ran to Ruth, who hugged her. Carlton stiffened up behind the counter. But he did not come around to greet Daddy, nor offer his hand, though Daddy had started smiling his big Gospel smile. I could tell that he was prepared to take up his ministry right where he had left off.

But, "They's been some changes in your absence," Carlton told him solemnly across the counter.

"What do you mean, 'changes'?" Daddy asked. He looked pretty much the same as ever, his white hair maybe a little shorter. He cut off a hunk of hoop cheese from the big round on the counter and ate it without taking his eyes off Carlton Duty.

Carlton reddened but held firm. "There's them, and I am among them, sir, who feels it was a sign from God, Fannie being took thataway, and Ruth getting hurt on the same day, and so we have laid the serpents down for the time being, until we hear different from the Lord."

"I'll tell you what the Lord says." Daddy's voice was as clear and deep and full of power as it had ever been, but Carlton shook his head.

"No sir, you will not," he said sternly, though he

blushed a fiery red. "The Lord can speak to me as good as He can speak to you. Why, he can speak to any one of us, just as He has spoke to your own daughter, Florida Grace."

Daddy looked at me good for the first time since he had come in the store. I had stopped dead in my tracks at the sight of him. My heart was beating like a jackhammer.

"Is this true, Grace?" he asked.

"I don't know," I said. I didn't want him to know anything about my gifts. I looked down at the counter, at my own hands on the counter, and wouldn't say. Everybody else got quiet too.

Daddy's big booming laugh rang out false in the silent store. "Well, well," he said. "Well, well. I reckon I can see how the land lays. I reckon we had best take this up with God at the next meeting, and see what He has to say about it. Come on, girls. Florida Grace, Billie Jean. Mind me now."

But Billie burst into tears and flung her apron up over her face. Ruth kept hugging her tight, and did not let her go. Ruth reached out with her other hand for me.

"All right," Daddy said shortly. "Come on, then, Grace." He raised his voice.

It was his voice that did it. For I thought then of Mama, and the light that came to her face whenever he spoke. I *had* to go to him then, I *had* to go with him, though my heart sank like a stone in my chest. I walked out from behind the counter.

Gravely, Carlton took one of the keys off the big ring he wore on his belt. He put it down on the counter. "Take the truck," he said.

Daddy looked at him.

"That boy took off in your car," Carlton said. "He's long gone now. He left right after—" Carlton bit his lip and looked down.

Daddy picked up the key. "Let's go, Grace," he said. He grabbed an orange soda out of the cooler as he left.

I followed him out the door into the dry golden afternoon. We got in the Arnold's Electric truck. "Billie and me have been staying with Ruth and Carlton," I told him. Without a word, Daddy drove the short distance to the Dutys' house and stopped in front. "Get your things," he said. I ran in. Their door was never locked. It did not take long. I came out with my arms full and got back in the truck, and Daddy drove up to Scrabble Creek. He parked at the foot of the hill but made no move to get out of the truck.

"How did she do it?" he asked me finally. He did not look at me but stared straight up the hill at the house.

"She hung herself on a piece of clothesline," I told him. "Out in the barn." I felt like I was talking about somebody I didn't even know.

Daddy shook his head. He looked pale and old and beat down.

We walked up the hill and into the house, where everything was pretty much the way Mama had left it, for Ruth and Carlton had been checking on things, and me and Billie had been in and out frequent too. Daddy kept looking around like he didn't know where he was. He kept picking things up and putting them down, such as the little statue of two dwarves that said "Rock City" on it, and Mama's sewing basket still where she'd left it on the sofa in the sitting room, and the blue willow teapot in the kitchen. There was no sign of Lamar to be found. He had vanished without a trace, as if he had never been there at all. Daddy walked back into his and Mama's bedroom, and I followed him and saw him open the wardrobe and bury his face in the folds of her few dresses hanging there. I watched him for a long time. Later I went into the kitchen and opened up a can of chicken noodle soup and poured it in a pan and measured a canful of water into it and put it on the stove to heat. Somebody had to do this, with Mama gone. I ate some soup and then Daddy ate some. As I was going to sleep, I heard him walking all around the house carrying on, calling out to God and praying. It sounded like there was a whole lot of people out there, but it was only Daddy.

I don't know if he ever went to sleep or not. Right before dawn he woke me up and said, "Come on, Grace. We're going." I sat up instantly, completely awake. I was not surprised, though he had not told me that we were leaving. Most of my clothes were still in the Arnold's Electric truck. I dressed in the dark and gathered up the rest of my clothes and went outside, where Daddy stood on the porch looking at the black outline of Coleman's Ridge against the lightening sky. We walked down the hill together. I didn't look back once. I didn't need to.

For I had my own picture of the house on the hill by Scrabble Creek which I had loved, my own picture safe in my mind already, like the little scene in the miraculous Easter egg which Marie Royal had kept on top of the dresser in her bedroom. This was a white sugar egg with a clear window in one end, where you could peep in to see a tiny castle, with a moat and a king and a dragon. This scene never, ever changed. Each time I peeped in, it was always the same. Our early years in the wonderful house on Scrabble Creek seemed to me perfect and everlasting in that same way, and I loved to think about them, peeping into the egg in my mind whenever I chose, as Daddy and I traveled the South. I remembered all the good things that had happened there, and sometimes right before I went to sleep, I even thought I could hear the musical waters of Scrabble Creek and feel Mama's soft good-night kiss on my cheek.

Traveling Light

ONCE DADDY AND me got on the road, it all came back to me, us being on the road before, when I was little, crammed into that old Studebaker. Back then, we surely could have used a nice big truck like the one from Arnold's Electric. We could have used the room. All of us kids could have been in the back under the camper top. We could have played there. But now it was just me and Daddy on the huge seat in the cab, rattling around like two peas in a pod. I felt so lonesome, like about a hundred people were missing. Daddy was not much for talking, at least not to me. He didn't seem to be that interested in me. He took me along because he needed me to read the Bible out for him to preach, the way Mama used to do.

I was an instrument of Daddy, the way he was an instrument of God. I understood this, and bore it without complaint. I felt like it was my due some way, my duty. This had to do with Lamar.

As Daddy and I drove along through Tennessee, I thought about Lamar constantly, though by then I couldn't even remember what his face looked like. I thought that he was the Devil, come to visit us and try to pull us down to his level, which he had done a pretty good job of. But then too I would remember how sweet he could be, how he'd watch out for me and make me go to school, and I'd get confused. I reckon the worst thing about it was how much I missed him. For I did. I did miss Lamar just awful in spite of everything, and this made me hate myself, and not mind going where I had to go, and doing what I had to do.

Which was whatever Daddy told me.

On the road, my main job was to read the map. As soon as it got full light on that morning we set out, Daddy handed it to me, soft and dog-eared around the edges from so much use. "God will tell us where He wants us to go," Daddy explained, "but He needs for you to be His navigator."

"All right." I unfolded the map and laid it across my lap. "Where does He want us to go first?" I asked.

"Newport, Tennessee," Daddy said.

I looked on the map. As the crow flies, Newport, Tennessee, was not too far away, but it was a long wiggly line on the map, because of all the mountains. "It looks to me like you just keep on going on this road we're on," I told Daddy, "and then you turn off to the left first chance you get, up at Hot Springs."

"Ah, Hot Springs," Daddy said. "We had us a grand meeting at Hot Springs, Grace, where many souls were brought into glory, it must of been, oh twenty years back, before you was even born. Before you was even a twinkle in your daddy's eye."

"Well, why don't we stop in there now?" I asked. "That was a mighty long time ago. I bet a lot of them have backslid and fell by the wayside since then. I bet they'd just love to see you coming." I said this in a mean tone, surprising myself. Sometimes it was like Lamar had planted a little seed of the Devil in me which would prompt me to speak up and make fun, or say the ugliest things.

Daddy looked at me hard. "Grace, Grace," he said sorrowfully, shaking his head. "God forgives you, honey, and I forgive you too."

Then I felt awful, of course. We rode along in silence for a while after that, me looking out the window as the beautiful countryside flowed past like water. The leaves were just starting to turn. Children stood out by the road waiting for the school bus, and smoke rose here and there up on the mountains, from little tucked-away houses you couldn't see. I wondered who all lived up there, and what they were doing, and if a creek ran down past their house like it had past ours. Later that morning it gave me a pang to see the slow yellow school buses, but I couldn't really connect myself with that earlier girl who had loved school so, and horses, and writing books. She was somebody I used to know a long time back. I went to sleep for a while, and woke up to find Daddy carrying on a big conversation with himself. He was talking about Mama a lot, and then sometimes it seemed like he was talking *to* Mama. "Fannie," he wailed. "Oh Fannie, oh my God, Lord, Lord." But when his pain moved me so much that I reached over to touch his shoulder, he jumped like he'd been shot, and his face darkened.

"Your mama was not what you thought," he said. "She was not what all she was cracked up to be." He clenched his teeth, looking straight ahead, but then he appeared to forget me and started up grieving for her again. This time I did not interrupt.

We stopped to eat lunch in a restaurant outside of Hot Springs, where Daddy embarrassed me by praying out loud over our sandwiches, but the owner of the restaurant seemed to like this, and when Daddy went up to the cash register to pay, she said it was on the house. Daddy grinned at me as we went out the door. "In that case, we should of eat more!" he said. "We should of loaded up!"

I couldn't help but grin back at him.

We got to Newport around sunset, with Daddy driving from memory as to which roads to take to get to the church house. It was a small plain cinder-block building with no steeple and no way you could tell it was a church except for the hand-lettered sign over the door which said ONE WAY CHURCH OF GOD. We pulled up into a gravel parking lot to the side and got out to stretch our legs. Daddy smoked a cigarette while I walked around. The One Way church house was way up a holler, built in the overhang of a big rocky mountain so steep you couldn't imagine anybody even climbing it. This location gave the church a forsaken, lonely feeling. I didn't like it. But I could tell from the way Daddy had been driving that he knew his way now, so I figured this was the place in Tennessee that he had visited so much with Evelyn. I got all excited at the thought that I might see Evelyn.

We waited in the parking lot until two men drove up in a shiny red truck. It was starting to get dark by then, and I figured they were coming to set up for the meeting, as this was a Wednesday night. Daddy stomped out his cigarette and cleared his throat as they pulled in. The truck came to a stop and they got out and walked over toward us. Daddy leaped across the lot to hug and bless them, as was his custom. "Brother Ben! Brother Loomis!" he shouted, pounding first one and then the other on the back. "It's good to see you! So good to be here, praise Jesus!"

Brother Ben, the tall one, embraced him in a half-hearted way, but Brother Loomis held himself real stiff, arms down at his sides. Brother Loomis had bushy black eyebrows that grew across his forehead in a line, and bristling hair. He looked kind of rough, a man that you might be scared of, but when he spoke his voice was soft.

"What brings you over this way, Virgil?" he asked.

Daddy smiled his big happy smile. "Why, I've come to stay with you-uns for a spell!" he said. "And I have brung my daughter Grace, here."

"Hidy," I said from over where I stood by the truck, but neither man so much as looked at me. They looked at each other instead, and something passed between them.

"Well, Virgil," Brother Loomis said, for evidently he was the spokesman, "the plain fact of it is, we would just as soon you'd move along right now. You've done a lot for us over here, no man could deny it. And we're grateful. But the word has got out about what all happened at your Homecoming—you know there was a right smart of our own people present—and the fact is that there is some of them that has took out agin you at this time. We have been having a lot of strife and prayer here our ownselves, sir, a-trying to determine what exactly the Lord has got in mind for us to do, what course He wants us to foller."

"You mean iffen He wants you to take them up or not," Daddy said.

"Yes sir, there's that, and there is other things besides." Brother Loomis kept looking at Daddy real steady. "I reckon we're just gonna have to thrash it out some way amongst ourselves."

"But the Bible don't give us no leeway!" Daddy started in. "The Word of God is real clear, to them that has ears. You've got ears, ain't ye?"

But Brother Loomis wouldn't smile. "I reckon you had best go on, sir," he said.

"Ben, where do you stand on all this?" Daddy asked the taller man, who took his cap off now and turned it around and around in his hands.

"We have done talked it over," Ben finally said. "It ain't just him, nor just me. I hope you will understand that, Virgil." He looked like he was worried to death.

"Well, boys," Daddy said heavily, "I'll remember this. God will remember this. Get in the truck, Grace," he said, and I did, and we pulled out of the One Way Church parking lot just as about five cars pulled in. Daddy drove out to the paved road and stopped and put his head down on the steering wheel.

"What are you doing?" I asked, for his behavior scared me.

"I'm asking God for directions." His voice was muffled by his arms. He prayed on the wheel that way for a good half-hour while cars came up behind and blew their horns and then drove around us, full of faces staring curiously at us. By then it was flat-out dark, I was afraid somebody was going to run into us. But finally Daddy straightened up and started the truck.

"What'd He say?" I asked.

"He said turn left," Daddy reported, turning, "and forgive them their trespasses, which I will do though it sticks in my craw, I don't mind telling you. Why, they would not of been nothing over here without me! They wouldn't have had nothing but a wide place in the road!" He talked on and on as we drove into the night, the red tip-end of his cigarette and the lights on the dashboard making his face just visible. The thought of Evelyn got smaller and smaller in my mind. I was hungry, but there was nothing to eat, so finally I went to sleep. I woke up later to find us bumping up a long rutted road, our truck lurching from side to side. We stopped next to a brick house which I could barely see. Daddy got out and knocked on the door. After a while a light came on, and I heard a woman's laughter.

"Why, Virgil Shepherd!" she said. "You big old sweet thing!" Daddy went in the house, slamming the door behind him. The light went out. I reached over the seat and started pulling clothes out of my sack until I had enough to make myself a kind of a nest on the seat, and slept there all night long.

That was in Newport, Tennessee, and that woman was named Marva Gail Drew. The next morning, she had a fit when she found out that I was with Daddy and had slept out in the truck. She clucked over me and patted me and dragged me in the house and cooked up a big breakfast of scrambled eggs and biscuits and sausage gravy for us. We ate every bite of it. Marva Gail Drew could cook as good as Ruth Duty. She was a skinny woman, though, with long dyed-blond hair. I thought she was probably older than she looked, because her eyes looked older than the rest of her. She didn't eat anything. She smoked a cigarette and watched us eat. Every now and then she'd dash into the front room to stare out her picture window and then glance at her sunburst clock.

"Now, you know I hate to rush you, Virgil," she said the minute we were done. "But Lucy is going to bring Mama over here before long, and you know I'd just as soon you wasn't here then, what with Bill on the road and all."

Of course I didn't know the people she was talking about, but I got the picture. I had been hoping to take a shower in her pretty pink-tile bathroom, but I could tell it wasn't going to happen.

Daddy drained his cup and wiped his mouth and stood up. "I thank you, Marva Gail," he said, "and God thanks you too."

"Well, you're both welcome." Marva Gail smiled real big at Daddy, crinkling her eyes. "My pleasure," she said.

We got back in the truck and I picked up the map again, but Daddy said he wouldn't have to have me read it out that day, as we were not going far, and he knew how to get there.

"But where is it?" I asked, opening up the map anyhow. "What is the name of the town?"

"It don't matter," Daddy said. "Everplace is the same in the sight of God, Grace, and He's the one in charge here. You're on the way to Heaven, and that's all you need to know."

"But I thought I got to be the navigator!" It occurred to me that maybe Daddy had just said that to make me think I was important, that neither God nor Daddy either one had any real use for me. I started crying like crazy, and couldn't hardly breathe. I spread the map out on my lap anyway, dropping big tears on it. I liked being the navigator, I liked the dots of the towns and the spiderwebby lines of the roads that connected them. I needed to know where we were on the map.

"Okay, okay. We're heading down here to Cosby, if you have to know, right here it is." He jabbed wildly at the map, but I had already found the dot that was Cosby. I settled back in my seat and stopped crying as we drove along, while Daddy sang "When the Roll Is Called Up Yonder I'll Be There." He *did* have the prettiest singing voice.

But they wouldn't take us in Cosby either, and for the same reason, as we were told in no uncertain terms by several members of that church and then by their preacher himself, after we tracked him down at his job at a power plant.

Daddy got back into the truck in a black mood, slamming the door.

I spread out my map. "Where to?" I said.

"Well, it looks to me like God is sending us farther afield," Daddy finally said. "We are going to spread His seed on new ground."

Somehow this seemed to pep us both up, though it was afternoon by then and we didn't even have a place to sleep that night. Daddy drove west and I read out the names of the places we were headed toward. "Jones Cove, Pigeon Forge, Cove Creek, Gatlinburg," I read.

"Gatlinburg is a place of sin and mammon," Daddy announced darkly. "Not Gatlinburg. Read me some more."

"Laurel," I read, skirting around the Great Smoky Mountains National Park. "Waterstown, Walland, Maryville."

"Ain't that a right big town?" Daddy said. "Maryville?"

"Yessir," I said. It was printed in darker letters than any of the others.

"Maryville." Daddy rolled the sound of it around in his mouth. "Maryville, then."

The moment which I had dreaded the most came that very afternoon. It was a sunny, windy day, with bright leaves plastering themselves on our windshield and dancing across the road. I was enjoying the ride. But all of a sudden, Daddy pulled off the road and braked to a jarring stop. I stared at him. "What are you stopping here for?" I asked, as there was no store, nor house, nor anything remarkable that I could see.

Daddy said something I couldn't understand. Then he jumped out of the truck and looked back in the window at me. "I won't be gone long. It's God's will, Grace," he said, his blue eyes snapping with energy and light. Then he disappeared from the window and I couldn't see anything but the steep rocky mountainside. For a while I could hear Daddy rooting around in the back of the truck, and then I couldn't hear him anymore and he was gone. I got out and sat on a rock by the side of the road, my heart pounding hard in my chest. I had known it was only a matter of time. I got light-headed as I sat there. Not a single car or truck passed by. I started to feel that I was the only person for miles and miles around, maybe the only person besides Daddy alive in the whole world. Right in front of me, yellow and orange leaves spun around and around in a circle, like a little tornado. It was a beautiful day. Still I found myself panting for breath. But before I could believe it, Daddy was back, grinning from ear to ear, holding a burlap towsack up high in the air. The sack wiggled and bulged.

"They was exactly where God said they would be, Grace!" Daddy was as excited as a boy on Christmas. "I was driving right along here when He spoke up plain as day in my ear, said, 'Pull over, Virgil, I have got something for you under a red rock on this here mountain,' and so I done it, and clumb up, and I swear I had not got but a yard or so past the tree line when I seed it, that big old red rock provided by the Lord, and God give me the strength to pry it up, which I thank Him for, and I done so to find two of them coiled up in a big knot under there just like He said they would be, and I reached over in there and plucked them up and popped them in the sack before they knowed what hit them. Easy as pie!" Daddy threw the heavy towsack into the back of the truck and then climbed in the front and started the engine. "Well, come on, girl!" he hollered. "We ain't got all day! We've got the Lord's work to do, Grace, and we'd best get on with it."

Sure enough, that night in Maryville, Daddy was anointed by God to take up those serpents, and in so doing he brought many souls to God, and a man came up and gave him a beautiful serpent box tooled in silver and engraved with the words of Mark 16. Daddy took this as a sign, of course, and said that his faith, which had wavered, was now fully restored. At the end of the service, Daddy and a bunch of them drove to the nearest river for a big baptizing, for he would not baptize in a lake or a pond, preferring running water as the Bible says.

I went home with some church people as was customary. When I went to the bathroom at their house, I saw the brownish-red stains in my white underpants, and I knew I had started my period at last. I was a real woman now. I did not feel any different, however, and it did not even seem very important in light of everything else that had happened. I rooted around in a bathroom drawer and found some Kotex.

I had to smile, thinking that God had provided both me and Daddy with what we needed that day.

I didn't feel any pain. I went out and told the woman that lived there what had happened, and asked could I have a couple more Kotex and a belt until I could get to a store to get some. This was a real poor blonde woman who sat in a kitchen chair nursing a baby while another child, a little girl, slept on the floor at her feet, pretty as an angel. She looked up from her baby to me, and her blue eyes slowly filled with tears. "Why, sure you can, honey," she said. "You can take the whole damn box," which I did.

WE STAYED WITH different people in every town. By November it was too cold to sleep in the truck. Sometimes after a meeting, I'd go home with one family and Daddy would go home with another. Sometimes I'd forget the name of the people I was staying with and have to ask them again in the morning. One time Daddy disappeared, leaving me with an old couple named Childress in Coeburn, Virginia, and showed up three days later to announce that he had backslid but had now patched it up with God. I was glad to hear this, as in his absence Mrs. Childress made me wash all her floors and her clothes and even her curtains.

Another time I stayed with a family that had some teenage twin girls who took me to a drive-in restaurant where the waitresses came on roller skates to take our order. We got a foot-long hot dog for each of us. It was a whole car full of girls who knew all the words to all the songs on the radio, and giggled a lot. I had a good time with them. This was in Big Stone Gap, Virginia.

It turned out to be true what Daddy so often said, that God's time is not man's time. I lost track of the days. Later I lost track of the weeks, and even the months sometimes. I called Carlton and Ruth Duty collect when I could. The big news from them was that Billie had turned out to be pregnant, though she had gotten so fat that nobody knew it until the baby was nearly due. Billie herself acted real surprised, and swore she didn't know how it had happened. I myself was certain that baby was Lamar's. If he would mess with me, then he would surely mess with Billie, especially since she couldn't remember things.

The baby, a little girl, was born in January. They named her Fannie after Mama, and said she looked like Mama, fair-complected and delicate. As far as Ruth and Carlton were concerned, this was the baby they had always wanted but never had. They believed that God had sent little Fannie to them as a gift for standing His test of faith. She was all they would talk about when I called them, from various points south, to see how they were doing. They always said they were doing fine, but I was not, and after a while I didn't call anymore. Hearing their voices made me miss them too much, and feel too bad. But they couldn't call or write to me, as I was on the road, and so we lost touch then.

Things went along okay in general, I guess, until Daddy got put in jail in Chattanooga, leaving me stranded on a street corner without a penny to my name. This happened after we left Alabama, where we stayed the longest. Anyway, Daddy had been preaching on the streets in the bigger towns in order to make cash money for our trip, but we didn't stay anywhere long enough to get to know anybody real good. This was certainly true in Chattanooga. So when they took him away, I didn't know anybody to call, nor have any place to stay. It was June, and already hot as blazes. I couldn't think what to do. The Arnold's Electric truck parked by the curb contained everything Daddy and me owned in the world. I stood there beside it, fanning myself with my straw hat for a while, and then I went over and sat on a stone bench under a big tree next to a statue of a soldier.

The only good thing I could think of was that the police had taken the serpents too when they took Daddy—for evidence, they said. I knew they would kill them, and I was glad, though I knew also that there would be others when Daddy got out of jail. There wasn't ever any shortage of serpents. I sat on that bench holding my Bible, which did not do me a bit of good with Daddy gone. I was not about to start preaching. People kept walking by, but none of them looked at me. I was getting real thirsty when the prettiest lady came walking right up to me and said, "You must be the preacher's daughter." She had soft, curly brown hair piled up on top of her head, and a blue and white seersucker dress, and red high-heel shoes. She talked funny, which was a Northern accent. I could smell her perfume.

"Well, yes ma'am, I am," I said. "My name is Gracie Shepherd."

She stuck out her hand and I shook it. I had never shook hands with a woman before. "I'm Mrs. Thoroughgood," she said, "and you're to come along with me."

I hesitated, though I *wanted* to go along with her. "What about our things?" I asked. "I can't just go off and leave the truck." I pointed to it.

She cocked her pretty head to the side like a bird and studied me. "No, of course not," she said. "Don't you have the keys? Why don't you just follow me? I'll be in that blue sedan."

Then I had to say that Daddy had the keys, and that I couldn't drive anyway, though I was old enough. Daddy did not hold with women driving. Then I busted out crying, to my surprise and embarrassment.

"There, there," Mrs. Thoroughgood said. "You just come with me, then. Dan will find out about the keys and send somebody for the truck." I didn't understand any of this, but I followed her along the busy sidewalk to her car, feeling like I was being pulled by a little tugboat.

"Dan" turned out to be Mrs. Thoroughgood's husband, who was rich and let his wife do whatever she pleased. I never did understand exactly how they found out about me, but I stayed with them until Daddy got out of jail. They had the most beautiful old house, which was full of antiques, plus a sweeping curled stairway in the front hall and lots of oil portraits of old-fashioned people staring out like ghosts from their fancy gold frames. I slept in a bed with a tent over it, which Mrs. Thoroughgood told me was a "canopy." It was the most beautiful bed in the world, with angels carved into the headboard.

But I did not feel that I deserved to sleep in that bed, or stay with the Thoroughgoods.

"Let me help you," I said on the first day. "I'd be glad to clean, or do whatever you want me to do around here."

"Well—" Mrs. Thoroughgood narrowed her eyes at me. "Clara comes in every day to clean, and I know you wouldn't want to take her job away from her, now would you?"

"Nome," I said. But then I started crying again. It was

crazy how much I cried the first few days I stayed with the Thoroughgoods, when I had never cried once about my mother during all those months previous, not even at her funeral, nor when we left Ruth and Carlton and Billie Jean on Scrabble Creek.

Mrs. Thoroughgood kept looking at me. "I'll tell you what," she said. "Your job will be to amuse the children after day camp." This did not sound like much of a job to me. "And you can help me clear away at dinner," she added. "Clara is gone by then."

I nodded, feeling better. It would have to do.

The Thoroughgoods' two girls, Amanda and Melissa, were little brats in spite of them having such a nice mother. They had everything they wanted, and no chores. Whenever they changed clothes, they dropped their dirty things down on the floor, where they stayed until Clara picked them up. I couldn't get over this, nor how many clothes they had. "They a mess," is what Clara said. Clara didn't like them, but she didn't like me much either. I heard her telling Mrs. Thoroughgood that they ought to have me checked for head lice, which hurt my feelings. Mrs. Thoroughgood never said anything about it, though.

Things soon fell into a routine. I'd get up every morning when Clara knocked on my door, and have a delicious breakfast which was always ready when I got downstairs, and then Mrs. Thoroughgood would take me with her on her errands all over town. She was teaching me to drive, and after a week, I was at the wheel.

"A woman needs to know how to drive," Mrs. Thoroughgood told me. "It is an *imperative*." She was very definite about this, and about other things as well. She had plenty of opinions, which I wasn't used to, and asked me a lot of questions. "I know you believe in Hell," she'd say, "but don't you believe in Heaven too? What's your concept of Heaven?" or "What is your earliest memory?" or "Don't you have any brothers and sisters? Tell me about your brothers and sisters," or "What's it like to have a father like yours?" I didn't say much. For I always felt like no matter how down I got on Daddy myself, I didn't want other people to get down on him. I felt like I had to protect him. Luckily, Mr. Thoroughgood just let me alone, for the most part. He was usually gone on business, and drank a lot when he was home. "Now, who are you again?" he asked me two or three times before he got me straight.

After I learned to drive, I got to drive Mrs. Thoroughgood everywhere. I'd wait for her in the car, reading a magazine. One day while she was in the beauty salon and I was doing this, I was startled to hear a voice say, "Well, hello there," right at my ear. I jumped a mile.

"Oh, sorry," the voice said.

I put the magazine down on the seat and turned around to find that it was the cutest boy, wearing khaki pants and a green knit shirt. "I'm sorry," I said. "I scare easy."

"Is that a fact?" The boy kept looking in the window at me. He had dark hair parted on the side, and very white, even teeth. For some reason, I was particularly taken with his teeth. He looked exactly like any of the boys in my magazine. "I've heard all about you," he said.

"From who?" I was astonished.

"Oh, everybody in town knows about you," he said. "Everybody always knows about Carol Thoroughgood's projects. But I've heard about you from Amanda too. I'm Amanda's swimming teacher."

So I am a project, I thought. "What do you think of Amanda?" I said.

"She's kind of spoiled." He was staring at me through the open window. I dropped my eyes, and felt my face turn red.

Mrs. Thoroughgood came back right then, with her hair too fixed-looking. "Well," she said uncertainly, squinting at us in the sunlight. She put a hand to her head.

The boy said, "I was just making the acquaintance of—"

"Gracie Shepherd," I said.

"Gracie Shepherd," he said easily. "And I'd love to come by and take her to the movie sometime."

"Why, Sammy!" Mrs. Thoroughgood seemed very surprised. "I think that would be lovely!" Only, I could tell that she didn't *really* think it, from the look on her face as I drove us home. Still, when Sammy called up on the telephone and asked me to go to the movie that coming weekend, she didn't say I couldn't go. She didn't say anything, though she pressed her red lips tight together.

I probably would have gotten to be too much for Mrs. Thoroughgood if I had stayed there any longer, I can see this now. People such as her think they want to help you, but then they don't know what to do with you after you start to get up on your own. I was beginning to notice this too. They like you a lot better when you're down-and-out.

But in any case, Daddy showed up on that rainy Saturday morning, the very day I was supposed to have the date with Sammy. Mrs. Thoroughgood was out at a meeting—she went to meetings all the time—and I was letting the girls watch TV instead of reading to them out loud as I was supposed to. They appreciated this, and never mentioned it to their mother, though they told on me for other things, such as sneaking one of Mr. Thoroughgood's cigarettes from time to time. They sat in front of the TV like little zombie statues, which gave me a chance to work on the jigsaw puzzle that was always set up on a Chinese table in the family room. I loved the Chinese table, I loved the family room, and I especially loved the jigsaw puzzle, which I was very good at. Mrs. Thoroughgood had showed me how to start with the pieces with straight sides to form the outline, and I took it from there. Since I had been at their house, I had done three whole puzzles. Number four was an ocean full of sailboats with bright sails and high, puffy clouds overhead. The water was the hardest part, with so many blue pieces, but the sky would be hard too. I was doing the water first. I had just filled up one corner of the puzzle when I heard Clara's voice saying, "No sir, now, you can't just—"

I kept right on fitting the pieces of water in place.

"What's going on?" Amanda asked. "Who's out there?"

"Nobody," I said. "Who's that?"

"That's the bad guy, dummy," Amanda said. "Now he's going to shoot the sheriff. Watch this."

"Grace!" he yelled. "Grace!"

I heard him in the hall, but I did not get up, I sat right there doing the puzzle and thinking about what I would wear that night for my date with Sammy Walker, my blue sundress or my yellow blouse and the madras plaid Bermuda shorts. All these clothes were new. "Grace!" he thundered. The bad guy galloped away. The little girls were screaming. Out in the hall, Clara was on the phone. I put three blue pieces of water together to make one giant piece. Then I turned it upside down and saw where it would fit. This is when Daddy turned the Chinese table over on the rug, scattering the puzzle pieces everywhere, and pulled me to my feet. "I'm talking to you, Grace," he said in that quiet voice which was even worse than the loud one. "Come on now."

"Good-bye, Amanda, good-bye, Melissa," I said. They were crying in Clara's arms. I knew that they would both grow up to be pretty and rich and happy, not because of anything that they would ever have to do. "Law, law," Clara said. I went upstairs and took the flowered pillowcase off one of my pillows and put my things in it, including the blue dress and the yellow blouse, but not the Bermuda shorts, which I would not be able to wear anymore. Then I came down the fancy staircase one step at a time, dragging the pillowcase. Daddy stood at the foot of the stairs looking too big and too rough for that house, wearing a shiny blue suit which did not fit good. "Get a move on, honey," he said.

I reached the bottom of the stairs.

"I never knowed you was staying over here among nigger lovers," Daddy said. "I'm just as sorry about it as I can be." Then he swung the pillowcase up over his shoulder and pulled me out into the rain.

I WAS NEVER to learn what happened to Daddy while he was in jail, but something did. He was wilder and moodier after that. About a day later after we left Chattanooga, as he was driving along smoking a cigarette, he hollered out, "Oh, Jesus! Sweet Jesus!" and ground the cigarette out into his own cheek while the truck jerked all over the road. We ended up in the other lane, but luckily there was nothing coming. Daddy got a terrible sore on his cheek which lasted for weeks and looked awful. Once he yelled at a lady in a parking lot for wearing gold jewelry, and another time he dumped a rack of potato chips on the floor of a Zippy Mart because a boy gave him back the wrong change. In meeting, he'd take up any serpent, anytime. He got bit repeatedly, and did not seem to mind or even notice. He was never hurt. At a camp meeting in Crab Orchard, Tennessee, a crown of flames sat on his head, and yet another time, a dancing green light shone in the trees by a river where he was baptizing. All these months have run together in my mind, since we traveled from one place to another, all over the South. We were traveling with three coolers full of serpents in the back of the truck, plus several boxes. In Coldwater, Tennessee, Daddy healed a woman that was about to die from internal bleeding, and drove the demons out of a poor young man that crawled into church on his hands and knees, speaking nonsense. After his healing, he walked out the door like a man, talking like anybody else. I was there. I saw these things. I read the Bible out loud for Daddy at each location. I did not offer to drive the truck, though. I did not mention that I could drive. I did not want to displease Daddy, for he was a real power in those days, and I could not have gone against him.

But Daddy did not seem to appreciate or even realize what all I did for him. He never said thank you. He took my help for granted, though others remarked to him in my presence how lucky he was to have such a nice big girl. Daddy's attitude hurt my feelings, even though I knew he had more important things on his mind, such as saving souls. It was not for me to call the shots. I told myself that Daddy was giving me as much attention as he could, as much as I deserved. I knew I did not deserve much, due to what I had done. I was sure everything was my fault. I often dreamed that I was being swept along down a great flooded river, and I'd feel that it was really true even when I woke up, like the earth was moving, turning to water beneath my feet. Still, Daddy and I did okay, I reckon, until we got back to Tennessee and Daddy got hooked up with Carlean.

He met her at church, which was where he met all of them. In Piney Ridge, it was the Hi-Way Tabernacle of God, though there wasn't any highway anywhere around that I could see. Somebody said they were going to build the highway through there, but then did not. Anyway, that was the name of the church. In looks it resembled so many others where we had preached in the past months, a little white frame building set up on cinder blocks, very plain, up a dirt road on a muddy lot beside an abandoned coal tipple. A slag heap on the mountain above it smelled like rotten eggs. It was some kind of an independent church with a mournful pastor named Travis Word. It used to have two pastors, but the other one, who was Travis Word's brother-in-law, had died. I believe Daddy saw this situation as an opportunity, and planned to seize it. Travis Word gave me the creeps. He was big and tall and looked like Abraham Lincoln. He could scare people into Christ, it was said. When we showed up in Piney Ridge, Travis Word seemed glad to see us at first, for his church had been declining, as there were a lot of people put off by his gloomy ways, while Daddy was ever one to get folks jacked up, laughing and shouting in the Spirit, full of joy. Daddy could bring them in. It was a church that used to follow the signs, but had not done so in years. This is something that comes and goes among congregations, depending upon who the preacher is, and how long he stays with them. Anyway, there were those that appeared to be just *waiting* for Daddy to show up. They all jumped out of the woodwork when we came.

One of these was Carlean Combs.

Carlean Combs was a tall redheaded woman as big as a man, as big as Daddy himself, with a jutting nose and a jutting chin and dark eyes set too close together. She looked like a witch. She had a big hard white body, and the longest legs. Her breasts jutted straight out, pointy as ice cream cones. At first I thought this was because of the bras she wore, but later when we lived with her I saw her breasts all the time and they were like that. They were really like that. Everything about Carlean was big except for her mouth, small and narrow as a slit in her face.

She showed up on the fourth or fifth night of the revival. Word had got out by then, so the church house was packed. Daddy had had me read from Peter Number Two as he called it, about false prophets and modern times. Daddy said he felt that he had been called to Piney Ridge for a special purpose, to bring the people back to the old-time religion and the old-time ways.

"Now I know there is churches down the road here that's got padded seats and wall-to-wall carpet," he said. "They've got colored windows and Lawrence Welk music and kitchens in the basement, Lord, Lord. They have got all these things, my beloved, but they ain't got the Lord Jesus Christ in their hearts tonight. No sir! And I'll tell you why not. Because the Lord don't need all them fancy things, that's why not. Why looky here, beloved, Hebrews tells us flat-out that God is the same yesterday, today, and forever. Yesterday, today, and forever! Now, don't that tell you something? Don't that tell you something important? Why, them old-timey people, they didn't have nothing like folks has today in their church houses. They didn't have nice rostrums nor gold crosses on the altar of God, nor fancy new cars to carry them to church. No sir. Them old-timey people, if they didn't have no way to get there, they'd walk miles down the muddy road. *Miles,* beloved, a-carrying the old lanterns in their hands, a-singing the old songs, with the knowledge and love of God in their hearts. And when they got to the church house, my beloved, why, it'd be the same thing. They'd fall on their knees where they was at, and pray till their hearts was *full,* praise God, full of that old-timey Spirit that Jesus loves. Now, I know that this old-timey Spirit has gone away from you-uns over here, but we're fixing to get it back. Well, we're *a-going* to get it back, praise Jesus! Praise Jesus, beloved—"

This was the first time I saw Carlean Combs, who kept working her way slowly forward through the crowded little church house, shouldering people aside. I noticed that whenever anybody turned and saw who it was, they would step back mighty fast to let her pass. She never took her squinty eyes off Daddy. When she finally got to the front, everybody was singing and dancing and clapping, and Daddy held a little copperhead in each hand. Two or three other men were dancing and handling in addition to Daddy, and the hot air in there was just crackling as the Spirit moved among them. I stood over by the wall watching, though I could not keep my feet still, the music was so good in that church.

Carlean—of course I didn't know her name yet— danced up into the cleared space at the front of the church. She was wearing a tight aqua-and-white-striped top, and aqua pants that looked like they'd been glued on her. Her hair was pinned up on top of her head.

It was easy to tell she had not been saved.

Everybody was singing "Jesus on the Main Line." Carlean moved her whole body as she danced forward. She didn't look at anybody but Daddy. A heavy woman to the right of her began shrieking out in tongues and sank to the floor, and several came forward to help her, but Carlean just stepped to the side, closer to Daddy, and kept on dancing. Her body rippled all over in rhythm. Then she let her head fall back, like a rag doll. In the light from the dangling bulb, her white neck and chest were slick and shining with sweat. It made me feel funny to see her neck exposed that way. It was like her throat had been cut.

I kept watching her. By then, Daddy was watching her too. Suddenly she let out a big whoop and reached up and started pulling bobby pins out of her hair and throwing them down on the floor. Her heavy hair flew out around her face, bouncing down her back in rhythm as she danced. Now she was right in front of Daddy, not yelling anymore but kind of whimpering, and I couldn't see her face, all I could see was that hair, which was like a live thing, as real and as alive as the copperhead she took from Daddy's hand and wrapped around her white wrist like a bracelet. I could see its markings real plain, and its triangular head, which darted back and forth in rhythm as she danced. The copperhead appeared to be jived up too.

Now the Spirit spread all over the room as visible as paint, so that even the skinny little guitar player cast his instrument down and ran forward to grab up a serpent. Daddy lit a kerosene rag stuck in a Pepsi bottle and held the flame to his face. People were screaming. Several women in the back fainted dead away and had to be carried out. So a lot was going on as you might imagine, but at some point during this meeting I glanced over to find the Reverend Travis Word staring at me steadily with a look I could not fathom. He stood near the opposite wall, right across the church house from me, comforting a pudgy woman who was clinging to him and crying, but he looked across her gray head at my face. I realized that he was younger than I'd thought, and not scary, just stiff and serious, the kind of preacher that could never bust loose like Daddy no matter how much he might wish to. It made you wonder how in the world he'd ever gotten called to be a preacher in the first place. When Travis Word saw me looking at him, he looked down and then away.

The Spirit moved off then, which left everybody praying at once, Daddy up at the front in a big gang of the newly saved, Carlean Combs among them. I looked back as I was going out the door, to see Daddy with his arms outstretched like Jesus on the cross, his shirt front and neck and face blackened by the fire, in wild contrast to his white hair.

I went home with a family named Rogers that we were staying with. Daddy never did come back that night, nor the next day.

Rose Rogers, a nice sickly woman, kept casting glances at me while I was helping her can some beans, but she didn't say anything. It was after supper the next night, almost dark, when Daddy finally came driving up to the house in the Arnold's Electric truck with Carlean Combs in the front seat. She stayed in the truck.

But Daddy came in like gangbusters, hugging Rose and Lucius Rogers, tousling the kids' hair and saying how pretty they were. The kids got to laughing and Rose and

Lucius lost their sour look. Nobody could stay mad at Daddy when he was right there in the room.

"Come on, Grace," he said to me as he had said so many times before. "Get your things," though he knew that they were mostly in the truck.

But I made no move to come. "Where are we going?" I asked him straight-out. "Are we going someplace with her?" I pointed out the front door at the truck.

Lucius Rogers cleared his throat and looked at Rose, who nodded.

"Brother Virgil," Lucius began, "we feel, me and Rose, that there is things you ought to know, sir, before you go rushing off into something." He held his head up and seemed determined to have his say.

"Such as what?" Daddy straightened up from where he'd been bent over tickling a child. He stared at Lucius Rogers.

"We have been knowing that there woman for a long time around here." Lucius spoke out strongly. "She does not go to our church, nor to any church, and she is not fit for a preacher like yourself. You will do us all harm, sir, to take up with such as that."

I felt a stab of fear at these words.

But Daddy gave Lucius a look that had made many before him quake. "Do you propose to tell me who is *good* and who is *not good* in the eyes of the Lord, Mr. Rogers? For there is only one that can say these things, and that one is our Lord and Savior Jesus Christ. And let me tell you another thing, Mr. Rogers. Jesus ain't stuck-up. Oh no, beloved. Oh no. He ain't too stuck-up to stoop for a poor sinner woman who has given herself over to Him in the hope of glory and the chance for a better life. Oh no, honey! Oh no! He has got a big house, beloved, and He's got a room for us all. Why, He's got a room for you-uns, and a room for me, and a room for my daughter Grace here, and a room for Carlean Combs. Yes, He has! Don't you doubt it! Why, don't you-uns remember the words He spoke to Simon the Pharisee, concerning that sinner woman? 'I entered your house,' He said, 'but you didn't give me no water for my feet, and here she has wet my feet with her tears and wiped them with her hair. You didn't give me no kiss, but from the time I came in here, she has not stopped a-kissing on my feet. You did not anoint my head with oil, and here she has come along and anointed my feet with ointment. So I'll tell you what. Her sins, which are many, are forgiven this minute, for she has loved much; but who is forgiven little, loves little.' Now what about that, my friends? Oh, you had better be careful now! You had better watch out! Remember the woman that they brought to Him in John Eight, why, she had committed the sin of adultery, beloved, and they was all ready to stone her, but Jesus said, 'Let him who is without sin among you be the first to throw a stone at her.' And you know what? They couldn't do it, beloved. And we can't do it today either!"

Daddy thundered at Rose and Lucius, who clung together as they listened to him. A picture of Jesus Himself hung on the wall behind them. They were good, God-fearing people, and their faces changed as they listened.

Finally Daddy lightened up. "But He will forgive you, beloved, just as He forgives us all for our manifold sins and wickedness on this earth, for His mercy is everlasting. Now let us pray together—Grace, have you got your things?—before we go." Daddy prayed a long prayer asking God's forgiveness for Rose and Lucius, who knew not what they'd done. He said that he himself had already forgiven them. Then he stood and beamed at everybody.

If he had left it at that, it would have been all right, but he could not resist saying one more thing from the door, and Lucius Rogers's conscience was so strong he could not resist answering.

"And I'll tell you what!" Daddy was smiling. "Carlean Combs is just as happy as she can be today, as a newborn child of God. Why, she's been shedding tears of pure joy! She will be joining the church directly, for she's just crazy about Jesus!"

"Sir, she is just crazy," Lucius said quite plain as Daddy closed the door. Daddy paused on the stoop but did not go back. He charged off down the steps muttering, and unlocked the back of the truck, and I had to get in there and ride amongst coolers and piles of stuff, while Carlean Combs rode up in the front with Daddy.

SHE *WAS* CRAZY, as it turned out. She had been in the hospital several times, and had had shock treatments. She took nerve pills. She had been married three or four times, nobody was exactly sure, nor was it clear where she had come from. I learned all this from the fat old man named

Mister Harnett Bean who ran a truck stop called the Volunteer Café, and employed Carlean as a waitress. When I asked him where the husbands were now, thinking of our own safety, he grinned at me in a funny way, shaking his head. He was so fat that his jaws flapped, and fat rose up on his neck like those collars on English queens. "Gone," he said. "She wore 'em out."

I nodded. I could see that. I was hoping she would wear Daddy out before long too. I hated Carlean, and I hated living out in the woods behind the Volunteer Café, in the little old beat-up trailer which Mister Harnett Bean had given her. Nobody decent would have lived out there. We did not even have water. We had to walk up the sandy path to the Café to take a shower. We hauled our drinking water out there in plastic jugs.

The trailer itself was dark green, with brown rusted-out places all over it. It looked like camouflage. One of the blocks it sat on had sunk into the swampy ground, so that the whole trailer was on a slant. I had to walk uphill to get to the tiny back room where I slept on a mattress on the floor, and all night long I'd feel like I was slipping off of it, and wake up numerous times, and in the mornings I'd be real tired.

Whenever I woke up in the night, I'd hear Daddy and Carlean Combs, still up, and still at it. Talking and carrying on. They never seemed to sleep. Whatever was wrong with her, it was wrong with him too. It was wrong with both of them. In the morning I'd find cigarette butts and clothes strewed all over the slanted linoleum floor, and sometimes beer bottles.

I knew that Daddy was backsliding, and that Carlean had not really been saved.

But the folks over at the Hi-Way Tabernacle had not figured it out yet, as both Daddy and Carlean put on a real show of holiness when they went over there for meeting, Carlean with her wild red hair pulled back so tight it gave her slant-eyes, in long plain dresses that made her look like she was in disguise. These dresses had belonged to Mr. Bean's dead wife, Belle. There was no end to them, as he was rich and had never touched a one of her things since she had died eight years before. Mr. Bean appeared to get a kick out of seeing them on Carlean.

Carlean became the one that read the Bible out for Daddy to preach, though she pronounced about half of it wrong.

I didn't even care. Sometimes I didn't even go to meeting. I felt that God didn't have much use for the likes of me, anyway. Mr. Bean had given me a job waiting tables at the truck stop, which made me real nervous at first, but then I started enjoying it. At least I enjoyed it when Carlean wasn't there, for she'd swoop by like an eagle, keeping an eye on me.

"I know what you're up to," she told me more than once. "You might fool your daddy, but you can't fool me." Close up, Carlean was cross-eyed. The awful thing was, I thought she might be right. For I felt that Carlean *did* know me, like Lamar had.

And it was true that I liked to talk to the truckers and the local men that came in there, I liked to kid with them all. I had also bought myself some pink Tangee lipstick and some Maybelline blush-on and mascara at the drugstore. I'd go in the ladies' room at the café and put them on to work my shift. I had a cute pink waitress uniform, and I knew the men were looking at me. Carlean was right. One of them was looking at me a lot. His name was Davey Street, and he was tall and gangly, with a big grin. He drove a truck for Wonder Bread, and came by four days a week, in the late afternoon. I knew he was going to ask me for a date before long, but he kept not quite doing it. He was not much older than me, and shy, though he liked to talk once you got him started. He'd order a piece of pie and a Pepsi and ask me a lot of questions, which made me real nervous, as I did not want him to find out anything much about my life. I did not intend to get into what Daddy did, nor what our situation was.

Over at the Tabernacle they were having a power struggle. This is what Daddy called it. What it was, was that some of the elders had begun to have their doubts about Daddy, but Daddy had the rest of them in the palm of his hand. So there was serious dissension among them, which is not good for working the signs. A woman named Lois Montreat was hurt at a home meeting by a canebrake rattler which Daddy handed to her, and then she went to the hospital and talked about it, with the result that Daddy was arrested in front of the Tabernacle one Sunday morning before the meeting even got started. They drove him away in an unmarked police car, while the church people gathered around by the church house steps, praying and talking among themselves. When the police car was out of sight, some people turned to go inside, which Travis Word was urging them to do, but a lot of them—the ones that had come just to see Daddy work the signs—turned around and left. Me and Carlean left too.

She drove me back to the trailer in the Arnold's Electric truck, with her skirt hiked way up on her thighs. It was hot that morning, and she had rings of sweat under the arms of Mr. Bean's dead wife's long-sleeved brown dress. She took it off the very minute she got inside the trailer, and dropped it on the floor. Then she walked over to the refrigerator in her half-slip and pointy bra to get a beer. She opened the bottle and looked at me. "You want a beer?" she asked.

"Yes," I said.

"I knew it." Carlean handed me one, and I opened it and licked off the foam, which tasted bitter and not at all the way I'd thought it would taste. I acted like I liked it, though. I took a big swallow and carried the bottle back with me, walking uphill to my room, where I figured I would change clothes and then go to the Volunteer Café and get the funny papers from Mr. Bean, who saved them for me.

I was putting my dress on a hanger when I heard the lock click behind me. I ran right over to the thin metal door and pounded on it. "Carlean!" I yelled. "Carlean! What are you doing?" I hadn't even known that my door could be locked.

Carlean was laughing and laughing on the other side of it. "Don't you go noplace now, you hear?" she cackled. Then I heard her moving around out there for a while longer, singing "This Ole House." Then I heard her slam the trailer door, and a little later I heard the truck start, way up the path where they kept it parked.

I did my best to get out of that place, but there was no way. There was no window, and though the door rattled, it would not give. Finally I got so hot and tired from pushing at it that I just laid down on the mattress and drank the rest of the beer. Everything began to spin around. Since all this was happening on a big slant anyway, I started to feel like I was going crazy. I swore I would not do it, that I would not go crazy like the rest of them, I swore it on the Bible which lay on the floor at my feet. The only light in the room came from a forty-watt bulb in the ceiling, so it was very dim in there. The walls were painted aqua. I laid there on the mattress and imagined myself as a fish swimming around in an aquarium. This was peaceful. But with another part of my mind I was thinking it was simply a matter of time until I did go crazy, whether I swore on the Bible or not. I prayed hard to God, saying that if He would just get me out of there, I would give in to Him and do His bidding from that day forward. I would open my heart to Him and let Him in, and join the church. I meant it too. I felt Him move in my heart then, a little flutter like a baby bird just learning how to fly. Then it started to rain, drumming on the trailer's metal roof. This was a sound which I loved. I took it as a sign that God had heard me, a sign of His care. I let Him comfort me with the sound of the rain. I closed my eyes and let go of everything until I was swimming free, beyond the aquarium, in and out of undersea caverns through shafts of light that pierced the beautiful blue water of the sea.

I don't know how long I slept, nor when they came back, nor why I didn't call out when I woke up and heard them. They were making a lot of noise, banging things around in the big part of the trailer. I was instantly, totally awake. It had quit raining. I felt all rested, like I had slept for hours and hours. I had to go to the bathroom real bad, but something made me hold it and lay still. It came to me that they were packing.

They were going to leave me.

Sure enough, it was not long before I heard the rusty front door of the trailer slap and then slap again, as they carried things out to the truck. One time there was a crash over in the kitchen part of the trailer, and the sound of breaking glass. Carlean yelled, "Shit!" Daddy said, "Leave it. What do you want all this stuff for, anyway? You ain't gonna need it. I've got all the stuff you need." Then there was a lot of laughing and breathing noise while, I guess, they kissed.

They took some more things out to the truck, and then I heard the jingle of keys. You can always tell what keys sound like. *Go, go, just go,* I was thinking. *Go to Hell.* The door slammed one more time and I could hear their voices getting fainter, moving away. I sat up on the mattress.

Then I heard the door again, and Carlean yelling, "Where the hell are you going?" and Daddy's voice saying, "Just a minute, honey, I forgot something," and Carlean saying, "Come on now, Virgil, you didn't forget nothing." The trailer shook as Daddy strode across it and up the slant toward my room. I lay back down on the mattress and closed my eyes. His footsteps stopped, and I could hear his heavy breathing outside the door. I thought he must have come back for the Bible. Then it crossed my mind that he might kill me. But what he did was flip the lock on my door. The trailer shook again as he went out.

"Never mind, I couldn't find it," he hollered to Carlean.

"You asshole," she yelled back.

As SOON AS I heard the truck leave, I jumped up and ran out into the dark, wet woods, not too far, and peed like crazy. The woods smelled wonderful, the way they do after it rains. I breathed in deep. I had been dying for air in that little room. Then I walked back to the trailer and sat on the steps enjoying the cool sweet smell of the night. After a while I went inside and ate some saltine crackers, which was all that I could find. I didn't care. I felt real good. But I did not want to sleep in the room where she had locked me for so long. I walked down the slope to the other end of the trailer and looked at their unmade bed, which was nasty. I found a half a pack of Camel cigarettes on the floor and went out on the steps to smoke them. Then I went inside and lay down on the old sofa and fell immediately asleep.

In the morning I got dressed and went to the Volunteer Café, where I took a shower and washed my hair and put on my uniform and makeup. Carlean was supposed to work that shift, not me, but I was here and she was gone.

Mr. Bean raised his eyebrows when he saw me come out of the washroom. He sat in his big chair by the cash register reading the paper, with his belly balanced on his spread-apart knees like a beach ball. "Where's Carlean?" he asked, and I told him.

"Son of a gun!" he said, slapping his leg. He laughed his wheezy laugh. "I never did think all that religion had took with her."

"Can I eat something before I start working?" I asked, and he looked at me good and then hollered at Don to fix me whatever I wanted. But he told me to bring him the phone first, and I did. Mr. Bean never got up if he didn't have to. I ate two fried eggs and some sausage and three pancakes while he talked on the phone. Then he asked me if there was anybody I wanted to call, and I said no. Even now I am not sure why I said that, or why I felt that way. I simply thought that I had come too far along the road that I was on, to turn back now. I had to keep on going. I could not imagine going back to live with Ruth and Carlton Duty and Billie Jean and that baby I had never seen, back there where everything awful had happened. I thought about it and thought about it, but I just could not bring myself to call them. Some truckers came in and I took their orders, and before long here came two elders from the Hi-Way Tabernacle that I had to talk to, and then the police, who were real respectful, calling me "Miss." I liked that. Daddy and Carlean had run off with as much Tabernacle money as they could lay their hands on, which did not surprise me, but I couldn't give the police any leads. I didn't have a clue as to where they'd gone.

Mr. Bean told everybody that I was welcome to stay out in his trailer and work at the Volunteer Café as long as I wanted to. This was a big relief to me, since I was broke, of course. Daddy had not left me a dime. I thought Mr. Bean was real nice. But then the next Wednesday when I got done with my shift, Marcia told me Mr. Bean had said for me to come over to his house and see him for a minute before I left for the night. He lived right next to the café in a nice white house, and so I walked on over there, thinking nothing of it, bone-tired but enjoying the early-evening breeze and the fireflies rising from the scrub grass along the path that went to his house. Out on the road, cars and trucks flashed back and forth. I enjoyed seeing them, too. I had big plans right then. I hoped it would not be very long before I could save up enough money to get some kind of a car myself. Then I would drive over to Scrabble Creek for a visit before heading out for parts unknown, where I would get a job, and make my fortune. For I had learned to be a good waitress at the café, and I could do that anywhere.

Now that things seemed to be working out, I had conveniently forgotten the promise I had made to God in my hour of need. It is real funny how strong you can mean a thing, and then how fast it will slip your mind. But I was young, and thought I could do anything, and have it all.

I walked across Mr. Bean's front porch and pushed his screen door open. By now it was pretty dark. "Mr. Bean," I hollered. "Mr. Bean?"

"Come on back here, honey," he wheezed out of the darkness. I could see a sliver of light under a door at the back of the room, so I walked toward that, through a dim parlor which smelled old and musty. I could barely make out the dark shapes of the furniture. When I opened the door, I could tell right off that there was a big difference between Mr. Bean's dead wife's parlor and that back room where I guess he stayed all the time. He sat on a ratty old sofa covered by a ratty old quilt, watching TV. He had the TV close enough so he could reach over and change the channels without getting up. Of course, he didn't get up when I came in either. He just looked at me, with something new and lively in his hooded eyes. "Sit down," he said. *"Sit down!"* cried a loud, cracked voice which made me jump, but it turned out to be only Mr. Bean's parrot, which sat in a big cage on top of a dresser in the corner. It was a scraggly, bad-looking parrot.

Mr. Bean patted the seat beside him. So I did sit down, but as far away from him as I could get, which was not too far since he took up most of the couch.

I looked around the room. He had a refrigerator in there, and a desk piled up with papers, and piles of clothes and papers all over the floor. It was a mess. That day's newspaper lay on the floor by his feet, with some pictures of naked girls spread out on top of it. At first I couldn't believe it. I looked again to see if that could possibly be right, which it was, and then I saw his old red thing hanging out of his pants. "Hiya, hiya," the parrot said. Mr. Bean leaned forward, grunting, to turn the sound all the way down on the TV. Then he looked at me.

"Now, Gracie," he said, "there's some things I need for you to do."

I was out of there so fast I don't even remember leaving! I don't remember anything until I was back in the trailer, where I slammed the door shut and pushed the sofa up against it even though I knew that was stupid, that Mr. Bean was not able to walk all the way out there. It was all he could do to get back and forth between his house and the café. But I was scared he would send somebody to get me, like Don the skinny cook with tattoos all over his arms. Of course I could not imagine Don doing this, but Mr. Bean was a rich man, in a place of poor people. People will do a lot for money. I didn't have any money myself, and wasn't supposed to get paid until Friday. Now I knew I would never get paid. I sat curled up in a ball on the couch wedged against the door, and sure enough, not ten minutes had passed before somebody was there, knocking at first and then banging on the door.

I Settle Down

I DIDN'T SAY a thing. I sat there with my eyes squeezed shut and my fingers in my ears while that metal door banged and rattled like Judgment, only inches away from me.

"Gracie!" a voice yelled. "Gracie Shepherd! I know you're in there! Gracie!"

I took my fingers out of my ears and sat up. It was not Mr. Bean. I couldn't tell who it was, though it was a voice I knew somehow, knew yet didn't know.

"Gracie, are you all right? Gracie Shepherd! Answer me, please. This is Travis Word."

The most profound relief rushed through me. I knew I had been saved.

"Just a minute," I called. I jumped up and straightened my waitress uniform the best I could, and pulled the sofa back from the door. Then I clicked the lock open.

And there he stood, so tall that he had to stoop to peer in the trailer door. He wore a white short-sleeved shirt and blue jeans. He was long and skinny. I realized that I had never seen him without that old dark suit coat he wore to meeting. Often he wore a wide-brimmed black hat too— then he really did look like a man from another time. But *that* night, standing on the cinder-block steps of Mr. Bean's trailer with the dark night behind him and the light from the open door shining on his pale concerned face, he seemed somewhat younger to me, and nicer than I had thought. He twisted his hands together and looked nervous.

"They're gone," I said.

He nodded, his Adam's apple jumping up and down, and a piece of his straight black hair fell down in his eyes. He pushed it back. "I heard," he said. "I heard it from Ray Keen—" This was one of the elders that had come to see me only that morning at the Volunteer Café, that morning which now seemed like years before. "That is why I came over here, to see if you was all right, and if you needed anything."

I tried to smile. "Well, I'm just fine," I said.

"And you don't need nothing?" Travis Word's dark eyes traveled all around the trailer. It was a wreck.

"Why no, I'm just fine," I said again. "Won't you sit down?" I asked as proper as if I had a real nice house with real nice furniture in it, and not a junked-up trailer with a sofa sitting crazy in the middle of the slanting floor. I had some idea of how a woman was supposed to act when the preacher came to call, you see. Then I turned to walk over to the sofa myself, but at this point a funny thing started happening to my legs, they simply would not work right. It was like the air had gotten too thick for me to walk through, like I was walking underwater. I tried to say something, but I couldn't talk right either.

I woke up to find myself lying on the sofa with Travis Word right there on his knees beside me, one hand on my forehead. "Dear Jesus," he was praying, "dear sweet Jesus, please bring this pretty girl back to us—" I was awake by then, but I kept my eyes closed. *Pretty!* I was thinking. *Pretty!*

"Have mercy on her, Jesus," Travis Word went on.

I opened my eyes and smiled at him. "I'm all right," I said.

He leaped back like he'd been shot, almost falling over. He had to put one hand down on the filthy floor to steady himself. "Praise the Lord!" he cried. "Oh, praise the Lord!" which is exactly what I had heard Daddy say upon many a similar occasion, but Travis Word said it different, like he really *was* giving all the praise to the Lord, and not keeping some for himself. He stayed on his knees and looked at me carefully, his eyes like searchlights. I guess I really had scared him.

"I'm sorry," I said. "I reckon I fainted."

"I reckon you did," he said. Then he smiled at me, a thing so rare it seemed as if his face would crack.

I realized that the skirt of my Uniform was all twisted up on my legs, so I struggled to pull it down. Travis Word looked away and cleared his throat.

Then we both started to say something at the same

time, which was funny. Of course neither one of us could understand what the other was saying. Travis Word turned bright red, and I started laughing.

"You go first," I told him.

"I was going to say, I reckon you will go on working over there at the Volunteer Café for Mr. Bean," he said.

Mr. Bean! I had clean forgot about Mr. Bean, but now the awful thought of him drove out whatever else it was that I had had it in mind to say. I closed my eyes again, I couldn't hardly speak. "I don't think so," I said. Then I opened my eyes to find that Travis Word was looking at me like I was a puzzle to solve.

"You don't think so," he repeated slowly. It was a question.

I sat up and shook my head. "Nope," I said. "I won't work for Mr. Bean no more."

Travis Word nodded gravely, as if he respected my judgment. Of course, being a preacher in that community, he might have heard some things about Mr. Bean that I didn't know. "Then you can't live here no more either," he said. He looked at me.

"I guess not," I said, and my heart sank, for I didn't know what I would do then. I guessed I would have to call the Dutys after all.

But Travis Word was still looking at me. "I want you to come home with me for a while." He turned red again. "It'll be all right, I live with my sister Helen, that is Helen Tate that was married to Thurman Tate, you know, the preacher, she is a widder woman now—" Still talking, he held out both his hands.

I put my hands in his. Travis Word had huge hands, rough and hard from work. They closed around mine. He pulled me to my feet. Standing as tall as I could, I only came up to his shoulders.

"Let's get out of here," he said.

We walked straight out of that trailer right then, leaving the door wide open and the lights on. We went down the dark, sandy path like Indians, single file, Travis in the lead. I never looked back, just straight ahead as I followed his white shirt through the gloomy woods. In no time we were in his truck, a black pickup as neat as he was, with a worn black Bible on the seat. He gunned the engine and we set off. We rode all the way to his sister's house without another word. I couldn't imagine what was in his mind. As for me, I was still feeling shaky, and wondering what in the world his sister would think of me showing up that-away in the middle of the night.

I need not have worried, though, She came to the door in her nightgown, with her long gray hair hanging down to her waist. "Travis?" she said, scarcely looking at me.

"Helen, you have seen Gracie Shepherd at church with her father. Now he is gone, and she'll be staying with us for a while."

This was all he had to say.

"Come on, then," Helen told me, and took me down the little hall to a spare bedroom with a chenille peacock bedspread on the bed. I used to see bedspreads like that for sale at some of the fruit stands where Daddy and I stopped on our long journey, and I had always admired them, especially the pink ones, which this one was. *Things are looking up,*

I thought. "Bathroom's at the end of the hall," Helen said. Then she shut the door behind her. I kicked off my shoes and laid down on the bed, feeling those little ridges on the chenille. I liked how it felt. Before I knew it, I was instantly, deeply asleep.

I woke up to find my clothes in two sacks just inside the door. I knew that Travis Word had gone back to the trailer and gathered them all up for me. I was so thankful for this, as it meant I would never have to see Mr. Bean again. But I *was* to see him, only once, a few years later, standing on the street over in Valleydale, at the Fourth of July parade. He wore a straw hat. Under it, his face was pasty gray and streaked with sweat, and I'll swear he was fatter than ever. He looked like he couldn't hardly walk. "Hello, Mr. Bean," I said, but all he did was spit tobacco juice off to the side, and act like he didn't know me.

THAT FIRST MORNING in Travis Word's house, I lay in bed for an hour or so after waking, just to get my bearings, and just because I *could*. I felt easy in mind, for the first time in months and months. It was August, high summer. So the window in my room was up, allowing fresh air and sunshine to stream across the bed. The peacock on the bedspread fairly glowed in the sunlight, strutting his stuff. The filmy white curtains, like dreams, moved gently in the breeze. The bedroom contained a chest of drawers with a beautiful china tray on top of it, a vanity with fancy woodwork and a three-part wavy mirror, an old chest bound with iron strips, and a cane-bottom rocking chair. A bright hooked rug with every color of the rainbow in it was on the floor. Three pictures hung on the wall: Jesus walking in the garden, Jesus praying in the desert, and Jesus with the woman at the well. Everything in the room was as neat as a pin. When I scooted sideways on the bed to look out the window, I saw a row of hollyhocks growing right there, up against the house. Bees flew in and out of the rosy blossoms closest to the window. Beyond that, I could see a well with a little red roof, and a great big shade tree with two aluminum lawn chairs under it, and a white picket fence beyond. I was thinking how I would admire to sit in one of those chairs in the afternoon, and just pleasure myself. Or maybe do some sewing. I had never done any. I had never pictured myself before as a girl who would sit and sew. As I lay there, I could smell coffee and hear women's voices talking somewhere in the house.

Finally I got up. I was still wearing my waitress uniform, which was all soiled and wrinkled by then, as you might imagine. But somebody had taken my tennis shoes and socks off, and placed them so neat at the foot of the bed. I was sure it had been Helen Tate. I knew enough about Travis Word already to know that he would never do this.

I opened the door and walked down the hall to the bathroom where I took a slow bath in the big claw-footed tub. I washed my long hair with the baby shampoo I found in the wooden cabinet over the sink. I puzzled over the shampoo, as there was no baby in the house. Later I would learn that Helen Tate used it herself on her own thin frizzy hair. I dried off on a big green towel which hung from a nail in the wall. This towel was hard and clean and smelled like sunshine. I could tell it had been dried outside on the line. I rubbed myself until my skin was red and tingling all over. I wrapped my hair up in the towel and squeezed. Then I wrapped the towel around myself and went back to the bedroom to dress, carrying my dirty uniform and underwear with me. I pulled things out of the sack until I found something clean: a long flowered skirt and an oxford-cloth shirt Mrs. Thoroughgood had given me. I parted my hair in the middle and spread it down over my shoulders to dry.

I looked in the mirror and scarcely knew the girl I saw reflected there. She didn't seem worried, or scared, or like she had terrible secrets to keep. She looked fine. She looked healthy and strong, and I winked at her as I left the bedroom, closing the door behind me. I felt like the events of the previous night had happened a hundred years before. I followed the smell of the coffee and the sound of the women's voices down the hall and into the kitchen.

Here I found Travis Word's sisters, all three of them, ready to inspect me, though they acted real nice about it.

"Well, looky here!" said Helen Tate. "I'll swear, you clean up pretty good, don't she, girls?"

Minnie and Vonda Louise nodded. They were not what I would call "girls." Helen, clearly the oldest, was in her sixties then. Her beloved husband, Thurman Tate—who had been the pastor of the Hi-Way Tabernacle for thirty years—had died a year before. She was still grieving for him, and would always be grieving for him. Helen dressed in black, with a little fluff of white lace at her throat. This morning her frizzy gray hair was plaited and wound up on her head. She had paper-white skin and sunken eyes like her brother Travis, eyes that seemed to see everything. "How you feeling now, Missy?" she asked, and I said, "Fine." She nodded, pleased. Helen was a pert no-nonsense woman who expected things to go the way they should. She had biscuits warming in the oven for me, wrapped in a tea towel so they'd stay soft, and sausage gravy on the stove. I am a fool for sausage gravy. She got up and split the biscuits for me and poured the sausage gravy over them and gave me a fork. It was a delicious breakfast! I ate as though my life depended upon it, and decided to stay there as long as I could.

"Well, she eats good, anyway," Minnie said. This was the next-oldest sister, who had been married once many years before to a boy she scarcely remembered, who had died of encephalitis before he was twenty. She lived in a little brick house down the road, and liked everything just so. For many years she had worked at the county library, where her job was to put all the books back on the shelf in the right place according to the Dewey Decimal System. Minnie loved the Dewey Decimal System. She never read any of the books.

Minnie and Vonda Louise—this was the third sister, Vonda Louise—did not get along very well, though they were all three united in their adoration of Travis and their dedication to the Hi-Way Tabernacle. If Minnie was brittle and bitter, Vonda Louise was too soft, too sad. A pale dumpling of a woman, she had never married, much to her dismay. She always imagined things, and thought that men were looking at her, and that people were against her. She lived in her own little brick house just down the road beyond Minnie's. Both houses had been built by Thurman Tate, who had been a bricklayer by trade—a trade which he had passed on to his beloved young brother-in-law. Helen and Thurman Tate had raised Travis, assisted by Minnie and Vonda Louise, their parents having died in a fiery car wreck when Travis was little. So no wonder all three sisters doted on Travis. They would do anything in the world for him.

"Where's Mr. Travis?" I asked when I had finished eating.

"Gone to work, of course!" Minnie snapped. "Been gone since daybreak."

"Now, now, there is no need to bite her head off, Minnie . . ." Vonda Louise had one of those voices that just trail off, so that each sentence ends in confusion.

All three sisters sat at the kitchen table drinking coffee and looking at me. "Can I have some coffee, please?" I asked, and Helen got up to get me a cup and saucer. Then she poured the steaming coffee into my cup from the blue speckled pot on the stove. I put a lot of sugar and cream in it, and stirred it up with a silver spoon. Usually I didn't even take sugar and cream. I was just doing it because it was there. I had gone for so long without anything much that everything in that house struck me as a miracle.

"God works in mysterious ways," Helen Tate offered as she sat back down.

"It is not for us to understand." Minnie pursed her lips. "It is not for us to say."

"The right hand don't know what the left hand doeth," chimed in Vonda Louise in her trembling voice, and we all looked at her.

"Just hush, you stupid fool," said Minnie.

"Now girls, now girls," Helen said.

I got so tickled at them, I had to smile.

"Pretty little thing, ain't she?" Minnie said.

"Why yes, yes she is," Helen Tate agreed. The three of them sat there sipping coffee and looking me over with those dark eyes in a way I would come to think of as the Word Look.

I grew uncomfortable. "Where is Mr. Travis working?" I asked, just to make conversation.

"He's building a patio on the other side of Valleydale," Helen said.

"For a contractor," Minnie said. "Oh, he does fine work."

"Fine work," Vonda Louise repeated.

"He works like a dog," Helen said.

"Dawn to dusk," Minnie added.

"Dawn to dusk," said Vonda Louise.

"But he'll go around visiting when he gets done, tired as he is," Helen said. "Visits the sick, done it for years."

"Visits the sick whether they ask him to or not," Minnie said.

"He's so good," Helen explained.

"Too good for his own good," Minnie said.

"He came to see me ever day when I had my hysterectomy out," said Vonda Louise. "Brought me some of those chocolate-covered cherries."

"Oh, he's good," Helen said.

"Good as gold," said Minnie.

I stood up and took my dishes to the sink and washed them, trying to be helpful. I peered out the kitchen window at those two chairs under that big shade tree. It looked like they were out there just waiting for me. It occurred to me to pick up the sisters' cups and saucers and wash them too. Then I started to wipe off the big oak table, but was stopped by Helen's firm hand on my arm.

"We don't use the dishrag for the table or the counters," she said. "That would be nasty. We put the dishrag right here on the drain rack to dry." She showed me. Then she opened the cabinet under the sink and got another rag off a hook. They looked just alike to me, but I kept my mouth shut. "*This* is the rag we use to wipe off the table," she said.

WHEN TRAVIS WORD came home from work that evening, I was sitting out under the shade tree in one of those aluminum chairs, enjoying the end of the day. I had already been out there earlier to let my hair dry, and it still hung loose all down my back and around my shoulders. I was a little bit sunburned. Helen Tate was sitting with me, but she disappeared when she heard his truck.

Travis Word walked over and stood grinning down at me, that grin which seemed to hurt him. "You look a lot better," he said.

"I feel a lot better," I told him. "I slept so good."

He eased his long self down into the other lawn chair,

which looked too small for him. He had on dirty khaki-colored work clothes and steel-toed boots. His face was streaked with sweat. "I have been thinking about your father," he announced in a preaching tone of voice, "and as far as I am concerned, what he done passeth understanding."

"Well, I have to say, it's the kind of thing he has done a lot before," I said. "Daddy would be the first to tell you what a backslider he has been upon occasion. But then he always comes back to God in the end, and apparently God is real glad to have him, every time. This is the part I can't figure out, how come God is so glad to have him. If I was God, I'd get tired of it." All this just came bursting out of me, for I had been thinking about it. Travis Word turned to look at me.

"It is not for you nor me to figure out the workings of the Almighty," he said, still in that preaching tone which made him sound sorrowful. "But I'll tell you what's the truth, from my own study of the Holy Word which I have read all my life, your daddy is flirting with fire, that's for sure. For it says real plain, 'Do you suppose, O man, that when you judge those who do such things and yet do them yourself, you will escape the judgment of God?' And yet again, 'For He will render to every man according to his works: to those who by patience in well-doing seek for glory and honor and immortality, he will give eternal life; but for those who are factious and do not obey the truth, but obey wickedness, there will be wrath and fury.' That sounds pretty plain to me." Travis shook his head, pitying Daddy.

Travis Word was the first preacher I ever ran into that placed works above grace in order of importance. As a person even then searching for hard ground in a world of shifting sands, I liked this. I was real glad to hear it. For privately I had always questioned Daddy's belief that a person could just go out and do whatsoever they damn well pleased, and then repent and get forgiven for it, over and over again. In my own mind this made God out to be too easy, a pushover. I had never really believed that that was the case. Travis Word's idea of the true nature of God came closer to my own image of Him as a great rock, eternal and unchanging. Even though I did not believe I was saved at that time, I did believe in Him, and I also felt that if He was worth His salt, He'd have no place prepared in Heaven for the likes of me.

Such was the state of my soul as I sat there in the lawn chairs with Travis Word in the sweet buzzing twilight of August 1959. I was at the end of my rope. I was damned, abandoned, and wore-out.

Travis Word's deep voice came to me with almighty force. "You need some rest," he said, "and a place to stay. You can stay here for a while if you want to."

"What about your sister?" I asked. "Are you sure she won't mind?" For she had seemed kind of distant to me, not mean, but not real warm either.

"Helen?" He laughed. "She won't mind. If I tell her, she won't mind. She just about drives me crazy trying to do for me, if you want to know. She doesn't have enough to do since Thurman died."

"I can tell that," I said.

"She's a fine woman," he added, and I said, "I can tell that too. But good intentions can be hard on a person sometimes." I knew this from my own experience with Mrs. Thoroughgood in Chattanooga.

Travis bobbed his long head up and down. "You're telling me!" He sounded a lot more human than he had so far.

"Have you always lived here?" I asked. "With her and Mr. Tate? You never got married?" I could not resist asking, though it was none of my business for sure.

Then he told me all about the car wreck that killed his parents, and how he had had burns over eighty percent of his body, and how he had had to lay stretched out in the bed with Crisco rubbed on him for months and months afterward, nursed by his sisters and sustained by their prayers, and then how Helen and her preacher husband had taken him to raise for their own. Except for a stint in the Navy during the war, he had always preached, and always lived with Helen and Thurman. He had thought of getting his own place when he got out of the Navy, but by then Thurman Tate was having heart trouble. "They needed me," he said, "so I knowed it was my duty to stay." He was not a man to shirk his duty, I could tell.

"So when did you start preaching? When did you get the call, I mean?"

"Back when I was not but a little boy," Travis answered earnestly, "down by the road here playing with some neighbor boys, and one of them said to come on home with him, that he had something he was going to show us, and I could tell just by the way he said it that it was something nasty. But I went right along with the rest of them, following them down the road here to his house, because I wanted to see what it was, you know." I nodded. I could tell by the way he spoke that this was a story he'd told many times. It was his testimony. "And so they all went in through that gate one by one, all of them in front of me, but when it come my turn to go through it, why, God slammed it shut and locked it. Scared all those other little boys to death! And then He spoke to me real plain out of the clouds, He said, 'Travis, you have not got no truck with any of that, go on home, for I am saving you for myself.' "

"God spoke to me one time too," I said. "I sat up in the night at a camp meeting, but I don't have any memory of it now." I did not mean to claim holiness in saying this, though I did want Travis to think well of me, of course. By this time I was thinking that he was probably the *best* man I had ever met. I was already deciding not to tell him that I had not been saved, for he'd naturally assume I had, and I figured I might as well let him think it. Right then I was more interested in Travis Word than in God, to tell the truth.

"Is that a fact?" he said in the stricken tone of wonder he reserved for direct communication from on high.

"Mm-hmmm," I said. I was playing with my hair, lifting it up to let the soft cool breeze blow on my neck. My face felt hot because of my sunburn. "Aren't you hungry?" I asked, for Helen Tate had given me my supper long before.

He snapped his fingers. "Well, for goodness' sakes!" he said. "I ain't eat yet, have I now?" He stood up and I stood up. We were real close to each other. He sucked in his breath and then I moved away.

Travis Word was forty-two then. I was not yet eighteen.

But it seemed like the most natural thing in the world when he put his arm around me and guided me toward the house. I was surprised to see a dark shadow move behind a curtain in the open parlor window closest to where we'd been sitting. Then the curtain fluttered. But before I could say anything about this, the back door opened and there stood Helen Tate, all smiles, welcoming us in. "Why, Brother!" she said. "I was wondering where you was at! Why don't you come along too, Missy?" she said to me. "You can sit with Brother while he eats."

I KNOW I would not have been the sisters' first choice as a wife for Travis, but I was the one they got. For I came along at a time when they had almost given up hope, fearing that he would never marry. As a boy, he had not been interested in girls, putting his energy into the church, his schoolwork, and basketball. He had been a high school star, I learned. In fact, he could have gone to college scot-free due to the basketball, but after struggling with it all, he decided not to, as he felt himself in danger of placing basketball above God, and other books above the Bible. Thurman Tate had supported him in this choice, citing Ecclesiastes 12: "The sayings of the wise are like goads, and like nails firmly fixed are the collected sayings which are given by one Shepherd. My son, beware of anything beyond these. Of making many books there is no end, and much study is a weariness of the flesh."

Travis was not much older than me when he started out preaching at the Hi-Way Tabernacle along with Thurman. Then he enlisted in the Navy for a while, stayed in for the war, and went to the Philippines, where he saw things that sent him into despair and made him question his faith for years afterward. He had to be born again when he got back to Tennessee, but even so, he said, it took him years to get back right with God. He would not really talk about his stint in the Navy, referring always to that time as his "dark night of the soul," but once he did admit that he had not only killed some Japs and witnessed some bloody and awful events, but also succumbed to the desires of the flesh, for which he was afraid he had a special weakness. This was news to me!

For by the time I knew him, I couldn't hardly get him to touch me.

I remarked it from the first, though I thought it would change when we married. I admired Travis Word for his restraint and the way he controlled his emotions, since I was just the opposite. No, that's wrong—I didn't just admire him. I worshipped him for his certainty, his faith, and his strength, as well as for his kindness, which never faltered.

I will never forget the day of our engagement, October 17, 1959. This was a Saturday, which was the only day Travis had off—until time for the evening service at church, that is. He usually spent the day doing work around the

house, or around his other sisters' houses, for if he did
something for one of them, he had to do it for all. They
were real jealous of each other when it came to Travis. Or
he would spend Saturday helping somebody in the church
do a job of work, as he called it—this might be moving
into a new house, or clearing a field, or building a barn.
He was the willingest man in the world to help other
people.

Now I knew by then that he loved me, or I *thought* he
did. It is something you can feel, and I had felt it many
times when we would catch each other's eye accidentally,
for instance at a meal, and he would blush and look away,
or when he would pause and pretend to be fixing the fence
post or something else, but he was actually waiting for me
to come out the door so he could walk with me wherever
I was going, down the road on an errand for Helen perhaps. She used to keep me busy by sending me to the store
and giving me little jobs around the house. I was glad to
do them. For I had never had it so good, and I knew it.

I couldn't imagine going back over to North Carolina
after what all had happened. It made me real sad to think
about it. Plus I knew Carlton and Ruth and Billie Jean
were busy taking care of little Fannie, and there was no
room for me now in that house. But here I had grown to
love my bedroom and the big grassy side yard and the wide
front porch where I sat for hours in the glider and waved
at everybody who drove by on the road. Everybody waved
back. They all knew who I was and how I had come to
be there. Sometimes I would string beans for Helen, or

crochet—she was teaching me how to crochet. Sometimes I would read a magazine if it was one that Helen approved of, like *Good Housekeeping* or *Life* or *Redbook*, which actually had more things in it than she realized, such as articles telling housewives how to improve their sex appeal! People were always dropping by to visit, and I was glad to pass the time with them. I got a reputation for sweetness, well deserved.

The fact is, for the first time in my whole life I was being *taken care of,* and I loved it. I ate it up! All I had to do, really, was be sweet and figure out how to get Travis Word to marry me.

This was harder than you might think. Every time I seemed to be getting someplace, he'd wise up and back off. For instance, he never went in the bathroom until he was pretty sure that both me and Helen had gone to sleep, so one night I laid awake on purpose and waited until I heard him go in there and close the door. Then I got up in my long flowered gown—which was not at all bare, that would have scared him to death—and stood behind my half-closed door until I heard him flush the toilet and open the door. At that moment I rushed out and ran right into him. "Oh!" I cried, like I was so surprised. I staggered back, clutching at his long-sleeved pajama shirt, so that he had to put his arms around me to keep me from falling. I nestled close to him, snuggling my head against his chest. "Oh, excuse me!" I said. For just one minute I could hear his furiously beating heart. I felt his lips on my hair. Then he gently but firmly picked me up and set me down at arm's length, and rushed off down the hall without a word. But I knew he wanted me—I knew it. I could feel it. There is no mistaking a thing like that. The next morning, though, I was amazed to find that Travis had gotten up and gone to work way before sunrise, according to Helen. He had told her that he wanted to get a good start on the day. Helen shook her head and watched me carefully as she told me this at breakfast, and I looked down at my plate. I was not about to tell her a thing, though I felt that she and I were on the same side of the matter.

After several incidents of this sort, I began to realize that Travis got real scared every time he had any emotion that was not directly linked to God, and that I would have to get around this some way if I wanted to get anyplace with him, which I did.

So back to that Saturday, October 17. This was the morning when Travis announced that he was going over to Claude Vickers's house to help him put a prefab utility shed together. "Will you be home for dinner?" Helen asked.

"I don't know if we'll be done by then or not," Travis said. "You all go on and eat when you get it ready. Don't wait on me." Then, without looking at me once, he was gone. "You all" included Minnie and Vonda Louise too, who always came for dinner, plus anybody else who happened by. That Saturday, it was a neighbor woman, Darnell Ball, who had a big story to tell about her sister in Ohio, who thought she had a tumor but it turned out to be a *baby, at her age*. Minnie and Vonda Louise just loved this story, so Darnell Ball drew it out as long as she could in the telling, during which I started to feel like I was going to jump out of my skin. For it was the most beautiful day outside, the clear sky as blue as a robin's egg, the gold leaves falling on the grass. It made me want to run, to jump, to—well, to kiss Travis Word! But Darnell Ball just went on and on. "And do you know," she said, leaning forward in a kitchen chair, one hand on each knee, "do you know, she was pregnant with that baby for ten months with no sign of labor, until the doctors gave up and done a Sicilian?"

"Well, was it all right, then? The baby, I mean?" Vonda Louise was hanging on every word.

"Honey, it was practically growed! Had a full head of curly blond hair and weighed ten and a half pounds! Why, it was practically talking! They named it Carol Elizabeth, for Mama. Isn't that sweet? Seeing as how the rest of us all had boys, I mean. . . . But you know what I wonder the most about all this? I wonder what would of happened if they had not been any doctor there to do the Sicilian, like in the olden days, I mean. I wonder if Carol Elizabeth would of just kept on a-growing in there."

"I'm sure that is not medically possible." Minnie sniffed. She was setting the table.

"Well, but don't you remember what happened to the Sloan girl?" Darnell said. "You can go on and set me a place too, Minnie, if you want to."

"Is that Bill Sloan's girl or Birdy's?" Vonda Louise asked. She picked up her fork so she'd be ready.

"Well, it's the one that worked at the health department," Darnell said.

I thought I was going to jump right out of my skin. "Listen," I told them, "if you all don't mind, I'd like to borrow the car." Helen had an old gray Mercury, which Travis drove them to town and to church in. It had an automatic shift, just like Mrs. Thoroughgood's car.

"Why, Missy, we didn't know you could drive!" Vonda Louise cried.

"Well, I can," I said. I couldn't even stand still in the kitchen. I was bouncing on the balls of my feet.

"Where do you want to go?" Helen looked at me carefully with a little frown between her eyes.

"Well—" Various answers ran through my mind, but in the end I told the truth. "Why don't I go over to Claude Vickers's and take Mr. Travis his dinner? You all have got enough chicken for an army."

Helen relaxed. She beamed at me. "I think that's a wonderful idea, dear. Let me just pack it up for you." So then I had to wait while she wrapped up the fried chicken and cornbread in waxed paper and put them in a paper bag. I stopped her when she got a Thermos and took it over to the stove.

"That's all right," I told her. "I'm going to buy us something to drink at the store."

"Travis likes his coffee," Helen said.

"I'm going to get some Coca-Colas," I said.

"Coca-Colas!" Vonda Louise sounded as if she had never heard of them.

"Waste of money," Minnie said.

But Helen took the key to the Mercury off its hook and gave it to me, along with a five-dollar bill.

* * *

Luck was with me. I found Travis working on the shed by himself, as Claude Vickers had had to take his wife to the doctor in Valleydale. I drove down their driveway and stopped in front of the shed and jumped out. Travis straightened up and grinned, real surprised. He looked from me to the car and back again. "Why, I didn't know you could drive a car!" he said.

"There's a lot you don't know about me," I said. Then before he got too embarrassed I added, "I brought your dinner."

Travis smiled the biggest smile. "That was mighty nice of you, Missy." He acted like he expected me to hand his dinner over to him, but I said, "Get in the car. We're going on a picnic."

Travis stood there dumbfounded, with his big hands hanging down empty at his sides.

"Get in!" I said again. "I have to eat too, don't I? Get in the car!"

He did, and after I drove to the Quik-Pik for Cokes, we went over to the Butler Dam, which was real nearby. I talked about one thing and then another on the way to the dam, keeping it light. I told him the whole story of Darnell Ball's sister's baby, thinking to amuse him, but he frowned. "Those women all talk too much," he said. I parked at the picnic area. We got out of the car and walked to one of the stone tables, and I put the bag of food down on it. The water was beautiful that day, rippled by the breeze. Red dogwood leaves had fallen on the table.

Travis looked around uneasily. "Claude Vickers is going to wonder where I am at," he said.

"You're on a picnic," I told him, starting to unwrap everything.

But Travis put his hand on mine. "Let us bless this food first." Then he took his hand off mine like it was a hot potato, and said grace. I unwrapped the food and served him, which seemed to embarrass yet please him at the same time. We ate in silence, looking out at the water which shone like a mirror in the sun.

"I don't know when's the last time I went on a picnic," Travis said suddenly. "I mean, I have eat outside, of course, on the job and after church and at the Homecoming when we all take dinner on the ground, but that ain't the same thing. I reckon it's been since grade school, when they took us in a bus to the endless caverns."

"Well, that's *too long*," I said. "You ought to enjoy yourself sometimes. You work too hard." It is true that I was amazed at how hard Travis worked at his day job and at his preaching both, especially since Daddy had never worked another job at all, trusting in the Lord and other people to provide for us.

"The Lord loves work," Travis said. "He loves a workingman. And so I had best be getting on back over there. Claude will think I have flew the coop." Travis smiled to think he would do such a wild thing. Then he stood up and stretched, and I knew I would have to hurry or I would miss my chance.

I took a deep breath and went around the table and hugged him. "I just wanted to talk to you by yourself for a minute," I said. "There's always so many people around you at the house and at church. I wanted to thank you." Then I stood on tiptoe and pulled his head down and got him—finally—to kiss me. I knew a lot about kissing due to Lamar, though this was completely different. Travis did not open his mouth at all, but I could tell he liked it.

"I have been wanting to do that," I said when we quit.

"Lord have mercy." Travis drew back and looked at me good. "I never meant—" he started, but I put my hand over his mouth. "I know you didn't," I said. "I just think you are cute, that's all." I realized "cute" was not a word that most people would apply to Travis.

He knew it too. He shook his head, smiling. "Missy, Missy," he said.

I got a great idea. "Turn around and shut your eyes," I told him.

He looked at me like I was crazy.

"Go on," I said. "Keep them shut till I tell you to turn around."

Of course he humored me in this, as in everything. While he turned his back to me, I took off my sweater and my bra and dropped them down onto the leaves. "Okay," I said.

Travis turned around and I smiled at him. "Lord God Almighty!" he burst out, horrified. "Girl, cover yourself!"

But he did not close his eyes.

I reached forward and took his hand and brought it up to touch me. He leaped back as if he had stuck it in the fire. I started giggling then. "Travis Word," I said, "I guess you'll just have to marry me now. What do you think?"

I will never forget how he looked at that moment, standing there in his work clothes at the Butler Dam, staring at me with his Adam's apple popping up and down—a man out of place on a picnic, a good man in a bad world. First he looked like he would faint. Then he swallowed hard a couple of times and grinned. "I reckon I will have to," he said. "Now put your clothes back on."

I did, which relieved him a lot, and then I drove him back to Claude Vickers's, where he worked for the rest of the afternoon before coming home to tell his sisters the news. Meanwhile I did this and that around the house, until Helen told me I had the fidgets. I was so scared he might change his mind. But when he got home he told them straightaway. He kept his arm around me and grinned the whole time he was telling them. The sisters had a fit, as you might imagine, with Vonda Louise in tears and Helen saying, "Well, I swan! I swan!" over and over. Minnie said she had a wedding dress that I could wear.

I was sorry to hear this, as I had hoped I could pick out my own wedding dress, but Travis nodded. "Let's see if it fits her," he said.

Minnie looked at me. "It'll fit," she said.

AND IT DID. It fit like it had been made for me instead of Minnie, and though I wondered privately whether it would be bad luck to wear it since her own short marriage had ended so tragically, finally I chose to say nothing about this and to count my blessings instead. The dress had a long full skirt with a dropped waist, and long puff sleeves tapering to little points at the wrist. Thirty tiny buttons ran up the back. After Helen told me what they were made of, I loved to say it over and over to myself—"Mother-of-pearl. Mother-of-pearl, mother-of-pearl." The dress was okay. It was a lot prettier than anything I would ever have expected Minnie to own. It must have been a much younger, sweeter, very *different* Minnie who had chosen it, I decided, and when I mentioned this to Travis, he nodded.

"We are put through some terrible tests," he admitted, "and some of us does better on them than others." He also told me that Minnie had been real pretty as a girl, which I could not even imagine until he found some old pictures and proved it to me. It was really true. During the brief period of our engagement, I was learning that my fiancé was not only good but wise. I loved that word "fiancé" too, saying it over and over as often as "mother-of-pearl." Helen heard me doing this in my bedroom one afternoon and knocked on the door. "Cut that out," she snapped. "Brother is *not* your fiancé. He is too old to be a fiancé."

Back to the dress. It had a deep V-neck, which both Helen and Minnie felt "showed too much," and so they decided to put a lace inset in it, though Vonda Louise voted with me to leave it alone.

"But *you* wore it like it is," I said to Minnie. "How come you wore it, if it shows too much?"

Helen snorted. "Minnie didn't have nothing to show."

This sent Vonda Louise off into a fit of giggles and embarrassed Travis so much that he bolted for the door, ending the argument. Minnie and Helen won, of course.

Mabel Reed drove the two of them to the fabric outlet in Valleydale, where they bought a pretty square of Belgian lace to sew in the neckline, plus a shoulder-length illusion veil attached to a white lace bow. The bow hid a barrette, so I could pin it on top of my hair, which I would wear up, of course. I would wear my hair back or up from that time forward, as a married woman, a preacher's wife. The veil was a surprise for me, and my first reaction was disappointment that I had not gotten to go along to Valleydale with Helen and Minnie, though they had explained to me that there was not enough room in Mabel Reed's car because she had a Volkswagen and she was going over there to buy drapery material which would take up a lot of room. I was a little bit mad at them when Mabel Reed dropped them off that afternoon.

But then Helen pulled the veil out of the bag and held it up high so that it floated out on the air like a cloud, and I caught my breath, it was so pretty.

"Oh, try it on her," Vonda Louise said. "Try it on her!" And they did, with me sitting in a chair so they could pin it in place. Then Vonda Louise pulled me over to the oval mirror which hung by the door, and I had to gasp again. I looked beautiful. Right beside my own reflection in the mirror appeared Helen's and Minnie's and Vonda Louise's, Helen and Minnie frowning, Vonda Louise all smiles.

"Do you like it?" Helen asked.

"Oh yes!" I threw my arms around her in a big hug. "I love it! Thank you so much!"

"Good," she said, stiffening up.

"Thank you too, Minnie." I turned toward her, but

Minnie was already gone, having slipped silently out the door. I looked at myself in the mirror for a good long while then, as all kind of things ran through my mind, such as the day Evelyn had played bride in the house up on Scrabble Creek, and how Mama had cried to see her. I wondered how Evelyn was, and where she was, and if she had worn a wedding gown when she got married. I thought about Billie Jean and how she had loved her paper dolls, and how many times we had walked the bride doll down the aisle. I smiled at myself in the wavy mirror, turning this way and that. I felt like a paper doll myself, all dressed up by Travis's sisters.

"Quick, quick! Take it off!" Helen said when we heard Travis's step on the porch. "He can't see you in that until the wedding, it's bad luck!" But I was still struggling to unhook the barrette when he came in.

"Don't look! Don't look!" Vonda Louise was nearly in tears.

But Travis did look. He stopped right where he was in the doorway and looked his fill.

"What do you think?" I said.

"I think you look like an angel," he said. "I believe that God has sent me an angel of my own." This made me blush, though I had to smile too.

"Oh go on, get in the kitchen, Travis!" Helen shooed him away, but it was already too late for luck.

TRAVIS'S SISTERS WERE not the only ones interested in the wedding. Everybody at the Hi-Way Tabernacle just had to get into the act. Garnet Keen volunteered to make the cake for free. It would be three layers high, with silver bells and pink icing. Marge Abernathy would make the mints, old Mrs. Friendly offered her famous cheese straws, Rose Rogers promised to make sausage balls, and John Green said he would donate anything we wanted from his grocery store, such as paper plates and cups and crepe-paper streamers. The wedding would be at the Tabernacle, of course, with the reception immediately following in the fellowship hall. Travis's senior youth group volunteered to go out to gather evergreens and holly for the church, and after worrying about this for a while, Travis said he believed that would be all right. He did not want people to do *too much*, Travis said, though it was clear by then that everybody was determined to do as much as they could.

By then it was also becoming clear to me how much everybody in that church and that community thought of Travis Word. They had loved his brother-in-law Thurman, and they loved him. My own daddy had come and left without a trace, like a bad dream. Nobody ever mentioned serpent handling. The only signs we followed were speaking in tongues, which comes natural to people anyway, and the special healing service that Travis always had on Sunday nights, the same as Thurman had had before him. I cannot tell you how many people came up to me—after meeting, or in the store, or on the street in Valleydale— and launched into some big story about how Travis had helped them out when their mother died, or when their baby was sick, or when they fell into debt or trouble or wrongdoing. Everybody seemed to be tickled to death that he was getting married, and wished us well, except for a few old biddies that couldn't get over the difference in our ages. Most people said it was nice that Travis Word would have a family after all. Helen planned to turn Travis's upstairs bedroom into the baby room, after he moved downstairs into my room with me. Travis would not move so much as one sock until after the wedding. Everything had to be proper.

During those weeks of the engagement, I got Travis to where he would kiss me for a long time every night after Helen went to bed, but that was all. That was *it!* though I could see the bulge in his pants, and feel his hot breath on my face. I was real excited, myself, and could scarcely wait, though Travis made it clear that we had to. However, Travis was more excited by *not* doing it than by doing it, as I would learn.

I would learn a lot of things.

But during the engagement, I worshipped him. He seemed perfect to me. All his decisions about the wedding were practical and wise. When I said that I wanted Carlton Duty to give me away—I would not have invited Daddy, even if I had known where he was—Travis said it might be best if him and me just stood up there together, and nobody gave me away. Otherwise, he said, if I let some complete stranger such as Carlton Duty be in the wedding, all his sisters would get their feelings hurt.

"But you don't think your sisters would ever *want* to be in it, do you?" I asked. That idea struck me so funny I couldn't help but laugh. I could just see Vonda Louise up there!

He grinned. "Well . . ." he said.

"Okay," I told him. "Carlton and Ruth can just sit in the front row, then, and be my family."

WHICH THEY DID, and the wedding went off without a hitch except for Vonda Louise fainting dead away from excitement before it even started. They stretched her out flat on a pew where she still lay—looking like a mountain range of purple polyester—when Travis and I walked down the aisle to the tune of "Here Comes the Bride" being played on the electric keyboard in a jazzed-up way by Bert Riggs, who worked with Travis and played rock-and-roll in his spare time, a habit which Travis was trying to break him of. Right as we were at the door, I heard Vonda Louise asking, "Is it over? Is Travis married yet?" but by then we were outside in the cold air and it *was* over. Robert Potter stood there waiting with the bell rope in his hands, and the minute he saw us he started pulling it like crazy, ringing that old bell loud enough to wake the dead. Travis went over and patted him on the back and said, "Thank you, son," and Robert nodded but did not slack off in his efforts, ringing the bell across the whole valley, through the frosty air.

Travis turned to me. "Missy, I love you," he said, very formal. He picked me up and kissed me so hard I saw stars before my eyes, and when he put me down, I was dizzy. I was so happy! I stood with my husband on the Hi-Way Tabernacle steps as he shook hands and hugged everybody that came pouring out of the church after us, which was exactly what he did after meeting. We were the last ones to walk around the church to the fellowship hall for our reception, along with old Forrest Knight, Thurman Tate's half brother, who had driven over to marry us. He pastored the church up at Mica Mountain. As we walked, he kept giving us advice from First Corinthians, all about being married, but I was far too excited to listen.

Now I wish I had.

A great cheer went up as we entered the fellowship hall, where everybody that Travis had ever known in his whole life, baby to man, was gathered. The only people I had there were Ruth and Carlton Duty and little Fannie. Ruth and Carlton were having a fine time and making a good impression, while Fannie had stolen every heart. You couldn't look at her without touching her hair, it was so pretty—the palest gold, and curly like a halo around her head. And she had the biggest blue eyes. I thought she looked exactly like Mama, but everybody from Piney Ridge claimed she looked like me, as they had never seen Mama, of course.

"But where is Billie?" I cried, when Ruth had finally quit hugging me and I could speak.

Ruth and Carlton looked at each other. "We couldn't get her to come," Ruth said, "but she sends you her love."

"Well, why not? What's the matter with her?" I asked.

Little Fannie spoke right up. "Mommy had to stay and watch TV," she said in her loud voice.

I looked at Ruth, who just shook her head. "Things have changed," she said. "Me and Carlton don't go to your daddy's old church no more. We have got a TV now, and go to the Church of Christ. But we can't hardly get Billie to go anyplace with us. She has gotten real fat," Ruth added, before she had to lean down and shush Fannie, who liked to talk all the time.

It hurt my feelings that Billie hadn't come to my wedding, though it didn't really surprise me. I was sure glad to see Ruth and Carlton, though, and to meet that tough little Fannie, who reminded me more of Evelyn, actually, than shy Billie Jean. Ruth looked exactly the same, except that her curls had turned to purest white. They sat like a crocheted cap on her head. Carlton was as thin and grave as ever, and I'll swear he was wearing the same old hat! He stood off to one side talking seriously to different men from Piney Ridge. I bet they were talking about Daddy, comparing notes. But I couldn't worry about them, I had to hug everybody, and cut the cake.

I was surprised and a little put-out to see that Garnet Keen had written "Glory to God Amen" in silver icing around the side of the bottom layer, instead of "Travis and Gracie in Love," which she had said she was going to write. Helen saw me looking at it, and whispered to me that she and Minnie had asked Garnet to put this, since the other was too undignified for a preacher. I realized she was right. Then Travis and I had to pose our hands together on the knife just so, while Lodge Hibbitts took a close-up picture of them, and then he took another one of me feeding the first piece of cake to Travis, which was real funny as I got icing all over his long chin. He was laughing too hard to chew. Several people remarked on this, on how nice it was to see Preacher Travis have a good time for once, and I believe that the sight of his happiness softened up some of those old biddies who had continued to take a dim view of me and of our marriage. Then everybody ate some cake and drank some punch, and Travis announced that the grand sum of one hundred and thirty-four dollars had been contributed to the Tabernacle in our honor. He had asked that people make a contribution to the church instead of giving us a wedding gift.

Standing right in front of the mostly eaten wedding cake, Travis stretched out his long arms to everybody. "I thank you!" he told one and all. "From the bottom of my heart, I thank you. This is the happiest day of my life." Nobody who saw him could doubt that this was true. I felt a sharp poke in the ribs just then, and Minnie whispered in my ear, "Say something." I knew I had to.

I stepped forward to stand with Travis, and said, "Thank you too," which sounded so funny that I got embarrassed, but it made everybody laugh. Then it was time to throw the bouquet, which was homemade, out of mistletoe and evergreens. In the end I could not pick among the hopeful old maids and sad widows in the church, and tossed it to the oldest Hibbitts girl, a trashy blonde.

Then we left, Travis and me, without changing clothes, since there was no place to change. People threw rice all over us as we ran out the door to his truck. It was freezing cold outside. I grabbed up my coat from the seat and wrapped it around myself. Travis turned on the heater.

I scooted over real close to him, like we were teenagers. Well, I *was* a teenager, but I had completely forgotten this fact. For I was also a married woman, and had spoken my first words in public as the preacher's wife. Just as Travis turned onto the main road it started to snow, big lacy flakes that stuck on the windshield before the wipers swept them away.

"There ain't no two of them snowflakes alike in the whole world," Travis said. "Think on that."

I thought on it. The snowflakes were so perfect that they reminded me of the ones we learned to make in grade school, where you would fold the construction paper just so and cut it, then unfold it slowly, and presto! you were dazzled.

"It all goes to show you the infinite variety of God," said Travis, who could find Him in anything.

I agreed. Then I told him what Ruth Duty had told me just before we left, and how much it had pleased me. She'd said, "Oh Gracie, your mama would be so proud of you! You know she would just be so happy to see this day!"

And as we rode along after the wedding with all those different snowflakes rushing at us from the close gray sky, I suddenly felt Mama's presence right there in the truck with us, I felt her warm kiss on my cheek as real as the stream of air from the heater, and I heard her soft voice say, "I love you, honey," right in my ear.

"WHERE ARE WE going?" I finally thought to ask. I knew we were not going to have a real honeymoon, as it would cost too much, but I had assumed that we would be going somewhere special for a night anyway, and had stuck a little traveling bag behind the seat accordingly. I had not asked exactly where we were going, since I would rather be surprised, but I secretly hoped it was Knoxville, which was the closest real city. All my hopes were pinned on Knoxville.

"Well," Travis said, "when I got to thinking about it, it just seemed to me like a sinful waste of money to spend twenty dollars on a motel room when we have got our own bed at home, where the price is right."

I couldn't believe it. "You mean we are not going *noplace*?" I asked. "Then what are you driving way out here for?" He had passed the road that led back home, and we were now on Highway 11, headed east.

"I thought we'd just drive around awhile," Travis said. "Give folks a chance to get back home, get settled down. Anyway, looky here at all this snow. Might be God is trying to tell us to go home anyway."

"It's not sticking," I said, which was true.

"What?" Travis turned his head to look at me.

"It's *not sticking*," I said, too loud. "It isn't supposed to stick. You didn't say a thing about it this morning when you read the paper."

"That's true enough," Travis said. Travis loved the weather report, he read it out loud to me and Helen every morning, and then the sisters would all talk about it for the rest of the day, deciding whether or not it had been right, or how far off it was. All of a sudden I realized how much I hated this, and then I was crying.

"Why, Missy, what's the matter?" Travis reached over and took my hand, which helped some, but I couldn't quit crying.

"I don't know," I said.

Travis Word did not have a clue what to do with a crying girl. First he cleared his throat a lot, and then he started patting my thigh like I was a dog. "There, there," he said.

I moved as far away from him on the seat as I could get. I put my hot face up against the cold glass of the window and kept on crying.

"Now, Missy," he finally said, "you are going to have to tell your old preacher man here what is the matter."

"Nothing," I managed to say.

"It don't look like 'nothing' to me," Travis allowed.

"Oh, it's just—well, I don't know. It's nothing, honest. I am just wore-out, is all. I am feeling kindly nervous."

At this, Travis brightened up. "Why I guess it's just a bad case of the nerves, then!" he said, as if this explained everything.

"Quit patting me!" I snapped, surprising myself. I have never been able to act like I wanted to, in all my life. It's like the Devil gets into me sometimes.

"What, honey?"

"*Quit patting me,*" I said again. At this he withdrew his hand, and we rode along in silence through the falling snow. But try as I might, I could not stop crying.

Still Travis did not turn back toward home, and I could tell he was thinking hard. "Okay," he said. "Okay, Missy, I have done changed my mind. We will drive over there and spend the night in Knoxville. Is that what you want to do? I should of thought this out better, I can see that. I'm sorry. You're just a girl, and sometimes I forget."

"Oh, Travis!" I had to hug him then, though his sweetness made me feel unworthy. I *was* unworthy. But I snuggled up close for the rest of the ride to Knoxville. It quit snowing and got dark and the stars came out.

"See?" I poked him in the side. "God wanted you to go to Knoxville after all."

We stopped once at a Shell Oil station for gas and took a lot of ribbing about being just married, because somebody had put a little note on the gas cap that told them, and also I still had my wedding dress on and I had to get out and go to the ladies' room. "Hey, honey," one of the gas station boys called to me as I hurried back to the truck with my coat wrapped up tight around me. "Excuse me, Miss, but can he really get it up? That old goat? Don't he have to get some *help*?" Then they all just about died laughing.

"Listen here," I said, whirling to face them, "he just wears me out, if you want to know!" I gave them a wink and a big happy grin, and they set up a cheer, and I jumped in the truck.

"What was all that about?" Travis asked, and I said, "Nothing, sugar," scooting closer.

I was so excited when we pulled up at the Holiday Inn.

"You can always trust a Holiday Inn," Travis told me. Now he was acting like he stayed at motels all the time and knew all about them. "You stay right here, honey." He patted my knee and went inside, and this time, I didn't mind being patted. But he was back out in a minute, his face a study. He walked around to my side of the truck and stood there drumming his long fingers on the window, lost in thought. I rolled the window down. "What is it now?" I asked.

"It costs moren I thought," he said.

"Why, how much is it?" I asked.

"Moren we've got." Travis did not believe in checking accounts, so I understood right away how this could be a problem.

"Wait a minute, Travis!" I thought of something. "It's all right, we've got a hundred and thirty-four dollars."

He looked blank.

"*In cash*. Back there in that sack. From the church, remember?"

"Oh Missy," Travis said. "That money belongs to the Lord."

"Well, I don't see why we can't *borrow* some of it," I said, "and pay the Lord back later."

Travis stood stock-still as cars came and went in the parking lot, and people passed back and forth through the thick glass doors. I could see a huge gold-foil Christmas tree just inside the lobby, glittering with lights.

He slapped his hand against the side of the truck and laughed out loud. "Hand it over, then," he said, and I fished around behind the seat until I found the sack, heavy with coins.

"I'll be back in a minute," Travis said. "I've got to take this in there so I can see to count out the money." He leaned in the window to kiss me quick on the lips and then was gone, striding across the parking lot on legs as long and black as stovepipes.

Now, I can't imagine what they thought as he counted out his dollars and change at the desk—twenty-two dollars and seventy-five cents, paid for in cash by God.

But our room was beautiful, all done up in shades of beige and blue and green, with the prettiest picture of a flower arrangement hanging over the bed. Travis put down my bag—he didn't have one—and peered all around, looking nervous. "Well, let's go eat," he said loudly, adding that the dining room closed in two hours. He said that he would wait for me outside while I changed my clothes, that he needed to lock up the truck anyway and call Helen from the pay phone.

I felt oddly shy walking into the restaurant with Travis a little while later, dressed in my gray pleated skirt and gray sweater with its detachable pearl collar that I had been so proud of—now the pearl collar seemed too girlish to me, and my stacked heels hurt my feet. The glamorous young hostess wore a ton of makeup. She seated us at a table with a pink tablecloth and a candle burning softly in a hurricane lamp. "Would you like something from the bar to start with?" she asked.

"*No ma'am,*" Travis said in such a definite way that she scurried off and came right back with menus for us to order from. I thought Travis should not call her "ma'am," as she was about twenty years younger than he was— nearer to *my* age! and how I wished I could wear some of that makeup!—but I was not about to say this. I would not have hurt his feelings for the world. He moved his lips as he read the menu straight through to himself, and then he smiled at me. "Order anything you want," he said. "This un is on the Lord too."

I ordered a veal cutlet with tomato sauce. Travis ordered the T-bone steak, well-done, with a baked potato. "What do you want to drink?" our waitress said, her pencil poised above her pad. She was about forty years old, skinny and disappointed-looking. It was not all that long before that I had been a waitress myself, and now I was already a wife. "Sweet milk," I said. She wrote it down. When our order came, we ate every bite, and then we both had brownie a la mode for dessert. I enjoyed just sitting in the pink dining room looking around at all the other people while Travis drank his coffee. A TV was on in the bar area, but they had soft piano music piped into the dining room. I remember they played "Unchained Melody," which I have always loved, and I thought to myself, *Now that will be our song. I will always remember this moment, and that will be our song.*

When we got back to our room, Travis asked me to please excuse him while he went in the bathroom. I just *knew* he would undress in there too, that he would not want to undress in front of me, so while he had the door closed, I went ahead and took off my clothes and put on the white nylon nightgown which Helen had bought for me at J. C. Penney's in Greeneville. I let my hair down. I was standing by the bed when he came out of the bathroom in his underwear, with his pants and his shirt hung up neat on a coat hanger. I had wondered about his burn scars, but they were not bad at all, just a white tracing like a spider web on his chest and shoulders. He looked at me. "Oh, Missy, Missy," he said like he was in terrible pain. He let the coat hanger fall to the floor as he came to me in one bound, and he loved me up even better than I had bragged to those boys at the gas station. It was like a great dam had given way in his soul. He could not get enough, nor do enough. By the time we were both laying flat on our backs, sweaty and exhausted, it was midnight.

"Why, look," I said, pointing to the clock, "it's already Sunday."

At that the most awful change came over Travis Word. His very face turned gray and his eyes rolled back in his head, and he sat straight up, with his black hair sticking out from his head in every direction. Before I knew it, he was down on his knees by the bed.

"Pray, Missy, pray!" he begged me.

"Why Travis, what in the world are you doing?" Though a chill went through my heart, I tried to keep things light. But his eyes were closed and his lips were already moving. "Come to Jesus, come to Jesus," he implored, and nothing would satisfy him but for me to get down then and there on my knees too, both of us buck naked, as he quoted from Romans about our sinful passions working in our members to bear fruit for death. He was attempting to purify us, he would explain, for "the mind that is set on the flesh is hostile to God; it does not submit to God's law, indeed it cannot; and those who are in the flesh cannot please God." He was trying to bring us back. It seemed like this was going to take him all night long, and I was going to freeze to death down there on the floor while he did it. Finally I climbed up in the bed by myself, making as little movement as I could, and lay there on my side watching him pray, until at last he finished and climbed up into the bed and turned his back to me without a word and fell instantly, deeply, asleep, snoring like a freight train. I had not known that he snored. Maybe it was the snoring, or maybe it was only that so much had happened to me that day, but I could not fall asleep, for the life of me. I was strung as tight as a guy wire. I got up and put on my coat and my shoes, and went out to stand on the balcony in the chilly air. The Holiday Inn was on a hill, so that I could look down upon the highway and beyond it, at the whole city of Knoxville spread out like a big sea of twinkling lights which seemed very, very far away.

OUR FIRST CHILD was born a year later, to general rejoicing. I don't think any young bride was ever watched more closely for signs of pregnancy, or treated better during those nine special months—which just *flew* past, it seemed like. Travis and his sisters spoiled me to death. At the beginning I felt real bad, with terrible morning sickness. I had to eat saltine crackers and drink flat ginger ale the minute I woke up, to keep from vomiting. Travis would hand me the crackers one by one, and hold the ginger ale up to my lips in a jelly glass.

"This is like Communion, isn't it?" I asked once just to tease him, but right away he turned so serious that I was sorry I'd spoken.

"Now, Missy, we are not to make a mockery of the Lord

in any way, not even of the practices of others that we don't believe in," he said, for we did not take Communion at the Tabernacle of course. I have never actually taken Communion in my life, I think it is a Catholic thing.

"It was just a joke," I said, still flat on my back.

"The worship of God is not something to joke about," Travis intoned, but I said, "Come here," and pulled him to me and kissed the deep sad wrinkles on his brow until he smiled at me. That early in the marriage, I could do this, though later it would get harder and harder to lift the gloom which settled on him so easy and stayed so long.

During the first three months, all I could stand to eat was chicken noodle soup and Pine State ice cream, which Helen was glad to fix for me. The sisters wouldn't let me lift a hand, which was okay with me since I felt so bad. Minnie brought me stacks of books from the public library to read, whatever I asked for, whatever new came in. The sisters viewed my reading as a harmless hobby, something to keep me occupied while the baby grew inside me. There was certainly no point in me making baby clothes or little blankets, since Helen and Vonda Louise were already hard at work on this, plus about half the women of the Tabernacle. So I got to sit up in bed drinking Coca-Colas and reading *Butterfield 8* and *Gone With the Wind* and *The View from Pompey's Head* and *Mandingo* and other books that would surely have shocked them if they'd known what went on between those covers. But I also read the Bible and *The Upper Room*, especially when Travis was in the house, which was not often. With his sisters right there to take care of me, he was free to minister to his flock with total dedication, as he had before our marriage. He was involved in every phase of their lives. After I burst into tears because he spent more time sitting with Lucius Rogers's dying mother than he did with me, he improved a little bit, but not much.

As the months passed, I felt better, though, and was able to dress and go over to the Tabernacle myself, though I never did take on all the regular duties of a preacher's wife. This was partly because I got pregnant right away and had such a hard pregnancy that nobody expected me to do much during it, and then they got *used* to me not doing much, but also because Helen Tate had always filled that role herself and continued to, taking a casserole to whoever was sick, a ham in the case of death. I got out of all that. Now I wonder if this was such a good thing or not. For if I had been more involved in the day-to-day life of the Tabernacle, perhaps I wouldn't have been so idle and restless. I don't know. I do know that there has never been a girl that was treated better in all this world than I was, this is true. I went through that pregnancy like a bird in a nest, protected and spoiled and loved. Yes, *loved!* There lies the hurt of it. And I hate myself still for what I would do to that little circle of loving, trusting faces—Helen and Minnie and Vonda Louise, and most of all, Travis.

MISTY WAS BORN on December 15, 1960, not long after our first anniversary. We were trimming the tree when my water broke. I didn't know what was happening, but Helen did. She told Travis, who happened to be home at the time, which was lucky, to start his truck. She told Minnie to get some blankets and then go in our bedroom and get my suitcase, which she had had packed for two weeks. She told Vonda Louise to hush and lay down, a good thing, as Vonda Louise had gotten so excited that she was crying and laughing by turns. First she started crying because my water breaking had messed up one of *her* presents, and then she started laughing that high-pitched "hee hee hee," which meant she was simply nervous. She was so nervous in fact that Minnie stayed home with her to calm her down, while Helen rode with Travis and me to the hospital.

Travis drove the fastest I ever knew him to drive, but we need not have rushed so, as it turned out, because my real labor was just coming on. The old doctor looked at me and said that it would be a while, but we might as well stay at the hospital since we were already there. So we all went upstairs to a room, where I put on a hospital gown. My pains started coming then, and they were awful, but as they were still far apart, Travis took this opportunity to go all around the hospital visiting the sick and their families. The nurse shaved and prepped me while Helen knitted. Travis was still gone when the nurse announced that I was dilated ten centimeters and they were going to take me to the delivery room.

"Travis," I said, "I want Travis," but they were wheeling me down the hall by then, and all I could see was the big round bright lights in the ceiling zooming overhead one by one, and all I could feel was the pain. The pain was terrible. I maintain that if a woman could remember how much it hurts to have a baby, she would never have another one. But we can't remember, of course. Our bodies make us forget.

I was in labor for twenty hours. About the last thing I really remember is the doctor saying, "Now, Mrs. Word, you are going to feel better after this shot," which they gave me in defiance of Travis's wishes, as he did not believe in medicine. But he gave in, the pain was so horrible. Poor Travis. I learned later that he was down on his knees in the waiting room praying the whole time.

Misty was a breech birth—what people call a britches baby—and it took all the prayer and medicine available to get her born, and to get me to stop bleeding. If we had not come to the hospital, we both might have died, is what the doctor said, and later Helen would be glad to relay this news to those who had thought the Words were uppity to use the hospital in Greeneville instead of relying on Mrs. Terrell's services. But it was more like an operation than a birth, finally. By the time I woke up and saw my baby, they had cleaned her up and put a little pink bow in her blond hair. She was the cutest thing I had ever seen! I took her and counted her tiny fingers and toes, and examined her all over. "She's perfect," I said to Travis, and she was. He leaned over the bed and held my hand and thanked the Lord for giving her to us, a prayer I joined in with all my heart.

"What is the name of the baby?" asked an older nurse

with a clipboard, and Travis and I looked at each other. We had been planning to name it Travis Junior, assuming it to be a boy, as this is what Travis had wanted and what all the old ladies had told us we would have, including the expert Mrs. Terrell. "If you can't tell she's pregnant from the back, it's a boy for sure," Mrs. Terrell had announced. "A girl baby will wrap all around you and show on the side." Since everybody had agreed you couldn't tell I was pregnant from the back, we didn't have any girl names picked out.

But right away Travis started flipping through his Bible to come up with some.

"What about Mary?" he suggested. "Or Ruth? How about Mary Ruth?"

"Mary Ruth is real pretty," Helen said.

"Misty," I said.

They both stared at me.

"Now, honey," Travis said.

"That sounds cheap," Helen said.

"Misty Celeste Word." It hit me like a revelation. Later I realized I must have gotten the Misty from *Misty of Chincoteague*, but I never did know where the Celeste came from.

Travis swallowed hard, his Adam's apple peeking above his shirt collar. "I think that's a real pretty name," he said.

"*Travis!*" Helen hissed, but it was too late.

"How do you spell 'Celeste'?" the nurse asked, and I told her. It was done.

"That is a mighty big name for such a tiny little girl," Travis said, touching her hair and smiling.

* * *

A WOMAN NEVER knows exactly how she will react to having a baby. I have known women that were just dying to have a child, to come home from the hospital and cry for a month. I have known others that hated to nurse and swore their babies bit them. I have known others that could not sleep. As for me, I am glad to say it all came natural. But I was so lucky—with Helen happy to fix meals for Travis and run the house, I could stay on Misty Celeste's schedule as long as I wanted to, and I did so for the longest time. I did everything she did. When she slept, I slept. When she got up, I got up. I ate when she ate. When spring came, I'd put her out on a blanket in the yard in the sunshine. Me and Misty both got a suntan, and each day seemed to stretch out full and golden, and last forever. I was the happiest I had ever been. That younger ornery me was like somebody I didn't even know anymore, and I was glad to drop her acquaintance.

Of course I was happy! I was living in a paradise. The sisters did everything. Travis came and went, busy with the Lord's work. When Misty was six months old, I got pregnant again, and before I knew it, the whole circle had started over, only I was not so sick and I had my Misty to keep me company. The second pregnancy passed in no time.

"Oh no!" the old doctor said when he saw us coming. "I reckon you're going to turn this whole hospital into a prayer meeting again," he said severely to Travis, who grinned at him. But this time my labor went like clockwork, and Sandra Annette Word was born in about three hours, and this time I was awake to see it. Birth *is* a miracle, I had to agree with Travis as he prayed beside the bed while I held the new baby in my arms. She was smaller than Misty and did not seem as well developed, startling easy. But she was just as pretty in the face as her sister. Travis let me name her too. I chose Sandra Annette. Sandra is a name I have always liked, and I got the Annette from Annette Funicello, who I had seen on *The Mickey Mouse Club* at Mrs. Thoroughgood's house. Later she was on *American Bandstand*, where everybody was so happy and had such a good time. I hoped that my Sandra Annette would be as cute and as perky as Annette Funicello, and as happy.

It worked. For the next few years, we were *all* happy. When you have babies, your whole life revolves around them. It has to. It's always time for a feeding, or it's time for a bath, or Misty has a fever, or Annette has colic—and then they start walking and the world gets so dangerous all of a sudden, you have to be right there, you have to snatch them up before they tumble down the Tabernacle steps or touch the eye of the stove, your job is to keep them safe. I took this real seriously too. Even Helen Tate came right out and told everybody that when Travis brought me home, she didn't know what to make of me, but I had turned out to be a fine little mother after all! I talked Travis into letting me enter the girls in the Little Miss Valleydale contest at the new shopping center when Misty was four and Annette was three, and Travis's sisters sewed pink princess outfits for them to wear in the contest, with tiny tiaras. They won first place and got their picture on the front page of the *Valleydale Record*, and though Travis sniffed, he was proud as punch. Misty was outgoing from the first, she had that kind of personality that doesn't know a stranger. But I had to watch her every minute, as I never knew what she might take it into her head to do next.

Annette was quieter, more like her father. She had huge dark eyes like those starving children in paintings of other countries. Her eyes seemed to soak up the whole world like a sponge. She didn't speak for the longest time, so long that we were all getting worried about her, and one woman in the church said we ought to have her tested, which made Minnie furious.

"Tested for what? She'll talk when she gets ready to talk!" Minnie said. "When she's got something to say."

Of course Annette did not really *need* to talk, with Misty right there to tell everybody what she wanted. "Annie want some Kool-Aid," she'd say, or "Annie sleepy now."

Sure enough, Minnie was right, because Annette *did* finally speak up when Misty had the flu and couldn't talk for her. Annette asked me to get her a drink of water, please, in a complete sentence. I thought I'd die! But my girls were both real smart.

They were my whole life in those years. I didn't really have any friends. There was one other young wife named DeeDee Burgess who used to bring her own little girls, the same age as mine, over to play while we sat out in the yard and watched them. In one way it was like no time had passed since Travis had brought me home and I had so longed to sit out there and while away the day, and yet in another way I felt like I had been there forever and ever, a thousand years. Life seemed to pass like a big slow river. For the most part, I was content to float along, or paddle in the shallows with my baby girls, looking out across its broad mysterious expanse.

But sometimes, something would happen to make me come up gasping for air.

I remember that summer day when DeeDee and me were sitting out in those chairs watching our little girls play in a plastic pool. Misty shrieked and splashed with DeeDee's girls, while Annette stood holding the hose, making a hole in the yard with the water. She was just as serious about this as if somebody was paying her to do it.

Then DeeDee said, "I'll swear, sometimes I wish Johnny would lay off of the sex for *just one day*. It gets old, you know what I mean? But Johnny, he wants to do everything the same way every day. He has to have meat for supper every night and watch the ten-o'clock news and get his loving and go to sleep. You can't read a magazine in bed. You can't watch the eleven-o'clock news. On Saturdays we do it in the morning too, while the girls look at the cartoons on TV. Then he goes hunting or fishing, depending on the season. Then we do it again on Saturday night. He is exactly like his daddy, who is the most boring man on earth. I've said to him, 'Honey, let's get a baby-sitter and go out sometime,' or 'Let's get your mama to keep the girls and we'll go over to the lake, just the two of us,' and he looks at me like I'm crazy. Oh, I don't know. I get tired of it, you know what I mean? I swear I do. I feel like we're real old, but we're not even thirty yet."

I was dumbstruck. Though I had never talked Travis into going on a picnic again, I had not yet gotten to the point of boredom. DeeDee was just enough older than me so that part of what she was saying was like a preview of things to come. But what really hit me about her outburst was the fact that they did it every day. DeeDee's husband Johnny was a man's man kind of guy who drove heavy equipment for the highway department and had a big gut. Now I had to picture him and DeeDee *doing it every day*— and on Saturdays, twice a day! I just couldn't get over this, considering my life with Travis Word. For I was still young then, something I had mostly forgotten about, and when you're young, you relate everything to yourself.

I guess I was staring. DeeDee pulled her red hair up into a ponytail and giggled and said, "Now don't you tell Travis what I was talking about, you hear?" because of course he was their preacher, and I had to smile as I said, "Don't worry, I won't." The fact was that I couldn't *imagine* talking about a thing like that with Travis Word, or discussing my own private life as Travis's wife with anyone. I was not even tempted to tell DeeDee about it. It was purely not possible. Also, I did not mind my situation that much. I loved my little girls, and I loved my life. From time to time I was still overcome by a feeling that I didn't deserve any of it, that I was there under false pretenses and might be discovered at any moment and thrown out, though I was unclear about what these false pretenses actually were. For I really *was* a wife now, and I had had two real babies. I was earning my keep.

The only problem was the one I touched on earlier—the

true nature of Travis Word. Now this is a thing which I had not even dared to think of before DeeDee made her comment. But then I couldn't stop thinking about it. Every day! I kept thinking. Twice on Saturday! I could count on my fingers the number of times Travis and I actually did it in any given month—or to be accurate, the number of times he *did it to me*. For he did not like me to move much, or say anything, while he was doing it. And when he was through, he would fling himself down on his knees, praying in anguish to be cleansed. I had thought he might ease up on this with time, but he had not. I had to kneel down there and pray too. After a while, I got to where I did not often try to tempt him, as it was not really worth it, if you see what I mean.

For a long time Travis's attitude toward bodily love did not seem too important, but then there came a time when it did, when I reckon my true nature came out too. For there are ways in which it is easier to live with a plaster saint like Daddy than with a real saint like Travis Word.

THE SERIOUS TROUBLES began when Misty was in school and I started volunteering there a lot, being the room mother and the candy drive chairperson and what have you. Travis and his sisters were real proud of me at first. Then Misty's teacher, Mrs. Browning—who had been at that school forever and ever—took me aside one day and said that her teacher's aide was going to quit because she was pregnant, and asked me if I would like to take her place. All I really had to do was apply for the job, Mrs.

Browning said, and she would make sure that I got it. I would make four thousand dollars a year.

Travis and his sisters hit the roof—or his sisters did, to be fair. They called me ungrateful, while Travis just looked sorrowful and said didn't I have everything in the world I could possibly want? I tried to stand my ground, explaining that since Helen did everything at home, I *needed* something to do. I gave the example of my friend DeeDee, now getting an associate degree in practical nursing at the community college. DeeDee drove over there for classes every day, so I never got to see her anymore. I was crying before I knew it, as I tried to explain. Vonda Louise started crying too, to keep me company. Minnie pinched her lips together and went to clean the bathroom, which was what she always did when she got mad. But Helen looked at me thoughtfully through her new glasses which made her eyes look as big and blank as plates. Travis began to quote at me from the Bible as was his wont, citing Proverbs, but Helen took his arm before he was done and pulled him outside to help her fix the chicken-wire fence around her vegetable garden. I stood at the window and watched old Helen talking to Travis while he worked, both of them glancing back at the house from time to time. I knew they were talking about me. Meanwhile Minnie splashed water around in the bathroom and Vonda Louise wept on the love seat.

"What's the matter with Auntie Vonda? What's the matter?" my girls cried, running into the room. I was short with them, saying, "Nothing," in a voice that made *them* cry too.

"Well, *shoot!*" I said out loud to myself. I gave them a hug and then got Helen's car keys and took the girls and Vonda Louise out on the interstate for a sundae at the Dairy Bar. Vonda Louise loved sweets and didn't get out much. Then we went to Kmart. We had a good time. Travis and Helen and Minnie were beside themselves with worry when we got back.

"I couldn't stand to lose you," Travis said, very dramatic.

"Oh, don't be silly," I told him, but I felt flattered all the same. That night Travis covered me all over in kisses, and I did something to him that had him down on his knees until dawn.

So I DID not take the job, to Mrs. Browning's dismay. But as I was soon pregnant again, it was a good thing I'd said no. A good thing for *her*, that is. Not for me. I've always wondered how things would have turned out if I had took that job. Different, I'll bet.

In any case, I lost the baby at eight months. It just died. It had been kicking a lot, and then it quit kicking. I knew immediately that something was wrong. I knew even before the old doctor told me. He was listening to my stomach, and then he put the stethoscope down and took my hand. "I'm sorry, Mrs. Word," he said. I started crying and couldn't stop. I was afraid my womb had turned poison and killed it.

"Now, now," the doctor said. "These things just happen."

But I had to go through labor anyway, and deliver the dead baby. That was the only way they could do it.

The baby was a boy, stone gray and perfectly formed.

We named him Travis Word Junior and buried him in the graveyard right next to the Tabernacle. He has the tiniest, prettiest stone, with a carved lamb on top and these words cut into the rose marble:

A LITTLE LAMB OF GOD
TRAVIS WORD JUNIOR
SEPTEMBER 10, 1966
BELOVED SON OF TRAVIS AND GRACE WORD

I know people talked about us for spending so much money on a stillborn baby, but Travis insisted. He was brokenhearted. This was the only son he would ever have, since the doctor said I couldn't have any more children after that. I don't think Travis *ever* got over the loss of Travis Junior, in fact, and I didn't either.

We buried our son on a drizzly afternoon in Indian summer. Little crystal drops of water clung to all the leaves, like jewels. I could not understand how a thing so awful could happen in such a beautiful world, nor could I understand how God could let such a thing happen in the first place. I was weak from loss of blood, and could not quit crying. I hated Him. As we left the graveyard, I kept looking back over my shoulder at that sad little grave with its tiny new stone and its tiny pile of red dirt. I hated to leave my baby there surrounded by old Words and McGlothlins he had never met and never heard of, all of them Travis's ancestors, going back for a hundred years. The cemetery was full of Travis's family, in fact it hit me as we were walking out that his family was more dead than alive in general.

When we got home, Travis went straight to bed in the middle of the day, an unheard-of thing to me. But Helen and Minnie raised their eyebrows and looked at each other when I told them what he was up to, and that he didn't want any supper. "Oh-oh," Minnie said, and Helen nodded. Then they told me that their father had done this from time to time, just simply gone to bed for weeks on end, refusing to speak to anybody. He had lost several jobs this way, and worried them all sick.

"Why did he do it?" I asked.

Helen shook her head. "Nobody ever knew."

"Runs in the family," Minnie said.

They went on to tell me that Travis had been known to do it too, his most recent bout having been right before Daddy came. But this was so long ago now that they had thought he was cured.

"Cured by love," said Vonda Louise, winking at me.

Though I smiled, I felt sick to my stomach. I couldn't stand to see Travis just lying around, a big man like that, doing nothing. All my old orneriness started coming back. I wanted to run around and act up and smash things. I scared myself.

The only thing worse than having Travis gone all the time was having him home all the time.

I brought his Bible to him as he lay in bed, thinking he might find some comfort in it, but after reading for a while, he announced that the "evil days" had come upon him as foretold in the last chapter of Ecclesiastes, when "the years draw nigh, and you will say, I have no pleasure in them, before the sun and the light and the moon and the stars are darkened and the clouds return after the rain, in the day when the keepers of the house tremble, and the strong men are bent, and the grinders cease because they are few, and those that look through the windows are dimmed, and the doors on the street are shut. . . ." Travis read on and on, through the part where the daughters of song are brought low, and terrors are in the way, and the grasshopper drags itself along and desire fails and the golden bowl is broken, all the way to "Vanity of vanities, all is vanity" at the end. He put the Bible down. He had big circles under his eyes.

"That's the most depressing thing I've ever heard," I said.

"So be it," he answered. "So be it."

He refused to look at me even when I kissed his neck. He shrugged me off like I was a buzzing fly that wouldn't leave him alone. This made me madder than anything else, the way he shut me out and wouldn't let me grieve with him, as I had pain and grief to spare. I was the one who had carried Travis Word Junior for eight months in my own body, after all. Every time I closed my eyes, I could still see my little gray baby. Now I didn't feel too good, and thought I deserved some attention. But no. Nothing doing. Travis turned his face to the wall.

He lay there neglecting us and neglecting all his duties for three weeks solid. Then Helen told him sternly that he had to get up or he would lose his congregation, that the

Faith Baptist Mission was holding a revival right now, and the whole Rogers family had been going to it. Helen said she would not be surprised if they quit the Tabernacle and joined up over there.

This got Travis up. Maybe he was ready to get up anyway. He started planning for a revival at the Tabernacle, and raising money for Mona and Harley White's daughter who had a brain tumor, and then he announced that the senior youth group was going on a trip to Rock City.

But the pattern was set. Travis would be brought low from time to time by those "evil days," when gloom sat heavy upon him and all was for naught. Then he would have periods of sixteen-hour workdays, when he spent every free minute in the service of the Lord. He tried to accept the evil days, often quoting Psalms 94:12, "Blessed is the man whom thou chasteneth, O Lord, and teachest him out of thy law."

Travis believed that everything in life happened for a purpose and fell into the great scheme of God, but I did not. I was still prone to question and agonize. I criticized God, and hardened my heart.

This went on for years.

I could never see why Mama had had to die so young, or the White girl, or Leonard Cartland, a high school boy who died in a wreck on his graduation night. He was an only child, whose parents never got over it. I particularly could not see why DeeDee's brother Rusty had to die in Vietnam while other boys wouldn't even go over there, running off to Canada and growing long hair and burning down their schools. We read about it in the paper. None of this made sense to me, and I could not detect God's purpose anywhere. I began to suspect that there was *no purpose at all*, in fact, but every time I thought this, a great bottomless empty feeling would rush through me, scaring me to death. Yet I had no one to share my thoughts with. Travis was growing farther away from me than ever. Either he was lying on the bed or he was working like a dog, and either way, there was no room for me in his life.

I tried to stay as busy as I could. My girls took up a lot of time, and I enjoyed every minute of it. When they got old enough to be Girl Scouts, I believe I enjoyed it even more than they did. I had never gotten to be one myself, so I got the biggest kick out of helping them earn their merit badges. I tried to be more active in the work of the Tabernacle too, going with Helen to every wake and birth and wedding that came along, helping with the youth group where I was a big hit, everybody agreed, since I was young enough for them to relate to. They all thought I was cool! I had to be careful not to relate *too* much, as a matter of fact, for there were a couple of boys in it that were real cute, and I was real lonely. But this was strictly my own fault, since I was surrounded all day long by so many people. It didn't make sense to me. Nothing did. But at least I had enough sense to quit the youth group after an incident where Doug Jones put his hand on mine for a minute too long when I handed him a piece of pizza.

I quit helping with the youth group right then and started visiting shut-ins and old people instead. One lady I visited was Mrs. Quigley. Her whole family hated her because she was so mean, but I kind of liked her. She was ninety-seven years old, and had thin white hair that stood up on end all over her head like she had been electrified, and brown age spots all over her face, and pale eyes covered by cataracts. They looked like milk glass.

I was supposed to read the Bible to her, but she loved the *National Enquirer* so I always brought that, hiding it from her family. She loved the lives of the stars.

One day as I was leaving, she grabbed my sleeve hard and hung on tight. I tried to pull away, as I was fixing to be late picking up my girls from school. "Listen!" she screeched at me. "Listen!" She had a voice like Mr. Bean's parrot. "Listen to me. Get out of here. Listen to me. Get out of here." She kept saying it over and over. She wouldn't let go of my sleeve. Her hand was like a claw.

Finally Mrs. Quigley's daughter came in and forced her fingers from my arm and said, "Now, Mama, let go of Mrs. Word. You run along, Mrs. Word, you're an angel, and we all appreciate you so much."

I got out of there. I never went back either. I knew she was just a crazy old woman, but I was no angel, and she had scared me. I was afraid I might turn into a mean old woman like that myself. In fact I thought I was in danger of doing so immediately. Though I was only thirty-three, I felt old as the hills. I felt ungrateful, and mean, and old.

I believe Helen guessed something about all this. One night when I was reading the paper, I glanced up to find her staring at me with a look that seemed to search my very soul. I could not help blushing, though I looked back down at the paper and continued to read, and never met her eyes.

It was soon after this that Helen decided we ought to redecorate the house.

"I want you to pick the colors," she said. "You're so good at things like that, and I'm too old. I want you to drive over to Sherwin-Williams in Knoxville and pick up some paint charts."

In spite of myself, I started to get interested. "What about wallpaper?" I asked, for I have always loved wallpaper.

"Wallpaper would be nice," Helen said.

A New
Paint Job

I STILL THINK that part of it was Travis's fault. He refused to let us call the contractor he worked for, Ed Goode, in Valleydale. Ed Goode would have charged us half price, or done it at cost, but Travis wouldn't have that. Oh no. Travis wouldn't take any favors. "I pay my own way" was one of his mottoes. Another was "Pay as you go," and he kept both us and the church on a cash basis at all times. Nor would he let us ask anybody from the Tabernacle to do it either, as he was sure they would do it for free.

"But that's all right," I tried to tell him at dinner one Sunday afternoon. "After everything you have done for them? You ought to let somebody do something for us sometime, Travis. It would make *them* feel better."

All those dark Word eyes turned in my direction, the way they did whenever I ventured to contradict Travis. It was the three sisters, plus Misty and Annette looking so pretty in their church dresses. Minnie's thin mouth hardened into a line, and Vonda Louise started biting her lip like she always did when she got nervous.

Travis put a forkful of mashed potatoes back down on his plate. "I am not too sure about all this redecoration anyhow," he said in that sincere way which meant he had been wrestling with it. "I don't know if it is meant to be."

"Meant to be?" I said. "What do you mean, *meant to be?* It is not an act of God, Travis. It is just some paint and some wallpaper. It's up to us. We can either do it or not do it."

But Travis shook his head gravely, as if it was all real serious. "If it ain't broke, don't fix it," he said in his deep voice—another one of his mottoes.

"Daddy, you promised!" This was Misty, who took after me, outspoken and headstrong and growing up too fast.

"You did, Daddy, you did." Annette was usually real quiet and good.

But Travis was genuinely worried. "I just don't know that a minister of God ought to do a thing like this," he said. "Maybe we ought to be satisfied with what we've got, and thank God for it, and leave well enough alone."

At these words I burst into tears.

"Mama, Mama," the girls cried, for this was not like me at all. Misty jumped up and ran around the table to hug me. I was so embarrassed, yet I couldn't stop. And I didn't even care about redecorating, not that much—it was all Helen's idea in the first place.

Travis sat there stiff as a poker.

"Oh, for Heaven's sakes!" Minnie started taking dishes

off the table. By then, of course, Vonda Louise was crying too, but Minnie made her help clear anyway.

"Can I be excused?" Annette asked, and when nobody answered her, she gulped and pushed back her chair and ran up the stairs two at a time.

Travis and Helen and I sat there looking at each other while Misty stood behind my chair and hugged me. I couldn't stop crying.

"Well, *shoot!*" Travis said finally. He cleared his throat and ran his finger around the inside of his white collar. "There's things a man just don't think of, I reckon. You go on then, Missy. You go on. Fix it up real pretty."

I DROVE TO the paint store in Knoxville by myself the next morning, a cold dreary March day, feeling blue and nervous. *Maybe I am entering the change of life*, I thought, *in spite of my age*. And to tell the truth, I wouldn't have minded the change of life either. It wouldn't have made a bit of difference to me.

First I had trouble finding the paint store, which had moved from the place where it used to be, beside the highway, to the big new mall outside town, and then I had trouble figuring out where to go once I got inside, as the store was huge. Eventually somebody directed me to the Decorating Center, a little carpeted island in the middle of the store with tables and chairs where you could sit and page through the big wallpaper books, and look at paint charts and pictures of rooms and swatches of drapery material and fancy venetian blinds, all of which was called window treatments. I sat down and started looking through the wallpaper books, but it was hard for me to concentrate. That new store had the brightest fluorescent lights—I hate how they buzz in your ears. They always make me feel like I'm going crazy. Maybe I *was* going crazy! I looked at stripes and tiny prints and velvet flocking and metallics. I had no idea there were so many different kinds of wallpaper in the world.

"If I can help you, just let me know."

I jumped a mile at the soft voice in my ear. The pretty blonde girl smiled. She was younger than me and appeared to have stepped straight out of a magazine in her coral pantsuit with bell-bottom legs.

"Are you looking for anything in particular?" Her name tag said "Miss Whittle, Home Design."

"Some wallpaper for my sitting room," I told her.

"This one has a lot of nice patterns for the living area." She pulled a huge book over toward me.

I felt dumb and country because I had said "sitting room" instead of "living area."

"Or maybe this one." She looked at me, then glided away, and I studied both the books. Her second choice offered a much cheaper line than the first. This showed what she thought of me! Well, I would show *her*. I closed that book and shoved it away. At least Travis was not cheap. Once he finally decided to buy something, he went whole-hog, He went for quality. Besides, I knew they had money saved up, him and his sisters. They owned property all around the county that had belonged to their parents. A lot of checks came in every month, people paying their rent I reckoned, though nobody ever talked to me about any of this. Minnie gathered up the checks and took them over to her house, where she did the bookkeeping. So money was not the problem. The problem was *progress*.

Travis was against progress in every way. He still would not let us have a television, nor could I wear pants or cut my hair—though I snuck and did it a little bit, of course, otherwise it would have been all the way down to my fanny, which it nearly was anyway. He never caught on to this. And he did let the girls wear jeans. He also let Misty go out for cheerleader and Annette join the Latin Club. But he had preached from the pulpit that man should not have gone to the moon, that we were not *meant* to, and the sisters swore that it had ruined the weather.

Anyway I could pick out whatever wallpaper I wanted.

What I wanted was an all-over pattern of red roses and green leaves. I had loved red roses ever since we lived in the house up on Scrabble Creek. I went through the books, but I couldn't find what I was looking for. And I was getting a terrible headache from those buzzing fluorescent lights.

Miss Whittle glided back, and I finally told her what I was after.

"Oh. You mean the English country look," she said.

"Exactly," I said, which surprised her.

So then she brought me more books, each page a garden, but I couldn't find any simple red roses. I broke down and asked her to help me look.

"Oh, red is *out*," she said. "Let me show you some really popular florals."

Before I knew it, I had ordered a tangerine/avocado/gold

print for the living area and gold paint for the kitchen, so the two rooms could flow into each other. Miss Whittle would arrange for the painter. I found myself standing out in the March wind, shaky and breathless as the glass doors of the paint store closed behind me, holding a color chart for the girls to pick from.

The sun ducked in and out of the racing clouds as I drove home, and my heart was racing too. Something was wrong with me. Now, I think this was when my old gift of discernment started coming back. I stopped by the Tabernacle to visit Travis Junior's grave, something I did often. For no particular reason, I went inside the Tabernacle first. The door was always open. Travis insisted upon leaving it unlocked, and nothing had ever been stolen.

Of course there wasn't much to steal.

Though the Tabernacle was not as poor as the churches which Daddy had pastored in my youth, the sanctuary was as honest and plain as Travis himself. There was nothing to distract you from Jesus. Rows of hard wooden benches on either side, no cushions, two windows with frosted-glass panes in them such as you might see in a public restroom, no carpet, just the old boards worn satin smooth from years of use, years of dancing in the Spirit, years of prayer. The church was built in 1888 by Methodists, but they had all died off and it was standing vacant when Thurman Tate took it over for his own ministry, which had started out as Church of God but became independent after Thurman fell out with somebody, I forget just who. Travis and Thurman did most of the work on it themselves back in the fifties, when they added on the meeting room and a bathroom at the rear.

I stood in the back and let my eyes adjust to the dim pearly light of the sanctuary. Here was where Travis and I had gotten married. Here was where Misty and Annette had accepted Christ as their personal savior at the revival the summer before, here was the bench where Travis's sisters sat right up front every Sunday morning come Hell or high water, wearing their best dresses and their old black hats. Wind came in the open door behind me and flapped my skirt around. I blinked, and blinked again. For I seemed to see a shadowy girl—who was she?—moving through the Tabernacle like a ghost. I saw her on a bench halfway back on the left, with her shadow husband and shadow children, then I saw her sitting there alone when her children grew up and left her and her husband died, then I saw her sitting with the other widows, way up front in order to hear, and then she was gone, all gone, nothing left of her but a little mist in the sanctuary, she was a shut-in someplace like Mrs. Quigley, and then she was dead and they had buried her in the graveyard beside the church.

Before I knew it, I had run out there and flung myself down sobbing on Travis Junior's grave. The cold grass was prickly against my face. The marble felt slick and wet and cold.

"Missy, Missy, what in the world are you doing, girl?" Suddenly Travis was there in his work jacket, helping me up. I was so surprised and glad to see him. He had been on his way home early and had stopped when he saw the

Tabernacle door standing wide open the way I'd left it. He held me while he prayed aloud for Travis Junior, and for us, and for everybody in the graveyard, and in the church, and in the world.

I wished he had stopped with us.

Then he squeezed me tight and said, "Let's go home," and we did.

HELEN DIDN'T WANT her room painted, and Travis wouldn't even think about getting our own room done. He liked for everything to stay exactly the way it was. But the girls picked Lavender Blue Dilly Dilly for theirs, and I called the paint store, and the painter showed up a week later.

This moment is fixed in my mind forever.

It was a morning like any other, March as I said. Travis had gone off to work and I had driven the girls to school and dropped by the store for milk and come back home to find Helen out on the porch waiting for me, clutching her coat around her. She had her pocketbook, so I knew she was fixing to go someplace.

"It's about time!" she said, grabbing the keys from me. "Where've you been, anyway?"

I held up the grocery bag. "At the store," I said. "We were just about out of milk."

"I *know* we were out of milk!" Helen said. She fished in her coat pocket and brought up a little list that had "milk" written at the top of it. "I was going to get some," she said then in a nicer voice.

"Well . . ." I stood there on the steps.

"Never mind," Helen said sharply. "We're fixing to be late, that's all. I'm taking Vonda Louise in to Valleydale to the doctor." She cast this news back over her shoulder as she hurried down the walk. "She's just about out of nerve pills."

I sat in the glider on the porch and watched Helen drive down the road to pick up Vonda Louise. It was cold, but somehow I could not stand to go inside, where there were beds to be made and dishes to wash and everything else that I had been doing every day for the past fifteen years.

I have always loved to sit in a glider. I love the way you kind of hover on the air, like you're not really sitting where you are, or not for long, like you might just stand up and walk out into the universe.

I was still sitting in the glider when a truck drove up about ten minutes later. It was coming real slow, looking for the right place I reckon, though there was not much on our road except for us and Vonda Louise's and Minnie's houses and those three ranch-style houses around the bend, which it would have already passed by the time it got to us. The truck stopped right in front of our house and the driver got out and opened the gate and walked up the walk without hesitating, all of this in slow motion, as if it was meant to be. I sat in the glider and watched him come. He walked to the bottom of the porch steps and stopped, looking at me.

This man was not like anybody I had ever seen.

He had long shaggy blond hair which came down almost to his shoulders beneath his Sherwin-Williams paint cap, and mirror shades. Nobody wearing mirror shades had ever come to our house before. He walked up the steps still looking at me. He held a burning cigarette in one hand. He wore a gold chain around his neck with a small gold rabbit hanging from it. I stood up. I could see myself reflected in his glasses, all wavy and shiny and out of whack. He took one last drag on his cigarette and threw it out in the yard.

"I'm Randy Newhouse," he said. "The painter? From Sherwin-Williams?"

"I'm Mrs. Travis Word," I said with as much dignity as I could muster.

"No shit." He grinned at me.

I laughed in spite of myself. I took him in the house and showed him the rooms to be redecorated.

"I thought you were ready for me," he said, looking around.

"I am," I said.

"No, you're not." But he was not mad at all, and he helped me move the furniture away from the walls in the living area and cover it all up with drop cloths. He started bringing things in from his truck while I took down the curtains.

"Here you go, honey," he said, stepping up behind me as I struggled with the last venetian blind. My heart began beating real fast even though I could tell he was the kind of guy that calls everybody honey. Then he reached around me and got hold of the venetian blind. "Careful now," he said, so close that his mustache tickled my neck and I could feel his hot breath in my ear. I had not felt this way since Lamar. I jumped aside like I'd been shot, and the venetian blind clattered to the floor. Randy Newhouse laughed. "Nervous little thing, ain't you?"

"No," I said. He was still laughing when I ran upstairs, where I made the beds and straightened the girls' room and then started ironing Travis's shirts furiously, pushing down as hard as I could. Randy turned on a portable radio downstairs while he worked, and the sound of rock-and-roll music filled the house. It was the Allman Brothers, though I didn't know their name yet. I couldn't keep from grinning as I ironed.

I knew Helen would have a fit when she got home.

SHE DID, OF course. She told Randy Newhouse he couldn't play the radio in our house, or smoke cigarettes on our property. He said, "Yes ma'am," and smiled at her until even she got nervous. Randy had a way of acting like he knew a secret joke, and the joke was on you.

But everybody liked him. My girls would not quit talking to him when they got home from school. He told them all about his band, which was called the Sheet Rockers. Misty came in the kitchen and whispered that he was cute. "Cute!" Helen snorted as if this was ridiculous, but she gave him a big hunk of the carrot cake she'd made the day before, and Randy ate every crumb, swearing it was the very best carrot cake he'd ever put in his mouth.

Travis never actually met him. During the six days Randy worked at our house, he was always gone by the time Travis got home. But Travis, who knew about such things, made an inspection each evening, and said that

Randy was doing a real good job. First he painted and papered the living area, then painted the girls' room, and then the kitchen. While he was doing the kitchen we had to go down to Minnie's house to eat. Vonda Louise was the most excited about the redecoration. She kept coming over to see what was going on, wearing bright crazy spots of blush-on which made her look like a clown. Randy always talked real nice to her, but I could tell that she amused him.

"Now, what have you been doing today, Miss Vonda Louise?" he asked on the second or third day, and she started in telling him everything she'd done, stuff so piddly I couldn't believe she could even remember it. She always went into too much detail anyway.

"Well, I went in the kitchen and had me a cup of coffee," she said, "but then I had to let it cool off some before I could drink it. I don't like my coffee too hot."

"You don't, huh?" Randy asked, winking at me.

"No sir!" Vonda Louise said. "Burns your mouth! One time I burned my mouth so bad I had to hold ice in it. That was back in 1968. It might of been 1969."

"That must have been real painful," Randy said.

"What?" Vonda Louise had what they call a short attention span.

"Your mouth. When you burned it."

"Well, it was," she said. "It sure was."

I'd laugh so hard at these conversations I'd almost wet my pants. But Vonda Louise was having the time of her life. Every day Randy came, she'd visit two or three times, always leaving in a flurry, all of a sudden.

"Where you going so fast, Miss Vonda Louise?" Randy Newhouse called out after her once, and I followed her outside just to find out what she would say.

"Missy, honey, come here." She motioned me over to her, and I went. The smell of her cheap perfume was almost more than I could take, as she whispered in my ear. "That painter feller is *looking at me*," she said.

"Well, maybe he is," I said. "You are still real pretty, Vonda Louise." This was a lie, but I knew it would please her. She sucked in her breath and took off, talking to herself. I stood outside in the cold wind, watching as she picked her way down the road to her own house with those mincy little steps, like she was walking on broken glass.

I had to smile.

For I knew he was looking at me.

WHILE RANDY WAS at the house, I got what Mama used to call the "all-overs," when she'd get too nervous to sit down and had to pace from room to room. I couldn't eat. I couldn't sleep. First I'd feel like I was on fire, and then like I was freezing. Helen asked me if I was sick, and Vonda Louise offered me one of her nerve pills. I said no thank you. A nerve pill was not what I needed. Randy Newhouse *was* looking at me, but nothing had happened so far.

I was the preacher's wife, after all.

And nothing ever would have happened if it hadn't of been for me. I did it, pure and simple. It was all my own doing, and all my own fault.

It happened on the last day he was there.

Randy had finished everything except for replacing the doors and the fronts of the cabinets and things such as switches and light fixtures. I was upstairs in the girls' room sitting on a straight-back chair I'd pulled over to the window, waiting for him to come. It was the only upstairs window with a good view of the front walk. My heart started pounding as the red truck with the ladders on top stopped at our house for the last time. He swung down from the cab and headed for the house with that cocky way he had of walking, I watched him come. Then right before he got to the steps, he looked up. I froze. But he saw me. He was looking up directly into my eyes, and a big grin spread all over his face. "Yahoo!" he yelled suddenly, scaring me to death. He took off his cap and slapped it against his thigh as I moved back from the window, my face hot as fire. But even in my embarrassment I had to go down and see him, I just *had* to.

I could hear Helen fussing at him as I went downstairs. "You crazy thing," she was saying. "What are you out there yelling about?" She treated him like she treated Misty and Annette, as if he was a child too. Well, he *was* a child, compared to Travis, who was nearing sixty by then. An old man.

Randy was not an old man. He was thirty, three years younger than me. The minute Helen turned her back, he gave me a big wink, and the minute she walked out to feed her chickens, he threw down his tools and ran in the bathroom where I was cleaning the sink, and whirled me around to kiss him, all prickly mustache and hot tongue. I got so lightheaded I dropped my can of Ajax on the floor and had to lean back against the sink for support. Out the corner of my eye I could see us in the mirror, and we looked young and beautiful, both of us, like movie stars.

The back door slammed.

"I'll call you," Randy whispered into my hair.

Then he was gone and I sank down onto the toilet-seat cover which I myself had crocheted, and wept. Finally I got up and washed my face in cold water, which did nothing to calm me down. I went upstairs, where I unfolded and refolded everything in the linen closet.

In another hour he was really gone. I could hear him saying good-bye to Helen and Vonda Louise in the kitchen, but I just yelled, "Thank you so much, you did a great job," down the stairs, and did not appear. I did not trust myself to face him in front of them. Later, when I had gotten ahold of myself, I went down and found Vonda Louise and Helen sitting in their parents' matching armchairs, which looked so old-fashioned now in the newly papered living area.

"You know what?" Helen said to me. She was knitting. "I believe Vonda has got a little crush on that hippie painter."

"I do not." Vonda Louise started crying.

I did not think he looked like a hippie, myself. I thought he looked like a cross between Jesus and Kris Kristofferson.

Helen peered all around the living area with satisfaction. "Well, I think he done a real good job," she said. "I think we got our money's worth."

Travis thought so too, when he came home from work. "Are you happy now, Missy?" he asked me.

"I'm real happy, honey," I said.

* * *

I WAS ON pins and needles waiting for Randy's call, which came three nights later, when I had almost given up. I was helping the girls with their homework. They always started it at the dinette table in the kitchen after supper while I cleaned up, and though Annette never really needed any help from anybody, one of us would usually have to help Misty, who was not studious. I believe we all have gifts, in the words of Travis, and being smart in school was never Misty's gift. Still, I was real proud of both my girls, who had gone farther in school than me. That night, Misty was supposed to write a paper on the Bermuda Triangle.

"Well, what in tarnation is it?" Helen asked, drying while I washed.

I smiled. I knew what it was.

"I'm going to read you from the book," Misty said. "Okay. Now listen, this is just amazing!" One of the cutest things about Misty was how excited she got about everything—this is why she was such a good cheerleader. She started reading. "'The Bermuda Triangle is an area located off the southeastern Atlantic coast of the United States which is noted for a high number of unexplained losses of ships, small boats, and aircraft. The apexes of the Triangle are generally accepted to be Bermuda, Miami, Florida, and San Juan, Puerto Rico.'"

Annette had looked up from her math to listen.

"'Since 1945, more than a hundred planes and ships have literally vanished into thin air. More than a thousand lives have been lost in this area within the past twenty-six years, without a single body or even a piece of wreckage from the vanishing planes or ships having been found.'"

"Shoot!" Helen finished drying and hung the dish towel on its hook. "Do you believe that?"

"Well, sure, Aunt Helen, it's right here in the book," Misty said.

"People that believe that would believe *anything*!" Helen stomped off into the living area, where I could hear her asking Travis if he believed in the Bermuda Triangle or not.

Misty giggled. Annette smiled and shook her head, going back to her math. I was wiping off the kitchen counter when the phone rang, so I was right there to get it.

"Hello?" I said.

"Is this you?" said Randy Newhouse.

"Yes, it is." I used an airy voice, as if I was talking to a complete stranger.

His deep chuckle came over the wire so close and real it sent an electric shock through my whole body. "Well, I want you to meet me at the Per-Flo Motel on the other side of Knoxville on Monday afternoon, can you do that? As soon after noon as you can get there. Just look for my truck."

"Yes," I said in that same voice. "It's just fine. *Yes*," I said again for emphasis.

Randy was still laughing when I hung up.

Both girls were looking at me, Annette with her little squint. She was so smart. "Who was that?" she asked.

"Oh it was just somebody from the electric company," I said right off the top of my head. "They're taking a poll." It was the first flat-out lie I had ever told in that house. But it was easy, easy as pie.

I went over and sat down beside Misty. "Now tell me some more about the Bermuda Triangle," I said. "What causes it?"

"They *don't know*, Mama. That's the point. Look here." Misty showed me a chart of possible explanations including sudden tidal waves, fireballs, sea monsters such as giant squids or sea serpents, a time-space warp leading to another dimension, capture by UFOs, and blue holes.

"What's a blue hole?" I asked. My heart was just pounding.

"It's this real deep hole in the ocean," Misty said. "Sometimes divers come upon them and start going down and keep on going down in them because they can't stop. They get confused. Fish even get confused in them sometimes, and swim upside down. Sometimes they find boats down there too, crammed up against the rock, like they got sucked down there by some enormous force. It's kind of like a big cave down there. Like a cavern." She showed me the picture. Then we looked at some more pictures, of whirlpools and waterspouts and some kind of Japanese wave. We read about the mysterious glowing streaks of white water in the Gulf Stream. We read about Atlantis and the Golden Age of Man.

"It's too much!" Misty threw down her pencil in despair. "It's too complicated. I don't know if I ought to make this report on the air part, or the water part. If it was just the air *or* the ocean, it would be a whole lot easier. This is too much. It's too hard." She stuck her bottom lip out the way she's done ever since she was a baby.

"Make a topic sentence," I said.

"It's too hard," she whined.

"No, you can do it. Come on. Just make a topic sentence." I remembered this much from school.

Misty picked her pencil up and bit it. Then she said, "The Bermuda Triangle is a place of mystery," and smiled, pleased with herself.

"Write it down," I told her.

Annette never looked up while all this was going on. She could concentrate like you wouldn't believe. She went on and did her math while I helped Misty write her report, which I was somehow able to do just like nothing had happened, just like he had never called, even though inside I felt like I was being whirled around and carried away by some mysterious current, sucked down down down into a deep blue hole of my own making.

I ARRIVED AT the Per-Flo Motel about twelve-fifteen that Monday, having lied to Travis that I had a gynecology appointment. I told him I'd been having some female problems, which was all I had to say. Female problems and gynecology made Travis so nervous that he never wanted to hear any more about them than he had to. If the sisters pressed me for details later, which I was sure they would, I planned to say I had endometriosis, which my friend DeeDee Burgess had had, and that it required a series of dry-ice treatments at the doctor's office.

My mood matched the sunshine as I pulled in beside Randy's truck. It was the only vehicle in the whole parking lot of the Per-Flo Motel, which turned out to be one of the worst-looking places I had ever seen, a nasty one-story cinder-block thing painted baby blue but peeling, with old boxes and trash piled in front of some of the rooms. Even this sight did not dismay me. It was what I had expected. In fact I welcomed it. For I knew that I was about to commit the worst sin a woman can commit, and I did not want it to be prettied up or glossed over. I parked right next to his truck for the same reason. I didn't care how obvious we looked. Of course it was not likely that anybody from home was going to drive along that ugly stretch of highway out by the chair plant on the other side of Knoxville anyway, but I didn't care if they did. I didn't care!

I may have been bad, but I am honest. That's the truth. And I cannot honestly say that I had struggled with this decision. I had *tried* to struggle. I had stood in the side yard in the cold blowing wind the night before and asked Jesus out loud to help me, to give me some sign not to go over there, but He didn't do a thing. Nothing. The wind kept on blowing and I got cold. So I went back inside and plucked my eyebrows and gave myself an egg facial. For the fact is, I was going to do what I was going to do long before I even knew I was going to do it.

And I started smiling the minute I got out of the car.

Then the door of Number Seven opened and there he was, shirt unbuttoned all the way down, holding a long-neck Bud. He drained it and set the bottle down on the sidewalk. "I been waiting for you, girl," he said. "Get on in here."

I went to him like a shot. He closed the door behind us with one hand and started unbuttoning my blouse with the other. We did it all afternoon. It was like Lamar and then some. We did it every way I had ever imagined or heard of and some I had not, in that tacky paneled room with no pictures on the walls and the ugly drapes pulled tight and nothing but snow on the TV. In fact the only light in the room came from the TV, a watery blue that made us look like we were in a movie. *A porno flick*, I thought, though I had never seen one.

When we finally quit, it looked like Number Seven had been hit by a hurricane, with the bedspread kicked to the floor and our clothes strewed all over the room. We lay on our backs, not touching, sweaty and too tired to move. Randy was smoking a cigarette.

"Mmmmm-hmmmm," he said. "There is nothing as good as a good woman."

"Don't make fun of me," I said.

"Missy, I'm not. Believe me, I'm not."

"My name is not Missy," I said.

"It's not?"

"No, it's not," I said.

Randy propped himself up on one elbow to look at me through the smoke. "Well, what the hell is it, then, honey?" he asked.

"Grace," I said.

"That's a old lady's name. You ain't a old lady yet, though you might have thought you was."

"My whole name is Florida Grace," I said.

"Florida," he said. "I been to Florida."

"Well, I haven't. I haven't been anywhere much. What's it like?"

"Hot," Randy said. "Just like you."

I giggled. I liked to think of myself as hot. Then he reached for me again, just as the whole bed began to shake beneath us. I started screaming.

"Hush up, hush up now." He put his hand over my mouth. "Don't scream like that. Have you done quit now?" I squirmed and nodded, and he took his hand off. The bed was still moving.

"*What is it?*" I said.

Randy laughed so hard he liked to have died. "It is nothing in the world but a Magic Fingers," he said. "Looky here." He pointed out the metal box on the nightstand, which I had not noticed before. "I swear, you ain't seen *nothing*, girl. It's like you been living in a time warp."

I relaxed then, and lay back and giggled while Randy fed a couple more quarters into the Magic Fingers and did me one last time slow while the bed moved beneath us. Then he stood up and started putting his clothes on. I lay there and watched him, memorizing his body. He swatted me with his shirt. "You better get a move on, girl," he said. "I'm talking to you, Miss Florida."

I did not want to leave that room, not ever, but I knew I had to. When I stood up, my knees felt real wobbly. Randy came and stood behind me and gathered up my hair and kissed it. Then I got dressed and braided my hair and wound the braid back up on top of my head.

"That turns me on." Randy was watching me in the mirror, by the dim light. "There's something about you that really turns me on. I could tell it the minute I saw you."

"Oh, you could not," I said. I knew I had caused all this myself, by looking out the window for him the way I had.

But, "Yeah I did," he said. "Oh, yeah. I did."

Though I was completely dressed by then, he came over and stood behind me and pulled up my skirt and started playing with my fanny. I leaned back against him as a wave of feeling swept through me. I would have taken off my clothes and laid down again, I would have stayed in that room forever. I would have told Travis and Helen any lie. I would do *anything*. And I knew I would get away with it.

"Tune in again next week," Randy said. "Same time, same station." He was trying to keep it light, so I did too. I blew him a kiss as I went out the door, something I had never done before in my whole life, but I must say, it came natural.

At first I was blinded by the sunshine and had to stand still shading my eyes, until I could see. It amazed me to find that Helen's old car was exactly where I'd left it, that the sun was low in the sky now, that a few more cars were parked down at the end of the motel lot—that the whole world, in fact, seemed to have gone on about its business while I was there in Number Seven with Randy Newhouse. A fat old man came out of the office and stared at me like he knew what I'd been doing, like he knew me. I would learn that this was Percy Odum, who ran the Per-Flo Motel by himself now since his wife Florence had left him. He ran it mostly for traveling salesmen and men who came in by the week to work at the chair plant and for people like Randy and me. Lovers.

I should have been exhausted but I was not even tired, driving back home. I had more energy than I had ever had, I was sizzling with it. On fire. I sang all the way home, though the only songs I knew were church songs—the old hymns. "If you can't bear the cross, then you can't wear the crown," I sang at the top of my lungs, with the window rolled down and the fresh air streaming in. "Glory hallelujah!"

I thought I had been born again.

I WAS SURE everybody could look at me and tell, but it was not so. Nobody could tell. Or maybe nobody ever really looks at anybody else. I have thought about this possibility too, that we are just ships passing in the night, as in the song, through a dark ocean. In any case, I got away with everything. It was so easy. The way I did it was by being extra nice to everybody, which made me realize something else. If you are real nice, you can do whatever you want. Anything! You can get away with murder!

First I said I had to have dry-ice treatments for endometriosis and then I said I was taking a class in first aid at the community college and then I said I was taking a how-to course in window treatments at the Sherwin-Williams store so I'd be able to make some new curtains for the living area. This was Randy's idea, because Sherwin-Williams really did offer such a class. I was not in it, of course. I was in Room Number Seven of the Per-Flo Motel with Randy Newhouse, fucking my brains out. Pardon my French. This is what Randy always said—"Pardon my French"—whenever he talked dirty. But actually I didn't mind him talking dirty to me, it turned me on. *Baby, you turn me on*. Randy used to say that to me all the time. Randy turned me on. He turned me on so much that I didn't care about anybody else or anything else in the whole world. I couldn't even think about anything beyond the next Monday, or Wednesday, or whatever day we had planned to meet at the Per-Flo Motel. I guess I went kind of crazy there for a while. This continued through April and May. I knew it was going to get harder when the girls got out of school for the summer, but I didn't care. I couldn't worry about that. I couldn't worry about them. I know this is awful, but I am trying to tell the truth here.

"HELLO," I CALLED as I came in from Knoxville late one Friday afternoon in early June and closed the front door behind me. "Helen, it's me, I'm back," I called, and then almost jumped clean out of my skin when I looked into the living area and found all three sisters in there dressed up and waiting for me. They sat real still in the semidarkness, sipping ice tea. None of that big old furniture went with the new wallpaper, I realized suddenly. The sisters looked like old statues left out in some wild garden gone to seed.

"Well, look who's here," Minnie said. "Look who decided to come home."

"Oh, she knows which side her bread is buttered on," Helen said in the meanest voice imaginable. "You can count on that."

"She thinks she can have it ever which way she wants it," Minnie said. "Ever way from Sunday."

"But she can't."

"Oh no."

"No she can't."

I stood paralyzed in the front hall while Helen and Minnie went back and forth. Vonda Louise sat in a great pastel heap on the sofa and didn't say a word. I couldn't think what to do. I knew they knew something, but I didn't know what. I didn't know how much they knew. Finally I walked in and turned the lights on, which caused them all to blink like three old toads.

"What in the world are you all doing in here?" I said. "What are you carrying on about now?" I tried hard for the joking tone I used with them.

"You can quit acting so nice." Helen spoke to me directly for the first time. "Just don't bother."

"We know all about it," Minnie said.

"Everything," said Helen.

"You whore of Babylon."

"You hussy."

"You little slut."

I felt like they were hitting me in the stomach. I sat down in the old rocker near the door.

"Get up from there," Helen said. "That rocking chair belonged to Mama, a saint on the earth."

But I could not move, and said so.

They showed me no mercy. I sat in their mother's rocker while they rained hard words on me like hail, like bullets. They told me how Helen had been talking to Garnet Keen after meeting last Sunday, just passing the time of day, and

Garnet had mentioned that she was having the time of her life taking a window treatment class at Sherwin-Williams over in Knoxville. "Oh," Helen had said, "that must be the class Missy is in." "No," Garnet Keen had said, "Missy's not in it. It's limited to six people, and she ain't in it." "Well, maybe she's in another one, then," Helen had offered, but Garnet had said no, that there was only the one, and it met on Saturday mornings. Well! Helen said her suspicions had been aroused, and she had said something to me about how did I like my class, and I had lied and said I loved it, that there were fifteen people in it and we were learning to make pleats.

"Pleats!" yelped Minnie, who couldn't keep quiet another minute.

"I would just like to know," Helen said, spacing her words out in a way that made it clear she had planned this whole conversation all out in her mind, "I would just like to know exactly what you intended to do, Missy, when it got down to where you had to produce some curtains?"

"Drapes is hard," said Minnie.

"Lying bitch," said Helen.

"Where is Travis?" I stood up.

"Laying down in the bed, as you might expect," Helen said. "He might not ever get up, after what you have done to him now." Then she told me how they had prayed over it all, and how it had been revealed to them through prayer that they had to tell Travis, which they had done, but he wouldn't believe them until he followed me over to Knoxville that very day and saw me go in the Per-Flo Motel.

"Claude Vickers seen it too," Minnie put in. "Claude Vickers went with him, Travis was too wrought up to go by himself."

At this news, my heart broke. I could not stand to think of hurting my poor sweet Travis. I had never understood that it would come to this. I raced down the back hall into our bedroom, and sure enough, there he was on the bed, lying flat as a board on top of that ancient peacock bedspread, with his hands joined in prayer on his chest like a dead person. His long face was as gray as his work clothes. He looked like he was a hundred years old.

When I burst in the door, he closed his eyes and turned his face away.

"Travis," I said, shaking him. "Travis, I know you're not asleep. Travis, I'm so sorry. I'm so sorry you drove over there, and got your feelings hurt. Oh Travis, I never wanted to hurt you. It didn't have a thing to do with you, honey, it never did. I can't stand to hurt you, I just can't stand it!" I threw myself across him, but he did not move a muscle, nor respond in any way. I kissed his face, which was as dark and lifeless as Travis Junior's had been.

"Come on now," Helen said from the door.

"Too late for that now," Minnie said behind her.

She was right. I got up and stuck the barrette back in my hair, which had tumbled down. Then I brushed past them into the hall, where I stopped dead as a sudden, awful thought came into my mind.

"Where's the girls?" I asked carefully. Even if Annette had stayed after school for 4-H, they should have been home by now.

"Never you mind," Helen said smugly.

"What do you mean?" I whirled on her, grabbing her shoulders. *"Where are my girls?"*

Then Helen said that they were both spending the night out, Annette at the Abernathys' and Misty with her best friend Heather Burgess, DeeDee's daughter. They were always asking if they could do this, but usually Helen said no. However, Helen went on to tell me, this time she herself had called up Claudia Abernathy and DeeDee Burgess and arranged it, saying that there was trouble in the home. Trouble in the home! I could just imagine everybody on the telephone already, talking about it. The news would be all over the valley by now.

"So now, Missy," Helen said. "What have you got to say for yourself? Aren't you sorry for what you done? Aren't you sorry for kicking people in the teeth that's been so nice to you?"

At this point, I surprised my own self by saying, "You never have liked me, have you, Helen? Not even after all these years. You never have either, Minnie. You haven't. You all ought to just go on and admit it."

"Shame on you!" Minnie said. "After everything we done for you."

"But you never *liked* me," I said. "Travis did, but you didn't." I thought about going back to see Travis again but decided there was no point in it right then. I went to the kitchen and called Randy Newhouse on the telephone. I knew his number by heart but had never called it, as we had made our arrangements in person so far.

"Hey now," Randy said after the first ring. I was so

glad to hear his voice. I told him he had to come over right away, that I had to talk to him. No, I couldn't do it over the phone! Helen and Minnie stood there listening while I talked to him.

Randy did not hesitate. He said he was on his way. But even with the way he drove, I knew it would take him at least half an hour to get there.

I left Helen and Minnie standing in the kitchen, and went out on the porch and sat in the glider to wait for him. They did not follow me out, thank goodness. I sat there hovering on the air and watching the most beautiful sunset I had ever seen, all pink and purple and gold streaks in the piled-up clouds over the mountain. I felt like I was seeing everything with brand-new eyes—that sunset, the white picket fence against the darkening fields, the long white curve of the road where it disappeared around the bend. I trembled on the breeze, waiting for Randy Newhouse.

After a while, Vonda Louise came outside and stood quivering before me in her pale green dress, like a giant moth. "I don't care what you all done, you and that painter feller," she said, "that *Randy*. I don't care where you went, nor what you done, nor if he kissed you on the lips, nor what you talked about. I don't want to know a thing about it," she said, and even though I didn't say anything to her, she stood right there until Randy pulled up in the road with his brakes squealing. Then Vonda covered up her face with her hands and went inside.

I was there before he could get out of the truck. I jumped up on the running board and stuck my head in the window and started kissing him. He pulled back. "What are you doing, honey, are you crazy? What's the matter?" he asked, and then I told him. "You mean your old man *knows*, then? The old preacher? He knows everything?" and I said yes. I told Randy he had to take me with him now. I said I couldn't go back in that house tonight.

"*Shit*." Randy pounded the side of the door with his hand. "Oh, shit. Now I reckon I'll have to tell Brenda."

BRENDA WAS HIS wife, of course. And she was not even his first wife either! I couldn't believe it. I just couldn't believe it. It simply had never occurred to me that Randy Newhouse might be married. It had never entered my head, due to him acting so young and all, and me feeling so old.

"But why didn't you tell me?" I asked over and over on that horrible ride from Piney Ridge to Knoxville.

None of his answers made any sense.

"Well, we aren't *very* married," he said. "We was drunk when we done it." And, "Hell, she's been running around on me anyway. She's been running around with her supervisor."

"Do you know that for a fact?" I asked. "Have you and her talked about it?"

"A man can always tell a thing like that," Randy said, and for a minute I hated him, he acted so superior.

"I can't believe you'd stay with her if you knew she was running around on you," I said. "I'd never do that."

"Oh hell, honey, ain't you ever heard of free love?" he asked.

"No," I said, and then he told me what it was, and I said I thought that was awful, but he said he believed in it.

"You mean to tell me you think people can go around and do whatever they want to?" I asked slowly. This sounded like some of Daddy's theories to me.

"Whatever feels good," Randy said. "Whatever feels right."

"Randy," I said, "don't you know *anything?* Don't you know that what we done is a mortal sin, and we are going to burn in Hell for it?" I was just as serious as I could be.

But Randy started laughing that wild free laugh of his, which was somehow catching. "Oh Miss Florida," he said. "Oh honey. You act like you have been living under a rock or something. I swear to God, girl! You need to come out in the sunshine and look around. You need to smell the daisies."

Randy was saying this while all the scenery of my life flowed backward past my open window, mountainside and fields giving way to open highway and then filling stations and 7-Elevens and then housing developments and strip malls. Randy went on to tell me his belief that there is no Heaven and no Hell either one! He furthermore believed that what is meant to be *will* be.

"Well, I don't," I snapped, for I still believed in choices and responsibility, even though I knew I was going to Hell for what I had done. Randy stopped at a 7-Eleven on the outskirts of Knoxville and got himself a six-pack of beer and three wine coolers for me. I had never had one, which I told him.

"Well, it's high time you did, then," he said. "Helps

your nerves." He opened a wine cooler for me with this special knife he always wore on his hip. We stood by his truck and stretched our legs. By then it was dark, but the arc lights above the parking lot cast a beautiful glow over everything. The wine cooler, which was a lemon-lime, tasted great. It did help my nerves. I finished it in a gulp and Randy opened another one for me. "That's my girl," he said. Then he pulled me to him and kissed me hard, and I remembered what all this was about, anyway.

We never did eat supper. We went back to the Per-Flo Motel and did it, and then while I was in the shower, I could hear him talking on the telephone and I figured he had called Brenda, but when I came out of the bathroom, he didn't say anything about her. I was so tired, tireder than I have ever been in my whole life. I snuggled in beside Randy to watch TV but went sound asleep at once and did not wake up until the middle of the night, when I was instantly horribly awake with my heart going in my chest like a jackhammer. I thought of Travis asleep in our bed at home, and my girls asleep at their friends' houses, and a wave of terror washed over me. "Randy! Randy!" I shook him good. "Randy, honey, *what are we doing to do?*" But Randy was sleeping like a baby, so I sat up in the bed by myself hugging my knees and crying as I realized what I'd done.

Randy who was so casual did not understand that there'd be no going back. But I did.

To MAKE A long sad story short, Helen packed up all my clothes in three cardboard boxes with my name printed on them in big red letters and got Claude Vickers to bring them over to Knoxville and leave them at the Sherwin-Williams store for me, which meant that everybody where Randy worked knew all about it, all about us, so Brenda took off in a huff, which she was apparently dying to do anyway. At that point I moved out of the motel, where I had been living for a week on a steady diet of Big Macs and free love, and moved into Brenda and Randy's apartment.

"Honey, I have got nothing but pity for you," Brenda said to me on the only occasion I ever met her, when she was driving away from their apartment at Creekside Green in Randy's flashy red Trans Am piled high with everything she could cram in there. I was upset to find that Brenda was so cute, with big blond hair and puffy lips like Sandra Dee. "And I'll tell you something else," she went on, "if he left *me*, you can bet your bottom dollar he'll leave *you*!"

Then she scratched off, while I stood out in the parking lot and pondered that one.

But Randy really loved me. I am convinced of this, even now. He loved me as much as he could love anybody. I know it. I knew it then. And he was fun—Lord, he was fun! We used to have the biggest times in spite of how heartbroken I was over losing my girls, or maybe *because* of it, if that makes any sense.

One of the worst things for me was that my girls didn't seem to miss me all that much.

"You can rest assured that we will take good care of these sweet little motherless girls! They will do just fine," Helen had told me on the phone right after I left, and this turned out to be true. Annette kept on making A's, and Misty was picked for the May Court. Living over there in Knoxville, I didn't even know what the May Court was! I was holed up in the Creekside Green Apartments, fucking my brains out.

But I missed them so much. And I missed the country too, I missed sitting out under that shade tree in the side yard, or in the glider on the front porch looking across at the mountains. There was no creek at Creekside Green, nothing green either. Nothing but cheap apartments and concrete. Somebody told me that there used to be a creek but they had paved it over to build the apartments, and then they named the apartments for it.

As for missing Travis himself, I could not even stand to think about him. I *didn't* think about him! I pushed him out of my head like a dream in the morning. Every time his face came into my mind, I would turn on the television or drink a wine cooler or smoke a joint—another thing Randy introduced me to—or go lay out in the sun by the swimming pool. The one thing I liked about Creekside Green was the pool, and even though I did not know how to swim, I loved to lay out in my purple bikini, which Randy had bought for me at the outlet mall, and marvel at all my skin which had never seen the sun before. I put lemon juice in my hair, which streaked it blond, and let it hang down to my waist. I liked the way the UT college boys and the other men around the pool looked at me, I knew they were lusting after me in their hearts. This turned me on.

When Randy came home from work, I'd jump on him

like a dog on a bone and then we'd go out and eat at Taco Bell, which I loved, and then we'd get high or drunk. I grew to like vodka in particular, as it was like you weren't hardly drinking at all. You couldn't even taste it. I never did any cooking to speak of at Creekside Green, or kept house much. About all we had was the waterbed and the TV anyway, and I didn't actually know how to cook, since Helen had done it all. I believe Randy was surprised to see that I was not interested in keeping house or buying things, and I know for a fact he got worried about my drinking. All I did for two months was drink vodka and get a tan. Finally Randy told me I would have to get a job if I was going to cost him that much in liquor, so I did. I got a job as a waitress at Halby's Olde English Pub, where Randy's band played sometimes after they got back together when his drummer, Marlon Johnson, got out of jail.

The Sheet Rockers were pretty good and had already started to get a big following. They were a Lynyrd Skynyrd, Allman Brothers type of band. I used to love to go hear them, and I went to all their gigs before Randy made me start working. I loved to watch Randy up there onstage flipping his hair around, leaning over the microphone like he was making love to it. When they played Halby's, I'd be behind the bar wearing my English serving-girl outfit with the black fishnet stockings, and in between sets Randy introduced me to everybody. "This here is Miss Florida," he liked to say. "Can you believe she was a preacher's wife?" This still turned him on. But Randy got moodier and moodier at home and was gone a lot when the band started to travel more. He gave up his day job. After a year or so, it got to where I loved him the most when I saw him up onstage performing. What happened eventually was, the Sheet Rockers started getting hot. They were doing gigs out of town. Marlon bought a van. They all put in some money to make a demo tape.

It was about this time that Misty ran away from home her senior year and arrived in Knoxville on the bus, to stay with Randy and me. At that point I came to my senses momentarily and made Randy marry me, which took all of five minutes down at the courthouse and didn't seem to mean what it ought to. This had also been true of my divorce, which consisted of a lawyer who had showed up one day with a paper for me to sign. When Misty came, I bought some furniture at Pier 1 and tried to cut back on my drinking and act more like somebody's mother, but by then it was pretty much too late for all concerned. Misty was fascinated by the Sheet Rockers and went to Atlanta with them for a gig, and before I knew it, she had married the bass player's little brother, just like that. He was in a country band. He and Misty got an apartment, and then Misty got a job at a dry cleaner's. I used to drive by there on my way to work to catch a glimpse of her through the plate-glass window, sorting clothes. She was still real pretty, and real enthusiastic. She loved her job, and she loved Johnny Jenkins, her young husband.

Annette, meanwhile, was a junior in high school, still making As. She used to write me a letter every month, which she signed "Your Daughter, Annette Word." I never heard a thing from Travis, though Annette would drop bits of news from time to time, such as that Helen had

found him a girlfriend. I couldn't imagine! In a way I felt
sorry for this girlfriend, but in another way the news broke
my heart. One good thing about it, though, was that the
Words eased up on Annette some. After she got her license,
for instance, they let her drive over to Knoxville so she
could meet Misty's husband, and we all ate supper together
at the Peddler Steak House. Annette never once looked
Randy in the eye. When she left, she gave me a hug and
said that she would pray for me. She had a little Bible with
her name on it in gold which she always carried in her
purse.

"Thank you, I could use some prayer," I said, though
Randy scowled at me.

But I was telling the truth.

The End of the
Love Tour

THE FACT IS, I was not real good at modern life. I didn't even look good anymore after five years with Randy Newhouse. I had circles under my eyes and a double chin. I had gained thirty pounds. I had cut my hair and gotten a permanent so it would be easier to take care of, and it *was* easier, but I don't think Randy liked me as much after that. He liked me back when I looked country, when I looked like a preacher's wife. This is what turned him on, Now that I was thirty-eight years old and had cellulite on my thighs and looked like everybody else in Knoxville, he was losing interest. The band was traveling a lot, and when he came home it wasn't the same. But I couldn't face this, because of course I had given up everything for him. So I just tried to keep busy, working at Halby's and helping Misty take care of the baby she had one year to the day after she got married. I'd keep him mornings while Misty went to school. First she got her GED, and then she

enrolled in a practical nursing program. I was amazed—
Misty had never been one bit practical as a child, and
always said she wanted to be a movie star. But she made
real high grades in the nursing program.

Annette had gotten a full scholarship to Carson-
Newman College, where she was majoring in Bible. Randy
used to make fun of Annette and say she went to Carci-
noma College. She made him real nervous by being so religious. But I was proud of both my girls. I have to admit, I
was not too crazy about being a grandmother at my age,
but I *was* crazy about Misty's little John-Boy, who was
named for his daddy.

Johnny Jenkins turned out to be a good boy, a hard
worker who gave up music entirely after the birth of John-
Boy, and advanced steadily in his job at Lowe's. He gave
Misty a diamond lavalliere for their second anniversary.

In many ways Johnny Jenkins was more mature than
Randy Newhouse, and a better provider. Still, I went on
pretending that things were all right for a long time, until
that winter day when my car was in the shop and I had to
drive Randy's old truck to work, and I opened up the glove
compartment and found a black lace bra inside. Not mine.
Thirty-two C, some skinny little nineteen-year-old with
big tits, I could just imagine.

That whole night I served food and drinks at Halby's
on automatic pilot, smiling at everyone. Nobody could
have guessed that anything was wrong.

When I walked in the door at home after work I still
didn't know what I was going to say to Randy, or how I
was going to put it, but he was gone anyway. I couldn't

remember where he was supposed to be, or who he had gotten a ride with. I couldn't remember if the band had a gig or not. In fact, I couldn't remember anything. It was like I had old-timer's disease. I couldn't remember how things had ever gotten to be this way. When had it happened? I thought about the Per-Flo Motel and the Magic Fingers, and how we used to be so much in love. I sat on the couch in the dark feeling real confused. Then I got up and got a beer and turned on Johnny Carson, but I couldn't understand the jokes, it was like it was all a babble in another language or something. I sat there on the couch in my Olde English outfit letting the television noise wash over me like water, at least it gave me some company. Johnny went off and then some old movie came on and went off.

My Randy showed up at three-thirty, with lipstick on his neck. He was drunk.

"Why, Florida!" he said like he had never seen me before. "What are you doing up, honey? I thought you'd be sound asleep by now."

"Well, I'm not," I said.

Randy stood in the middle of the floor breathing hard, his gut going in and out. He had put on some weight too. Then his face started getting red the way it always did when he got mad. "What the hell is the matter with you?" he said.

I couldn't tell him. Nor could I look at him. I looked down at my hands instead, crying. I wished I wouldn't cry but I couldn't help it, though I knew it made him furious. Anything that made Randy feel bad made him furious. He couldn't stand to feel bad. Finally I opened up my hand, where I had been holding the wadded-up black lace bra ever since I got home.

"So?" Randy said. "So what?" He grabbed the bra and stuck it in his pocket and tried a loud laugh. "Big deal, baby. Could be anybody's, you know? How the hell do I know whose it is? Where'd you find it, anyway?"

"You know." I could barely talk. I could not quit crying. Randy tried to touch me but I pulled away. He sat down on the couch beside me and put his head down on his knees. "Shit," he said. "I wish you hadn't of done this, Florida. You ought to know what men are like, their nature, I mean. It's normal. But you're not normal. You never were normal. It's all black-and-white with you."

I didn't know what he meant. I couldn't imagine how else I was supposed to act in this situation. This situation was not supposed to happen.

We sat there a while longer. Neither one of us had anything to say to the other. Randy kept his head down. I really thought he had gone to sleep, when he said, "Give me the keys, then."

"What?" I said.

"The truck keys. *The-keys-to-my-goddamn-truck*." He said this real mean, like I was retarded, I gave him the keys and he left, not looking back. He slammed the door behind him. By then all the channels had gone off the TV, and I sat there and stared at the snow until finally it started getting light outside, and one of the worst nights of my life was over.

* * *

ONE OF THEM. The other is the one I am fixing to tell about next.

I intend to tell everything, as I said. Randy did not come back home or call. I got my car out of the shop two days later, and after not sleeping at all, I went over to Marlon's early in the morning. It was real cold, and hardly even light. I had to ring the bell for a long time. When Marlon finally cracked the door and saw me standing there, a look came over his face like he wished he could just close it.

"Where is he?" I did not have time to beat around the bush.

"Hell, Florida, I don't know," Marlon said. He kept the door open just a little bit, and did not ask me in.

"Is he in there?" I tried to look over Marlon's shoulder, where, sure enough, a girl appeared behind him, a black-haired girl I'd seen around but did not know.

"He's not here, honey," she said. "He's really not." I could tell from her voice that she was feeling sorry for me.

"You know where he is, though," I told Marlon. "You're bound to," which was true, as I knew they were supposed to go to Atlanta the following week. Randy might leave me, but he would never leave the Sheet Rockers. This was sad but true, and I knew it. Marlon knew I knew it too.

"I'm sorry, Florida," he said, closing the door.

But behind him, the girl said, "Gatlinburg, honey. They're in Gatlinburg," and then Marlon said, "God damn it, Shirley," and slammed the door.

I stood there crying. Then I went home and called Bill Halby and said I had the flu and would not be coming in to work that evening, and called Misty and told her the truth. I said I was going over to Gatlinburg to find Randy and get him back.

"Mama, that's crazy," Misty said, and I could hear my little grandson John-Boy in the background. I told her I couldn't keep John-Boy that day, that she would have to take him to his other grandmother, Johnny's mother, or leave him with a friend. She said John-Boy didn't like to go to Johnny's mother's, and I said well, she'd have to figure out something else then, that I was going to Gatlinburg.

"Mama, I think you ought to get some counseling, I really do," said Misty, "and some other kind of job where you don't have to dress up in an outfit." Now Misty thought she knew all about such things, since she was in nurses' school. She thought she knew everything!

I hung up.

I went in and washed my hair and put on my makeup real careful. I meant to look good. I wore some new jeans and my red high-heel boots and my white angora sweater with sequin snowflakes on it and took my car coat in case it actually did snow. Then I got in my car and left immediately, hoping my old Toyota would make it over the mountains to Gatlinburg, where Randy and I had been together in better days.

GATLINBURG IS A resort town with everything that you can think of to do there such as restaurants, shopping, mountain crafts, chair lift up the mountain, a giant needle, movie theaters and souvenir shops and outlet stores and fudge factories and even a Ripley's Believe It or Not.

They call it the jewel of the mountains.

I got over there in the early afternoon but then I didn't know where to start looking. Somehow I had forgotten how many motels there were, plus I had not expected the town to be so packed with people in the middle of the winter. There were big banners saying SANTA DAYS stretched across every street, and big Christmas sales going on in every store. It was a real winter wonderland too, with Christmas decorations everywhere, including the cutest automatic angel choir singing carols right in the middle of town. Gatlinburg sits in a ring of mountains, and all of them were topped with snow. But it was hard driving through town—lots of traffic, lots of people. You had to keep stopping for jaywalkers. All of the people looked red-faced and happy, their arms full of packages. I drove slow, looking for Randy—looking for his new black Stetson with the silver band. Time after time my heart would race wildly as I thought I saw him, but it always turned out to be some other cowboy. Some other cowboy with a blond mustache and a big grin like Randy Newhouse, with some other girl by his side.

I'm not sure where the time went, but before I knew it, it was starting to get dark, and beautiful Christmas lights came on all over town, including lights strung all the way up the chair-lift cable. A big star on top of the mountain shone over everything. Now it was getting colder, and my breath hung in the air like a cloud when I stopped to buy gas, which took just about every cent I had. I was real hungry by then, but I only had enough money for a Tab. I had decided to go on a diet anyway. The guy that waited on me at the gas station was dressed up like an Indian, so I asked him if he was a Cherokee, but he said no, he was from Charlotte. I finished my Tab and got back in the car, my heart hammering. I figured the best thing to do was to drive around Gatlinburg looking for Randy's truck in motel parking lots, and so this is what I did for the next two or three hours, with no success. Motel after motel— TraveLodge, Alpine Chalets, Holiday Inn, Howard Johnson's, Rocky Top Motor Lodge, Bear Village, Park Vista, you name it. Even when it started snowing, I didn't stop.

I had given up everything for Randy Newhouse, and I was determined to get him back. I still believed that if I acted nice and tried hard, I could have anything I wanted. So I kept driving around. I drove past the tiny wedding chapel just in time to see a bride and groom come out the front door smiling while another wedding party waited in the parking lot at the back. By then it was snowing steadily. Somehow I lost track of the time. When my car slid into a snowy bank in the turn-around at the Mountaineer Inn, I was amazed to look at the lighted dial of my clock on the dashboard and find that it said ten-thirty. How did it get to be ten-thirty? My tires spun around and around on the ice, and I could smell rubber burning. I turned off the ignition and got out of the car, stiff from tension. My nerves were shot.

I went into the Mountaineer Inn and found the bar, where I ordered a vodka on the rocks.

Two men sitting on the bar stools next to mine quit

talking to each other and turned around to look at me. They both wore leisure suits and name tags.

"Well hello, honey," one of them said. I thought, *I'll show that Randy Newhouse a thing or two!*

"Hi there," I told them, smiling.

THE NEXT MORNING when I woke up, I felt the worst I have ever felt in my whole life, both spiritually and physically. I went in the bathroom and threw up and then got dressed and got out of there, carrying my boots in my hand all the way down to the lobby, where I sat next to the big Christmas tree to put them on. It was still dark outside, and I was the only one in the lobby, thank God. The boy at the desk was watching me real close.

"Is there anything I can do to help, ma'am?" he asked.

I hate it when anybody calls me "ma'am."

Also I was having some trouble getting my boots on as my feet had swollen up in the night, but finally I succeeded and then walked over and put one of the twenty-dollar bills down on the desk. "Well, yes there is," I said. "I believe my car is stuck."

When we went out there to look at it, the cold wind hit me in the face like a fist. At least it woke me up.

"You're not stuck too bad," the boy said. "Why don't you get in and start it, and let me get in front here and push? If that don't work, we can call the filling station."

It worked. I set off real slow around the driveway and picked up speed once I got out to the main road, which had been cleared pretty good. It was just starting to get light. A glow seemed to rise from the snow all around, and the silver sky was streaked with rose, then gold, and then the sun itself came up like a fried egg over the mountains, and the snow turned dazzling, like diamonds. I could see clearly then. I knew I would never find Randy. I knew I had lost him forever. I drove past all those motels with snow on their roofs and still-dark rooms where men and women lay tangled together on king-size beds.

I had lost my gloves, and my heater didn't seem to be working. Just before I got to the highway, I pulled off at a little café which was lighted up and friendly-looking. UNCLE SLIDELL'S DINER, the sign read: A CHRISTIAN RESTAURANT.

All right, I thought.

I went inside and ordered a cup of coffee and two sausage biscuits to go, paying for it all with the other twenty-dollar bill. No matter what is wrong with you, a sausage biscuit will make you feel better.

"Ma'am, are you all right?" the young girl behind the counter asked me when she handed me my food. "I don't mean to bother you or nothing, but you don't look too good. You could come in the back room here and lay down for a little while if you wanted to." Her broad freckled face was serious, and her brown eyes shone out big and honest behind her glasses. A nice girl. A good girl. I used to be a good girl myself, about a million years ago.

"Thanks but no thanks," I said.

"Well, you come on back if you change your mind," she said as I went out. "We'll be here."

The door closed behind me. I took one bite of a biscuit

and then threw both of them into a trashcan. The wind had died down. I looked to the east where that glorious sun hung right over Gatlinburg, shooting out rays like the spokes of a golden wheel. Sunlight glanced off the windshields of the cars and the windows of the diner. Sunlight danced on the snow everywhere, blinding me.

I stopped dead in my tracks as suddenly—over the sound of the trucks rumbling past on the road and my own heart banging in my ears—I heard it, very faint—a baby's cry. I looked all around. I was alone in the parking lot except for two boys that came out of the diner at that moment and got in a black pickup and drove off. I heard it again. There were five other vehicles in the lot, two cars and three trucks. I went and looked into each one, shading my eyes with my cold hands pressed against the glass. No baby. But as I headed across the packed snow to my own car, I heard it again, louder. If you have ever been a mother, you cannot stand to hear such a cry. So I walked around the side of the diner to the back, where they had several trailers and a putt-putt golf course, closed for the winter. A man came out of one of the trailers and got in his truck and pulled out, stopping long enough to roll down his window and say, "You got a problem, lady?"

"No," I said.

He shook his head and rolled his window back up, the chains on his tires crunching into the snow as he left. It looked like nobody lived in the other trailer, which had sheets of wavy plastic, like you see over carports, stacked against the door. But then I heard the cry again. The blinding light from the snow was giving me a headache as

I walked over to the putt-putt course, which had a big sign that said UNCLE SLIDELL'S CHRISTIAN FUN GOLF. This was a homemade sign, and it looked like it might have been made by Uncle Slidell himself. I pushed open the chain-link gate and walked in. THE LOVE TOUR, another sign said, STARTS HERE. Hole Number One was the Garden of Eden, with Adam and Eve painted on plyboard and a red rubber snake coiled halfway up a plastic palm tree which had plastic fruit such as bananas fastened all over it. The bananas had icicles hanging off of them. Hole Number One was beside this tree, full of snow.

I heard the sound again, closer now. I walked on, picking my way over little walls and around shrubs and plyboard structures. It was all very confusing and the sun was so bright and the air was so cold and my head hurt and the holes didn't seem to go in any order and I couldn't figure it out. Number Six was The Cross. It featured a huge wooden cross made of railroad ties with barbed wire wrapped around it and a hand-lettered sign that said HELLO MY NAME IS OLD RUGED CROSS, CAN YOU PICK ME UP? On Hole Number Eight, The Ten Commandments, you were supposed to hit the ball up a mountain and then it would bounce down a series of steps that had a commandment printed on each one—no ADULTRY, NO OTHER GODS, NO SWEARING. I didn't think NO SWEARING was really a commandment, but I was so cold and I had such a headache and I couldn't think good.

The girl from the diner stood by the Fun Golf gate. "Ma'am," she was saying.

I ignored her and went on because I could hear that baby

real clear now. Real clear and real close. I walked past Number Three, Daniel in the Lion's Den, and Number Eleven, The Wedding at Cana, and Number Four, The Tomb. Here you hit your ball past the centurion into the tomb and it came out on the other side, where the big stone had been rolled away and the angels were waiting. The baby cried like he was hungry or like his little heart would break. And then finally I was there, Number Ten, The First Christmas, with enormous plyboard cutouts of the Wise Men and ceramic barnyard animals such as chickens and ducks and a sign that said TO:YOU FROM:GOD and the whole heavenly host of angels hanging from a clothesline over the manger. Dirty snow dripped into His face as He lay in Mary's lap, but the glory of God shone all around as He held out His chubby little arms to me, still crying.

I remember the girl from the diner saying, "Ma'am, I'm sorry, but you will have to get out of there now," but I don't remember leaving Him or walking back through the snowy Fun Golf to my car, where a man stood waiting with his arms folded, watching us come toward him. He opened the car door for me.

"Are you Uncle Slidell?" I asked him as I got in.

He laughed shortly. "There ain't no Uncle Slidell," he said, and turned away. I do not remember the drive back onto the interstate, or the longer drive across the snowy mountains as I headed back toward home.

I DIDN'T NEED much time to pack up. Me and Randy Newhouse never had taken to housekeeping in a big way, as I said. There wasn't much of me there in Creekside Green to start off with, and when I got finished, there wasn't anything left. Misty and Johnny came over and helped me load up my car, while John-Boy toddled around the apartment. He is the most precious child, with white-blond hair just like the girls had when they were little. It seems like only yesterday when they were that small themselves and I was Misty's age, sitting out in those lawn chairs in the Words' side yard. Now Misty is so grown-up you can't believe it, all serious and sensible. She went from being a girl to a wife in no time flat, just like me. When Misty is smiling, she's still beautiful, but when she's not, her eyes are sad, too old for her face, which is already tired-looking. It's real hard, what she's doing. Going to school and being a mother both. I had it so easy myself, I swear I don't see how she does it. How any of them do it. Modern life is a lot harder than it used to be.

"Why don't you take the toaster oven?" I told her. "Go ahead, take it. Randy'll never use it. Take the Crock-Pot too."

"Well, I don't know if you ought to do that now, honey," said Johnny, who is even more serious than Misty.

With her arms full, Misty stopped in the doorway and looked back at him. "Are you *kidding?*" she said. "After what he did to Mama?"

"Well, shoot." Johnny shook his head.

Misty grinned at him. "Honey, don't let John-Boy get on the steps," she called back over her shoulder.

"Excuse me a minute," I said.

I left Johnny and John-Boy playing pat-a-cake in the

living room, and went in the bedroom and pulled open the dresser drawer and cut up all of Randy's underwear into ribbons with the scissors. He always liked to wear these nasty little bikini briefs in different colors. I also cut up a whole box of rubbers which I found under the underwear. Ha! He had never used them with me. Then I put the scissors in the last box of odds and ends from the bedroom, including the clock radio, which I had bought myself from Stereo Sound only a week before, and carried the box to my car. I left all my Olde English outfits in a pile in the corner, along with my red boots, which were worn-out anyway.

"I reckon that about does it," I said. "But don't forget the coffee table."

Misty had always loved our coffee table, which was nothing but this Indian-looking ceramic elephant from Pier 1 with a big thick sheet of glass on top of it, one of the things I had gone out and bought when she showed up to live with us. They had already put the papa-san chair and the armchair and the end tables and Misty's white wicker dresser in their truck. *I am almost gone,* I thought. It was the funniest feeling. I was leaving Randy with the TV and the couch and his tape deck and the waterbed, about what he had to begin with. I went down the steps real slow, holding John-Boy's hand. Johnny passed me as he went back up for the elephant. When John-Boy and I got to the bottom of the steps, Misty threw herself on me and started crying.

"Now, honey," I told her, "you quit that. You have not got a thing to cry about. Not a thing! Come on now."

"Oh Mama," she said. She said it again and again. Johnny came over and patted her hair, while John-Boy clung to her thin legs.

"Don't, baby, don't," I said. "I am going to be just fine. In fact, I am going to be a lot better off."

"But where will you go?" Misty wailed. "What will you do?" She acted like it was the end of the world. Misty is still dramatic, in spite of nursing school.

"The first thing I am going to do is drive over to North Carolina to see Ruth and Carlton Duty," I told her. "I already called them. They're expecting me."

At this, Misty sniffed and gulped and looked at me. Her face was all streaky from crying. "They are?"

"Of course," I said. "I'll probably stay over there for a while. Then I'll let you know what I'm going to do next. I'll call you."

"Promise me you won't go back to Randy! He's so trashy. I never could see why you married him in the first place." *Because of you,* I did not say. *And you used to like Randy just fine before you went to school and got so uppity,* I did not say. I wasn't going to get into all that.

"Honey, right now Randy Newhouse is the last thing on my mind," I told her honestly.

"Okay then," Misty said. She let go of me. "I still wish you'd stay here with me and Johnny and John-Boy and get some peer counseling. Plenty of other women have dealt with these same problems. Plenty of other women have been in your shoes."

I patted Misty's shoulder and tried not to smile. I didn't

want to be the one to tell her, but there is some conditions that counseling can't cure.

And I had to do what I had to do, a thing that did not involve counseling or Randy Newhouse either one.

"I'll be back over here before you know it," I said lightly. "Somebody's got to keep an eye on this mean little boy!" I picked John-Boy up. "Give Mamaw some sugar now. I've got to go." He gave me the biggest, wettest kiss. He loves to kiss people. I handed him over to Johnny.

At that moment, I meant every word I said. I expected to be back in Knoxville before long, to get another place to live and another job and another divorce, but I wasn't worried about it. A good waitress can always find a job. Plus I had cleaned out Randy's and my bank accounts, which gave me four thousand two hundred and ten dollars in cash, some of which he had been saving toward a bass boat. Ha!

So I figured I'd take me a little trip, and consequently I was leaving in kind of a hurry, before Randy got back. "I don't think he would have the nerve to call you all," I said to Misty and Johnny. "But if he does, don't you tell him a thing." They nodded.

"Be sure to get your oil changed and your antifreeze checked when you stop for gas," Johnny told me. "You'd better stop on your way out of town." He is one of those boys that is so earnest he looks cross-eyed. His ears were red in the cold. John-Boy was waving and waving. He loves to wave. All of them were waving, Misty and her family. They were so young and sweet and hopeful and determined, it just about killed me. They were the only people in the parking lot, dwarfed by the huge buildings of Creekside Green. They got smaller and smaller in my rearview mirror as I drove away. Then I turned into the street and they were gone.

Now YOU MIGHT think it is pretty pitiful if everything you own in the whole world will fit into your car, but I didn't mind it. In fact I felt surprisingly good, better than I had in months, maybe years, as I drove out of town. I stopped for gas at an Exxon station. I did need oil and antifreeze both, as it turned out.

I needed everything.

The sky was low and gray and puckered-looking, like insulation, but it never snowed as I drove the winding roads into North Carolina that afternoon. They had never built an interstate across those mountains. Though the road was okay, there were icy patches on the shoulder, and piles of gray snow where the snowplows had pushed it up against the mountainside. So I drove slow. I was not in a hurry. I had not told them any particular time that I would get there, so nobody was waiting on me. The snow on the mountains was pure white, broken only by the black trees and the dark patches of pines. Sometimes I'd see a little faraway house with smoke coming out of its chimney. The snowy slopes stretched right up into the pale gray mist, so I couldn't make any distinction between the earth and the sky. It looked like you could just walk up the mountain and into Heaven without any trouble. Once I looked way down the mountainside and saw three deer in a line, posed like statues against the snow, but when I blinked and looked back again, they were gone. Of course my heater still didn't work, but I was not even cold. I rolled my window down to let the sharp clear air fill my lungs, and it felt great. I felt suddenly, completely *alive* in a new way, a way that made me realize I had only been walking through my life.

The light was nearly gone by the time I reached the Scrabble Creek area. I couldn't even see the Little Dove River, which ran along beside the road now in the darkness. I could imagine it though, deep and black and mysterious, cutting through the snow, disappearing under ice. I knew it was there.

I couldn't wait to see Ruth and Carlton! It had been so long. Ruth had given me what-for on the telephone back when I left Travis, and said my mother would just die if she knew about my trashy behavior.

"She did die," I had said to Ruth then, and she hung up on me.

But when I'd called to tell her I was coming, she had sounded nice again, and said that they would be glad to see me, but that Billie Jean wouldn't be there, as she was in a home now. "A home," I'd repeated. "What do you mean, a home?" "Over in Asheville with some other people like herself," Ruth had said. "It's working out just fine. She likes it over there. They do things together, go to the mall, you know. Everybody has a chore. It's in a big old stone house."

"I can't believe Billie would want to go to Asheville," I

had said. "She never wanted to go anywhere. She liked to stay home."

"Well, Gracie, she *is* home. This is what I'm trying to tell you. They call it the Blue Ridge Home."

"But—" I'd started.

Then Ruth had cut me off. "Florida Grace Shepherd," she said sternly, sounding old and cranky, "you cannot just waltz back into your sister's life and start calling the shots. Why, she's all right! But things is different now, honey, I'm telling you."

But I was still not prepared for the sight that met my eyes when I came around the bend. There sat a huge Food Lion supermarket, right where the Dutys' grocery used to be. An enormous paved parking lot full of cars completely covered the place where we'd held the Homecoming, the place where I'd had my vision, the place where Daddy's church had stood. I couldn't believe it. I pulled into a parking space to get a better look. Clearly this was a brand-new Food Lion, very modern, with drive-thru pick-up and everything. It was open and doing a great business. People streamed out of the automatic doors, their carts piled high with paper Food Lion bags. Kids ran all around. Violet arc lights shone over the parking lot where—four spaces over—a long-haired teenage boy and a girl were backed up against a truck, kissing like crazy. Their legs were pressed tight together. I sat there in my car for almost fifteen minutes and watched the crowd without seeing a soul I knew. I couldn't take it all in. Then I drove on up the road a ways to the Dutys' house, which was still right where it had been, thank goodness. The house looked as warm and welcoming as ever. Yellow light spilled from its windows onto the front porch and the frosty grass and their new patio, which I noticed as I came in the driveway. I turned off my car just as the back door popped open and Ruth herself emerged like a woman coming out of a clock, to wrap me up in a big hug that made me start crying.

"Oh, honey!" she said. "Oh, Florida Grace! I am so glad to see you, honey, and I'm so glad you've come to your senses at last."

I pulled back and blinked at that, and Ruth squeezed me again.

"Come on in this house right now," she said. "You must be froze! Now I want to see some pictures of those youn-guns!" Meaning of course Annette and Misty. She had not seen any pictures of them since I ran off with Randy New-house. The Words used to take pictures all the time—Helen kept a scrapbook—but I had never bought a camera once I got to Knoxville. It's a funny thing how you only want to take pictures when you're proud of yourself. But I had brought Annette's yearbook picture from Carson-Newman and Misty's wedding pictures and my "Bragging Album" full of pictures of John-Boy, so we settled on the couch to look at these.

"Law, law!" Ruth kept exclaiming as she peered at him. "Ain't he the dickens, now! Ain't he a cutie-pie!" Ruth had really aged. Her big wrinkled hands were splotched with liver spots, and one arm was discolored from that long-ago bite. Her wide kind face was crosshatched with wrin-kles. She still wore her hose rolled down around her heavy ankles, and those sturdy black shoes. "I swan! I swan!"

she said over and over as she looked at John-Boy's pictures.

Meanwhile I walked around the living room, where every surface was covered with framed photographs of little Fannie. She looked a *lot* like Evelyn. Fannie in a dress with a sailor collar, Fannie in a ballerina costume, Fannie winning a beauty contest, Fannie in a cap and gown. I looked at that one for a long time.

"Where is she now?" I asked.

"Roanoke, Virginia," Ruth announced like she was saying London, England. "She's a dancing teacher now. She specializes in tap, but she does ballet and modern too, modern is where they wear leotards. Plus poise and how to walk. Oh Gracie, can you believe it?"

Frankly I could not. I thought back to my day, when nobody was allowed to dance except in church. "When did she start all this dancing?" I asked.

"Well, there was a girl that came over here every Tuesday," Ruth said, "and she held a class after school, and so we signed Fannie up, and she just took to it. Oh, she did! She was a natural! Everybody said so. She'd star in all the recitals. Gracie, you should have seen her in the Teddy Bears' Picnic! I will never get over it. Well then, after she had learned all she could there, we signed her up at the academy over in Waynesville, and then she went to the Shenandoah Institute of Dance in Roanoke after she graduated. And she's still there! She loves it. Why—"

Ruth went on and on about Fannie while I looked at the pictures. I have to say, the grown-up Fannie struck me as kind of stuck-up, posing just so in each frame. Now I might not of been everybody's idea of a good mother, but I raised two good girls in spite of myself. Fannie's pictures were everywhere, but so were old pictures of us. I kept looking at one of me and Billie holding hands and smiling into the camera as if we owned the world. That picture had been taken out by the big quartz rock at the old house up on Scrabble Creek. There was another one of us kids all fixed up for church, Billie and me in matching dresses Ruth had made for us. Evelyn looked like a little movie star, holding Troy Lee on her lap, while Joe Allen stood straight and tall behind us all, squinting into the sun. There was a picture of Mama and Ruth together, wearing wide-brimmed hats, posing on the porch by the roses, then another picture of Mama by herself, seated in a chair with the big Bible open on her lap, smiling at the camera.

There were no pictures of Daddy, and I asked Ruth about this. "Law, no!" she said, slapping her hands on her knees. "Honey, it was a dark day when we fell in with him, this is what me and Carlton have come to understand now. I know he was your daddy, but he was a bad un, I'll tell you straight out, Gracie. Why, he took advantage of everybody around here, not to mention what he done to your poor sweet mother, rest her soul. He was a blot on the church of God, if you ask me."

"Was," I repeated. "You mean he's dead now?" I had long figured that this must be so, but Ruth went on to say that he had died only eight years before, down in Mississippi someplace.

I went ahead and asked it. "Did he die of serpent bite?"

She nodded, her white curls flopping. "Yes indeed he did,"

she said. "At a meeting in somebody's house. It was what he wanted, I reckon. They wrote it all up in the papers, and Doyle and some of them went down there for the funeral."

"Who?" I asked.

"Doyle Stacy. Don't you remember him? The one that got bit in the face? Well, he's still carrying on, him and Dillard Jones and a few more, they're still at it, though they have been run out of first one place and then another. Nobody wants to have them around here anyone, it's an embarrassment. It ain't civic. Folks got up a petition, drove them out of town. I hear they've got a little old cinder-block building someplace on the Zion Hill Road, but I don't know nothing about it. *Nothing!* I don't want to know. Doyle Stacy works right over here in the Food Lion now, and he always tries to act real nice to me when I go in there, but I just turn my face. I've got nothing to say to the likes of Doyle Stacy." Ruth was laying down the law now, in her old grand style. "And furthermore, I do not want Fannie to be told anything about your daddy, nor that Carlton and me was ever in such a church, it is not anything she needs to know."

"I get it," I said.

Ruth nodded. "We have tried to give Fannie every advantage. And we can afford to, ever since we sold the land." Then Ruth looked at me sharply. "What about you?" she asked. "Don't you need some money?"

"No," I said. "Thanks, but no thanks." I could not keep from grinning at the thought of how mad Randy Newhouse must be by now.

I packed up a Christmas card with a picture of the nicest-looking family, taken in front of a brick house with white columns and a beautiful wreath on the front door, which had a fanlight over it. Three blonde girls, dressed all alike in plaid dresses with fur muffs, stood in a row on the stoop, along with a handsome man in a suit and a blonde woman who looked familiar. "Evelyn?" I asked, and Ruth said yes. I kept on looking at it.

"You should of got a card from her too," Ruth said. "She has been sending one out ever year since she got hooked up with this feller. She wrote me for your address some time back, and I sent it to her."

"When what that?" I asked. "What address did you give her?"

"Well, the Words' address, of course," Ruth said. "I never had no other. You never did send me the one in Knoxville." This was true, and I rued the day when I trade in my whole family for Randy Newhouse. "Now this here is Evelyn's fourth husband, actually," Ruth went on. "She sells Mary Kay, and lives in Charlotte. Don't she look good, though? I reckon it is all that Mary Kay. Don't she look good, Gracie?"

"Oh yes," I finally said. I was trying to take this in. Evelyn did look good. She looked like Mama. Or she looked like Mama would have looked if her life had turned out different, and she had not met Daddy or been so poor.

"I can't believe you never have got a card from Evelyn." Ruth was shaking her head.

I said I guessed that Helen had never forwarded my mail because they were so mad at me.

Then Ruth stood up and stared at me, her mouth open. "Then you don't know," she said. She took a step toward me.

I was still going around the room looking at everything, such as the crocheted antimacassars on the chair arms which I remembered from childhood. I remembered how they'd leave little pushed-in dots on the inside of your arms. Ruth had those same old ugly ball-fringe curtains too, but a big new TV.

"Don't know what?" I asked her.

"You don't know about Joe Allen, then." Ruth said.

"I know he was in the Marines, is all." I reached over to pick up a photograph of him in his uniform. He looked as sturdy and dependable as ever, a square-jawed grown-up version of the boy he'd been. I was thinking how we don't really change at all as we grow up, any of us—that whatever we are, we just become *more so*. *Look at Evelyn*, I was thinking. *Look at Joe Allen*.

"Oh, Florida Grace," Ruth said, coming closer to take my hand. "Joe Allen is dead, honey. He's dead. He died in a freak accident at Camp Lejeune three years ago. I wrote you, honey. I even sent you the piece out of the paper."

I felt like I had been shot. "I never got it. I didn't know." I sat back down on the couch.

"I can't believe she done that." Ruth meant Helen.

I sat there holding the picture and looking at Joe Allen's face, remembering how good he was, how he brought the money to Mama every week on his bicycle, how he saved Troy Lee. I always wanted to know what had happened to Troy Lee.

Ruth got some medals out of a drawer and showed them to me. "Joe Allen was a hero in Vietnam," she said.

"Who cares?" I said. "He's dead anyway, isn't he?"

"Gracie, Gracie." Ruth was shaking her head. "You always did have the worst attitude."

I just sat there. I couldn't stand for Joe Allen to be dead. I had always thought, someplace in the back of my mind, that no matter what I might be doing, no matter how bad off I got, Joe Allen was somewhere in the world doing okay. I had been thinking this all during the last few years when he'd been dead. Now I felt like somebody had played an awful trick on me.

"Well, anyway, Troy Lee is in San Francisco, California," Ruth went on. "He says he is coming back this summer to find his roots, so I reckon we'll see him. He says he's fixing to go on to school."

"What kind of school?" I asked automatically. I could not get Joe Allen's face out of my mind, how he'd looked the day he left for good.

"He didn't say. Well, look who's here!" Ruth cried as the kitchen door opened, and there stood Carlton at last, back from prayer meeting. He paused in the doorway to catch his breath, and I ran over to hug him. He felt bony and thin to me under that big coat, like a stick man. His health had failed a lot, I could see that.

"Hello, Grace," Carlton said, wheezing. "Me and Ruth has been praying for you."

Now this made me feel awful, of course. I hated to think of these old people praying for me.

Carlton wheezed some more as he crossed the kitchen to put one of those tubs of fried chicken on the table.

"I told him to get some chicken," Ruth said. "We didn't know if you'd eat yet."

It was a funny thing, but I didn't know if I'd eaten or not either. I couldn't remember. But I wasn't hungry. And now I was dead tired, so tired I couldn't even speak when Ruth led me to the bedroom. I have never slept so hard in my life, and the next day I didn't wake up until Carlton had already gone on his mail route, which Ruth said he liked to do just to keep busy. This was the same room where Billie Jean and I had stayed as children sometimes when Mama and Daddy went off preaching, the same room where Billie had lived for years after that. I reached back and ran my fingers along the satiny wood of the old spool bed, something I had always loved to do. Then I stretched again and ran my hands down my own body, which felt different now. Thinner. Heartbreak is a terrific diet. Bright sunlight came in the window and fell in a great shining patch on the bed, but there was a big black hole in my mind where Joe Allen used to be. Finally I got up and dressed and went out to the living room, where Ruth sat drinking coffee and watching Phil Donahue.

She smiled and hugged me. "Well, looky here," she said. "I thought you was going to sleep all day!"

"I guess I just about did."

I followed her into the kitchen and sat at the table while she scrambled me some eggs and got the toast and bacon out of the oven, where she'd been keeping them warm for me. Obviously Ruth liked to feed people as much as ever, though she said she hardly cooked anymore. "I just ain't got the strength," she told me.

The breakfast tasted wonderful, but I couldn't finish it, which disappointed Ruth. "Why, Gracie, you used to be such a good eater," she said. Finally she quit coaxing me, and took my plate and dumped the rest of the food down the disposal. Then she poured us both a cup of coffee and sat down across the table and eyed me, stirring her coffee. There was no mistaking it when Ruth meant business.

"What I want to know, Florida Grace," she said, "is what you are planning to do now."

"I don't know," I said, which was certainly true, although so far I had known enough to leave Randy Newhouse and come over here. I was waiting to find out what I had to do next, but I was beginning to understand that there was an order to everything, a pattern which would be vouchsafed to me in due time.

"I thought so," Ruth said. "Well, honey, you have come to the right house, as I am fixing to tell you! Now listen good."

"Okay," I said. I was in the market for directions.

"First off, let me tell you how lucky you are. You always was a lucky girl, Florida Grace, and I don't know whether you appreciate that fact or not. You was *very, very* lucky to marry that nice Travis Word, and you are very, very lucky that he ain't married nobody else in the meantime, while you have been so busy going off the deep end."

"What are you talking about, Ruth?" I said. "I can't go back over there. It's too late. They *hate* me now."

"Listen to me," Ruth said. "You ain't bad, honey. You have just got too much nature, that's all. Why, Travis don't hate you! Those sisters of his, well, that's another story. But it don't matter. They're old, Florida Grace." Ruth's eyes never left my face as she drank her coffee. "You might've made a big mess of your life so far, honey, but at least it ain't too late to straighten it out. It's not many that's given a second chance in this world, and you're still young."

"I'm not young," I said.

Ruth just looked at me. "Honey, you're young," she said.

I KNEW I could do a lot worse than to follow Ruth Duty's directions.

So the upshot of it was that I got in my car and drove over to Piney Ridge that very afternoon, stopping only to buy gas. It took me about three hours.

First I went by the Tabernacle to see Travis Junior's grave. The snow on it did not look cold. It looked like the softest blanket in the world. *Maybe he was* lucky, I thought, *to die as a baby, and not have to walk through this vale of tears*. I was horrified to think this. I stayed there in the cemetery as long as I could stand it, and then got back in my car and sat parked up the road from the Words' house waiting for Travis's truck to show up. I did not doubt that Helen would shut the door in my face if I knocked. She had already turned on the porch lights and it was nearly dark when his old black truck came around the curve. My heart rose as I saw those headlights cut across the snow. I had the biggest urge to run to him that minute. *Travis! Travis!* I would cry.

But something held me back.

Instead, I got out of my car and walked along the fence in darkness, with only the pale eerie glow of the snow to light my way. I heard the hollow sound of the truck door closing, then the creak of the toolhouse door. I knew Travis was putting his tools away. He had done this every night when we were married, even though he had to get them right back out the next morning. I used to ask him why he didn't leave them in the truck, which would have been a lot easier, but he'd just say, "In the truck?" and look at me like I was crazy. He *loved* to put his tools in the toolhouse, is what it boiled down to. He liked to hang them up on the pegboard where they went. I crept around to where I could watch him. I stood hidden behind the cedar trees and looked at him—at his tall thin body, his long jaw, his beaked nose, his black hat, his strong wide shoulders. A strong man. A good man. I had left a good man, a man who loved me, for a bad one. Now I couldn't even remember why I had done it, it all seemed so long ago.

Then Travis locked the toolhouse door and turned so that the hard white light fell directly on his face, that familiar face so full of bones and hollows, a skeleton's face. Travis stood staring intently into the winter night with his dark eyes fixed on some distant point beyond the light, beyond me, even beyond the mountains. His was the saddest, most terrible face I have ever gazed upon. I understood then that he was still looking for me, still waiting for me to come back. But in that moment I also knew that I could *not* go back. Ruth was wrong. For me there would be no going back.

It was given to me to see Travis Word's whole life as days of duty stretching in a long unbroken line into the future, to that evil day when he would end it abruptly and for all time, end it himself in that very toolhouse by putting his staple gun to his head, oh it would be awful. I saw it as clear as anything. The gift of discernment is a gift you do not want to have.

The cold wind moaned through the cedar trees as I stood there. My feet were blocks of ice.

Then Helen opened the back door. "Travis?" she called in her nasal voice.

"Coming," Travis said.

I waited until he was inside the warm house before I left the safety of the trees and made my way back to my car through the bitter cold.

I spent that night at the new Howard Johnson's out on the highway. I had an English muffin the next morning before heading across the mountains toward Waynesville. Somehow a plan had been forming itself in my mind while I slept, so that I awoke full of purpose, and knew what to do next. I left my waitress a big tip and then paid for the room in cash, thanks to Randy Newhouse.

By the time I pulled into the Food Lion parking lot, the snow had melted to form big gray slushy puddles.

I knew I would need supplies.

I WALTZED THROUGH the Food Lion like somebody that has won a giveaway, tossing everything I wanted into my cart. Bananas, cereal, milk, Cokes, soup, bread, stuff for sandwiches, hand lotion, toothpaste, shampoo and rinse, you name it! The lights in there were very bright and gave off that buzzing sound which was getting me all keyed up.

I smiled at everybody, though I didn't see a single soul I knew.

Until I got to the meat department, that is.

"Can I help you, ma'am?" A voice broke into my thoughts as I studied the different grades of hamburger.

"Well, I don't know," I said. Then I started talking too much. "I am just figuring out which kind of hamburger I want. It used to be that they only had one kind, just plain old hamburger. Do you remember that? It sure was easier then."

"Gracie?" the voice said.

I was so shocked I almost fell over dead. Then I realized it was Doyle Stacy, as gawky and sweet-looking as ever, one side of his face hanging slack though the other half appeared real glad to see me. He wore a bloodstained white apron over a nice blue oxford-cloth shirt and a tie.

"Well, this sure is a blast from the past!" I said stupidly, sounding like Randy Newhouse, which embarrassed me as you might imagine. But you cannot lay down with a pig and come up smelling like a rose, that's for sure.

Doyle Stacy smiled at me with his good side. "I swan," he said. "I was just thinking about you the other day, and wondering where you had got to, and how you was getting along."

"I'm fine," I said too fast, juggling my cart.

Doyle's steady gray eye, the good one, took me in slow. "We heard you was married to a preacher man over in Tennessee," he said.

"That's true," I told him. "I was." I watched this register on him.

"Children?" he asked then.

"I've got two," I said. "Two girls. One's married and one's in college."

Doyle nodded. "That's good," he said.

The fluorescent lights buzzed overhead as people kept pushing me aside to get to the meat counter.

Doyle jerked a thumb at my cart. "Looks like you're stocking up," he said.

"I am," I told him. "I need to be ready."

Doyle did not ask, Ready for what? He just nodded. "That's always a good idea," he said.

The two of us stood like islands in the fast-flowing stream of shoppers, staring intently at each other across all the cellophane-wrapped packages of meat. Though I knew he was several years older than me, Doyle looked strangely boyish—maybe because of the paralysis. The left side of his face had not aged at all, and the right side had not aged much. He had plenty of hair, which was still sandy-colored and wavy, a nice straight nose, not much chin, and the biggest, whitest buckteeth you ever saw. He would not win a poster contest, that's for sure!—another one of Randy's expressions. I put two packages of Holly Farms chicken in my cart. I knew there wouldn't be any electricity up there, but it was so cold I figured I could put the meat outside someplace, maybe down in the smokehouse as was done in the olden days. Doyle was watching me closely with a sweet little half-smile on his face. I remembered all about him then, how nice he was, and what good care he took of his mother. I picked up some hot dogs.

"Grace Shepherd," he said. "I would have known you anywhere."

I put the hot dogs into my cart and looked at him. He did know me, I could see that, just like Lamar had known me, only Doyle knew the other side of me, which Lamar had never seen.

"You're coming back, ain't you?" he said.

I said I didn't know what I was going to do, that I was waiting to find out, Waiting to hear. "I guess I sound like I'm crazy," I told him, "but I'm not. I swear I'm not. I am recently separated from my husband, is all, which has made me kind of nervous."

"That'll do it," Doyle said, fixing me with his good eye. "But my Lord Jesus Christ has got the best nerve pill available, and it's called salvation."

I started backing up. "I don't know if I'm ready for that," I said. My heart started beating too fast.

Doyle nodded, all business. "Well, He's ready when you're ready. We're holding services ever Wednesday night, ever Saturday night, ever Sunday. Same as always." He paused. "I reckon you remember all that. We're out the Zion Hill Road now, in that stone building that used to be Darrell Dotson's small-engine-repair shop, in fact that's what the sign still says to this day, 'Small Engine Repair.'" He smiled at me, a smile so full of joy that I was seized by wonder and fear.

"He's waiting for you right now," Doyle said. "He's been waiting a long time, but He's real patient, and He's got all the time in the world. He'll wait for eternity if eternity is what it takes."

By then the fear had expanded to panic. "I don't have the slightest intention of going over there," I said. "You must be crazy."

"They call us crazy, but that's all right. It don't matter what anybody calls us. You know that, Gracie."

"I don't know any such thing. As a matter of fact, I have to get back to Knoxville in a few days. I've got a new job over there, and a new boyfriend, and a lot of things to take care of."

Doyle smiled at me like he didn't believe a word I was saying. "Can I come up there and visit with you?" he asked.

"*No*," I said.

"I could bring you down to church, Gracie. I'm asking you to come worship with us, that's all. It's the same old church. It's the same old God. There ain't no other way."

I thought about the other ways I had tried—living a lie with Travis, worshipping flesh and the things of the world with Randy Newhouse. Yet I resisted. "I've got my own car, thank you," I said. "But as far as me coming over there to Zion Hill, you can just forget it. You hear me, Doyle? *Forget it!*"

Doyle stretched his arms out across the meat counter and kept smiling at me, his face shining like sun on the snow. "I'll see you," he said softly.

I wheeled my cart away in a rage, not looking back, though I could feel Doyle's eyes boring into me, all the way down the long buzzing aisle. I went through the checkout and left, still furious.

* * *

THAT WAS A week or so ago, I forget exactly. I am losing track of the time up here. In fact there is not any time up here now, not really, except for the day and the night, and the different light of the sun and the moon on the long white sweep of the snow. Lord it is cold too. The well is froze. I could not break the ice so I am drinking out of the creek now. Daddy always said he liked the water up here, that the water up here is better than anyplace else.

When Carlton drove up the road I walked down there to see him. He was like a tall black stick against the snow, standing beside his car.

"Honey, you come on back with me now," Carlton said.

"I will be down directly," I told him, but I knew I wouldn't. "Don't worry about me, I am just fine," I said. "I have got some things to work out in my mind, is all. I am just taking a break."

Carlton nodded and blew his breath out like clouds in the air. "Well yes, I see that," he said. "But you ought to know that Misty has been talking to Ruth on the telephone and they are so worried, they are going to get up a little posse and come after you if you won't leave. Why, Ruth would of been with me right now if she was well enough to make the trip," he said. "And Misty says she can't believe you would want to miss Christmas thisaway, miss seeing your only little grandbaby on Christmas Day."

Carlton was leaning forward peering into my face, trying to see what I was thinking, but I am wearing these old sunglasses now which belonged to Evelyn I believe. I have to protect my eyes from all this light. I found Evelyn's sunglasses in a dresser drawer along with her old movie magazines. Some of the big stars then you can't hardly remember now, such as Deborah Kerr, what ever happened to her? What ever happened to us? Carlton I know will be dead in a year. I could see the cancer in his chest like a bunch of dark grapes. I do not want to see what I see nor know what I know. I hugged old Carlton as hard as I could.

"You are getting so thin," he said.

"I have been on a diet," I told him. "You know I needed to go on one!"

"What about that old heatstove? Is it working okay?"

We both looked up the hill at the house, at the feather of smoke from the chimney. "Sure," I said. "And there's lots of coal."

"Well." It was clear Carlton hated to leave.

"Listen," I said. "You tell Ruth that you have seen me and I am fine. You tell her to call Misty. It won't be long, I swear. And I am just fine. You tell them that."

Carlton nodded. "Okay, honey. But you come on down in a day or so, and quit worrying us all to death, you hear me?"

"I hear you," I said. "I will."

And so Carlton left, and I stood there at the bottom of the holler and watched him go, his green car creeping along the packed snow of the road which actually is not slick at all if you go slow enough. I got in my own car and started it and let it run awhile, something I have been doing every day or so just to keep the batteries up. This is a good little car though Randy hated it, he likes

American cars. But who cares now what Randy Newhouse thinks?

I turned the engine off and climbed back up the hill, stopping by the barn to call the two horses somebody is keeping up here now, two big old rawboned work horses. He comes by here to feed them every two or three days, but I don't know who he is nor if he has leased this barn and pasture or what. In fact I don't even know who this farm belongs to. It doesn't matter to me as I am interested in the fruits of the spirit now, not the things of the world. The old horses came over blowing plumes of their breath in the frosty air, to eat the apples I brought them. Their lips curled back and showed their long yellow teeth. Among serpents we find the rattlesnake, moccasin, and copperhead. Among true believers we find the Word. Travis Word looked like a horse, I always thought. These horses are as big as trucks, their hair all matted and dirty. No one is taking care of them. They are only good for work I guess, or this is what he thinks anyway, the one that keeps them here. From the front room window I have seen him come, a fat man, a square black shape in the snow.

AND NOW IT is Sunday morning days and days later, I forget. I know it is Sunday though because I wake to hear a bell. I hear a church bell ringing, the sound carries for miles of course across the frozen snow. I sleep in Mama and Daddy's old bed where Mama has come to me in a dream. So I lie still now, trying hard to keep her. I love how the screen of her hair falls around my face when she whispers in my ear.

Come to me, Gracie, she says. *Oh come to Jesus, honey. It is time now, it is never too late.* Oh come to him it is time though I do not know what time it is exactly, the only clock up here that works is the one in my Toyota at the foot of the hill. The china clock has stopped at a quarter to two of some other day of some other year and I don't have a watch anymore, I believe I left it in Gatlinburg.

But I have always minded Mama. Wrapping the blankets around me I drag them into the sitting room where it is a little warmer though the fire in the old stove has died down now. I shovel in more coal and leave the stove door open pulling the old rocker up close to it. Daddy used to pour kerosene right in the stove, how the flames would roar! though it scared us all to death. The velvet easy chair has disappeared. The old horsehair sofa is still yet here but now its springs stick out in every direction, you can't sit on it. And the lamps are gone and most of the china. Thieves have been here, I reckon. Though they did not take Mama's blue willow teapot nor her sewing basket nor this statue of the two dwarves that says "Rock City" on it. It is so ugly, I don't blame them a bit for leaving it. It has been here as long as I can remember. I reckon it belonged to Elvie Mayhew, God rest her crazy soul. First she left this house in a hurry, and then we did. Our linens are mostly rotted now. All returns to the earth, and the Spirit returns to God who gave it. I believe I will go to church today. I believe it is time.

But what will I wear? The clothes I have here are way too

big for me now. I have got a safety pin in my jeans but they hang on my hips even so. You cannot wear jeans to church anyway, certainly not at your age. It is not respectful.

The fire roars in the stove and Mama whispers again in my ear. Okay. I leave my jeans in a pile and walk naked across the old heart-pine floor to her bedroom and open the wardrobe and sure enough, it is a regular boutique of the dead. I choose one of the four dresses hanging there, a navy blue gabardine dress with long sleeves and little white dots in the material. I take some time with my hair, brushing it all out like a cloud around my head. It is growing out now. I put on my tights and my boots but no makeup. Fear God and keep His commandments, for this is the whole duty of man. For God will bring every deed into judgment, with every secret thing, whether good or evil. Every secret thing. This means you, girl. I have never been baptized, a fact which would surprise many who have known me in my life. A secret. It does not take me long to pack up. I am traveling light.

But it is still early, too early for church, so I will sit here yet awhile in the heat from the stove, which is a comfort as Mama always said.

When I leave here this time, it will be for good.

Oh but I remember the day when we first came into North Carolina, me and Billie and Evelyn and Joe Allen and Mama and Daddy and Troy Lee, all of us sitting in a circle in the dirt eating Ruth Duty's coconut cake while our car burned up before our very eyes and black-eyed Susans were blooming by the side of the road and yellow butterflies fluttered all around. It is so hard for me to believe that Joe Allen is dead now. I can still see that one piece of straight brown hair falling down on his forehead no matter how often he pushed it back. Joe Allen was the best of us all.

I close my eyes to see him drifting in time and maybe I sleep for a little while but then I am awake, suddenly terribly terribly awake, and it is time. The Spirit comes down on me hard like a blow to the top of my head and runs all over my body like lightning. My fingers and toes are on fire. Oh Lord it is hard to breathe and I am scared Lord, I am so scared but I will let my hands do what they are drawing now to do and it does not hurt, it is a joy in the Lord as she said. It is a joy which spreads all through my body, all through this sinful old body of mine.

Now it is time to go. I close the stove door and bolt the house door though anybody could get in here that wanted to but there is nothing left to steal. Snow lies out before me like a field of diamonds. You cannot even see the big quartz rock now, it is under a drift by the sycamore tree. The snow is a smooth dazzling stretch all the way up to the dark tree line. Everything is black and white up here today. Oh where are Evelyn's sunglasses? I have to protect my eyes from all this light.

The morning Randy Newhouse first came to me he was wearing those mirror shades, I saw myself reflected so wavy and shiny and out of whack. And Daddy stood on this very porch at dawn in the pearly light with serpents running like water over his arms and hands. Lamar too, I can see him yet, leaning like a big dark cat against the rail, the bright forsythia now covered up by the snow.

I will go down these steps one by one. I am leaving here now.

And I cannot help but laugh as I start down the hill, for the Spirit is a joyful thing. There was nothing to be afraid of after all and I *am* happy, Mama, I am. I would even run if my boots did not sink and stick in the snow. I have got an awful lot of energy though I have not been sleeping too good and I believe I skipped breakfast this morning, it's hard to remember for so much has happened. I always made sure my girls got a good breakfast.

I stop for one last time to kneel by the icy rushing waters of Scrabble Creek. The sweetest sound I ever heard, it has stayed in my head all these years. I drink to my heart's content. When I raise my dripping chin to look back up the hill, our house appears small to me now. I once thought it so big and so fine. But it is a good thing I am leaving as it is starting to snow again though not hard, big lacy flakes drifting down from the sky like little angels. My gray angel baby Travis sleeps in peace beneath a lacy blanket of snow right now, over in Tennessee. The only light in that room in the Per-Flo Motel came from snow on the TV but it was plenty for me and Randy, we didn't need much light.

It's funny how sound will carry in this cold air. I hear an axe ring out, a bell, a baby's cry. Or maybe it is Troy Lee's cat, we never did find that cat. It could be anyplace around here, it could be down in the old barn someplace with those old horses. We never solved any of the mysteries, me and Spice. I know myself as the girl I was, who used to love stories so much. Well this is the story of light

Mama, this is the story of snow. That baby is crying again, you know I left him outside crying in the dirty snow but I am coming now, I am really coming Jesus though I cannot hear him now because all the bells are ringing, ringing, ringing as they did upon the occasion of my wedding to Travis Word, ringing across the whole valley.

I clean off the windshield and my car starts up fine. In the beat between the wipers, snowflakes cover the windshield like lace, no two of them alike in the whole world, Travis said. Travis called me Missy but my name is Florida Grace, Florida for the state I was born in, Grace for the grace of God. Just before I drive around the bend, I stop to look back one more time at the little house by Scrabble Creek and the long white sweep of snowy ground where me and Billie Jean made angels in the snow.

NOTES

In a way my writing is a lifelong search for belief. I have always been particularly interested in expressions of religious ecstasy, and in those moments when we are most truly "out of ourselves" and experience the Spirit directly. I visited several serpent-handling congregations near my hometown of Grundy, Virginia, as a girl, and became interested in their beliefs again recently when writing the introduction to Shelby Lee Adams's book of photographs of residents of eastern Kentucky, *Appalachian Portraits* (University Press of Mississippi, 1993).

I am indebted to Thomas Burton's fine book *Serpent-Handling Believers* (University of Tennessee Press, 1993). Several scenes in this novel are based on events described there. I was struck especially by Anna Prince's narration, which inspired my own fictional narrator. I learned a lot also from the films of Karen Kramer, Eleanor Dickinson, and Thomas Burton. Steven M. Kane's extensive work on serpent handling includes "Appalachian Snake Handlers" in volume 4 of *Perspectives on the American South*, edited by James C. Cobb and Charles R. Wilson (Gordon and Breach, 1987), as well as numerous articles, among them "Snake Handlers" in *Encyclopedia of Southern Culture*, edited by Charles R. Wilson and William Ferris (University of North Carolina Press, 1989). Jeff Todd Titon's *Powerhouse for God* (University of Texas Press, 1988) was valuable, especially for its study of religious language.

Saving Grace is a work of the imagination entirely, though I have tried to make it as true as I know how.

Readers might like to know the key passage of Scripture (Mark 16:17–20) upon which serpent handlers base their worship:

> And these signs shall follow them that believe; In my name shall they cast out devils; they shall speak with new tongues; They shall take up serpents; and if they drink any deadly thing, it shall not hurt them; they shall lay hands on the sick, and they shall recover. . . . And they went forth, and preached every where, and the Lord working with them, and confirming the word with signs following.